ABOVE THE LAW

ABOVE THE LAW

A NOVEL BY

J. F. FREEDMAN

A DUTTON BOOK

DUTTON
Published by the Penguin Group
Penguin Putnam Inc., 375 Hudson Street, New York, New York 10014, U.S.A.
Penguin Books Ltd, 27 Wrights Lane, London W8 5TZ, England
Penguin Books Australia Ltd, Ringwood, Victoria, Australia
Penguin Books Canada Ltd, 10 Alcorn Avenue, Toronto, Ontario, Canada M4V 3B2
Penguin Books (N.Z.) Ltd, 182–190 Wairau Road, Auckland 10, New Zealand

Penguin Books Ltd, Registered Offices:
Harmondsworth, Middlesex, England

First published by Dutton, a member of Penguin Putnam Inc.

 REGISTERED TRADEMARK—MARCA REGISTRADA

ISBN 0-525-94479-6

Printed in the United States of America
Set in Sabon
Designed by Leonard Telesca

PUBLISHER'S NOTE

To Georgia Rose Freedman

Your arrival into this world changed my life forever

Foreword for
Above the Law

Everyone seems to want to do two things in life: direct movies and write a novel. In 1987, I had been a successful film and television director and writer for 15 years. I wrote and directed several feature films and TV pilots, including *McGyver,* but I wasn't artistically satisfied because of the compromises inherent in that business: Only a handful of artists in film and television have creative autonomy.

I'd covered the director part of the fantasy. The idea of trying to write a novel, while daunting, was very appealing. Film writing is restrictive—there's no inner monologue, no description, no characterization, no flights of imagination.

One afternoon over coffee, I was browsing through the extension catalog for the University of California at Santa Barbara, the city in which I live. A particular course being offered in the writing department caught my eye. It was called *Novel Beginnings*. The class would meet 10 consecutive Saturday mornings. The object was to try to write the first 100 pages of a novel. I signed up.

There were a dozen wannabe novelists in the class. After a couple of weeks of talking about structure, characterization, etc., Shelley Lowenkopf, our instructor, sent us off to start writing and to come back in two weeks with some pages.

Of course, one had to have something to write about and I hadn't given that much thought. Now I had to. I recalled conversations my brother and I had had 15 years earlier about some cases he'd participated in as a young lawyer in Albuquerque, New Mexico. These cases involved outlaw motorcyclists, prison riots, perjured evidence, police corruption. Rich material. I took these basic elements, invented others and wove them around a series of fictitious characters I created spearheaded by a down-on-his-luck semi-alcoholic lawyer who gets hired by the bikers. I wrote 30 pages, turned them in and a week later heard them read aloud, by Shelley, to the class. The pages were well-received and I was off and running.

It took me almost four years to write that first novel, *Against the Wind*. I'd go off and direct a movie or TV pilot then, between assignments, come back to the book. When I finished, I presented it to my film agent, who, after recovering from his shock at being handed a 600-page manuscript he had no idea was being written—I'd told no one I was doing it except my wife—sent it along to his literary counterpart in New York. A month later, I had six offers for the book and a year after that it was published and became a bestseller. Now I was a writer, with film directing taking a secondary role, which has been the case to this day, almost 10 years later.

During the writing of *Against the Wind,* I developed characteristics as a novelist which have been consistent throughout all my books. I write from character and let events unfold as experienced by the people in my books. The expression "the book writes itself" is absolute for me. My characters drive the story along and I hang on for dear life, doing my best to guide them on their voyage, through perilous and often uncharted waters, to an ultimate safe harbor. This does not mean that all my books have happy endings. Some do and some don't; but the endings are the inevitable consequences of the characters I've developed and the story which comes from that development.

Like most writers, I have certain themes and tendencies I return to. I write flawed characters who are going through crises in their lives—personal, professional and emotional. Working out their problems, learning who they are, their core values, is the driving force behind my own motivation to write.

Above the Law is my sixth novel, my fourth legal thriller. (I'm not a lawyer; I have lawyer friends who help guide me through the labyrinths of the profession.) It's different from my previous books in two significant ways: one, I use central characters I've used in other books, the first time I've repeated characters. The protagonist, Luke Garrison, was the protagonist in *The Disappearance, The New York Times* bestseller I published before this one. And Kate Blanchard, his lead detective, was the core character in an earlier novel of mine, *House of Smoke.* Both those books are set in Santa Barbara.

The second change is that Garrison, a defense attorney (who was once a DA), takes on the role of prosecutor. I wanted to write a story in which a defense lawyer, someone who is used to going up against the establishment, now works for it. In my other legal thrillers my leading character has been on the defense side, which is traditional in this genre. Despite the move across the aisle Luke is, however, still battling evil, corruption and human weakness.

As is true in all my other books, *Above the Law* is a tale of imperfect human beings trying to find the light at the end of their personal tunnels and come out better people for having gone through the experience. It's the journey that interests and engages me as a person and as a writer, and I trust interests readers of my novels as well.

J. F. Freedman
Santa Barbara, CA

PART
ONE

SANDSTORM

The telephone rang. Riva answered it. "Luke," she called. "It's for you."

"You the fella looking t'buy a vintage Triumph motorcycle in decent to excellent running condition?" It was a man's voice, old-sounding, rheumy, wheezy. Decades of cigarettes and cheap whiskey had gone into fine-tuning that voice, which had a mocking tone on the "decent to excellent" part.

I felt a quick heartbeat skip, but I didn't want to get too worked up—I'd drilled this well a couple times already, but the holes had been dry.

My old ride had been trashed a few years back by someone who didn't like what I was doing, which was defending a very unpopular man on a murder charge. That my client ultimately wasn't guilty of the crime for which he was charged didn't bring my bike back to life. But what with getting married and having my son and all, I hadn't done anything about replacing it. Now, with my life settled into a comfortably predictable existence, I wanted to straddle two wheels again, if only on the weekends. I live in Santa Barbara, but nothing available here turned me on. So last week I placed ads in the *L.A. Times, Long Beach Telegram,* and the *San Fernando Valley Daily News:*

Wanted: Vintage Triumph Bonneville motorcycle. In decent to excellent running condition, or capable of being restored at a reasonable price.

I had some responses the first couple of days the ad ran, but either the price was too high or the motorcycles needed too much work. What I'd thought would be an easy transaction was becoming increasingly frustrating.

"Yes, that's me," I answered, probably too eagerly. The price just went up a couple hundred, I thought, but what the hell.

"Ain't got one." A kind of chuckle-wheeze-phlegmy cough. The connection wasn't great, so it was most likely not as bad as it sounded, but this was not a well man.

Ah, well. Life's full of little jokes.

"Thanks for calling," I told the prankster. Maybe he was an old shut-in, this could have been the high point of his day. Maybe even his week. I started to hang up.

"Got a Vincent."

The receiver was halfway to its cradle, but I heard that.

"Black Shadow, '53. She runs smooth, I ain't jerking yer chain."

I brought the receiver back to my ear. I didn't immediately reply, because now I was discombobulated. I was actually tingling, as if I'd stuck my finger in a light socket. Except for an ancient Harley I'd had as a kid, which threatened to snap my ankle every time I kick-started it, I've always owned British motorcycles, mostly Triumphs. It's the feel, I can't explain it. Like preferring blondes over brunettes, strawberry over butter pecan.

I'd been looking for a replacement for my old Triumph, a great old motorcycle for its time, but not the stuff of legends. This guy was talking about a legend. In its day this was the fastest, meanest, coolest motorcycle in the world, the motorcycle of every James Dean wanna-be's dreams. They were the most expensive bikes of their time, and there hadn't been many of them made, which made each one valuable and special.

I had only seen a few Black Shadows in my lifetime, in motorcycle museums. Now here's some old guy telling he's got one that runs, and he's willing to sell it?

"You still there?"

"Yes," I answered hurriedly, before he hung up. I had no phone number for this character, nothing. If I lost this connection, it could be lost forever.

"So you want to look at 'er, or what?" Spoken with an edge, a throwing down of the gauntlet: Are you man enough for a machine of this magnitude, both physically and spiritually?

* * *

I hitched a rental trailer to my old truck and headed southeast. End of September, early autumn, the beginning of the best time of year in California. Balmy, dry days, cool nights. When the weather's this good, it's hard to roust myself out of bed and go to the office in the morning; I want to lie on the beach with my wife, Riva, and Bucky, our two-year-old, hike up Figueroa Mountain, cruise the bookstores, in the shank of a twilight evening sit outside on the patio of one of the beachfront restaurants, drink margaritas with like-minded friends, and watch the melting sun die into the ocean.

Occasionally I'll take half a day off, jump on the golf course (my game is pathetic), or play with Riva and Bucky in the waves off Butterfly Beach. Once or twice a month, that's about all I'll allow myself. I can work as much or as little as I want, I'm a lawyer practicing solo, I answer to no one as far as my business is concerned; but I'm a lifer workaholic. Except for a brief hiatus when I left Santa Barbara under a cloud of immense funk and fucked off in the northern California forests, smoking weed, drinking good wine, and making love with the woman who would later grace me by becoming my wife, I've gone into the office and done the job. I'm reliable, you can set your watch by me. Everyone who knows me or knows of me (which is just about everyone in Santa Barbara who's in the loop), both from the years when I was the district attorney here, to now, as a lawyer specializing in criminal defense, knows they can count on me. Which can be a burden sometimes, but it's my burden, so I bear it. Generally with decent enough goodwill.

Over the last year and a half, though, pushing that metaphorical rock up the mountain's gotten harder. I've been losing passion. Not for the big picture—life's better than it's ever been. For my work. It's been a gradual thing, an erosion of faith in the law as it's happening in America today. It's not the people I represent. They're criminals, of course, almost all of them—that's a given. You don't hire a defense attorney and pay him good money unless you're in trouble, and if you're in trouble, it's usually because you've done something wrong. There aren't a lot of innocent people in jail, forget all those country-western songs. And I am a diamond-hard believer that a good defense for all is one of the best things about this country. But the line is becoming too blurred between what's right and what's wrong, to the point where almost nothing is "right" or "wrong." Things have become so "situational"—one of those words modern psychologists love to use—that people convince not only themselves, but plenty of others, that virtually anything is justifiable, up to and including murder.

What started my feeling this way was a notorious incident that occurred here in Santa Barbara, three years ago. I defended a man accused of kidnapping and murdering the fourteen-year-old daughter of a prominent local family. I got the case by default; no decent criminal lawyer in the city would take it, because of the awfulness of it, and because the girl's parents were big movers and shakers and no one wanted to offend them or bring them any more pain. I was dragooned down from my retreat up north and talked into looking into this morass, then finally, with great reluctance, signed on, more because of personal demons I needed to exorcise than the specifics of the case, which were truly terrible.

The trial was sensational, a classic Roman circus. At one point all three major network anchormen, as well as senior reporters from CNN, CNBC, and Court TV, were in Santa Barbara, reporting on it live. One of those media mosh pits that wind up being more important than the trials themselves. It took a lot of focusing and discipline not to get sucked into the giddy maelstrom in which everyone involved—defendant, lawyers, family members—became an instant celebrity and lost all sense of proportion and reality. I managed to restrain my baser instincts in that regard; most of the time. Riva, a practical and forceful woman, is good about stopping me from stepping in my own shit.

It was touch and go until the end, but I got my client off. Since he was innocent of the crime of which he'd been accused, that was a good thing. But that was all he was innocent of; he'd done so many bad things around the periphery, that had made the young girl's death almost inevitable, that he was almost an accomplice. Morally and ethically he was; by my sense of morality, anyway. I'm old-fashioned that way. I'm forty-seven years old and in some ways I'm from another time. It's inconvenient for a lot of people, but it's a quality I hope I never lose.

The upshot was, I've been drifting away from straight criminal law, which had been my life's work on both sides of the aisle. Riva and I had long discussions about it. What did I really believe in, what did I want to do, where did I see my future heading? Where did I want to be in five years?

I didn't know those answers. I knew I needed to do something different, but not so different that I was throwing the baby out with the bathwater. Fortunately, I was in good shape financially. The father of the murdered girl had sent me a huge check when the trial was over—he had offered a reward for finding out who had killed his daughter, and in defending my own client I had discovered who that was. I had qualms about taking his money, but he'd been so ugly in his conduct toward me before the truth was ultimately revealed that in the end I accepted the reward, as compensation for the grief he'd caused me. I'm no psychiatrist, but I think that my taking his money absolved him of some of his own guilt, in that his ex-wife, his child's mother, had turned out to be the murderer.

My compromise regarding my work was to branch out into less stressful areas—environmental law, personal injury, class action, things that came across my desk that seemed reasonable, not boilerplate boring, and covered my nut. Still good cases, but the kind you can leave on your desk at the end of the day. Because of my new notoriety, a fair amount of work was coming from out of town, L.A. and San Francisco. Those cases pay really good money, so finances weren't an issue. But practicing law wasn't my life anymore. It was part of my life, but it wasn't my life.

Which is the long and short of why I was going to the desert to buy another motorcycle.

The owner of the Vincent lived in the high desert outside of Joshua Tree, half a day's drive from Santa Barbara. He'd sent me a Polaroid; it looked okay, but who could tell for sure? The picture could be ten years old. But it was good enough to send me out on the road.

I cruised down Highway 101, the ocean on my right, surfers out in force at Rincon and around the piers south of Mussel Shoals. When I'd first come back to this area, I'd surf those spots as well as up north at Hollister Ranch, a real surfing mecca, but during that trial I mentioned, someone tried to kill me while I was out on the water. It was scary, the most frightened I've ever been in my life—the closest to dying. You don't forget something like that, it's indelible in the deepest levels of your unconscious, even though rationally you know it will never happen again. But rationality and what's in your gut are two different things, entirely.

What happened that night turned me off surfing, which is too bad, it's one of the greatest pleasures in the world, but the painful memories got in the way. I tried it once, some months afterward. I stood at the water's edge, and I couldn't go out. I was anchored to the shore, no wind in my sails. So I had to let it go. Now I swim inside the buoys, with my boy.

At Ventura I cut inland, through Santa Paula, Fillmore, Piru, at Valencia dropping down on Interstate 5 past Magic Mountain for a short run, then east again, Highway 14 to Highway 18, the signposts along the way flashing by through my grimy windshield, then it was dry, open country, cactus and sagebrush, the two-lane blacktop leading me into the shimmering distance, my companions on the road eighteen-wheelers, Highway Patrol Dodges, locals making their way from one small town to another, Canadian snowbirds in their blocky motor homes coming south for the winter. About the time the sun peaked, it was beginning to blow hard, a hot, dry wind, swirling dust against my windows and tumbleweeds into my bumper and radiator. The Santa Ana season had started the week before all over southern and central California, hot, strong gusts coming at forty or more miles an hour out of the northeast. Fire season. At home we'd had two bad fires already this summer, and the prediction was for several more weeks of the same risky situation. Out here, there's nothing to burn, so it's more an irritation than a life-threatening situation. I drove through it, the windows in the truck rolled up tight, the aftermarket air conditioner I'd installed huffing and puffing like an asthmatic.

Riva had laid on water and snacks in the truck, so my pit stops were a fill-up and a piss. I was motoring as fast as I felt comfortable pushing the old truck—my goal was to get there by noon, spend an hour or so checking out the Vincent (or a few minutes, if it turned out to be a wild-goose chase), work out the deal, load the motorcycle in the trailer, and be home at night. It would be late getting back, but it would be easy driving, no heavy traffic.

I made good time, but then I got lost and had to backtrack thirty miles, so it was almost two in the afternoon by the time I located his place, which was three miles of bad road off the highway. I felt like I was riding a washboard, driving up that road. A steady diet of coming and going would blow your kidneys, if it didn't blow your vehicle's suspension first. Finally, I rounded one last corner, and his place came into sight.

The house was a desert rat's enclave—an old double-wide on cinder blocks that had been in one place for so long it was almost petrified at the base. The paint job was original, in some places the metal worn so thin you could almost see through it to the inside. Twenty paces to the rear of the dwelling a corrugated metal shed, which would be the garage and all-around storage barn, listed ten degrees to the side. Unless I was badly mistaken, there would be a mountain of junk in that shed, decades of useless crap tossed in there. And if I was lucky, one real special vintage British motorcycle.

I drove up in a cloud of dust and jumped out. He was a dark, shadowy figure, sitting in an old, springy metal chair in front of the trailer, the one place that had shade.

"You're late." A stream of dark brown tobacco juice pocked the dust at his feet.

"I know, I'm sorry. I took a wrong turn coming out of Paradise Valley and wound up in the middle of nowhere," I apologized. I didn't want to mess up the deal before we'd even started trying to make one.

"I reckoned that's what happened. You ain't the first one. Not that I get a shitload of company." A sound wheezed out of his throat, the closest he could come to a laugh. "Most people think this sorry piece of dirt you're standing on is the original middle of nowhere."

I'd had that thought, but I wasn't about to voice it. I walked closer to him, close enough that I could make out his features. He wasn't that old, mid-fifties probably, but he had the weathered face of someone who'd been out in the sun all his life, leather and lines. It made him look decades older than his true age. His hands fit his face—bone-dry claws. What you'd imagine a mummy would look like. Except he was talking, breathing, moving. Moving slowly; he hadn't gotten out of his chair.

So much for the amenities. "Can I look at the motorcycle?"

"That's what you came for, ain't it?"

He reached behind him for a pair of crutches, and that's when I saw he was missing his right foot, above the ankle. The stump was wrapped all around with elastic bandages, bulging out under his pants leg. He hove to his one good foot with great effort, fighting for balance.

"Gangrene. Lost it four months ago. Circulation went bad from too much drinkin', but I didn't take care of it till it was too late. 'Cause I was drinking too much to notice." He lifted one crutch and pointed toward the shed. "Which is why I'm selling my pride and joy, instead of riding it."

The Vincent was a bit dusty under the protective drop cloth, some rust spots on the chassis—but it looked damn fine for a forty-five-year-old machine. I fired her up—she roared to life on my first attempt.

I nursed the old motorcycle down to the highway, but once I got to the public blacktop, I opened it up and let it sing. It needed work:

shocks, brakes, clutch, new chain, tires; but it was a running machine—not fast off the blocks like a new BMW, Kawasaki, or Yamaha. But fast enough. The handling was heavy but comfortable. And it had that great pedigree. The old desert rat hadn't been jerking my chain.

I was going to ride it for fifteen, twenty minutes, long enough to get a feel for it, what was right and wrong, and if it was worth buying. I wound up riding it an hour. I couldn't stop. I was having too much fun, even though the wind was howling. By the time I got back to his place, it was going on four o'clock. Time to make the deal, load up, and head for home. I'd phone Riva from the road, let her know I'd be late. She worries otherwise.

We haggled over the price. Gentle Ben Loomis, my motorcycle guru in Santa Barbara had instructed me that if the bike was a piece of shit but salvageable, try to get it for under fifteen thousand; in decent shape, twenty thousand, but be prepared to go to twenty-five. I didn't want to spend that much, but I would if I couldn't resist it.

This one was in the middle tier of the decent-shape category. He started at thirty-five, I countered at fifteen, he came back at twenty-five, I raised to twenty. We settled on twenty-two thousand five hundred. Much more than I wanted to spend, but this was irresistible, a once-in-a-lifetime chance.

It was five o'clock by the time we finished the deal. I counted out the cash, 225 crisp hundred-dollar bills, and he signed over the papers. We had a beer to celebrate. His suggestion, I didn't want to offend him. I was the only company he was going to see for weeks, except for the boy who delivered his groceries. He watched as I ramped the classic motorcycle into the U-Haul, strapped it down, and secured the doors. He wasn't happy, but he was philosophical about it.

"Ride 'er good."

"I will. Thanks."

We shook hands. It felt like I was shaking a rattlesnake, his skin was so dry and tough. I climbed into the truck and started driving home.

If I had been smart and checked the weather before heading back to Santa Barbara, I'd have known I was heading for trouble. But I didn't. I was like a kid on Christmas morning, so flush with excitement over his newest possession that he's oblivious to everything else. With images swimming in my mind of a man and his motorcycle, which would be the envy of every biker he knew, navigating back-country roads, I slipped a

Coltrane CD into the truck's stereo and motored along, grinning like a madman.

The sandstorm came up without warning. All of a sudden the wind arose with the force of a tornado, sweeping up the entire terrain and sending it into the air in a monstrous cloud that was extending clear to the horizon on all sides.

I was trapped. Worse, I was imperiled. I couldn't see ten feet in front of me. Driving was going to be nearly impossible, but I couldn't simply park here and wait it out. Some eighteen-wheeler on a schedule and a mission could come barreling out of the gloom and flatten me, and there was no shoulder to pull onto; on either side of the road there were steep ditches, four or five feet deep, built to catch runoff during heavy rains. I'd seen those movies about sandstorms, *Lawrence of Arabia* and *The English Patient*. I don't know if California sandstorms are that brutal, but the thought of being buried under forty feet of sand and suffocating to death was extremely frightening.

Even with the windows rolled up as tight as I could get them, the sand sifted in, pinprick needles biting at my face and hands. It's an old truck, the rubber weather-stripping is cracked and brittle. The wind was howling, it felt as strong as those pictures you see of the Gulf Coast being flattened by hurricanes. And it was deafening, a banshee-singing, the sound almost human-like; now I know why people in the Sahara think storms like these are accompanied by demons, shaitans, the devil in the wind.

My only option was to inch forward, headlights on high beam and flashing lights blinking, until I found a safe haven. I started off, inching along at five miles an hour, guiding by the yellow line in the middle of the road. I ejected Coltrane and fiddled with the radio, trying to get some news of what was going on, but there was only static. All I could hope for was that somewhere up ahead, close, there'd be an oasis. Filling station, motel, restaurant, any port in this storm.

I'd driven about ten minutes when I saw the car off to the side, nose down in the drainage ditch. It was a small car, a Honda or a Toyota— with the almost zero visibility, I couldn't tell. Whoever had been driving it had lost control of the steering and been blown off the road. It would be easy to do; the gale-force wind was coming every which way. My truck is heavy and solid, but steering it was really hard, partly because the trailer I was towing was fishtailing back and forth like a bullwhip. I, at least, had lots of ballast; still, just fighting the wheel for ten minutes had my forearms burning. And I'm in shape. A small car like that, one extra-strong gust would pick it up and drop it anywhere it wanted to. Already, sand was drifting over it, starting to cover it. In ten or fifteen minutes it would be buried under a mound of sand, invisible from the road.

Stopping was suicide. Every minute I dawdled out there lessened my chances of surviving. But if there were occupants stuck in that car, not stopping was tantamount to being an accessory to murder.

I pulled as far off to the side of the road as I could without risking losing traction and going over. I keep flares under my seat. I reached down and grabbed a handful, and a box of matches with them. Still sitting in the relative safety of the truck's cab, I put on my full-face helmet. (For some quirky reason that I didn't even remember, but was thankful for now, I'd brought both my helmets, the brain-bucket and the sensible one, which has a full visor.) I pulled my jacket collar as tight as I could up against it. Lastly, I pulled on my motorcycle gloves. Holding the flares in one fist, I lit them simultaneously. As soon as they caught, I jammed open my door and jumped out.

One step out of the truck and I was blown back ten feet. It was like I was in a wind tunnel. I'd never encountered weather this hostile before. Holding onto the side of the truck and bracing myself against the wind, I fought my way to the back, where I jammed my flares against the back tires. I didn't know if anyone coming my way would see them, but at least I'd given them a chance.

I worked my way to the front of the truck and rested for a minute. The wind was blowing dead down the road from behind me, so while I was in this position, I had some protection. Pulling my jacket tighter around me, I looked over at the car in the ditch. Already, in just a few minutes, it was almost invisible from the coating of sand that was cocooning it. If I had come by five minutes later, I would have driven right by it.

Taking a deep breath, I broke for the stranded car. As soon as I left my cover, the wind picked me up and lifted me clean off my feet, flipping me onto my side, hard, and I felt the rough tarmac as I scraped along it. I'd have a strawberry tomorrow from my shoulder to my hip. It's the same kind of roadburn you get when you go down on your motorcycle. I've had them, they're painful as hell.

Staying low seemed to work marginally better, so I crawled the rest of the way across to the car. Sliding down the embankment, I brushed some sand off the side window, enough to look inside.

Three pairs of eyes stared back at me. Women's eyes, wide with astonishment, fear, and relief. I'm sure they had figured this was it, they were going to die out here in this godforsaken place.

Between their pushing and my pulling, we pried the driver's-side door open. They were young, dressed skimpily, tank tops and jeans. Not enough clothes for out here this time of year. They had all been crying, their faces were smeared with makeup and dirt. But thanks to the Good Samaritan, they were alive.

"Grab hold of each other arm to arm," I yelled into the wind.

They grabbed their wallets and backpacks and we formed a human chain and worked our way up the ditch to my truck. They all piled into the cab along with me, slamming the doors against the biting sand. We were all scrunched together, two of them jammed up against me and each other, the third sitting on the shotgun sitter's lap. You couldn't have shoehorned another body into the little cab.

I pulled off my helmet, and we took a look at each other. Then they were all trying to hug me at the same time, almost hysterical in their gratitude.

I waited a minute for them to calm down, then we exchanged stories. They were college students, UC Riverside. They had been in Phoenix, visiting the sister of one of them, and had decided to take the scenic route home, stopping at the Spa in Twentynine Palms for a night. They had heard that a Santa Ana might be coming, but no one could imagine anything like this. It was like driving in a whiteout combined with a tornado.

They had been in the ditch for almost an hour. Initially, they had debated about getting out and walking, but that seemed more suicidal than staying where they were and hoping help would come. As time passed, their hopes faded, slowly at first, then faster. They thought they heard a few cars and trucks passing—in the howl of this wind you couldn't be sure of hearing anything—but as far as they knew, mine was the only car who had seen them.

"Or stopped to see if there was anyone inside." Said with anger by Marilyn (from "you know who"—she smiled—"my mother's idea"). She was sitting next to me, in the middle. Pretty, a voluptuous cheerleader's body topped by a classic Irish face and a full head of dark auburn hair.

They were all pretty. Which meant nothing to me, particularly at this moment.

"If you hadn't stopped, we would have died." This from Pauline, the lapsitter.

I didn't know what answer to give them. There was none, because it was true.

"You're not going to die now," I assured them (and myself). "We're going to find someplace where we can wait this out."

I started the truck and put it in gear. We inched forward. The needle on the speedometer was barely registering, but we were moving, that was the important thing. I hoped nobody coming upon where I had stopped would be spooked by the flares I'd left behind. I wasn't about to go back and get them.

We lucked out. The Brigadoon Bar & Grill was less than a mile up the highway from where I'd rescued the girls. We were almost by it before we saw it, but, man, what a welcome sight! I jerked the truck against the wind and skidded into the gravel lot, pulling into an empty parking spot. Several vehicles parked along the front—a few cars and pickups that looked local, a Dodge minivan with bumper stickers advertising every attraction west of the Mississippi, a Lincoln Navigator, and two boxy motor homes with Utah plates. Bracing ourselves against the storm, the girls and I ran for the entrance and staggered in.

The place was one big, barnlike rectangle. Dark wood, rough-paneled walls, black-and-white-checked linoleum floor that rippled from years of seepage. Opposite the entrance was a long bar, with an impressive old back-bar behind it against the wall. This was a serious drinking place, judging by the quantity of the bottles stacked on the shelves. Lots of bourbons, blended whiskeys, and vodkas. A few token bottles of wine, the corks stuck in them for God knows how long, sat in a corner. Several beer taps adorned the bar, in front of which were a row of red Naugahyde-covered stools. High-backed booths, covered in the same Naugahyde, aligned the front and side walls, with freestanding tables in the center. In one corner sat a classic Wurlitzer jukebox circa 1955, and a TV, tuned to a local station, was mounted halfway up the wall. Like a few other old bars I'd come across in my travels—Barney's Beanery in Los Angeles being one well-known example—old California license plates going back to the 1930s had been hammered onto all the walls, wherever there was an inch of free space. Your basic roadside tavern.

In the short moment it took to get from my truck to the entrance, the storm had blown a coating of fine sand over all of us. We looked like pieces of chicken that had been dipped in bread crumbs. The sand had penetrated under my shirt as well, making my skin feel like it had been rubbed with a Brillo pad. Shaking off as much of it as I could, I looked around.

There were over a dozen people in here, not counting the bartender, cook, and waitress, who, although chronologically somewhere in her middle age, looked like she'd stepped out of an old Robert Mitchum B movie, the ones where the good girls are bad and the bad girls are worse. She had a friendly smile, though, warm and welcoming.

"Here's another litter the cat dragged in," she exclaimed with gusto. "You girls look like you've been put through the wringer," she went on, looking at them more closely.

"We were stranded out there," Marilyn told her.

"Luke rescued us." This from Jo Ellen, the third girl.

The waitress gave me the once-over. "A good man is hard to find," she informed the girls.

"The voice of experience?" Marilyn asked, winking at her. Marilyn was the boldest of the three, the ringleader who could get them into trouble, if the opportunity arose.

"Definitely," the waitress responded in a tone of hard-earned wisdom. "How's it blowing out there?"

"Bad," I replied. "The roads're about impassable now. Couple more minutes, nothing'll be moving out there."

"Well, you made it to here, so you're okay. We've got plenty of food, the TV works, and we just pumped out the septic, so we're prepared for the long haul."

The cook called out from the kitchen, "Order up, Deedee."

She left to take care of business. While the girls, who'd brought their packs with them, retired to the ladies' room to clean up, I checked out the others who were sheltering from the storm. A few of them looked like regulars—men who drink in bars like this one; the others were refugees, like us. A family sat at one of the big tables in the center of the room, chowing down on cheeseburgers and fries: mother, father, two little girls, and a little boy, all big and blond like their parents. They reminded me of people I'd known from the upper Midwest, Scandinavian stock. They seemed to be holding up well, considering the circumstances. In a booth, nursing beers, were three middle-aged men who looked like upper-management executives, even though they were casually dressed. On the way to or from a hunting or fishing trip, I guessed. The remaining outsiders, the motor-homers, were three older couples who sat at two pushed-together tables, talking earnestly, eating large meals, laughing quietly at each other's jokes.

Considering how lousy things were outside, everyone seemed to be in decent spirits. Most of them had been here when the storm had struck or had been close, minutes away. The conscientious ones had listened to the weather station and had been warned that the storm was coming. Like the girls and me, they were grateful to have found a refuge where they could wait out the storm in comfort.

I approached the bartender. "Pay phone?" I had to call Riva, let her know I was all right.

He shook his head. "Phone lines are out. Got a generator and a propane backup in case we lose our gas and electric, but no phone. I'd let you use mine, but it's dead, too. Sorry." As if to make amends for my disappointment, which he had nothing to do with, he plunked an old-fashioned glass on the counter. "First one's on the house. Name it."

After what I'd been through, a drink was what the doctor ordered. "Johnnie Walker Black?"

"Ice?"

"Neat's fine."

He took down a bottle from the back bar, poured generously. I sipped—it burned going down, the good burn. I raised my glass in toast.

The girls, having changed their tops and generally freshened up, emerged from the bathroom. They flopped into one of the free booths. Marilyn patted the empty seat next to her, an invitation to sit down.

"I've got to get something out of the truck," I said. "Order me . . ." I glanced at the menu. The specialty of the house was chicken-fried steak with mashed potatoes, country gravy, and choice of two veg. Not today. "A western omelet easy, hash browns, sourdough toast. And coffee."

"You're going back out? That's crazy," Marilyn said.

I swallowed the rest of my drink. "If I'm not back in an hour, send the St. Bernards."

The wind was howling as badly as it had been earlier, maybe worse. Large drifts were forming against the sides of the restaurant and the vehicles. Even bigger ones were pyramiding in the parking lot and on the highway, creating sand dunes.

I fought my way to the truck, yanked open the door, and grabbed my cell phone out of the glove compartment. Dropping it into my pocket, I fought my way back to the safe harbor.

The highway was shut down. Nothing was going to be moving until the storm was over and the road was cleared; at least overnight, maybe longer. We were stuck in Brigadoon, home of the high desert's best chicken-fried steak.

Riva's voice on the telephone was thick with relief. "I've been worried sick. This storm's all over the news. Is there a television where you are?"

"Yes." I hadn't paid it any attention. Looking up at it, from where I was standing at the bar, I could see pictures of sand blowing. If I didn't know the storm was right on top of me, I would have thought they were shots of the Sahara.

"They say it's the worst sandstorm ever recorded in California," she said. "It's not supposed to stop until late tonight or tomorrow."

"I believe it." Looking outside, I couldn't see anything, not the cars in the parking lot, the highway, it was all sand. It was evening now, but it could have been high noon, there still wouldn't have been any sunlight. I explained where I was, the circumstances of getting here, a quick description of the Brigadoon and my fellow stranded pilgrims.

"Sounds like you've got it made." In the background I could hear Bucky making impatient noises. It was dinnertime, she had been in the middle of feeding him when I called. "Three college babes hot for your bod and a well-stocked bar."

"This is true."

"Keep your hands to yourself and don't get too drunk."

"I can do that." That was the last thing on my mind, either of those possibilities.

"Here, talk to your son."

Bucky's voice sang to me. "Daddy, when are you coming home?"

"As soon as I can."

"I love you, Daddy. Come home now."

"I love you, too, sweet boy. I'll be home just as fast as I can."

Riva came back on. "It sounds like you won't get home until tomorrow, if then."

"I guess. Even after it stops, the roads'll have to be cleared."

"Don't push it. Be safe. And cautious."

I've been known to take risks against the odds—but being a husband and father is very tempering against that. "Of course I will."

"Okay, then. I love you."

"I love you, too. I'll call you tomorrow morning."

"Oh, before I hang up. Did you?"

"Did I what?"

"Buy the motorcycle."

With everything else going on, I'd forgotten about that. "Yes. It's outside in the trailer, even as we speak."

"It was worth it, then."

"I guess."

We said our good-byes and hung up. Everything was okay now. It was only a storm, and I had shelter.

"You know what's a bitch?" Deedee the waitress said. She was sitting on a bar stool, shoes off, rubbing her stockinged feet.

"What?" Pauline asked. The girls had moved to the bar, where they had a better view of the television. The news was on: pileups on the freeway, a bank robbery in Palm Springs, and of course, the sandstorm, which got most of the airplay.

"I can't go outside to smoke, 'cause of this storm, and I can't smoke in here, 'cause of the stupid antismoking lobby and the chickenshits up in Sacramento."

Marilyn told her, "It's brutal."

My group had been in the Brigadoon for a couple of hours now, the last to find refuge. Nothing was moving outside; nothing human, anyway. Time passed slowly. We'd eaten, including decent blueberry pie à la mode for dessert (homemade). Most of us were sprawled out around the room, watching *The Simpsons,* which the kids had turned to, except for the motor-homers, who had brought a Scrabble game in with them and were playing a spirited four-handed game, and the executives, who were playing liar's poker.

A general torpor permeated the place. Wally the bartender, Ray the cook, and Deedee had joined the rest of us in the restaurant proper. We had nowhere to go and nothing to do, and plenty of time for both. I wished I'd brought a book along, but who knew?

Pauline leaned across the bar and helped herself to a draft. For the last hour, since everyone had finished their dinners, Wally had stopped bartending and had come around to the civilian side. Those who wanted a drink got their own and dropped bills, honor-system style, into a jug he'd placed on the counter.

The room was close—the windows were shut as tightly as possible and the air-conditioning had gotten clogged up from sand blowing into the filter. We were beginning to breathe each other's air, smell each other's body odors. Before dinner I had given myself a half-assed sponge bath with paper towels, but I still felt grimy and oily. It was getting to be a ripe environment and would get more aromatic before it was over.

The towheaded boy heard the noise outside first. He'd gotten bored with watching television and was standing near the door, staring at the patterns of sand blowing against the window, like snowflakes in a winter storm.

"Daddy, come here."

His father walked over to him.

"Do you see that, Dad?"

"What, Roger?" The man looked out the window.

"I thought I saw something outside." The boy pressed his face to a pane of glass.

His father leaned in next to him. "No, I don't see . . ." He paused; then: "What is that?" he exclaimed, loudly enough that it caught my attention.

I walked over to them.

The father turned to me. "I thought I saw something moving."

I leaned forward and joined him, our heads almost touching. Then we looked at each other, startled expressions on our faces.

Sheer visceral reaction—I tore open the door and rushed outside, the father hot on my heels. It was murky black out, no moon, no stars: only sand, an endless blowing veil. I hollered into the wind, "Where are you?"

From somewhere, a man's ragged voice answered, "Here."

"Where?" I was staggering forward, blind, my hands stretched out in front of me.

"Here," the voice feebly called again, and as I looked in what seemed to be the direction it was coming from, I saw a form.

"We're coming," I yelled, my voice whipping back on me.

The wind was howling. Fine grains of needle-sharp sand were stinging my face like wasps. It was almost impossible to remain erect; the father and I held onto each other for dear life. I had a hand over my eyes for protection, squinting out between my fingers.

Two apparitions, so phantom-like in the turbid darkness they almost seemed to be holograms, not actual flesh and blood, were swaying in front of us. We rushed toward them, the force of the wind so strong it was like running through tar. As we reached the ghost-like figures, both of whom were men, they slowly collapsed to their hands and knees—they had managed, by force of will, to survive long enough to find help and now had nothing left in reserve.

The father called back toward the doorway. "We need help out here!"

His cry galvanized some of the others, who came running out. Pulling the bedraggled survivors to their feet, we dragged them into the restaurant, and safety.

Their names were Joe and Bill. They looked to be in their late twenties; clean-shaven, decent-looking fellows. They were dressed in jeans and sweatshirts, which were completely trashed.

More than anything else, they were badly dehydrated. The kitchen staff provided wet towels and pitcherfuls of water, while the girls immediately and efficiently took over the nursing chores, wiping them down, propping their heads up while they drank, cleaning the dozens of tiny pitted wounds on their faces, necks, and hands caused by the exposure to the storm. The rest of us hovered like a swarm of ants, until we were sure they were in no serious danger.

After large doses of tender loving care from the girls, the two men recuperated sufficiently to tell us what had happened to them.

They had been hiking for ten days in Death Valley, moving from location to location—Zabriskie Point, Telescope Peak, Funeral Peak, breathtakingly beautiful places, desolate and forlorn, where you can go for days without seeing anyone and you have to carry everything in, including your water. They were seasoned hikers, they went out on long, remote trips frequently.

As hard-core hikers will do, they had brought precisely as much in the way of supplies as they'd figured they'd need, based on past experience (when you start out with sixty or seventy pounds on your back, you don't want to carry any extra weight), so that on their last day, a long, strenuous hike back to their car, they had run out of supplies. No food, no water. That didn't matter, in fact it proved they'd calculated their needs almost exactly, a point of pride. Within an hour they would be back in civilization and could stock up on what they needed—snacks, bottles of water, and gasoline—to get them home to San Diego.

Two things went wrong. First, while trying to make better time by driving on an off-road shortcut to the main highway, they had run over some particularly rocky terrain and had punctured the gas tank on their old Wrangler, but they didn't know it, until all of a sudden the needle on the fuel gauge had plunged to empty, and they were stopped dead in their tracks.

That was a bitch, particularly since they hadn't eaten or had anything to drink for almost a day. But they had a phone in the car, they could call for help.

Except that out of nowhere, with virtually no warning, the sandstorm descended upon them with all of its immediate and terrible fury, as it had done to the rest of us.

They were in an impossible situation, and they knew it. They had two options, both dismal: they could hunker down in their vehicle and hope to wait it out, or they could leave it and try to walk to safety. In reality, the first option was no choice at all. If they stayed in their old Jeep, especially without water, they would die, that was as absolute as if it were carved in stone tablets. Help wouldn't get to them in time. The car would be covered, they'd be entombed. Maybe found in a week, maybe not for a month. Whatever the time, they would die.

The girls shivered as they heard this. "Like we would have been," Jo Ellen said.

Joe looked at her. His partner was the principal storyteller; he'd sat there quietly, adding a detail here and there. He'd had his eye on Jo Ellen since he had recovered—she'd been his principal Florence Nightingale. She wasn't bothered by the attention; she was a sexy young woman who had been ogled by men since before she was a teenager and could handle anything a Joe like this could throw at her.

"You were lost out there, too?" Joe asked.

"Luke saved us," Pauline informed him, pointing at me. "Our car was stuck in a ditch."

Joe gave me the once-over. "You get a merit badge for that."

That was an unnecessary remark, but it was no big deal. He had inaccurately sized me up as a potential rival. He didn't know what had happened, and it didn't matter. Not to me, anyway.

"I never got past webelos," I said, smiling to defuse any possible tension. We were all stuck here together for a long time, there'd be enough natural uptightness without letting egos get in the way. At least my ego; I couldn't speak for anyone else's.

"He saved you, too." This from the father, who was a big guy, a good six-three, 225, oak-solid. If he'd said he played linebacker for the Vikings, I wouldn't have been surprised. "In case you'd forgotten."

Joe blinked. He realized he'd overstepped himself. "I know. I appreciate it, believe me. We both do."

Bill went on with their story. They shouldered their packs, which didn't weigh much now, but contained their wallets, Swiss Army knives, etc., and took off on foot. They walked on the highway, following the broken yellow line, at times actually crawling on their hands and knees away from the direction they'd come, because they knew there was nothing behind them for miles. Their only hope was that some civilized outpost lay ahead.

"And you found it," Deedee said.

Bill nodded solemnly. "We found it." He smiled at Roger, the little boy who had first seen them through the window. "It found us."

Roger grinned, ducking his head, shy and self-conscious.

"You're safe now," said one of the executives. "That's the important thing."

Deedee, garrulous and inquisitive, asked, "How long were you out there, out of your car?"

Bill turned to her. "What time is it now?"

She craned her neck to look at a wall clock that hung over the kitchen stove, back in the service area. "Five till ten."

"And we've been in here about forty-five minutes?"

"About that."

Bill calculated in his head. "About three hours. Three hours and change."

The collective gasp sucked all the air out of the room.

"Praise be to God," one of the lady motor-homers sang out fervently from where she was sitting with her husband and friends. They, like everyone else, had stopped what they were doing when we brought the two in and were listening intently.

Joe looked at her. "Amen."

The new arrivals cleaned up as best they could. Ray the cook, a heavyset man with a high, squeaky voice who reminded me of Andy Devine, the old western-movie character actor, fixed two chicken-fried steak specials. They devoured the food, washing it down with pitchers of beer.

It was getting late. The parents laid out makeshift beds for their children. Most of the rest of us would be up all night, zombie-watching a succession of talk shows and old movies.

Deedee had brought out her manicure kit and was polishing the girls' nails. "I used to do this for a living," she told Marilyn as she carefully applied a coat of dark crimson lacquer. "I've done a bunch of things in my time."

"Why'd you quit?" Marilyn examined the nails of one hand as Deedee switched to the other. "You're good."

"Of course I am." Deedee snipped a piece of cuticle. "I got tired of it, especially feet. Sooner or later you get tired of everything, then it's time to pack up and move on."

Bill and Joe finished their dinners and carried the dishes into the kitchen. Ray made a move for them, but they stopped him.

"Least we can do, after all your hospitality."

They washed their plates and glasses and set them in the drain. Then they came back into the main room. Joe wandered over to the jukebox, scanned the titles. " 'Blue Suede Shoes'? 'That'll Be the Day'? Don't you have anything more modern?"

"It's a fifties jukebox," Deedee instructed him. "It plays fifties music."

Joe fished a quarter out of his pocket, dropped it in the slot, punched up some titles. He walked over to Pauline. "Want to dance?"

She glanced at her friends. "Sure."

A slow ballad came on. Joe pushed a few tables to the side to clear room and pulled Pauline to him. They started gliding around the floor, barely moving. More pelvis-grinding than dancing. Bill, not to be left out, cocked his head at Marilyn. She blew on her nails to make sure they were dry, then slid onto the floor with him.

It was real honky-tonk, the whole scene. The fellows kept feeding the jukebox. They switched off dancing with the girls, fast ones as well as ballads. They were all decent swing dancers—the activity was hot and heavy and fun to watch. Between each selection they were all knocking down the beers with regularity. The men held their alcohol fine, but the girls were getting sloppy.

"You're not going to be able to sleep if you drink too much," I mentioned casually to Marilyn, during one of the times when she was the odd dancer out.

"I couldn't sleep anyway," she replied, taking a swallow off a fresh cold one. "This is like being at a fraternity party. You're not supposed to sleep, don't you remember? Or was it too long ago?" she joshed me.

"The memories are growing faint, but yes," I said.

A slow song started up. She grabbed my hand. "Dance with me."

She had a lush, womanly body, which she pressed tighter against me than I needed. Her head rested against my shoulder, her lips brushing against my ear. "Don't worry," she whispered, "I won't tell your wife on you."

I was getting aroused in spite of myself. Mercifully, the song ended before she could feel anything; I hoped.

"Another?" she asked, her hand moving lightly in mine.

A couple of the executives had been watching us—enviously, I realized, with a hit of ego-stroking. I'd been body to body with this lovely young thing, and they hadn't. That was enough.

"I'll sit this one out."

"Chicken."

"You betcha."

She segued over to Joe as the next number came on. I took a stool next to Wally, at the bar. He poured me a couple of fingers of my favorite libation. I was drinking moderately; I wanted to stay sharp.

"Give me twenty years," he said, hoisting his own drink. "Hell, give me ten." He watched the dancers.

"Maybe you should turn off the tap soon," I suggested.

He looked at me. "You think?"

"They're underage. It's going to hit them all of a sudden."

"Okay." He glanced around the room. Everyone else was settled in for the night, as best they could. "It's only them, anyway." He sipped his vodka slowly, still watching the action. "Those guys're sure lucky to be alive. They're pretty damn tough, to have survived what they did." He grinned. "Holding on to a pretty girl, I'll bet that was the last thing on their minds." He watched them dance some more. "So what'd you think of that crappy-ass story they laid on us?"

"What story?"

"Hard-core hikers out in the wilds for ten days, fighting their way back to civilization, all that jazz."

"What's not to believe?"

He shook his head. "You're out ten days, you don't have any food or water, but you take the time to shave and change clothes? Then your ride breaks down and you leave it and walk three hours in this blizzard?"

He had a point there.

"Know what I think?"

I shook my head.

"They're weekend pleasure hikers who got in over their heads and panicked," he said. "But they don't want to look like doofuses, especially in front of these luscious young babes, so they concoct a symphony out of an eight-bar riff."

Something had been tickling the back of my brain, the incongruity between their story and their appearance, now that I thought about it.

"That makes sense," I said. "Not that it matters."

"Life's eternal mating ritual. Mine's bigger than his. Ten days is ten times more macho than one. It has been forever thus," said he, the sagebrush philosopher.

The song ended. Wally wiped the bar dry. "Last call," he announced.

Joe turned to him in surprise. "What for?"

Wally leaned up against the bar. " 'Cause I want to, that's why. In my establishment, I make the rules." He smiled friendly-like at Joe. "And you follow them."

"You don't have to barkeep," Bill said, seconding his friend. "We can pour our own. You want to grab some sleep or whatever, don't worry." He smiled back at Wally. "We won't shortchange you, if that's what you're worried about."

Wally shook his head. "Bar's closed in five minutes. If this was how things are normally, you'd all be saying your Good Night Irenes and making your graceful exits."

"But it's not a normal night," Bill persisted.

Wally stood his ground. "The rules're still the same."

Bill started to say something in return, then held his tongue. "It's your place, man. You say those are the rules, fine. I think they're dumb, but I'm not going to fight you about it."

"That's good," Wally said, " 'cause fighting ain't permitted in here. Last call," he announced loudly. He walked back around to the other side of the bar.

People drifted over, calling their preferences. Wally dispensed on the house. Without my asking, he took down a dusty bottle of Courvoisier XO and poured me a snifterful. "For special company." He winked.

"I'll have a Jack Daniel's on the rocks," Joe said. He didn't like being dictated to, particularly by a fossil like Wally. "A double." Then he asked, "What happens when there is a fight in here?"

"I call the cops. They get here lickety-split."

Joe was leaning away from the bar. "They wouldn't be getting here lickety-split tonight." He shook his head. "They wouldn't be able to get here at all."

Wally put a glass with ice on the bar in front of Joe, poured him his drink. "Then I'd have to call on my ol' pal Brewster," Wally said, turning away and replacing the bottle on the back-bar.

"Who's Brewster?" Joe asked, bringing his glass to his lips.

"This." With a motion as fluid and sudden as a magician's, Wally reached under the counter and pulled out a sawed-off, pump-action twelve-gauge, double-barrel.

Joe almost jumped out of his clothes. Half his drink spilled down his shirtfront. "Jesus, man!"

"You wanted to know who Brewster is." Wally smiled. "Now you do."

The girls were wide-eyed, staring at the menacing weapon.

"Is that loaded?" Pauline asked timorously.

Wally nodded. "Ain't much good if it ain't. Number-twelve birdshot. Makes a large hole in one's anatomy."

Deedee pushed the gun aside, so that the business end was pointing at the ceiling. "Put that stupid thing away, Wally," she commanded. "You're scaring the bejesus out of these girls."

"And me," I added. This was a serious piece of armament. Years ago, when I was the D.A., we'd confiscated similar weapons, before the advent of assault rifles. They're lethal beasts. One pump, the first barrel goes. Another pump, the second. Both barrels can be discharged in less than a second. I've seen wounds caused by shotguns set up like this—they're nasty.

Bill put his hands up in a peace-offering gesture. "Look, man, we don't want any trouble. We're grateful to be here, and we'll be grateful when we can leave."

"Amen to that, brother," Wally agreed. "We could all use some space around us. My suggestion is, we put 'er to bed for the night, and ever'-body take care of his own self." He opened the cash register, scooped the paper money into a bank-deposit bag, and carried the bag and the shotgun back into the kitchen area.

"Good night, folks," Ray said in his high, scratchy voice, waving to us. He followed Wally into the back.

The jokebox was silent now, but the television was still on for the night owls, the sound turned low. Deedee doused most of the house-lights, leaving a few on over the bar, so people wouldn't hurt themselves if they had to go to the bathroom or move around later on.

"Time for me to turn in," she announced. She stretched languidly, her body language clearly saying, *I'm available—anyone care to join me?* She had her eye on the executives, who were oblivious to her. Realizing there would be no takers to her offer, she spread a blanket under one of the booths and lay down.

I wouldn't sleep; a catnap at best. The weather reports had predicted that the storm would be over sometime after midnight. I wanted to be awake if it stopped, so that I could go outside and feel the essence of it, the spiritual force. Something this powerful in nature is a statement. I wanted to find out if, by placing myself in it, I could discover what that was.

The various groups informally separated themselves into their own spaces, gravitating away from the center of the room, so as to have a modicum of privacy. The local men had taken over two booths. They were already dozing in their seats in a slumped-over sitting position, like passengers on a long-haul Greyhound bus. The motor-homers were where they'd been when I arrived. Some were trying to sleep, while the others were still at their board game. The executives, too, were in the same booth they'd been occupying for hours, talking quietly amongst themselves, passively watching television. And the family was in a corner booth near the door, the kids and mother sleeping, all entwined together; the father had moved near the bar, where he was reading a paperback and occasionally glancing up at the television set.

I walked over to a window and looked out. The wind was dying down. I could see the shapes of the cars and trucks, now covered with sand, parked in a haphazard line in front. The sound wasn't deafening anymore, more a hollow whistle than a deep roar. It was still blowing too hard to go outside, but it wasn't nearly as fierce as it had been as recently as an hour ago, the last time I'd checked.

When I turned back to the room, I saw that the inevitable was happening. Jo Ellen and Pauline had paired off with Bill and Joe; Pauline with Bill, Jo Ellen with Joe. Each couple had retreated to a remote corner of the restaurant, as far away as they could get from prying eyes. Marilyn, who was sitting alone at the bar drinking coffee, waved me over. I sat down next to her.

"Romance is in the air," she said, looking at Jo Ellen and Joe, who were making out like bandits, oblivious to everyone else. His hand was under her top, massaging her breast. Across the room, Pauline and Bill were going at it, too, but less conspicuously.

I looked away.

"You don't approve."

"It's none of my business," I told her, feeling prudish.

"You still don't approve."

"In public like that? No." I changed the subject. "Where'd you get the coffee?"

She pointed into the kitchen. "There's some hot in the urn." She handed me her cup. "Would you get me a refill? With a little milk?"

I went into the kitchen, drew myself a fresh cup, refilled Marilyn's. I added some milk to hers, carried the cups back to the bar. I didn't want to, but I couldn't stop myself from looking in the direction of Joe and Jo Ellen.

They weren't where they had been.

"In the bathroom," Marilyn said, cocking her thumb toward the back. "They must have felt your disapproving look."

"I'll be glad when we can get out of here," I said. "I'll be glad when the sun comes up."

"Can I say something?" She sipped her coffee; it was hot, she put the cup down on the bar.

"Sure."

"Your wife's a lucky woman."

I could feel a blush coming on. She had moved on her stool, so our hips were touching. "Thanks," I said. "You don't know me, but thanks."

"I know you well enough to know you're a nice guy. What you did for us." She put her hand on my thigh. It felt good, I can't deny it. "I owe you," she continued. "You saved my life, that's going to be there forever."

"You don't owe me anything, Marilyn. I mean that." This was taking too personal a turn; but I didn't move her hand from my thigh.

"What I mean is, if you wanted to . . . you know . . ." She fixed her look on me.

I looked back at her. God, she was appealing. In another life. "It's a tempting offer. You're very attractive. But I couldn't handle the guilt, and anyway, I wouldn't be that nice guy you like. The one whose wife is a lucky woman."

She smiled at that. "You're right." She moved her hand off my thigh. "You're not mad, are you?"

"No. I'm flattered."

A woman's voice cut through from somewhere in the bowels of the restaurant. "Don't!"

My antennae rose. As I stood from my barstool, turning in the direction of the bathrooms, Jo Ellen stormed into the restaurant. Her tank top was off, her makeup was smeared, and her skimpy bra didn't leave much to the imagination.

Marilyn rushed over to her. "What happened?" she asked in alarm.

Joe came out from where they'd been doing whatever they'd been doing. He was holding her top. "You forgot something."

This had gone too far. "Give her her clothes," I said.

He turned to me. "This doesn't have anything to do with you. It's none of your business."

Everyone, except the mother and children, who were sound asleep, came to life. I looked at Joe. They'd all had too much to drink. This was alcohol talking.

"I'm making it my business," I told him forcefully. "You're out of line, Joe. Now give her back her top."

The father got up and stood next to me, a gesture of solidarity. It was a comforting feeling.

Joe ignored me. "Fucking cocktease," he said to Jo Ellen.

She got right in his face. "I don't even know you, Joe. You're just a diversion," she added spitefully.

His face reddened. "You're full of shit, Jo Ellen."

The father of the children moved close to him. "Watch your language," he admonished Joe. "There are children here." He looked back at his sleeping kids.

"Like I give a rat's ass," Joe sneered. He took a step back, giving himself space.

I'd had it. "Walk away from her," I ordered Joe. "Now. And stop cursing." I started for the kitchen, to roust Wally and get him out here with his shotgun.

Bill's voice came out of nowhere. "Don't be going back there."

I had lost track of him. He was standing in the doorway leading to the bathrooms. One hand was on Pauline's biceps, holding her tight against his body. She was shaking like a leaf, for good reason: in his other hand he held a monstrous automatic.

"You're crazy." The words were out of my mouth before I could stop them.

"You'd better hope I'm not."

I took a deep breath. "Okay," I said , trying to sound as under control as possible. What the hell was all this about? A heavy-duty automatic? Who were these two?

"You're not crazy, you're just frustrated. We all are. We're in a bad situation and we've got to make the best of it." I was churning inside. "Put your gun away, we all take a deep breath, and pretty soon we're out of here."

Bill shook his head. "Pretty soon we're out of here, that's right. Some of us, anyway," he added ominously. He turned to his mate. "Go get the cook and bartender. Make sure you bring the bartender's shotgun."

Joe tossed Jo Ellen's tank top on one of the tables. She snatched it up and put it on. On his way to the back he picked his pack up off the floor, reached inside, and brought out another automatic, a companion piece to his friend's.

Wally had been right to have doubts about these two. But his misgivings had been benign. This was a potential cancer.

"Nobody messes up," Bill addressed us, "nobody gets hurt." He looked around the room. "Everyone move over here," he said, pointing in front of him, "where I can see you."

The others moved into his line of sight. Most of them, especially the older people, were trembling. For once, Deedee was speechless.

"Don't shoot us, mister, please," one of the old lady motor-homers begged.

"Christ Almighty, I don't want to shoot anybody," Bill said irritably. His gun was pointed at Pauline. "Just shut up and do like we tell you and you'll be all right, all right?"

Pauline was hysterical. "Don't point that at me like that," she whimpered.

"I am not going to shoot you. Do you understand?" He looked at her. "Do you?"

She was shaking so hard she could barely stand up, let alone answer him.

I stepped forward. "I'll be your hostage, if you feel you need one. Let her go."

Bill laughed. "You've got power, man. I let my guard down a moment, who knows? I want someone who's powerless."

The talking had awakened the children and their mother. They got up from their sleep, staring wide-eyed at Bill and his weapon. The little boy walked over to his father. "Is that a real gun, Dad?"

"I'm sure it is, Roger." His father was remarkably calm, considering that his wife and three children, all under ten years old, were sharing the same space with a couple of armed, seemingly irrational men. He stood like a mighty oak, drawing his family to him. They all huddled in the comfort of his arms.

Joe came out of the kitchen, pushing Wally and Ray in front of him. He had the shotgun in his hand. Wally and Ray stood in the crowd, next to me.

"You were right," I said to Wally, keeping my voice low.

"Small consolation," he answered.

"Is that shotgun of yours really loaded?" I whispered.

"Fuckin' aye," he whispered back. "Pump, pump; adios, amigos."

Joe hooked a rung of a chair with his foot, pulled it toward him. "Sit down here," he ordered Jo Ellen.

She slunk over to him and sat down. Joe leveled his automatic at her neck. "See what happens when you piss me off?"

She didn't answer.

Bill gave the rest of us the once-over. "Keep an eye on them," he told Joe. He walked over to the front windows and looked out. "It's letting up. We're going to be able to get out of here soon," he said, turning back to his partner.

To go where? I thought to myself. There was something ugly about these two, dangerous beyond the immediacy of this situation. Who were they? Escaped convicts? Professional hit men? And what was the point of this? Nobody was threatening them.

Bill came back to the group. "Anybody here got a cell phone on him, I want them now." He looked specifically at me. "Don't make me search you—if I find one on anyone, it won't go easy."

That killed one possibility of getting out of this mess. I placed my phone on the table. One of the executives did the same. Bill looked at everyone else. "Any others?"

"Mine's in my motor home," volunteered a man.

"We have one, too, in ours," said another.

"We'll leave them there," Bill said, scooping up the phones and stuffing them in his pack. "That's a good place for them." He turned to Joe. "You want the honors?"

"Whatever." Joe's hand, the one holding the shotgun, was resting on Jo Ellen's head. She was taking deep, slow breaths, trying not to hyperventilate. Her knee was vibrating like crazy, tap-dancing on the floor.

Bill looked at the motor-homers. "Who owns the big Winnebago parked by the door?"

"I do," quickly answered one of the men.

"Give Joe the keys."

The man reached into his pocket and drew out a key ring. Joe snatched it. He handed the shotgun to Bill, who cradled it in his lap.

"Don't take forever," Bill said. He laughed. "Knowing you, ninety seconds is a stretch."

"Very funny," Joe said sourly. He yanked Jo Ellen out of the chair, started pulling her toward the door.

We all got the picture. He was going to rape her.

I felt sick, physically nauseated. "Don't do this. You don't need to do this."

"We don't need to?" Bill cocked his head, like a hawk investigating a dead mouse at its feet. "We don't need to? What does that mean?"

Jo Ellen was screaming. "Don't! Please!" She beat on his chest with her fists. "I didn't do anything to you!" Then she collapsed to the floor, sobbing hysterically.

Joe jerked her limp body upright. "Don't freak out on me, goddamnit. It's not the end of the world."

Everyone was frozen, unable to move. Even when I was shot at, during the kidnapping/murder trial, I didn't feel this helpless. Then, at least, I could duck and dodge. Here, I was a fish in a barrel, with a dozen other fish.

I didn't know if I could do anything to stop this, but I had to try. "So far, you haven't done anything, not really." I was playing for time, hoping that I, or any of us, could figure something out that would forestall the imminent horror. "You've harassed us, that's all. Under these circumstances, nobody's going to press charges. But if you . . ." I couldn't say the rest.

My plea wasn't going to work.

"Don't take forever," Bill repeated to his partner. "This storm lets up a little more, we're history."

There was no way to stop them. They had enough ammunition in their two guns to shoot all of us.

Joe pushed Jo Ellen out the door. It slammed shut behind them. Next to me, Marilyn and Pauline were crying, not only for their friend, but for each other.

Everyone else was stunned. Glancing around, I could see that they were all withdrawing into themselves. No one wanted this to happen; but if it had to, they didn't want it to happen to them.

Marilyn looked at me, her eyes red. "You shouldn't have saved us," she whispered.

"Don't say that."

I looked at Bill. He was sitting in a hardback chair, alert, watchful. Pivoting slowly, I saw the parents and their children, huddled up against each other. The parents had formed a human barricade between their children and Bill. If things escalated, they would give themselves up for their kids.

For a moment I was light-headed, seeing this. That could be my son standing there. My wife.

Images from CNN on the television screen caught my eye. The worst of the sandstorm was over. The California Highway Patrol expected to have roads opened by mid-morning. Several people were missing, not accounted for.

Looking away from the tube, I caught Bill's eye. He smiled and pointed one of the guns at me. *Don't even think about it,* he was signaling me.

I turned to the television again. Reruns of stories from earlier in the evening. Storm-related accidents on the freeway: grisly pictures of cars piled up. A bank robbery in Palm Springs. Two million dollars in cash, a guard killed. Robbers were two men, Caucasians. The race for governor was tightening up. It was almost a dead heat now, too close to call.

A bank robbery in Palm Springs. Two Caucasian men.

I turned from the set and looked at Bill. He hadn't seen the television, his back was to it.

My peripheral vision caught the father's eye. He, too, had seen it. After I'd quickly glanced around at the others, it was evident we were the only ones who had.

Bill and Joe were the bank robbers. It fit—on the run, trying to get out of the country, not making it, having to find temporary shelter. It explained why they weren't dressed for the kind of hiking they'd said they'd been doing, why they had been out in the storm so long, risking their lives.

My mind went into overdrive. They had robbed a bank, a federal felony; compounding that, they had murdered a guard. Once this storm was over, the FBI would be swarming all over the desert, looking for them. They knew that. If they were caught, they'd be facing the death penalty. Which was why they were taking their pleasure now. If you're going to be hunted down for murder, you might as well knock off a piece of ass on your way out of town.

I didn't think they would kill us, but it was possible. They weren't afraid to kill people, that was the bottom line. They'd already proved that. I didn't know what was going to happen. The only thing I positively knew was that I didn't want to die. And I didn't want anyone else to.

They hadn't seen the news. That was vital. If they did, it could push them over the edge. They were hovering there already.

The front door opened. Jo Ellen staggered in, Joe on her heels, pushing her. She'd been crying—her face was streaked with makeup—but it was blank now, a death mask. Slowly, like she was walking on two broken legs, she came over to where her friends were sitting and collapsed in a heap on the floor.

Marilyn cradled her head in her arms. She turned to Joe. "You're a bastard."

He favored her with a smirk. "Really? That makes me feel terrible." He turned to Bill. "You're up."

Bill stood up. He cocked a finger at Pauline.

"*No!*" She started screaming. "Please, God, please. No!"

It was awful, hearing her. I was enraged at my own impotence and fear. Then Marilyn did something incredibly brave. Rising to her feet, she said to Bill, "Take me."

He looked at her like she was insane. We all did. Man, what guts, I thought.

She had unnerved him, that was obvious. He pulled himself together, trying to come on cool. "I want her."

"Yeah, right. You want me, but you don't have the balls." She threw down her trump card. "I'm too much woman for you."

His face blossomed so crimson it was almost blue. Reaching out, he slapped her as hard as he could. She flew across the room, landing hard on the floor. Shaking the cobwebs from her head, she looked up at him.

"Is that the best you can do?"

He almost choked in rage. "I'll show you what I can do." He turned to Joe. "Hold the fort." Grabbing her by the throat, he shoved her out the door.

While this was going on, I had my eyes fixed on Joe. He was holding his gun in his right hand, the shotgun dangling in his left. There was a nervous look in his eye, a signal to me that he was concerned about controlling the situation.

"Sit down!" he ordered us. He hefted his gun.

I remained standing. I didn't know how far I could push him, but I had to find out. If I, or any combination of us, were going to try something, it would have to be while Bill wasn't around. He was the brains in this operation, the leader. There was no question in my mind that he would pull the trigger, if he had to. Joe I wasn't sure about. He might panic and go off unexpectedly; but he might freeze up, afraid to take action without Bill's approval.

He looked at me. "Sit down."

I motioned toward the bathrooms. "I've got to hit the john."

He shook his head. "Hold it."

"I can't much longer. I've been holding it for hours."

The kids' parents caught my drift. "The children have to use the toilet, too," the father told Joe, standing next to me.

Joe was flummoxed. "Shit."

"We all have to go," the mother said. She looked around the room. "Who else has to use the facilities?"

Almost everyone raised their hands. Joe squirmed in his chair.

"I can't have you all going at the same time," he complained.

"If you don't let me go, I'll piddle on the floor," Deedee said.

He threw up his hands. "All right. You can go." He thought for a minute. "One man and one woman at a time." He pointed to the kids. "Them first."

"May I go with them?" the mother asked, her arms around her brood.

Joe nodded. "Yeah, okay. You can take two of them now, then the other one." His eyes darted to me, then back to the kids. "The other one stays here with me. When you come back, we'll switch."

"No!" A sharp intake of breath from the mother.

The father leaned over, whispered in her ear. He turned to Joe. "We'll do that. I'll be with her. That's all right, isn't it?" Without waiting for a reply, he walked one of his daughters over to where Joe was standing.

Joe's brain was stalled. "Yeah, it's okay." Trying to turn the momentum back: "Sit down," he told the little girl, pulling another chair close to his.

She looked at her dad. "It's okay, Sarah," he assured her.

The girl, who was no older than eight, sat down primly, her little hands folded in her lap. Joe's gun was resting on his thigh, almost touching hers. "Nobody wants to see anyone get hurt, do they?" he asked, his eyes roaming around the room.

The father didn't flinch. He stood behind his daughter, his hand resting lightly on her shoulder. The man was made of steel; I was admiring him more by the minute.

"Be careful where you're pointing that gun," he told Joe.

"Nobody's gonna get hurt," Joe reiterated almost defensively. "As long as nobody does anything stupid."

The mother escorted the other two children to the bathroom. They all used the ladies' room, including Roger, the little boy—she wasn't about to let either of them out of her sight.

After they came out and the mother rotated with Sarah, her other daughter, I took my turn. Standing at the urinal, my mind was racing. If I was going to make any move at all, it would have to be while Bill was outside in the Winnebago, with Marilyn. Given some help, or luck, I might be able to distract Joe and disarm him. With both of them there, it couldn't happen.

I came back out. The news on CNN was recycling. The story of the storm was playing, the cars piling up on the freeway.

Joe had shifted his chair. He could see the television now. He wasn't watching—his attention was on us, his hostages—but in about thirty seconds, the story of the bank robbery would be on. If he glanced up and saw that . . . I didn't know what the consequences would be, but they wouldn't be good.

The remote for the TV was sitting on the corner of the bar. As casually as I could, I drifted in that direction. My movement caught Joe's scanning eye.

"What're you doing?" he demanded.

"This old news is boring. Let's find something more entertaining," I said as nonchalantly as I could.

I was almost to the bar. The remote was five feet from my hand. Joe looked up at the television. The storm/car-crash story was almost over. The bank robbery was about to roll.

He took it in for two or three seconds, looked back at me. "Yeah, go ahead."

As I lunged for the remote and grabbed hold of it, the story changed. There was the robbery. As quickly as I could, I hit a button.

Comedy Central came on—an old Richard Pryor show from fifteen years ago.

And Joe exclaimed, "What the hell!"

I turned to him. He was locked onto the screen.

"Turn back to the other channel." He had risen to his feet, his eyes riveted on the screen. Then to us, then back to the screen. One hand holding his gun, the shotgun tucked under his other arm. Next to him, Sarah had resumed her place in the hot seat. Her father was right behind her, his hand firmly on her shoulder.

"Which other channel?" I said, playing dumb.

"The one that was just on, that you changed."

By now, everyone was looking at the screen. Richard Pryor was strutting back and forth across the stage, his audience falling out of their seats in laughter.

"I don't know what channel that was," I said straight-faced. "I'm just surfing."

He was shaking. "Give me that thing. Bring it over here."

I had to play Joe very carefully. He was a man out of control who was holding a gun near a little girl's head. Slowly, I walked toward him, the remote in hand. As I got within five feet of him, the father and I locked in. Be careful, his eyes were telling me.

Okay, I thought to myself, as much as I could think with a gun pointed to a kid's head, somebody's going to die here today. Or a lot of us, maybe everyone. So doing something to try to stop that, even if it's reckless, is better than doing nothing, and ultimately, no more dangerous. The most dangerous thing would be to do nothing.

"Here you go," I said to Joe, as I tossed him the remote.

His instinct took over, as I'd prayed it would. He reached out to grab the remote on the fly.

Everything happened in slow motion, dreamlike, a Sam Peckinpah movie for real. Joe was reaching to catch the remote control, the shotgun was sliding from under his arm to the floor, the father was pushing his daughter out of her chair, away from the direction Joe's big gun was pointing. I was lunging toward Joe, catching the shotgun before it hit the floor.

All this transpired in two, three seconds.

If Joe had pulled the trigger on his automatic right away, he might have hit Sarah before she was out of her chair. But he didn't, because I was going for the shotgun. My movement reflexively compelled him to turn and swing his weapon toward me.

The force of the explosion was unbelievable. It sounded like a bomb going off.

The top half of Joe's head wasn't there anymore. The pieces of it, and the pellets that had blown it off, were embedded in the wall.

Everyone started screaming and hitting the floor. The father was protectively lying on top of his daughter. Fragments of Joe's flesh were splattered across his back.

My reaction was delayed, seeing the carnage before me. Then it hit me. I started shaking so hard I fell to my knees, almost keeling over onto my stomach. I'm sure I would have thrown up, or even passed out, if the adrenaline wasn't flowing so hard.

The front door flew open. Buck naked, brandishing his big automatic, Bill came roaring in. "What the hell hap—" He stopped in midsentence: having heard the shot, he had assumed it was Joe, pulling the trigger on one of us.

In disbelief, he stared down at me.

It wasn't until mid-morning that the weather cleared enough for the helicopters to land. When they finally arrived, it was in a long-line cluster, one after the other, like ducks heading south for the winter. Along with law enforcement—county sheriff, CHP, FBI—there were news helicopters: the networks, CNN, Fox News, local southern California stations, too.

Long before then I had called Riva and told her what had happened. It took several minutes, once I'd recited my story, to calm her down and reassure her that I was all right, unharmed, safe. I promised her I'd get home as soon as I could—it would depend on how fast they cleared the roads.

In truth, I was extremely rocky. I was alive, and unharmed; but I had killed two men, and the enormity of that, in so many ramifications, was beginning to hit me. Yes, it was self-defense, not only for me but for all the other hostages, and yes, it was completely justified. Nevertheless, I had looked into the eyes of two human beings and killed them.

During my days as a district attorney, I had sent a few men to death row. One of them had been falsely executed. He'd been innocent, as he had claimed all along, which most of them do; you don't even listen to that stuff. Some years afterward, we found out, to our horror and shame, that someone else had done the crime we'd put him to death for.

All the evidence in the case had pointed to him, and no one ever blamed me; but the experience had weighed heavily on me, so much so that I eventually resigned.

That had been a sobering occurrence; but this hit me harder, even though it was infinitely more justifiable. This was immediate, and there was no refuge, none of the walls we build up as a society to shelter us from such stark reality and ugliness. There's a formal and rigorous protocol when the state kills someone. It's as antiseptic and bloodless as we can make it. And it's still a painful process. In this situation, though, there were no walls. It was primitive and basic, an instinctive reaction. Kill or be killed.

I'd had nightmares for years after that false execution. I knew I was going to have them for this.

Given my status as a former county district attorney, I did the briefing for the law enforcement agencies. Before I told them the whole sordid story, though, they came forth with a piece of information that staggered us.

Bill and Joe were cops. Not anymore; but until recently, they'd worn the badge.

They'd met up as MPs in the army and had stuck together since. In less than eight years they'd done stints with the Border Patrol, a couple of county sheriff departments in Nevada and Arizona, and the Roswell, New Mexico, police department. They didn't last long anywhere—they stood at the extreme edge of violence-prone behavior, way beyond the unspoken but allowable limit most forces tolerate in their officers. To these two, a badge and a gun conferred unlimited authority to trample people's civil rights—and they did. The records were full of allegations of beatings, extortions, attempts at blackmail, all kinds of ugly stuff. Including accusations of rape, none of which ever got beyond a disciplinary committee. They had managed to land on their feet after each jurisdiction let them go; they used police unions, threats of lawsuits, whatever they could to stop the unit they were leaving from vigorously informing others about their true natures. The agencies they were leaving were happy to see them go, be someone else's problem—the old "I'm okay, fuck you" syndrome.

All good things must come to an end. They had finally run out of departments who would hire them, so they went to work as rent-a-cops.

While working for a security agency in Palm Springs, they'd concocted their bank robbery scheme. They knew everything about the security procedures at the bank they robbed—they worked there, it was the ultimate inside job. Except that like most crimes of that nature, it didn't go according to plan, so they'd had to shoot their way out. They were going to escape over the border into Mexico, get lost in the mountains, eventually make their way down to Nicaragua, El Salvador, or parts south. Two million dollars can last a lifetime in Central America. And they might have made it, if the wind hadn't started blowing.

"Brutal story," I said to Keller, the FBI agent in charge of the task force.

"Incredible," he agreed. "Thank God none of you got hurt. Or killed. You all made it through intact."

A young woman was raped, another almost, three little children were traumatized, possibly for life. I don't consider that making it through intact, but I kept quiet about it with him. It was over, Bill and Joe were dead, the toothpaste wasn't going back into the tube.

The father and I finally got around to formally introducing ourselves. "That was incredible, what you did," he praised me. He had his youngest in his arms. She was holding onto him fiercely.

"You're the one who's incredible. You're a rock, man. You can share my foxhole anytime. That whole way you handled it with Sarah . . . I wouldn't have had those guts."

"They were going to kill us in the end, anyhow," he answered. "We gave ourselves a chance. I wasn't going to let them kill my family without trying to stop them."

———————

I was interviewed by dozens of reporters. My face would be plastered all over the tube tonight, tomorrow, for days to come. Newspapers and magazines, too. It was nothing I desired; I've had enough notoriety to last me the rest of my life. But this had been a huge big deal. For a week or so, I and my fellow hostages were going to be famous.

The question that hit me the most was asked by a reporter for the *Los Angeles Times:* "Given all the problems these two fugitives had— the storm, running from the authorities—why do you think they raped these women? What was their point?"

I looked at the dozens of cameras and microphones all pointing at me, all waiting to hear what I had to say. "It's a disease of arrogance certain people in authority get," I ventured. "They want something—like these two wanted that money they robbed—so they convince themselves that they're entitled to it. It's a belief—a dangerous, erroneous belief—that the law doesn't apply to you like it does to civilians, and you can choose not to obey it, and that's all right. The rationale is that you're out there on the streets, putting your life on the line, and you deserve some payback. Which is a very dangerous concept, if you follow it through. Like we saw here."

The girls were airlifted out on a medevac helicopter. The rest of us would have to wait until the roads were cleared and we could drive. Before they left, the four of us shared a private moment.

"We're going to be okay," Marilyn assured me. Once Bill had forced her into the Winnebago, she had taken a cunning tack; instead of fighting him, which would have resulted not only in rape but a brutal beating as well, she had shifted gears and made nice to him, prolonging the foreplay as long as she could. It had worked; she had escaped being raped.

I gave her my card. "Keep in touch. Let me know how Jo Ellen's doing."

"I will."

She lingered a moment while the other two boarded the chopper. "You saved my life," she said once again. "We're bonded for eternity." She smiled. "In many cultures, you're responsible for us for the rest of your life. Do you think you could handle that?"

I smiled back. I could smile, now that our ordeal was over. "Are you going to hold me to that?"

She shook her head. "We're not one of those cultures, unfortunately. Anyway . . . like I said, your wife is a lucky woman. A very lucky woman."

One kiss before parting, maybe never to see each other again. It was a good kiss, not the kiss a married man should be having with a beautiful woman half his age. But somehow it didn't feel bad, or wrong. It felt bonded, the right farewell.

Bill's and Joe's backpacks were propped up on a table in the middle of the room. Behind them stood all the law enforcement people, while the gathered media were on the other side, cameras at the ready.

"Here we go," Keller said. He upended the bags, spilling the contents onto the tabletop. The money came tumbling out. Packets of it, tens, twenties, fifties, hundreds. The cameras clicked and whirred like crazy. If this picture didn't make the covers of *Time* and *Newsweek,* for sure it would be on the front of next week's *Enquirer.*

"That's what two million dollars looks like?" Deedee said.

Keller laughed. "More like half a mil. The banks always exaggerate, 'cause they know Lloyd's of London will try to squeeze them."

The FBI people loaded everything, including the corpses, into their helicopters and took off. The CHP and county boys waited with us. Deedee washed down most of the carnage, Ray cooked up a hellacious banquet, and the drinks were on the house. The clock had not yet struck twelve, but no one was holding back. We all had great cause for celebration.

The roads were cleared for travel by midafternoon. Everyone departed; I was the last one left.

"Thank God for 'ol Brewster," I told Wally.

"Thank God for 'ol Luke who had the guts to use 'ol Brewster," he replied.

I broomed the sand off my ancient truck. It started without a hiccup, a deep growl rumbling from the muffler. They're great beasts of burden, these old American pickups. Letting it idle to warm up, I walked to the rear and pried opened the doors to the trailer.

The seals on the trailer were good. My new prize possession was sitting there all perky, barely a speck of sand on it. I jumped inside, ran my hand along the smooth gas tank, the worn leather seat.

"We're going to have fun," I told it. "We've earned it. By the way, your name is Marilyn, from you know who, and I am going to ride you hard."

I closed the trailer up tight, got into the cab of the truck, and pulled out. Deedee, Wally, and Ray were standing in front, waving good-bye. I waved back. For a few moments I could see them in my side-view mirror, receding in the distance. Then I followed the curve of the road, and they were gone.

AMBUSH

The old man stood apart from the others in a grove of old-growth California live oaks, smoking a hand-rolled. The only things here more ancient than me, he thought as he looked at them, their twisted limbs skeletal-like, black against the not-as-black sky of the night still two hours away from the beginnings of a crisp early autumn dawn. He squinted against the smoke as it curled up from the cigarette that was tucked into the corner of his mouth. His eyes, a startling desert-sky pale blue, were narrow anyway. He had been looking at things critically for over fifty years.

The location that he and the others in this raiding party had come to was a heavily wooded area of Muir County, the least-populated and poorest county in the state, situated in the far north, bordering Oregon, Nevada, and nowhere. Over thirty million people live in California, but less than twenty thousand of them live in Muir County, and that's a generous census. It's a vast place and difficult to get to. There are no interstate or federal highways running through it, and the county and state roads are poorly maintained; in winter, when there are storms every week, or during spring floods that originate from the rivers that flow down from the Sierras, access in and out can border on the impossible, except by private airplane—the nearest commercial airfield is in Reno, hours away. At any time during the year, you can be driving on one of the county roads and not encounter another car, or see another person, for several miles.

This is the unglamorous underside of rural America, as one finds in pockets of Mississippi or Arkansas and other benighted places; an over-all feeling more like Appalachia than California. If you went up to some family sitting on their front porch, took their picture on black-and-white film, and then compared it, side by side, with a photo taken by Dorothea Lange in the 1930s, you'd see strong similarities.

Because of the inbredness of the area, there is a tremendous suspicion of outsiders. Still, it is America at the beginning of the new millennium, with cable television systems and satellite dishes and Internet providers.

A sizable segment of the population is Native American, scattered among four reservations. In recent years, particularly since the passage, in 1998, of Proposition Five, which legalized a myriad of types of gambling on Indian land with virtually no government control or oversight, the tribes have become militant regarding land-use issues, particularly gambling. There have been discussions amongst the various tribal heavies in the county about building a huge, multimillion-dollar resort to attract some of the money that flows into Tahoe, two hundred miles to the south, even though this is a remote area. If you build it, the feeling is, they will come. The gamblers.

There are no other minorities here to speak of. The last census did not list one African-American, and hardly any Latinos or Asians.

Over thirty percent of the permanent residents are on some form of welfare or government assistance. Despite the overall poverty, though, there are pockets of considerable money, based around mining, logging, and ranching operations. That's the legal stuff. Then there are the illegal enterprises—marijuana growing, a huge industry, one of the largest farming industries in California, major meth labs, similar nefarious enterprises. The remoteness of the region lends itself to such clandestine activities.

This is the underbelly of the modern West: not the duded-up version, the West of the rugged and suspicious individual. There are no proponents of gun control around here, none that are vocal, anyway—these are fiercely independent people. Radical fringe groups abound, the kinds of groups you read about and see on television, hard-core fundamentalism crossed with hatred of anything smelling of government, where revelation is at hand and the fire next time is now.

The old man looked up at the sky, at the millions of stars clustering over his head.

His name was Tom Miller, and he had recently celebrated his seventy-ninth birthday. "Celebrated" is an ironic way of putting it; he had not celebrated anything, in the sense of a joyous occasion, for a long time. Even before his wife died, going on a decade now, he hadn't celebrated. The closest he would come then was to take her out to dinner on her birthday. But that wasn't a celebration, it was a ceremony, a ritual from the long-distant past, when there had been cause in his life for celebration.

Which is not to say he didn't find pleasure in life. He loved his work. It brought him gratification, almost every day. But that wasn't celebration, that was satisfaction. That he did a good job and knew it, and others knew it, too.

His job was sheriff of Muir County. Forever, it seemed like to most, but in truth, it had been the last thirty years. His story was one of triumph emerging phoenix-like from the ashes of personal tragedy and adversary. Forged from the ashes, because he had rebuilt his life himself, made it happen by hard, dogged work, self-belief, and mental toughness.

In 1949, freshly graduated from George Washington University Law School after serving with distinction as a marine lieutenant in the Pacific during World War II, Tom Miller joined the FBI. Right from the start he attracted Hoover's eye. He was smart, he was tough, he was incorruptible, and most importantly, he was loyal. He rose through the ranks like a shot, so that by 1965 he was among the boss's most trusted aides, one of a handful thought to be a candidate to succeed the little bulldog if and when he ever stepped down (or more likely, as actually happened, died). He loved Washington, the perks of his office, the closeness to power. Although they lived modestly on a middle-class civil-service salary, he and his wife, Dorothy, had a great life in the capital of the greatest country in the world.

And then it all fell apart, overnight. His son, James, his only child, an honors student at MIT, good athlete and musician, wonderful kid, defected to Canada rather than go to Vietnam.

Miller was contaminated. His chance at the big time in the Bureau was over.

He wasn't fired—there were no grounds for it. Instead, he was exiled. Hoover sent Miller to head the most desolate, out-of-the-way field office that was available: the handful of small-population northern California counties, which included Muir County. He would work in the one-man office, in anonymity and disgrace, for the rest of his professional life.

But something unexpected happened. Miller discovered that he loved the place. The physicality, the enormity of it. The serenity. An urban person his entire life, he learned to fish and hunt, to enjoy long, peaceful hikes in the mountains, to sleep outdoors under a canopy of stars. To his great surprise, he had found his home.

The Bureau's office was a wasteland. Boring, tedious, unnecessary. He endured it long enough to accumulate the minimum years of service that kicked in his pension; then he quit and ran for the sheriff's job. The reigning sheriff, a lazy, corrupt bastard who had lost contact with everyone, even the rich guys who ran things, never knew what hit him. Miller ran a vigorous, grassroots, door-to-door campaign, in two months putting twenty thousand miles on his car as he crisscrossed the county, meeting and greeting, listening to people's concerns.

In June of 1969, Tom Miller was elected sheriff of Muir County, California. He's been reelected seven times since. This is his county, which he runs with unchallenged authority.

But not tonight.

Tonight belonged to the feds, specifically the Drug Enforcement Administration. They were poised to storm a large, low-slung house in the middle of a compound that sprawled out over several acres in the wash below the forest. Ostensibly it was a hunting lodge built by an out-of-state millionaire (what the county was told when it and the adjacent airstrip were permitted and built). In reality, it was a safe house, a refuge for members of one of the biggest drug rings in the country. The men who came and went here with some regularity, about a dozen according to the DEA's intelligence, were the nucleus of this criminal conspiracy.

The compound is an armed camp, but the men inside have come to assume that they're safe, because they have taken great precautions to camouflage their being here. This place is too far out of the way to attract attention, and they keep a low profile. Everything comes in and out by airplane, via their own private runway, which is big enough to accommodate jets up to the size of a 737.

This bust had been almost a year in the making. It was going to be one of the biggest in the history of the DEA, a classic the world will be talking about for the ages. It would go like this: A Gulfstream 4 was coming in from Los Angeles with one hundred million dollars in cash, untraceable. Right behind it, a similar Gulfstream, carrying ten tons of Colombian cocaine, was going to fly in from Mexico. No flight plan, nothing on the screen. The coke was coming from this drug ring; the money from a former Iranian arms dealer who now lived in Los Angeles.

The way it was going to go down was, the money people would check out the cocaine, the dope people would check out the money, the pilots would switch airplanes, and then fly away. The entire transaction would take less than an hour.

There was only one problem with this well-oiled plan, which the dopers didn't know. The Iranian arms dealer was really a federal agent, who'd been playing with federal money in the drug trade, two million so far in smaller buys. Now they were going for the whole enchilada, in one gigantic bite.

Off to the side, one of the agents, an imposing man who had the air of being a leader, talked on a cell phone. He was animated, upset. He listened, made a final comment, shut the phone down in disgust, then strode toward the others.

"Listen up now. This is serious, I shit you not."

His name was Sterling Jerome. He headed up the DEA's Western States Task Force. This was his baby—he'd been the money supplier, he was the man behind this entire operation. Now he was ready to move in for the kill.

Dozens of special agents experienced in operations like this one, who had been brought here from all over the country, gathered around him. All were dressed in black, down to black running shoes or hiking boots, black watch caps, and black windbreakers with the letters DEA stenciled on the backs, in Day-Glo orange, over their Kevlar vests. Each was armed with his own weapon—heavy-duty automatics, Sig Sauers, and Glocks.

Miller fieldstripped his smoke and joined his chief deputy, Wayne Bearpaw, a member of the White Horse Nation, the biggest tribe in the area. They stood outside the circle at some distance from the others.

No reporters were present. That the operation hadn't leaked to the press was a miraculous feat in itself. Afterward, when it was all over and a success, they'd bring in the cameras. They'd been burned too many times with premature expectations.

Jerome was a mean man. Like many of his brother federal agents, he disdained local law enforcement people. His attitude had always been, I've got a job to do, so get the hell out of my way, amateur. His file had more reprimands than it should have, given his status in the department. But he got results.

Miller had known Jerome for years. There was no love lost between the two. Jerome is an arrogant prick in Miller's opinion, an opinion shared by most local cops who have had the misfortune of dealing with him. He had a habit of taking actions in local jurisdictions without checking in first, a normal courtesy. Although this bust had been incubated for over a year, Miller hadn't known anything about it until a couple hours ago, a bad breach of ethics. Not that Jerome gave a shit, the sheriff knew. Jerome preferred it that way.

"This isn't Waco or Ruby Ridge, or any so-called Freeman group," Jerome reminded his charges, some of them veterans of those fiascoes. "There are no women or children inside. This has nothing to do with religion or politics or strongly held cult beliefs or the moon being in Aquarius or any such bullshit. These men we're about to take down are major criminals. Period."

He paused, looked around. For a brief moment, he and Miller made eye contact. Jerome broke it off.

"They have a good security system, but they've become lax about paying close attention to it. It was shut down earlier tonight, but they don't know that." He looked behind him. "Our man here took care of that."

Standing off to the side, apart from the group, was a rough-looking man who Miller knew was not officially part of the task force. His name was Luis Lopez; he was a member of the drug ring's inner circle, now turned informant. Lopez had been sitting in a federal pen, awaiting trial on a murder charge that was going to put him away for the rest of his life, when he made Jerome an offer—drop the charge, and I'll give you the operation. Jerome persuaded his superiors to make the deal (which included a quarter million in cash to Lopez and immunity from prosecution) and got into bed with the devil. They came up with a cover story for Lopez about having to drop the case for insufficient evidence and set him to work.

Lopez was high enough in this operation that he could come and go without arousing suspicion. He'd been on Jerome's payroll for over a year, providing vital intelligence about the security, the number of men inside, all the information the task force needed to mount a successful attack. Lopez had been inside until late last night, when he'd snuck out, unnoticed, after disabling the alarm system. He had assured Jerome that the time was ripe to strike.

Miller knew of Lopez's reputation, which was that the man was an unreliable liar. If this was his operation, he wouldn't be using a scumbag like Lopez.

Jerome blew his nose. "This pollen's killing me," he said as an aside. Turning back to business: "They're heavily armed, we know that, it's to be expected; but we're going to catch them flat-footed. They've been untouchables for so long they think they're bulletproof."

He glanced back at Lopez, who nodded. Then he reached into his briefcase and took out an FBI most-wanted poster.

"It isn't a secret that the politicos back in Washington are getting anxious. They want a feather for their caps. We all do." He brandished the poster. "And even more than shutting these bastards down, we want this man." He looked at the poster himself. "Reynaldo Juarez, born in Mexico, now naturalized, age approximately forty. He's one of the worst characters you're ever going to encounter. He's also one of the great shadow figures of all time, a Howard Hughes of bad guys. He comes and goes like an ill wind, never sleeping in the same place more than a few days at a time. But he's in there tonight, right now." He pointed down to the compound. "We know that for an indisputable fact."

He looked over his shoulder at Lopez, who nodded that this was so.

Given the source of Jerome's information, Miller wasn't convinced.

"We know he's in there," Jerome repeated defensively, as if to quell his own concerns that if this got fucked up, it would be the worst snafu in recent history. "If he wasn't," he added stoutly, "we wouldn't be going in tonight."

Good luck, Miller thought. If Lopez is your primary source, God help the United States of America. He glanced over at his deputy. Bearpaw shook his head—he was thinking the same thing.

"Unfortunately, we've just had a major fucking disaster."

Miller's ears pricked up.

"The airplanes aren't coming in. Neither of them, ours or theirs. Everything's fogged in, from Bakersfield clear to the Mexican border. The deal is off."

Miller looked around. No one was moving; they were barely even breathing. Now what? he thought.

"So here's what's going to happen." Jerome paused. "We're going to go in and take Juarez anyway. We have a legitimate reason to do so: there's an outstanding reward on his head from the Mexican government for being involved in the murder of one of their federal agents. He escaped arrest down there, and no one's been able to lay a glove on him, mainly because no one can pin him down. But we've done it. If we don't take him now, we could lose him forever, *which is not going to happen on my watch*!"

Miller could feel the pit growing in his stomach. This was wrong; you do these things the right way, by the book. You don't cowboy something this important. He was glad, now, that he wasn't involved in this decision.

Jerome went on, "Here's the ticklish part. We want him alive. The word's come down from the powers that be. If he's captured, he can detail myriad drug-smuggling and arms-running operations, stuff that's going on all over the country; hell, all over the world. Dozens of operations we've been trying to break for years—he's an important key to our doing that."

Jerome's gaze swept the assemblage. "When I say taking him alive is our supreme objective, ladies, that's from Janet Reno's mouth to your ears. That's how serious this man is to the Justice Department. If this guy dies, they'll hang the tail right on our sasses. We'll be fucking roadkill."

He paused to let his words sink in. Even though these men were battle-tested veterans of the drug and arms wars, for many of them this would be the most important, blood-pounding encounter they would be involved in in their careers.

Jerome spread out a diagram of their target.

"We've gone over this, you have your own copies. The advance team goes in first, takes out any sentries they might have posted. Once they give us the all-clear, the rest of us go in. We overwhelm them—alive, let me once more stress that—and we are heroes to a grateful nation."

Clenched fists all around. They could feel their blood pulsing harder.

Jerome folded up his diagram and looked at his watch. "Let's coordinate. I've got three forty-one and thirty seconds."

Sixty other men looked at their watches. They were all digital watches, not an analog among them, except for Miller, who wore the same Longines he'd had since his wife had given it to him as a present upon his graduation from the FBI Academy, fifty years ago.

What a crock, the sheriff thought as he watched this hoary exercise. Almost 2000 and these guys are still setting their watches the way they did back in World War II.

"Eighteen minutes," Jerome said.

The agents dispersed, spreading around the perimeter. They were an overwhelming force, who would be in the compound and the house before the men inside knew what had hit them.

Miller approached Jerome. "What's our assignment?" He gestured toward Bearpaw, his deputy, standing a few feet from them.

Jerome looked at him. This was awkward, and annoying. "You observe."

"From where?"

Jerome looked around. Miller was here as an obligatory courtesy, because he was the local sheriff, a former FBI agent, it's his county, and he's not a man you deny—basically, he'd forced his way into this. But this was a federal bust, Miller had no standing, and everyone knew it, including him. If it was up to Jerome, Miller would be home in bed, sound asleep.

Jerome pointed to a hill that overlooked the compound. "There."

Miller looked at where the DEA honcho had pointed. He shook his head.

"That's too far away. I can't observe anything from there."

Jerome could feel his gut tightening. This was an incredibly delicate and dangerous undertaking; he needed grief from some eighty-year-old has-been like he needed the Tijuana runs. But he held his tongue—he didn't have time to get into a personality riff with this old man.

"What do you suggest, Sheriff?"

They're trapped in there. Hunker down and starve 'em out, Miller wanted to say. But that wasn't the point of this exercise. If they went that route, establishing a beachhead and digging in for the long haul, it would become a public siege, with all the attendant problems that had befallen those of recent history. Press up the wazoo. Pro and con interest groups. Meddlesome congressmen. The goal here was surprise, overwhelm, get in and get out.

One caution Miller wanted to give Jerome—if Lopez is your only source of information, you could be so far up shit's creek all the paddles in California won't save you. His reliability quotient is zero. And never let him out of your sight.

Miller said none of that. The question had been rhetorical. "Where are you going to be?" he asked the honcho.

"First one in the door," Jerome told him.

Miller nodded. Jerome had to lead the parade, his ego wouldn't let him do otherwise.

"How's about I follow you in?" Miller suggested. He gestured toward Bearpaw. "My deputy can stay up here, see the overall picture."

Jerome had been blindsided—he should have realized this crafty old soldier would try to finagle a way to be in the middle of the action. But he wasn't going to allow that to happen.

"No." He shook his head firmly. "This is a federal takedown. We told you that when we briefed you. You're not part of the game plan," he added bitingly.

The sheriff didn't acknowledge the insult. "I'll find my own spot, then," he assured Jerome. "Away from the center."

"Good." Jerome turned away.

Miller looked at Jerome's retreating back. Goddamnit, he was uneasy about this raid. Part of his trepidation was historical—government agencies, particularly these agencies, had screwed up too many times. They were too arrogant, cocksure. And they were bulls in a china shop, their instinct was always to charge in, especially if the plan wasn't working as they'd penciled it.

More ominously, their mission was at cross-purposes with itself. Breaking into an armed citadel and physically destroying a major crime ring was one thing; taking a prisoner alive was entirely different. One was a balls-to-the-wall enterprise, no holds barred, individual consequences be damned. The other was an act of extreme delicacy. The two were antithetical, 180 degrees.

He also felt, in his bones, that Jerome had badly downplayed the possibility of armed resistance. Men like those inside the compound don't fall asleep at the wheel. They may be sloppy around the edges, but they're always on the alert. Their survival depends on it.

Hubris. The man's ego was too damn big. Jerome felt that he was impervious, that he had it knocked.

Miller was a student of the history of war. He'd analyzed the classic battle philosophies, Thucydides, Sun-Tzu, Bismarck, Robert E. Lee, his personal hero. Attacks on an unknown enemy, without having reliable sources of intelligence, often led to crushing defeats: witness Lee's at Gettysburg, caused by Jeb Stuart's not being on time with the correct information about the size and scope of the Union Army.

He would not have authorized this raid based on nothing but information provided by a turncoat like Lopez. Snitches are fundamentally unreliable. He would have found a way to get his own mole inside.

But this was not his operation.

He thought about something else, peripheral but related to this action, something no one knew, not even Bearpaw, whom he trusted like a son: he had decided to hang it up. The next election was coming in a year, and he wasn't going to run again—he was going to retire. Time to pass the torch.

From Bearpaw and resignation, his thoughts turned to his son, James. They had fallen out over Vietnam and had never reconciled. Miller blamed James for the loss of his career with the Bureau and had hardened his heart against him.

He had not heard from James since Dorothy's funeral. He didn't know if he ever would again.

He came back to the present. He would be all right—since Jerome had rebuffed him, he wasn't going to be in any direct line of fire; and he had no need to be a hero and disregard Jerome's directive. Still, there was always risk in something this dicey, and he was going on eighty. You shouldn't be doing something this risky, this physical, at his age, even if you're in great shape and could pass for being a decade and a half younger.

For all the action he was likely to see, he might as well go home; but he had to be here. This was taking place in his county; he was responsible to his constituents for law enforcement in his county, even if it was being performed by an outside agency.

There was something else, too, more important. More personal. This would be the last big operation he'd ever be involved in. If there was trouble, and he went out in a blaze of glory, it would be a good way to die. He was going to die soon anyway; whether tonight or in a few years, it was there, looming before him. This would be an honorable way, fulfilling on many levels. But that was to be denied him now.

Miller walked over to where the others were congregating. Sixty men in the party. The assault teams comprised fifty of them, the other ten would be at the fence line, manning the artillery that could level every building if it came to that. Which wasn't going to happen, but they had to prepare for it. Their dogs, in portable kennels, were far enough back from the compound that the sounds of barking wouldn't be heard inside, although they were trained to be silent except when on the scent.

The advance contingent slipped into the compound. The perimeter was fifty yards all around the main building, clear, unprotected ground. This was the most dangerous part, bridging that distance.

Time was another dimension now, slowed almost to a standstill. Seconds drifted by like leaves on a quiescent stream; five minutes: an eternity.

Everyone was on edge, waiting. Miller could feel the collective adrenaline pumping. His own pulse was quickening, a rare occurrence. Looking toward the target, he saw that the advance party had safely crossed no-man's-land and were closing in on the house, protected by the shadows cast off from the light of the moon.

Miller looked at Jerome. The man was standing in place, but his body was quivering—you could almost see electrical charges zapping out from him, he was so wired. He was going to explode from his inner pressure if this didn't come off, and soon.

Jerome put up a hand for silence, even though there was no sound, no movement anywhere near him. He listened over his earpiece.

"All quiet on the western front," he relayed in a whisper. "Time to rock and roll."

They filtered into the compound and spread out, Jerome leading the frontal assault, two more teams on either flank, a fourth going around to the back.

Miller had taken a position on the high ground on the other side of the fence, two hundred yards away, where he had an unobstructed view. Standing next to his deputy, he watched through his binoculars. This is dangerous and stupid, he thought to himself, you don't put yourself in a cross fire, the way Jerome had them spread out. Jerome was too sure of this operation, he wasn't taking all the proper precautions.

He watched through the glasses as the men inside moved closer to the target. Maybe I'm wrong, he grudgingly had to admit to himself, intently surveying the action. A part of him did not want this to go perfectly. Being shut out didn't suit him—he was a man who wanted to be in the middle of the action. Even if he was too damn old.

He kept watching. In a few seconds Jerome would be leading the charge through the front door. With any luck, it would all be over before—

The sound was first: an all-points alarm, an earsplitting, pulsing siren, like a maximum-security penitentiary signaling an escape. And then, within seconds, the rest of all hell broke loose. The entire compound was lit up: one moment everything was in darkness; the next brought on dozens of high-density lights that lit the place up like a night game at Yankee Stadium.

The agents in the compound were caught totally off-guard, frozen in their tracks like a herd of deer caught in headlights. Then before they could react further there commenced a firestorm of gunfire from within the house, so deafening it almost obliterated the sound of the alarm.

Miller watched the debacle unfolding, for the first few seconds as dumbfounded and paralyzed as the men inside. Then he came unstuck. Jesus Christ! he thought. They've walked into an ambush!

A lifetime of reflex took over. He began running toward the action. He was almost eighty years old, but he could still run pretty well when he had to. Out of the corner of his eye he saw Bearpaw, running with him stride for stride.

Inside the compound, the agents were scrambling for cover. Half a dozen were down, wounded or dead, their screams of pain louder even than the cacophony from the siren and the gunfire. The rest were running, crawling, whatever they could do to get out of the line of fire.

Jerome had reached the cover of the edge of the main building and was shrieking into his headset: "Fuck taking them alive, take this fucking building out! Fire! Fire! Fire!"

Immediately, from outside the compound, the rear-guard agents started laying down a carpet-bomb barrage of mortars at the building. Shells and tear gas. Within seconds they'd hit their target, shattering windows and blowing huge holes in the roof. The inside of the building burst into flame, fire and black, tarry smoke pouring out from all sides. There was a brief pause, no more than a few seconds; then came the sounds of bullets and other munitions going off inside.

They've got ammunition in there, Miller realized. By now he and Bearpaw had breached the perimeter and were about forty yards from the house. "It's going to blow sky-high!" he screamed to his deputy above the clamor. "We've got to get out of here!"

They turned and started hightailing it back toward the safety of the woods.

Jerome had the same realization. "This place is going to explode!" he cried out. "Everybody get the hell out!"

His men scrambled to their feet and started running for cover. Disregarding their own safety, pockets of agents picked up their wounded comrades and dragged them along the ground, away from the house.

Miller and Bearpaw reached the safety of their former viewing place. They watched the debacle unfolding. Miller was bent over double, gasping for breath. "Bastard Lopez double-crossed us," he cursed. The first goddamn rule of informants—never trust them.

Bearpaw nodded grimly. Turning their focus to the house, they saw the fugitives staggering out, running in every direction, assault rifles and other state-of-the-art weapons in their hands, firing wildly. Most of them had been blinded by the tear gas—they ran like rabid dogs, weaving incoherent patterns.

Jerome and the remaining agents had safely retreated to the edge of the compound. "Secure the perimeter!" Jerome screamed at his men. "Don't let them break your ranks!"

Dazed and frightened from the unexpected counterattack, his people managed to form a raggedy circle, forcing themselves to be professional in the face of this world-class snafu. They began returning fire.

Miller had dropped his field glasses. He didn't need them to view this carnage.

"What a disaster," he said softly, more to himself than to his deputy, who had never seen such a bloodbath. Miller was both angry and regretful. Men were dead down there who didn't have to be.

The house blew. Sections went, then in one tremendous blast, a fireball billowed up to the sky, pieces of the structure flying hundreds of feet into the air, then crashing to earth, scattering burning debris all around, some of it falling on the men, federal agents and fugitives indiscriminately.

The DEA agents were badly bloodied, but their enemy was worse off. They couldn't see, and several of them had been wounded by the force of the explosion of their stored ammunition, and the fallout from the burning rubble.

Jerome was on the bullhorn now. "Drop your weapons and stand in place!" he ordered the surrounded fugitives.

The men who had been inside the house knew when to be brave and when to be smart.

Three federal agents dead, three wounded. Four fugitives killed.

Juarez was not among the captured.

Jerome was birthing a hippopotamus. "Where the fuck is he?" he screamed into the night sky.

The prisoners, lying facedown on the hard dirt, arms and legs spread wide in the prone position, were being handcuffed. Some were bleeding. Their wounds would not be attended to until this was over and they were brought back to civilization, which was going to take a while. Hours, at least.

Jerome bent down to one of the prisoners whom he knew to be Juarez's second-in-command.

"Was there anyone left inside?" Jerome questioned the man, grabbing him roughly by the throat. Fuck their civil rights and all that other fucking protocol, these motherfuckers were going to give it up.

The man shook his head. "No one stayed inside." He coughed. "The place was blowing up. We're not stupid."

"What about Reynaldo Juarez?"

Another head-shake. "Ain't been there. Some time now."

"We *know* he was in there!" Jerome insisted, his rising voice betraying his desperation.

The prisoner spat blood from the inside of his mouth onto the ground at Jerome's feet. "You know wrong."

Jerome and his senior agents circled around Lopez. "You said he was in there," Jerome braced Lopez. His voice had a rasp that could cut glass. "You swore that you saw him."

"He was in there," Lopez defended himself.

"Then where the fuck is he?"

Lopez backed up a step so as not to catch on fire from Jerome's breath. "Still in there, probably. Probably dead. You guys were so fucking gung ho, you killed his ass."

Miller, standing nearby, listening, silently agreed with the informant. Not about Juarez's presence—that had been a classic shuck on Lopez's part. But regarding the tactics Jerome had employed, he was in accord with this slime. Jerome, like all cornered animals of prey, had reverted to his true nature. When in doubt, destroy. Even if you go down with your captive.

"He'd better be in there," Jerome warned Lopez.

"Or what?" Lopez countered.

Jerome flared crimson. "Don't push my buttons, man. I'm close to committing justifiable homicide, right here on the fucking spot."

"He was in there when I left." Lopez dialed his attitude down a scosh. "That's all I know. That's all I promised. The rest was your shit, kemo sabe."

Fire hoses cooled the burning areas inside. The agents went inside, looking around. Miller tagged after, checking the place out. This is plush, he thought. And why not? These people were making tens of millions of dollars a month, they could afford the Taj Mahal.

The dogs were brought in. They began sniffing around, going from room to room. There were no bodies anywhere. Nothing human could be seen. Luckily the electricity was still running.

The action moved into the kitchen. A huge room, like something out of an English castle. Against one wall there was a bank of refrigerators and walk-in freezers, as big as those in a meatpacking plant.

Jerome watched the dogs sniffing around aimlessly, becoming increasingly agitated. Time was slipping out of their hands.

Miller, posting nearby, watched him. This is how careers are ended, he thought with no regrets for the man. Good men had died tonight because of this shitheel's decisions. You reap, you sow. His own career had been snuffed for a transgression far less egregious and not even of his own making.

A cacophony of dog-howling broke his reverie.

"Might have something, chief!" one of the handlers called to Jerome.

All the dogs had converged at one of the freezer doors, straining like crazy at their leashes, baying like banshees.

"Open that door!" Jerome yelled.

The door was pried open. A blast of cold air hit those closest to the entrance; then the dogs, pulling their handlers, led the search party inside.

It was icicle-forming cold. Uncovered lightbulbs hung from the high ceiling, casting pale pools of light in the dim chamber. Jerome, leading the rush into the cavernous compartment, noticed a thermometer on a wall: thirty degrees below freezing.

The agents' shadows leaped against the dark walls as they made their way into the room. Even with their jackets on, they immediately began shaking from the sudden glacial blast.

"Back here!" one of the handlers was calling, holding onto his dog for dear life, the eager animal barking nonstop at something in the far back of the freezer.

Jerome ran toward them, pushing past the dogs.

In the farthest corner of the deep space, huddled behind some pallets, a man was crouching, hunched up into a tight, embryonic ball. He had a blanket wrapped tightly around him, but he was shivering uncontrollably. Frost had formed on his hair, his eyebrows, his neatly trimmed mustache and beard. He looked up as his captors converged on him, his eyes red and watery from near freezing.

The feather was back in Jerome's cap. It was tarnished, because of the deaths incurred. But he had accomplished his mission: criminal ring busted, mastermind caught alive.

Jerome called the head of his agency in Washington, who patched him into the Justice Department. The attorney general came on the line, offering congratulations for their success and condolences for their losses, which were terrible, but this was a war and regrettably there are casualties in war. It could not be denied—this was a big win. After all the disasters and fiascoes of the last decade, it was great to have a win.

The night was still shrouded in darkness, but not for long, Miller calculated, looking at his watch and then at the sky. In less than half an hour false dawn would begin to show in the east. Bearpaw had gone home—they had come in separate vehicles. There was nothing for him to do anymore.

Miller couldn't bring himself to leave. It was almost as if he didn't believe Jerome and his men had pulled this off.

He'd been rooting for them to have blown it. Part of him, anyway. The part that distrusted and disliked men like Jerome, whose careers will forever be on the ascendancy, even when they fuck up. And this had been a fuckup, no doubt about that. It had been dumb luck that Juarez had been captured and alive to boot.

They locked the ringleader in the command trailer. He was given a quick grilling by Jerome and his top lieutenants. The prisoner gave them nothing. That was all right; there would be plenty of time to get what they wanted. Years.

The agents herded their prisoners into the heavily armed vans, preparing to caravan out. Everyone was bone-tired, more so emotionally than physically; this had been a hellish experience. Jerome came out of the command center momentarily to confer with his seconds-in-command about final preparations for their leave-taking. The men discussed the fastest route out. Jerome would ride with his star prisoner in an isolated van. He wasn't about to let Juarez out of his sight.

How it happened, nobody knew. Not then, not later, when they desperately tried to reconstruct it. Juarez had been handcuffed—everyone involved would testify to that. There was a slight noise to their rear, like a tree falling to the ground. As Jerome and the others reflexively turned their heads to look, the door to the trailer burst open and Juarez, miraculously unmanacled, came flying out, taking off like a bat out of hell for the cover of the nearby forest.

His break, so surreal and unexpected, froze everyone just enough to give the prisoner a few precious seconds to a good fifty yards between himself and his captors.

Jerome found his voice. "Don't let him get away from us," he screamed. He started running, stopped, turned back, almost tripping over his own feet, he was so out of control. "Some of you stay here, guard the prisoners! Come on, everyone, the rest of you!" He was already running in Juarez's direction.

It took a moment for the confusion to end—men running, then stopping, trying to make sense of this, whom to go, whom to stay; then half of them started chasing after Juarez, yelling unintelligibly at each other.

Jerome, leading the pack, was bellowing the loudest of all. "How the fuck did he get loose?" he screamed, charging into the darkness after Juarez.

Miller, hanging around on the periphery, heard Jerome's shouts, then saw Juarez fleeing. He began running after the escapee himself. He knew this territory better than anyone else, but this was like chasing a rabbit in a thicket.

It was too dark to see with any clarity. Men crashed through the woods, tripping and falling over rocks and tree roots, cursing.

Then a single shot rang out, echoing like distant cannon fire.

Everyone ran in the direction of the sound.

There were more than thirty men in the chase, and they had more than thirty stories. Not one of them saw who fired the shot. But when they came upon Juarez's body, they saw that it had been a clean kill, through the head and out.

They formed a circle around him. For a moment everything—the men, their breathing, the wind in the trees, even the movement of the clouds in the sky—was frozen. Then Jerome knelt down and shook the lifeless figure, yelling, "Don't die, don't die on me, you fuck, don't!"

He was shaking a rag doll. He dropped the body back onto the dark ground, looking around wildly, frantic with anger, panic, and fear. "Who shot him?" he screamed almost tearfully. "What stupid fuck . . . who the fuck . . . who the fuck . . . *did this?*"

His men watched him slump to his knees, his head buried in his hands. They knew he had won the prize of his life—lucked into it, to be cold about it—but still, he had done the deed; capturing Juarez was going to be his career-maker, and then, without warning, it had been taken away from him. Not just taken away, ripped away. Deliberately. Someone had wanted this man dead. And got him dead.

He was fucked, fucked, fucked. How was he going to explain this to his bosses?

All their weapons, their 9mm Sig Sauers and Glocks, had tremendous velocity—no skull and handful of brains was going to stop the bullet, a clean in and out, which was later found lodged in a tree by the body, stripped of its casing so ballistics couldn't match it to any particular gun. An incredibly important federal prisoner had been murdered, and not one of the men there had a clue as to who had done it.

PART
TWO
SIX MONTHS LATER

GHOSTS

The telephone rang. Riva answered it. "Luke," she called. "It's for you."

She said this in the distracted tone of a woman who has more important things to do than answer the telephone, especially when the call isn't for her. The important thing of this particular moment was that she had her hands full with our son, getting him ready for his bath. He likes them fine, splashing around and playing with his rubber duckies, but there's a ritual involved. You don't just say, "It's bath-time," and he plops right in. There are steps along the way that must be strictly adhered to: undressing steps, drawing-the-bathwater steps, placing the toys in the tub, etc. Each in its own time and sequence. If a step gets out of sequence, it's back to the beginning.

Naturally, these things can take time. You learn to adjust to his clock—you have to, he won't and can't fit into yours. I have discovered, over the past year and a half, since Buck motored his first crawls across the living-room rug, that his life revolves around rituals such as this one. Everything in his existence has a ritual, some quite elaborate and complex. They keep his parents hopping. I'm fond of them all, but I go to bed earlier now and sleep like a felled log. If Riva and I lay each other once a week, we feel we're doing pretty up-and-walkin' good.

I took the receiver. It was wet and soap-filmy. I dried it on my T-shirt. "Hello?"

"Luke?" It was a woman's voice. Not one I recognized. It sounded like someone who, even knowing who was on the other end of the line, was still surprised. "Garrison?" There was a hesitancy in her pause beyond the mere saying of my name. The hesitancy, I realized, had personal rubbing up against it.

"Yes."

"It's Nora Sherman. Nora Sherman Ray."

I almost fell over. Literally.

Some history. Nora Sherman was the Hillary Rodham of our Stanford Law School class. She was the smart, driven, motivated hotshot woman/feminist law student, top five percent of the class—*Law Review* coeditor, etc.—who fell in love with and married Dennis Ray, the smart, driven, even more highly motivated hotshot male law student: *first* in our class, *Law Review editor*, etc., etc., etc.

Unlike most of us, who came from cities and suburbs, Dennis was an old-fashioned country boy. Born and raised in Blue River—the main town, if you're charitable in your designating, of Muir County, a three-traffic-light bump on one of those county roads up at the top of northern California that goes from nowhere to nowhere. The kind of place that defines itself by those who have left it, which is anyone who has any ambitions and dreams.

Dennis had dreams, and ambition to burn. A hardscrabble kid from the remote sticks, he joined the marines the day after high school graduation, because that's what you did if you wanted to get out. Even before he was sent to Vietnam, which was a successful tour of duty in that he survived the experience intact, he soon figured out that he had more brains than any of the people his path crossed, including his officers. He was counseled by a savvy major he served under to go to college; in short order he applied to Berkeley, won a Regents scholarship, graduated magna cum laude, Phi Beta Kappa, you name the honor, he won it. Then on to Stanford Law, where he met his future wife.

There was a kind of wild, old-fashioned American-style romanticism to Dennis's life—the poor rural background that evoked Steinbeck, the up-by-the-bootstraps saga he'd lived thus far. He was older than most of us—he'd been to Vietnam, an experience those of us who hadn't seen war, which was almost all of us, couldn't begin to understand—and he had this great, empathetic charisma. Everyone was attracted to him.

The man was lightning in a bottle. He could go days without sleep and be as coherent and original and brilliant at the end as he'd been in the first hour. You can, of course, pay a price for that kind of intensity—it's called crash-and-burn. Which he would do, but then he'd be up and at 'em again.

Nora didn't have that kind of energy, but she had almost as many smarts.

Even though I was considered the real deal myself, I was far behind Dennis and Nora, those two shining constellations. We all were. In a school where everyone was expected to make it—however you define that—they stood out.

Dennis got the plum job out of our class: a clerkship for Justice Rehnquist (himself a Stanford Law grad) on the Supreme Court. During his two-year stint he impressed the hell out of everybody—his fingerprints were all over his most important writings, despite his being politically and philosophically in the opposite corner from the justice. He was able to park his own impulses and open a door to his brain, it seemed, ferret out his thoughts, then elucidate them in lovely, precise, muscular language. Many watchers of the court felt that his writing was at its most vibrant and important during the time when Dennis Ray was his chief clerk.

Nora followed him to Washington, of course. His career would always come first. She taught at Georgetown and did pro bono work for Legal Aid.

They were primed to go. They moved west to Denver—her hometown, where her family was well-connected—ready to take the world by storm. The master plan was that Dennis would work for a few years in the D.A.'s office (starting at a very high level, as befitting his credentials), getting practical, hands-on experience, particularly in trial work, the glamour post, then either go into private practice with some big firm, making more money than he'd ever dreamed of, or go into politics.

Dennis was received like a returning prodigal. It was as if Denver had been waiting for his arrival—six months after he and Nora moved there, he was a native son. Those in the local know figured he was the one who would make the world forget Gary Hart; that's how highly esteemed he was, starting out.

Nora joined Johnson, Pitcher, & Gross, Denver's biggest firm. She was on the partner track from the start. If, as was likely, her husband did go the political route, she'd be making more than enough money to support them in the style to which she was accustomed and he aspired to. They bought an old Victorian downtown, cherried it out, acquired a female golden retriever puppy from a reputable breeder, and started living good.

And then, the unimaginable happened. Dennis failed. He tanked, utterly, completely. A genius in the classroom or in an appellate judge's chambers, a theoretical wizard who could dissect any case and cut to the

heart of the matter with unfailing precision and incisiveness, he was a
very different person in the hurly-burly, gritty, smelly world of court-
rooms and backrooms and corridors where the real, nasty, harsh decisions are made—the world where not only his brain but his wits and ass
were on the line, not under some senior's protection.

He left the D.A.'s office without fanfare. He'd been there fourteen
months and never won a case that went to trial; after three losses, at
least two of which he should arguably have won—the prosecution's
overall success rate was over ninety percent—they moved him into another division. Which he was good in, particularly with analysis, as he'd
always been, but this obviously wasn't where he belonged.

So he moved. To a hot, relatively new, medium-sized firm that was
on the upswing. One of their founding partners was a former U.S. sen-
ator, another an ex-member of President Ford's cabinet. Twenty-five
lawyers, all sharks and bright in the firmament—you could camp out
under their collective light. Dennis would be the backroom brain, the
wizard who pulled the invisible strings.

But again, something went wrong. Or, more accurately, it never went
right. He couldn't cut it, even with all these heavies pulling for him, supporting him, covering for him. Something had gone wrong with Dennis.
He was a classic case—a man who shone under certain circumstances
that were nurturing and protective, but couldn't transfer his talent elsewhere. Like the class president whose destiny is the stars and winds up
teaching junior high school history.

Looking back, it was predictable, if almost inexplicable. The manic
depression, which had been misdiagnosed as the inevitable fruits of genius, the impossible expectations—he had fought mightily to overcome
his hard-wiring and his background, but blood will out. Blood and generations. Underneath the gorgeous facade there was a heartbreaking
fragility—an eagle's body on a sparrow's frame.

Some people, notably his in-laws, trying to be charitable and at the
same time to salvage some honor from this Olympian fall, implied that
Vietnam had done him in—a delayed reaction to the horrors of war. But
that wasn't true, and Dennis didn't like being labeled a burned-out war
casualty. To his credit, he wouldn't use it as an excuse.

The firm let him go. He was devastated, even though he and Nora
had seen it coming for months. His failures, as crushing as they could
be, were doubly hard to take because by then Nora had become a star
in her own right. Their paths were moving in completely opposite di-

rections. By the time Dennis was out on the street, she was a full partner in her firm, the youngest they'd ever had.

He had nowhere to go in Denver. He was a marked man, a public failure. His life became a daily series of encounters that played out, in his increasingly suspicious mind, as intentional humiliations. He had to leave, try to make it fresh somewhere else. If such a place existed.

Nora was his wife. She had married him for better or worse; she took those vows seriously. Her parents and other family, her blooming career, it didn't matter. She loved Dennis, way more passionately than anyone could understand. She left with him.

At that point they dropped off the face of the earth, as far as their friends and colleagues were concerned. By the time our tenth class reunion rolled around, not one of us had heard from them in years, although several of their friends, including me, had tried to find out what had happened to them. They had pulled a full-on B. Traven—vanished without a trace.

Until this moment.

All this flashed through my mind in about two seconds. "Hello, Nora," I said. "How are you?" This was a banal response, I knew, but I'd been thrown off-balance.

"I'm fine," she said. "I'm doing fine."

Her tone of voice seemed, to my ear, to belie her words, but it had been a long time. I couldn't recall exactly what she did sound like under various circumstances, such as happy or sad.

"This is amazing," I told her. "No one's heard from you guys in years."

Her muted reply was, "I know."

"So," I went on, excited at reestablishing contact with them after all these years, "how's Dennis? Where are you living, anyway?"

There was a pause on her end. She was collecting herself. I don't know why I knew that, but I did.

"Dennis is dead. I'm living in Blue River. I've been living here for almost fifteen years." She paused. "This was our last stop. After we left Denver and a few other places. It took us a while . . ." I could feel the hesitation, the searching for the right words. Truthful but not totally debasing. ". . . to figure out where it was right for us to be."

I thought I was going to go into shock—I'm not exaggerating. I was light-headed, my skin felt clammy, my lunch started boiling in my stomach. I started to shake; I leaned against the wall to support myself. Looking over, I could see Riva and Bucky through the open bathroom door. They were in the bathtub, playing with his toys, splashing water on each other. Two happy people, oblivious to me, thank God. If Riva had seen me, it would have scared the shit out of her.

What the hell had happened? When? Dennis and Nora had been living in Blue River—for fifteen years? The backwater Dennis had worked so hard to leave behind, like a snake sheds a dead skin?

When they left Denver, all of their friends, yours truly included, stopped hearing from and about them. Now I knew why. But Dennis dead? That doesn't happen to men in the prime of their lives. Not to any I'd even known, outside the battlefield. Not to one of your heroes.

"I . . . I'm sorry," I stammered. Shit, that was a lame reply. "I didn't know . . ."

"That's okay," she responded quickly—she was braced for this. "No one knew. None of our old crowd. Stanford or the other places."

My breathing was coming easier, although I still felt nauseous. "How long has it been?" I couldn't bring myself to say the word *die, dead,* any derivative.

"Four years."

This was sounding worse and worse. "Was it . . . ?" Shit, what? An accident, murder, self-inflicted? I felt like a ghoul. "Forget I asked that." I had to change the subject, this one was too overwhelming, especially without any warning. "What're you up to? Are you working, do you have kids?"

"We never had children." Another pause; another painful subject? "And yes, of course I'm working, I'll always work, I'm the repository of ten generations of Protestant guilt. If I hadn't been working, I don't know what would have happened. To me, how I would've coped."

Abruptly, her tone of voice changed. "Hey, you know what, you don't need to hear this now. Not over the telephone, after almost twenty years. Anyway, that's not why I called, Luke, to talk about Dennis or any of that. If we get together—which I hope we will—we can talk about it. Wine helps, and vodka's even better."

"Uh-huh." Where is this going? I thought, having recovered, at least partially, from this two-ton safe that had just been dropped on my head.

"So, to amplify your question about 'am I working?' I've been with the district attorney's office for eight years. In fact, for the past four years, I'm the man."

"You're the D.A. of . . . ?" This was an interesting twist, the big-city sophisticate running the show in some obscure, backwater county. The last job anyone would've expected to happen to a woman like Nora. Where the hell was Blue River, anyway? Up north in the tules, but I couldn't remember what county, exactly.

"Muir County. Blue River's the county seat."

"Oh, yeah." Something jogged my brain. "Wasn't that were that DEA bust that went south happened?"

"That's us. Not our operation, but we were tarred by it nevertheless, once the press got hold of it. They tried to keep it hush-hush, since it was such a fiasco, but you can't avoid the press these days, not even in an out-of-the-way place like Blue River. And the press can be brutal."

I knew the feeling—between the publicity from the killings six months ago, and my kidnapping trial a couple years before, if I never saw my name in the newspapers or on the boob tube again I'd be a happy man. "Yes, I know."

"It was awful." She hesitated. "You were the D.A. for some time down there, weren't you?"

I finally figured out where this call was going. "Ten years, about."

She corroborated my hunch. "I need to talk to somebody about this, who has your kind of experience."

"It's been a while," I told her, not wanting her to get the wrong notion of my present understanding of or involvement in the prosecutorial area. "I don't know if I'm the right person to give you whatever help or advice it is you might be needing."

Another pause from her end. Then she came right at me. "Do you not want to see me, Luke?"

Why the hell do people have feelings, anyway? Life would be so much simpler without them. "I'm sorry, Nora. If I gave you that impression, I didn't mean to."

"I've developed a thick hide over the years. There's almost nothing anyone can say or do to me anymore that I can't handle."

I told her the truth. "I would love to see you."

"Thank you." Her tension dissipated—I could feel the hum of relief over the wire. "Have you ever been up here?"

"Not in Muir County itself, no."

"Most people haven't. No reason to." She got to it. "Could you come up here for a day or so? We'd pay your expenses, of course. The county."

I wasn't lying when I told her I'd love to see her. But going up to Muir County and seeing her as the D.A., rather than meeting somewhere as two old friends, those were two separate and different issues.

"When would you like me to come up?"

"As soon as you can."

"Run this by me again," Riva said.

I told her. As far as the back story, Dennis and Nora and all that, she got the abridged version. It wasn't that I was hiding anything—Nora and I'd never had anything going, she was Dennis's woman from the moment they met—but it wasn't about Riva and me, in the present. Those were different times, I was a different person. Part of my reticence, I guess, was not wanting to examine old skeletons. And what, if anything, Dennis Ray's life and death meant to me. Or about me.

"I still don't get it." Riva was chewing on this. "What does this woman want from you, Luke? Contacting you after umpteen years of no word at all?"

Obviously, I'd thought about this. "Someone to talk to. Someone who's walked a mile in her shoes, to coin an expression. Dennis and her and I were good friends back then. Also, I'm probably the only one from our circle who became a D.A. Stanford Law Review honchos don't usually go into the public sector. Not on the prosecutor's side." I had been the exception—the odd man out.

We'd put Buck to bed. He's a good sleeper, he usually goes down without too much fuss and doesn't wake up until five or six—his motor runs so hard when he's awake that when the switch is turned off, boom, dreamland. Now we were sitting in Adirondack chairs, side by side on the deck of our house, which overlooks the Mission to the immediate west, the city below, the ocean beyond that. Killer views, which we paid through the nose for. After that big kidnapping trial of mine, a few years before, we decided to live the best we could afford, even stretch it some. When you've almost been killed, the future is now. The horror show out in the desert earlier in the year had confirmed that feeling.

It was chilly out. February nights are generally cold and moist in Santa Barbara. The thick, wet fog covered most of the deep view, but we could see down as far as the lights in the harbor. Both of us, bundled up in sweaters, blankets around our legs, were drinking Irish coffee from thick mugs I'd bought years before at the Buena Vista in San Francisco, when I was young and naïve/dumb enough to think it was a cool place.

Riva was still skeptical. "It's about that messed-up FBI operation up there."

"DEA, but yeah."

"Wouldn't the DEA be handling it? It was federal, wasn't it?"

Riva used to write bail bonds. She knows the law better than most lawyers, especially in criminal matters.

"From what I know"—I nodded—"but I know what I read in the papers, which I didn't pay that much attention to. Another government screwup; like, what's new? Let's face it, they fuck up all the time, especially the alphabet agencies. Maybe she's got something going on her own—which she doesn't feel like sharing with them."

"But wants to with you? Who she hasn't seen or spoken to in almost twenty years? Doesn't that seem odd to you?"

It did seem odd, put that way. Nora Sherman Ray and I didn't know each other anymore. Law school, twenty years ago? Such ancient history. But who knows how someone else thinks? Our shared three years at Stanford had been one of the high points of her late husband's life, and by extension, hers. It probably meant a lot more to her than it did to me.

"I think she wants to talk to someone about Dennis. My guess is she hasn't done that with satisfaction. Not to someone who knew him when he was a champion. And this comes up, which is a convenient and permissible venue. Meeting on a professional level, I mean."

"I know what you mean." Riva's hand was on mine, under the blanket. "You're not a shrink, Luke, a priest, her brother, cousin, father. You're not even her friend, I've never once heard her name out of your mouth."

"I was, though. A friend."

"Maybe you're a lifeline."

Maybe. I'd thought that could be it. I didn't want to be.

"She said she wanted to pick my brain about this case." I held firm. "So that's what I'm going to talk to her about."

Riva grinned, nudged me with her foot. "Yeah, sure. She'll be meeting you at the station, in widow's weeds. Grace Kelly hanging fire on Gary Cooper."

My wife cut me no slack, none. She also watches too many old movies on cable—home alone with a kid, you can fall into that.

"This is doing an old friend a favor, honey." I nudged her back. "Anyway, Amtrak doesn't run anywhere near Blue River. This is going to be a puddle jump and a rental car and a day with . . ." I shrugged.

"With?" She prompted me with another foot nudge. Not delicately.

"A fellow professional."

With old memories, is what had flashed through my mind. Riva's, too, I'm sure.

* * *

Since the incident in the desert, I'd been lying low. You kill a couple of rogue cops, you save a dozen lives, you become famous for a little while. Everybody wants a piece of you, whether it's *People,* Larry King, Oprah, whoever. Senators and governors. It lasts a couple of weeks and then dies down, but still, your face has been out there.

So I hadn't been working much, taking stock of my life, which was good, by and large, but I need to work, it defines me, I'm too old and set to change professions and I'm way too young to retire. Maybe I could spend a few days helping out on someone else's problem and let that ease me back into the lawyering racket.

I flew into Reno, the closest city to Muir County that had a commercial airport, and headed up Highway 395 in my rental Dodge. In a short while I'd left the populated world in my rearview mirror—except for Susanville, a fast hour's drive from the airport (population 7,300), there were no towns of consequence before or behind me for hundreds of miles.

As I've mentioned, I'd lived in the northwestern part of the state a few years back, up in the old-growth redwood area around Ukiah, not far from the ocean, which is where I met Riva. By any rational reckoning that is a weird, one-of-a-kind area—you have that much dope being grown, manufactured, and distributed, it has to be. Law and order is a hit-and-miss proposition, more to be honored in the breach than for real. It's a sixties kind of thing, I guess, the whole place is a throwback of a kind, but not so much peace, love, and understanding as paranoia against the man and all things organizational. Bunker mentality, the kind that bedrocked that old communes once they turned squirrelly and insular. Some of them still exist pretty much as they did back then, when the urban kids came from the Eastern cities with Bob Dylan playing in their heads. Thirty-five years later the answer is still blowin' in the wind, and you never need to be a weatherman to know which way the wind blows.

I was too young for that, and I wouldn't have gone for it anyway, I'm too square to feel comfortable in that life. But I see their point.

The thing is, I know what it's like to inhabit an environment that's abnormal, physically and emotionally. Riva and I thought we were fairly isolated there, which by my urbanized standards we were—but compared to this region of the state, we were absolutely cosmopolitan. Everywhere here was rawer, way more forsaken. Starting out, my drive took me through landscape similar to that of other places in northern California—massive stands of timber, towering skyscrapers jammed shoulder to shoulder that reached to the clouds and beyond, far past my seeing their tops out the windshield as I drove along the narrow boulevard that the highway created through them, occasionally broken up by stretches of raw grassy-mossy range. Unspoiled, majestic.

Then the landscape changed. Dramatically. From an abundance of foliage to terrain that was stark, dry, lifeless. The farther north I drove, the more featureless the territory became. Barren, dry, a lunar-looking landscape that went on and on, like that Dalí painting with the melting watch. But no melted watch, no bright colors. Which is not to say it wasn't beautiful; eerily, it was—on its own stripped-down terms. But so far from the world of people. It was almost impossible to conceive of two young, gung ho professionals leaving a place like Denver for this. Their circumstances had to have been dire in the extreme to have made this spot their home; more than I could ever have realized from hearing stories about it.

I stopped at a mom-and-pop gasoline station and filled the tank. They hardly exist anymore, even as far out in the boonies as this. It was comforting, being there; it reminded me that America hasn't gone completely corporate yet.

Lemon Snapple, mint Milanos, and Altoids in hand to fortify me the rest of the way, I handed a twenty-dollar-bill to the cashier, a weathered older lady with a bad homemade henna job. "How much longer to Blue River?" I asked.

"Hour and a half, about, if you pedal to the metal," she answered, making my change. She gave me a serious look-see. "Do I know you? You look kinda familiar."

"I've never been here in my life." Not a lie. I didn't want to be identified, too much hassle, and it could mess up whatever help I might be able to give Nora.

"You're not with the DEA?" she persisted.

"No. Do I look like I am?"

"They're about the only outsiders been around here, last bunch of months. Swarming the place. Looking for who did that murder. That drug kingpin. You seen it on TV? It was big news."

"I'm just passing through," I lied. I wasn't ready for anyone other than Nora to know I was coming. "Did the DEA catch who committed the murder?"

"Get serious." Her look at me said, *How feeble are you, anyway?* "When was the last time the DEA caught anything except a cold?"

She wasn't a fan of the bureaucracy, obviously. "I don't know," I told her. "I don't keep up on those things."

"Check out the *Enquirer,*" she advised me, pointing to the newsrack next to the register. The featured papers were the *Enquirer,* the *Globe,* the *Star,* and for serious newsies, *USA Today.* "It's a rag, they all are," she allowed, "but they get the scoop more often than not, and they don't wallow in their own pretentious bullshit, like those pathetic talking heads on CNBC."

"I'll keep that in mind." She placed my snacks in a plastic carry-bag. "So who does the *Enquirer* say did it?"

"They don't. Ain't spicy enough."

Well, I thought, I've got a captive audience here in front of me—might as well try my luck, see if I could get a finger on the local pulse. "Who do you think did it? You must hear talk."

"Do I look like Sherlock Holmes?" she parried. She didn't know me, my agenda, if I had one, despite my lame disclaimer to be "just passing through." "The man who got himself murdered was a drug lord, so he'd have made plenty of enemies." She hesitated, then said, "I'll bet you this—if they ever do find out, which is not likely, given the quality of law enforcement these days in general—I'll lay odds it won't be one of the usual suspects."

Dusk. The faded wooden guide-sign at the Blue River city-limit line informed me that this was the Muir County seat, that the population as of the latest census was 2,225. There were the standard civic organizations: Lions Club, Masonic Lodge, Knights of Columbus, a handful of lesser ones. A few churches were advertised, some establishment, some fundamentalist. The elevation was six thousand six hundred feet. It had been close to or over six thousand feet from shortly after I'd passed through Susanville. I could feel it in my lungs, the sparseness of the air.

Off to my right, looming over the small buildings of the town, a mountain range, nameless to me, was glimmering orange and violet in the fading sunlight. It looked fairly close, but it could have been a hundred miles away, distances are deceiving in vast landscapes such as this. A thin scattering of gnarly trees clung stubbornly to the side. A light covering of snow mantled it haphazardly in spots, where the sun never reached. Not a skier's or climber's mountain. Rocky, inhospitable. This entire region was a mighty force of nature, a raw, enormous gut of country. One of those places that isn't that different from when the first white settlers moved through it a hundred and fifty years ago. They rode horses, I was driving a car, but in both cases the land ruled. I knew it could overwhelm you in a heartbeat if you turned your back on it.

The courthouse shared space in the same building with the various county agencies. It was a squat concrete structure, located a block from the center of town, built in the boring one-size-fits-all mold from the fifties. Business was finished for the day, so plenty of parking spaces were available. In small towns like this they roll the sidewalks up early. I parked in front and went inside.

Quiet. I looked up the number of the prosecutor's office on the information board. First floor, the far end of the hall. I walked toward it.

Halfway there, a door opened. Nora had heard me, my footsteps echoing faintly in the empty corridor. I knew she had been awaiting my arrival, getting antsy as the day slipped away, and now there she was. It hit me that she had seen me out her window, my headlights as I pulled up. Watching for me.

The light from inside the office was behind her—she was in silhouette. Standing there motionless, erect, looking at me. Even from a distance it felt as if she wanted to come toward me; but she didn't. She held herself in check, waiting for me to reach her.

It had been almost twenty years. We hugged awkwardly, trying to fit our bodies together without being sloppy. Then we stepped back and looked at each other.

She spoke first—she was more nervous than I was. "You look good, Luke. You look . . . you haven't changed much at all."

"You're too kind." I smiled. "Full of it, but that's okay. I'll take it. You look good yourself, Nora."

"Thanks." Her eyes were on my face. Looking for . . . ? Now she smiled back; a shy smile. "It's been a long time since a man said something nice about my looks. The men around here, they don't look at women like me as . . ."

"As?"

"Women." She shrugged. "It's the culture. For me, that's good. I wouldn't want . . ." She tailed off again.

To get involved with a man here: I read her mind. She could feel it—the vibe was oscillating like a tuning fork. "How did we get on this track?" she asked, backing up a step.

"We're not on any track," I said to put her at ease.

She nodded. "Good."

Her office was standard government issue. At least she had a corner, windows on two walls. One view was of the street, the other of a parking lot. She grabbed her purse and an old leather briefcase from her desk.

"I got a room for you at the Holiday Express. It's the best motel in town." Another smile, this one not awkward. "Also the only motel in town. And it's Western, sort of. Game trophies on the coffee-shop walls. Stagecoach wheels, too. Except they're plastic. The wheels, not the heads." As we went back into the corridor, she said, "You're registered under my office. I didn't want anyone to know you were coming. On the off chance somebody might recognize your name and make some kind of connection."

"How likely is that?" I asked, surprised.

"The feds might. They're lurking around, although officially they aren't here anymore. You have been in the media, even up here."

"It's not like we're in Fiji, Nora."

"Fiji. God—that would be heaven."

We were outside, in the darkness of early evening. "Is this yours?" she asked, spotting the Avis sticker on my rental windshield. Off my nod: "I drive an Explorer. I'll pull around, follow me to the motel. We'll get you checked in, then we'll have dinner, and I'll give you my spiel."

At the motel I didn't have to sign in or leave a credit-card imprint— I was handed a key and told to enjoy my stay. Nora waited outside; it wouldn't do to have her standing there next to a strange man, even if this was official business. Although I had a feeling that if it hadn't been me, but just some regular guy she hadn't known in another life, it wouldn't have been the same. But maybe I was wrong.

The motel was one-story stucco, a horseshoe around a swimming pool that was empty, fenced off with a lock and chain. Nora waited in the doorway while I tossed my bag onto the bed. I travel light; I had a sports coat in the car in case, but I wouldn't need it. We weren't going to be doing anything that required me to dress up. I already knew that if Nora could help it, I was going to be invisible.

I got into her car. "Are you hungry?" she asked, starting the car.

"I could eat. Where're we going?"

"My house. There aren't any good restaurants around here, nothing even halfway decent. Like Burger King is Epicurean. And we can talk without worrying about being eavesdropped on. Is that okay?"

"That's fine," I said nonchalantly. Inside, though, I was a tad concerned. The way she had registered me at the motel, now this. She was more than a little paranoid. Was it this situation, or who she was? I hoped the former, which made sense, the feds can do that to you. Otherwise, it could be a long, uncomfortable night.

"I'm a good cook."

"In that case, I'm famished."

She didn't live in town. "It isn't far. Dinner won't be long, I came home at lunchtime and got most of it ready."

We drove in silence. I looked over at her, checking her out in the low light from the instrument panel. She was dressed professionally, off-white blouse, navy skirt and matching jacket, low heels, hose. I would have recognized her on the street, I was fairly sure of that, but she had changed. She'd been a thin, athletic woman—now she was heavier, mostly from the waist down. When men gain weight it's the gut; women do it on their thighs and behind. It wasn't unattractive on Nora, just spread out. Lines spidered her eyes, her temples. No makeup, not even lipstick. She had been pretty in a Nordic, Liv Ullmannesque kind of way, and she still was. But twenty years had gone by, almost half our lifetimes. She had gone through some damn hard times, all the sadness with Dennis, of which I could only imagine.

It was her eyes that gave her away—even when she smiled, as she'd done a couple times so far, her eyes didn't. They held the truth of what was going on inside.

Her house was set well back from the road, fifty yards. She had five acres, she told me, with a stream running along the property line.

It was new, but old-looking, done mission-style. I followed her inside.

"Very nice," I complimented her, looking around. The place surprised and impressed me, both architecturally and in its furnishings. I mentally calculated what a setup like this would cost in Santa Barbara. Over a million. In Montecito, two million, maybe more, with five acres.

"You live well, lady."

She smiled. "It's much cheaper here than where you live, I'm sure. And what else am I going to spend my money on? I'm not saving up to put my kids through college. My parents helped," she confided. "I'm their only child. Plus I made good money the years I was working in Denver."

I was quite impressed.

"You'll have to come back during the day, when you can see the outside," she said, kicking her shoes off on her way through the living room to the kitchen, tossing her purse and briefcase onto the couch. "It's the best feature of this place."

"Sure," I said, "okay." How long was I going to be here? I thought. And how much was going to be done outside the office?

I smelled dinner cooking. A rich, full-bodied smell. I wondered how often she cooked dinner, living alone as she did. I didn't know that for a fact, but I figured she would have told me if she was living with someone, a roommate or someone more intimate.

"You're not a vegetarian, I hope."

"I eat everything without discrimination," I assured her. Dinner was meat of some kind. I was hungrier than I'd realized, smelling it. Except for the snacks I'd bought back at the filling station, I hadn't eaten since leaving home early in the morning.

"Around here there's no such thing as a vegetarian, except way back in the mountains, what's left of the old communes from the sixties. And they cheat, when it's full winter and freezing out."

She lifted the lid off a large iron pot, checked inside. "Almost ready."

She got down a bottle of wine from a cupboard. "If you eat meat, you drink red wine. Make yourself useful." She handed me the bottle and a corkscrew. "I'll be a minute. Glasses are in the dining-room breakfront."

Grabbing her shoes off the floor, she headed down a hallway toward what I assumed was her bedroom.

"Okay if I call home?" I asked after her. I needed to check in with Riva, let her know I'd arrived safe and sound. Ever since my sojourn into the desert I did this religiously whenever I traveled. And I wanted to hear my son's voice.

"*Mi casa es su casa.*" An unseen door closed.

I popped the cork on the wine, a decent Napa cabernet. Pouring two glasses, I took a sip, a second because it tasted good and I'd been on the road all day, dialed my number.

Riva picked up on the second ring. "It's me," I told her.

"Oh good. I was beginning to wonder."

"The drive took longer than I expected. This is big country."

"And you're a big man, so it should be a good fit."

"Something like that." I took my motel key out of my pocket, read the phone number off to her, along with the room number. "We're going to have dinner, then Nora will start filling me in. Whatever it is she wants to talk about." In the background I could hear my son. It sounded like he was beating on his high chair with a spoon, or a hammer. Maybe he'll be a drummer. "How's the heir?"

"Kicking ass, of course. Here."

The phone was silent for a moment, then Buck's little voice came across the line. "Daddy? Where are you, Daddy? When are you coming home, Daddy?"

"I'm on business, honey. I'll be home real soon. Maybe tomorrow, or the next day." God, do I love that voice.

"When are you coming home, Daddy?"

"As soon as I can. What did you do today? Did you go to Mrs. Ferguson's and play with Jesse?" Mrs. Ferguson is the day-care lady he spends a couple mornings a week with, so Riva can do the rest of her life. Jesse's his best friend, another boy his age.

I listened to my voice as I talked to him. My voice was slower, more deliberate. I try not to talk young, but it's hard not to. It feels easier to talk on his frequency.

"When are you coming home, Daddy?" He had that fixed in his head, and that was all he wanted or cared to ask.

"As soon as I can." I repeated. "Let me talk to Mommy now, honey. I'll see you soon. I love you."

"I love you, too, Daddy. When are you coming home?"

"It's me." Riva was back on the line. "So to answer his question . . ."

"Day after tomorrow. Unless we talk out whatever has to be said tonight and that's it, but I don't expect that." I changed the subject. "Anything happening I need to know?"

"Nope, all quiet on the western front. Where're you eating dinner?" she asked, making conversation, not wanting me to hang up yet.

"Some restaurant. I don't know. Whatever she chooses." Riva assumed I was in my motel room, that Nora and I would be going to dinner in a public restaurant.

"I'm sure the choices are many and varied."

"I've got a feeling not." I was vamping. I didn't want to tell my wife that I was eating Nora's home-cooked meal, that it was only the two of us in Nora's house, out in the countryside.

I didn't know why I didn't want to tell her, I wasn't trying to hide anything, nothing was going on, or would. It just didn't feel right to tell her; anyone who's ever been on the road has had this feeling at some time or another. Nora was a part of my life Riva didn't know about. That Nora and I had never in any way been romantic didn't matter—

she was a woman, she was out of my past. Any explanation, no matter how benign, might not be a satisfactory one.

Nothing was going to happen, so why build a nest of doubt in her head?

Nora's bedroom door was opening. "We're about to go have dinner," I said into the phone. "I'll call you tomorrow, around this time."

"Is she there?" Not suspicious, but suddenly curious.

"I see her car pulling up, out the window." An actual lie, now. Fuck me.

"We'll be here."

She'd believed me, of course. Which was the way it should be. I was clean as a whistle. Why give her a reason to feel there's any mistrust when there is none? Why risk hurt, even if it's only a paper cut? "Give Buck a kiss for me."

"I will."

Nora came into the kitchen. She'd exchanged her work clothes for a loose sweater and jeans. Wool socks, no shoes. I smiled at her, held up a finger. "And you, too," I told the telephone.

"I love you, Luke," Riva told me from six hundred miles away.

"Me, too," I told her back. And hung up.

"Everything okay on the home front?" Nora asked, obviously not wanting to pry.

"Fine and dandy." I handed her the other glass I'd poured. We clinked, each taking a sip. To twenty years: long time ago.

I sipped my wine in the living room and watched a few minutes of what passes for the news on television these days while Nora put the finishing touches on dinner, then joined her at the table in the kitchen alcove when she announced it was ready: stew over rice, green salad, Pillsbury Doughboy biscuits thawed in the microwave—a working woman has to use some shortcuts, even my gourmet-chef wife rarely makes biscuits from scratch anymore. I was flattered that Nora had gone to the trouble to cook at all. Of course, I'd traveled several hundred miles to do her a favor, so I guess she thought she should try to please me, and here was a way.

I sat down, placed my napkin on my lap like the little gentleman my mother taught me to be, took a taste. Nora watched, waiting for me to pass judgment on her culinary talents.

The flavors exploded in my mouth. "This is . . . talk about finger-lickin' good!" I didn't have to pretend—it was delicious. A rich mélange of meat, potatoes, tomatoes, other vegetables, thick brown biscuit-sopping gravy. "Range-fed, the beef? Not from some grocery-store meat counter." I'm a connoisseur of this shit. I can tell.

"It's venison." She smiled back. "Deer. Like, you know . . . ?" She made antlers on her forehead with her fingers.

I looked at a square of meat on the prongs of my fork. "How out-doorsy. Did you hunt it?" Making a life up here, wearing lumberjack socks, why not?

She shook her head. "I can eat Bambi, but I can't kill him. All the guys hunt. One of the sheriff's deputies bagged this one. I bought half a side off him. Stew meat, steaks, hamburger. I've got a big freezer in the garage—de rigueur around here. Nice break from eating cow shot up with steroids, raised in some feedlot."

"It's very good," I said, properly chastised. "My compliments to the chef."

She smiled—the best smile I'd seen on her face. Even her eyes smiled with this smile.

"It's nice to cook for someone who appreciates it. Unless I'm having a working dinner, I usually eat alone, a sandwich over the kitchen sink." She brought the pot over from the stove, ladled me out another helping without asking if I wanted it.

When dinner was over and I was full-and-well-stuffed, we took the bottle and our glasses into the living room. We sat on the couch, discreetly apart, no body parts touching. "Can we talk some business?" she asked. "I didn't wipe you out with that heavy meal?"

"I'm fine. All I'm doing is listening, right?"

"Okay. Get comfortable."

She opened her briefcase, pulled out a thick stack of papers. "Tonight's homework assignment." She smiled at me. "I'll tell you what's in it later. For now I'll fill you in on what's happened, what I think." She plunked the papers on the coffee table, swung around on the couch so that her back was against one edge, drew her legs up. I did the same, so that we were both comfy and facing each other.

It was all very domestic. You wouldn't have known, looking at us, that we hadn't laid eyes on each other for almost two decades. You'd probably think we were an old married couple, settled in for the duration, sharing each other's end-of-the-workday trials and tribulations, the way Riva and I do.

"What do you know about this case?" she began.

"Not much. Big government bust that went south and got some people killed on both sides."

She nodded. "It falls under the category of 'you can't teach an old dog new tricks,' which they own the patent on. But in this case it was particularly pathetic because they violated a direct order from the top of their own food chain."

She had my attention. "How?"

"The prisoner who escaped, if you want to dignify what happened, wasn't supposed to be killed. He was supposed to be brought in alive. That was the entire point of the stupid operation, which was ill-conceived from the get-go. Catch him and bring him back alive. If you can't, abort. This from her ladyship Reno, no less."

"So maybe someone wanted him dead, bad enough to incur the wrath of the A.G. herself?" That followed logically, anyone could see where that was going. "Because it's a tar brush that has to splatter everyone who comes anywhere near contact with it."

"Which is happening, although the DEA's been doing their best to paint a happy face on it."

Now she really had my attention. "How the hell could they do that? The guy was their prisoner, wasn't he? In their custody?"

"Yes."

"So . . . ?" If the government was spin-doctoring this, they were really desperate to cover something up. But what? "Hasn't the DEA been investigating this? This was a federal bust."

"Oh, yeah." She was pissed, I could hear it, see it in the wrinkles in her face. "They've been investigating the crap out of it for almost six months. You couldn't walk down a street in this town without encountering a federal agent. Charming men, the locals were in tears when the last stage rolled out of town. They only pulled out a couple of weeks ago. There's a token unit down in Reno still, but they're done. Signed, sealed, and delivered."

"So what did they find out? They do a good enough job with that stuff."

"Yes. Unless it's their own people who might be in play, which doesn't only mean their agency, it can be any alphabet agency, as long as they're federal. Then maybe they don't find out what they should."

"Are you saying there's been a cover-up?"

I needed to slow this down—she'd had six months to build up a head of steam, and now, with a captive and friendly audience, the lid was blowing.

"Let's put it this way. If you go into an investigation with a particular theory, you can find facts that support that theory, to the exclusion of others that might be the right ones."

"Which is what, in this case?"

"It could be a couple of things. Or more. One is that one of the agents shot the prisoner and won't admit it."

"On purpose or accidentally?"

"Not exactly accidentally. More in the heat of the moment. Your blood's up, you've been in this incredible firefight which was a horrible miscalculation, some of your friends have been killed, you finally catch your target and then he manages to escape, which is a story unto itself, maybe part of the killing, maybe not. You're running through the woods like a blind pig, it's unfamiliar terrain, you're wired and scared, you aren't wearing your Kevlar vest anymore because the chase was over, the quarry was taken down, you were relaxing your guard. And you're the first one to stumble across him and the fear kicks in, you're not thinking straight, you can't, you're scared you're going to shit your pants your adrenaline's running so high. You see him and he sees you and you know for sure he's armed—if he could escape from the heavy custody you had him in, he has to have a gun, too, right? So you take him down. And immediately realize you made a big boo-boo, and you fade away with the rest of the troops and pray they can't connect you."

She paused. She was almost out of breath, reliving this plotline.

I stared at her, trying to catch up. "That's a lot of coincidences that have to come together."

She nodded in agreement.

"Tantamount to a whitewash, almost."

"Yes," Nora agreed. "It is."

My stomach felt queasy.

"However, that's not their main theory, fortunately. It's a backup." She pivoted and swung her feet onto the floor. "Do you want coffee?"

"If it's no trouble."

"It's already made. How do you take it?"

"A little milk. Black's fine if you don't have any milk."

"I've got milk." She padded off into the kitchen.

I sat back, digesting what she'd told me so far. It wasn't much. I didn't think the DEA would run with that theory, unless they were truly desperate. Not after all the other calamities that have gone down this past decade and a half. But you never can tell—arrogance, of which they are not in short supply, can bring forth great strangeness in men and institutions.

"Want a toot in your coffee?" Nora called out from the kitchen.

"Are you?"

"On the side. It's domestic brandy; a sophisticate like you might prefer it masqueraded in java."

"I'll go with the flow."

She came back in from the kitchen carrying a tray with two thick coffee mugs, a small pitcher of milk, sugar, spoons, two Hennessy promotional snifters, a bottle of brandy. I know the brand. It's fine for cooking. She placed the tray on the coffee table.

"I'll take mine in my coffee after all," I told her.

She smiled as she handed me the bottle. Again with her eyes as well. My presence was having a salubrious effect on her. She was hungry for a connection, that was obvious—a touchstone from her earlier life, when times were good and horizons were limitless.

I laced my coffee, handed her the bottle. She poured a couple of fingers into a snifter. I wondered if she was a solitary drinker, imbibing her evening wine—or stronger stuff—in the company of one, a middle-aged woman alone in a world she could not have, in her wildest dreams, expected to live in.

She swung her legs up, coffee mug in her lap, the snifter on the table, an easy arm's reach. "Okay." She squiggled herself comfortable. "Here comes the theory they're selling. Ready?"

I tasted my coffee. It was good—the brandy gave it the right combination of oomph and smoothness. "I'm . . ."

Our toes were touching. The tippies, socks to socks. Unconscious on her part. Her toes were warm. I guess mine were, too. I'm sure she didn't notice. She had nothing to feel guilty about.

If I moved my feet away, though, she might notice. And then she might be embarrassed that I was thinking something she wasn't intending, which could lead to further embarrassment, which could lead to . . . so I didn't move them.

"I'm ready," I told her.

"One of Juarez's own people greased him." She reached for her brandy and knocked down half, eyeballing me over the rim of the snifter.

Evidently I'd missed something. "I don't get it. The baddies were either under arrest by then, or dead." I paused. "Weren't they?"

"Well, yes. Then again, maybe not." She leaned forward, elbows on knees. The toe-pressure increased a tad, but she was too deep into her recitation to notice.

"Juarez almost wasn't found. If they hadn't had dogs, he wouldn't have been. And this was with the troops knowing he was there. Their snitch put him there. But they didn't know who all the other players were, who they were, how many there were."

I took a hit off my coffee. I was glad there was brandy in it, listening to this. "Okay. I'm with you so far. And therefore, the conclusion is . . ."

"One or more of Juarez's people didn't get caught or killed," Nora continued, "even though the house was a killing field. Wait'll you see the pictures and the video. It was a firefight like you see in footage on Vietnam or Cambodia. They survived the attack and . . ."

I made a *T* with my hands—time-out. "So these survivors managed to sneak into a heavily guarded area, let him loose—then kill him. His compadres. That's where this is going?" Shit, man, the world is getting way too surreal if anyone can spin a yarn like this, much less think anyone's ever going to believe it. Or even worse, believe it themselves.

"Give that man a panda." She finished her brandy, helped herself to more. I could've used something straight and strong myself; if I came back for dinner again, I thought, I'd bring a decent bottle. Not that I had plans to spend another evening with Nora in her house.

"Aside from the difficulty of the logistics," I asked, "why would they do that? What's the brilliant DEA theory there?"

"There's two."

"Which are?"

"One is that his own people were afraid that if Juarez were captured, he'd blow the entire operation out of the water. We're talking hundreds of millions of dollars, thousands of arrests worldwide. So they had an internal understanding—an agreement, really, like an old Mafia blood oath—that if he or any big cheese got taken down like this, they'd have to be eliminated."

"I have a hard time with that theory," I said. "Mainly because it's full of shit."

"It's happened before," Nora informed me, "so there's precedent."

"In this case, given what I know, it's still full of shit. That would mean the security that night was shit. Was it?"

"It wasn't a well-run operation. Isn't that obvious, even knowing the little you do know?"

This was getting interesting. Could the DEA have actually fucked up that badly? It was possible—they hadn't done very well in storming the palace, why not go for the trifecta?

"People who were there were appalled at how it all went down." She pointed to the thick stack of paper on the table. "It's in there. You can interview them, if you want."

She was spinning a web. Wanting more than advice.

"I'll look this over and we can talk about it, but I can't put in that kind of time." I needed to head this off at the pass—I wasn't getting involved. Advice, support. Not involvement.

Nora nodded, didn't say anything in reply or argument.

"So what's the other theory?"

"That Juarez was a double agent working for the government, his people found out, and used the bust as a pretext to kill him."

"Um." That made more sense. The hills are alive with subterfuge. "But if his people knew he'd turned, why do it this way? You want to get rid of someone, you don't wait around hoping for a convenient excuse. You strike at the earliest opportunity, fit him out for a concrete garment, adios, double-crosser."

"Unless you want to make it look like the feds did it. And knew the bust was coming down."

"Which brings us back to go." Finally.

She nodded. "Yep."

"I guess . . . yeah, that could work." Stuff was happening in my head, I needed to let it settle, so I took a minute. Then I went on. "But that still doesn't explain how they broke him loose after he'd been captured. If you buy that idea, they should've killed him during the firefight. Cleaner, more believable, more certain."

My mug was getting low. Nora reached over and topped it up. "That, my dear Watson, is the sixty-four-thousand-dollar question."

I swirled some of the brandy in my mouth before swallowing. The stuff wasn't so bad. It was growing on me.

"So what's the answer?"

I knew what I thought she believed, but I wanted to hear it from her. My role was to be a sounding board, corroborate her instincts. Not lead them. "What's your true feeling?"

"He was assassinated." She knocked back the dregs of her drink. "What else could it be?"

*   *   *

A federal agent, countermanding a direct order from the attorney general of the United States, murdered a prisoner who had been captured and was being held for transit. If that was true, and came out into the open, it would be an incredible scandal, rippling through not only the DEA but every federal law-enforcement agency, leaving bodies, policies, public trust, in its wake.

If it was true.

My motel room was not conducive to deep, focused thinking. It was clean—that's all you could say in its favor. Lifeless, sad-sack décor. The television was bolted to the wall, the remote was chained to the pressed-wood console between the two double beds, which sagged in the middle like a swaybacked gelding from the weight of years of transient overnighters. I'd bet those mattresses hadn't been turned since Dewey defeated Truman. Everything was plastic, down to and including the sheets, which were a raspy poly/cotton blend. I hate the sensation of that stuff on my body; it gives me an itchy feeling, like the bed's full of fleas. When Riva travels with me, especially to out-of-the-way places like this, she sometimes brings her own sheets, pillows, blankets, towels. She always brings along bedding for Buck—God forbid the tender flesh of her son, the young prince, should ever touch anything but three-hundred-count percale.

I lay propped up on top of the bedspread, wearing my boxers and a T-shirt. The papers Nora had given me were scattered about in paper-clipped piles. Our parting, by my motel door, had been somber. No hugs. The heaviness of her charge hung in the air, like a rain cloud about to let loose.

After she dropped me off and said she'd see me in the morning, I'd walked across the street to an open 7-Eleven and bought a six-pack of Cokes. The motel provided the Styrofoam cooler and the ice machine was out back, by the empty swimming pool, which was covered across the bottom with six months' worth of dead leaves. Now, Coke on ice at the ready, I looked over the documents.

Most of them were the accounts and summaries of the DEA's investigation into the killing. Nora had arranged the reports chronologically, from the beginning of the inquiry to the present. I began plowing my way through. Contrary to what Nora had implied, they hadn't ruled out that one or more agents in the task force were dirty. After conducting hundred of interviews with everyone involved, though, there simply was no evidence that pointed in that direction. No serious candidate for the shooting had emerged, despite what looked, from the stacks of paper-work, like a Herculean effort to find one. Every agent at the raid had been handpicked for the assignment, not only for its high profile in law-enforcement terms, but also because of the sensitive nature of the polit-ical ramifications. Not one of those men had a bad mark on his record, not even a mild reprimand. All forty-odd of them were Boy Scouts, through and through. Each one of them proclaimed his innocence, not only of killing Juarez, but of knowing who did, or why. All of them, also, were outraged that it had happened. It was a smear on them, as people and as an agency. More than anyone, they wanted this case solved.

I kept reading. Since the investigators had no evidence that the killing had been done by an agent, they started pursuing other possibilities, the ones Nora had told me over dinner. The idea that one of Juarez's peo-ple had killed him to silence him had been floated and discussed, but that theory didn't hold much water. I didn't need a DEA report to tell me that.

The other theory she'd mentioned was kind of intriguing—that Juarez had secretly been working for the man, his people knew it or were suspicious, that the bust confirmed it, and they took him down. The problem was that everyone involved in the organization flatly de-nied that was the case. Juarez was not working their side of the street. There were no records of meetings, no payoffs, nothing to link him to them. But still, that hypothesis had its appeal. If he had turned for them, they wouldn't want anyone to know it.

But there was a big hole in that theory. If Juarez had been turned, why would they kill him? Especially since they'd been flat-out warned not to. Alive, he could do considerable damage to dozens of like opera-tions, globally. Dead, he told no tales.

On the other hand—a case like this has several hands, many more than two—who else besides a federal agent could have sprung Juarez from the trailer where he was being held? I kept coming back to that. At the least, it seemed to me, there had to be someone from the DEA in-volved, if only to help the prisoner escape, Maybe whoever did that—because somebody did, Juarez was not Harry Houdini—might have thought, or hoped, that Juarez could pull off an escape, in the dark and confusion. And when Juarez didn't, that person killed him and then went to cover.

Not only the agents, but everyone at the crime scene, had been extensively interviewed: The county sheriff and his deputy, who had been on the scene but not active participants—the Washington boys didn't want the locals involved, something the sheriff resented, naturally—as well as all the arrestees, who were now languishing in the federal penitentiary in Nevada, awaiting trial on the drug charges, had been grilled, for weeks in some cases. Over and over again. The agency had a hard-on for them that wouldn't quit, you could read that in braille.

Their trial was a long ways off; it was a big, complex case, with heavy repercussions. Discovery and depositions alone would take more than a year. And the government people figured that if they were held long enough, one of them might be persuaded to cut himself a sweet deal, turn state's evidence in exchange for a big pile of cash and lifetime anonymity in the Witness Relocation Program, and give up the information needed to make a case.

Personally, I didn't see that happening. You can't lose somebody anymore like in the old days. Computer information can track anyone down, if someone wants him badly enough. Maybe down the line a weak link would turn up, but I wouldn't want to build a case on that. These fellows were all tough nuts; if it came down that they had to do time, they'd do it.

Luis Lopez, the informant who had set this in motion, had been questioned up one side and down the other. He stuck to his story like white on rice. Nobody inside should have known the bust was coming down, and as far as he's concerned, no one did. The men inside were more prepared than he and Jerome, the senior agent he had reported to, thought they'd be. Human error. A bad fuckup, definitely. But that had nothing to do with Juarez being killed. Lopez had no idea where that was coming from.

And so on. No one knew anything. No one who had been interviewed, which was everyone who had been there, had killed Juarez, nor had they helped him escape from the trailer. Nor did they know who did either.

The case had become a classic dog chases tail. Which was why the agency was taking a breaker. They certainly weren't going to let this case go dormant; it was too dangerous to them and their allied federal agencies not to solve it. But for now, they were stymied—they were looking to catch a break.

I didn't read everything, but I'd read enough to assume that someone on the inside was dirty. The combination of the bust turning to shit, the prisoner who was supposed to be protected from harm at all counts escaping from tight security and then being killed, the lack of any hard evidence against any single person or group of people; somewhere a cover-up was going on. Off the top of my head I came to my own conclusion, which was hardly original: One or more people had wanted Juarez dead. Someone connected with him. He or they figured out how to botch the attack so Juarez would be killed during the firefight. When he wasn't, they helped, or forced, him to escape. And then he, or they, killed him.

I didn't have any answers for Nora, and I didn't know what she wanted from me, besides a sympathetic ear and some professional advice. But I did know that she was sitting on a powder keg. A prominent killing, probably a murder, probably premeditated, had occurred in her jurisdiction. She had a stake in this.

Why it has happened wasn't her business, unless something weird or unexpected unfolded. But *who*—that was hers. When I was the Santa Barbara D.A., any crime that happened on my turf was my crime. Every D.A. in the country feels that way. All murders are local, just like politics.

Which was why I was far from home and family, lying on a cheap motel bed, going blind from reading garbage. Nora had to act, and she wanted someone who'd been there to tell her she should. Someone she felt she could trust.

We didn't know each other, except from a distant, blurry past. But she needed someone to turn to, and there was no one else but me.

Nora picked me up promptly at eight. She had a bran muffin and coffee in a paper sack for me.

"Some of your basic food groups," she said as she pulled out of the motel parking lot.

"My favorite kinds. What's our agenda?"

We pulled out onto the highway. "Did you get to read it?" she asked, ignoring my question.

"Enough."

"What do you think?"

"Somebody killed Juarez." I took a bite out of my muffin. It was good, fresh. "You make this, too?" I asked, wondering how heavy a full-court press she was putting on me.

"Get real. I work for a living." She passed a semi, swung back into the proper traffic lane. "One quality thing we have in our little town is a decent bakery."

We were in what I assumed passed for rush-hour traffic. Pretty sparse. "What else do you think?" she asked.

"I don't know if the DEA investigators tried to sweep anything under the rug. They've done a competent, by-the-book job with what they had. Nobody admits to anything. There's so much you can do when that happens."

"But what do *you* think?"

"Like, who did it?"

Her voice started to take on an exasperated tone. "Not *who* specifically, but don't you think it was someone from the task force?"

"Instead of one of his own people? If those are the two alternatives, I'd say yes. That other theory's fairy dust. But the lines get blurred."

"Okay." She relaxed. "That's . . . okay."

We were heading away from town. "Where're we going?" I asked, watching the scenery pass by. I stuffed the last of the muffin into my mouth, sipped at the coffee, which wasn't as good as the muffin. I hadn't seen a Starbucks for a couple hundred miles; back home they've taken over the world, but I assumed they hadn't gotten this far into the interior.

"The scene of the crime. Sit back, it'll take a while. Here." Without taking her eyes off the road she reached behind her and grabbed some computer printouts from the backseat, dropped them in my lap. "*New York Times.* Front section and sports. I access it first thing in the morning. I printed up the sports for you, in case you're interested in them."

"Thank you."

She was working hard to make me as happy as I could be, given the circumstances. I started with the sports first, per usual. Basketball was in full swing; Stanford, the university with which Nora and I shared an allegiance—actually the only tie that bound us—was a favorite to take it all. Baseball was about to begin spring training. I could've learned this from ESPN—the motel wasn't so prehistoric as to not have cable—but reading the *Times,* now that's civilized.

Half an hour later, the car pulled off the two-lane and headed down a gravel road bordered on both sides by walls of tall firs. I looked up, jarred from reading about the world's problems.

"The entrance was obscured when the druggies were in business," Nora explained. "If you didn't know to look for it, you never would have known. It took the DEA guys weeks to find it." She inched ahead, bouncing in and out of potholes. "If they had asked my people, they could have found it a lot faster," she added, her voice full of rancor. "But we're local yokels, what do we know?"

"You knew about this operation?" I asked, surprised.

She shrugged. "Not really. We knew that an airstrip was being built. The sheriff wanted to get inside, put a man in undercover. But nothing ever happened."

"Why not?"

"For one thing, this is federal land, which gets sticky. I'm sure you know how that works."

I nodded. Anything in your county is in your jurisdiction, but when there are competing agencies, the whales tend to swallow the minnows.

"It used to be tribal," she continued. "The tribe swapped land with the government during World War Two. The boundary lines are all screwed up, the area hasn't been properly surveyed for fifty years."

We emerged into a clearing. Nora parked her Explorer and we got out. I looked around. "Here?"

A rhetorical question—this was the killing field. Down below, in a shallow ravine, were the remains of the compound's main house.

"Place really blew," I commented, looking at the remains, about half, that were left standing.

"It really blew."

"They didn't know what was inside."

She snorted. "Obviously not." She shrugged. "Or maybe they didn't give a damn."

Agents killed, buildings blown sky-high. This had been a disastrous raid on every level. Could Juarez have been murdered by one of the agents whose frustration level was pushed too far? I wondered. Instinctive human nature takes over in situations like this, even with professionals. So-called professionals. Whoever had killed Juarez, regardless of who he was or what he'd done, was no professional in my book.

Nora showed me around the location, told me how the raid had developed and then unraveled, where Juarez had been held in custody and escaped. She walked confidently from place to place.

"You know your way around well," I observed.

"I do now. I'd never been here before the killing, but in the last six months, I've come quite often, trying to dope this out, pardon the expression."

We went into the house. I looked into Juarez's hidey-hole in the kitchen freezer. Pretty secure place; without dogs he wouldn't have been found.

Coming out again, we headed toward the wooded area in the direction Juarez had run, trying to escape. The ground under our feet was damp. Spring was in the air. There was dogwood, wild peach and cherry amongst the oak and fir, the blossoms just beginning to bloom. It was pretty here. And extremely isolated, the drug operation could have thrived here for years before they were detected.

A thought about that came to mind. "How did the DEA know about this place, anyway, if they weren't consulting with you?"

"The usual way. They busted one of them, a guy named Lopez, on something else, and he gave them the operation to save his hide."

"Snitch-driven."

"Yep."

We came to the place where the body had been found, about a quarter mile from where Juarez had been held and then escaped—a small clear area surrounded by thick trees. DEA stakes had been planted in the ground to signify where the body had been. I checked out the tree where the bullet had been found—an old live oak. Someone had spray-painted a white circle around the area where the bullet had hit.

"Who found him?" I asked. I put my finger in the bullet hole.

"No one seems to know. Another curious black hole. A bunch of them got here at roughly the same time." She made a face. "That's their story, anyway."

"And he was already dead." All this was in the report, but seeing it live made a difference. I tried to visualize the body, lying there, still warm, blood oozing from the head wound. It was an ugly picture—like the one from the desert I'd carry to my grave.

"Dead as he was ever going to get." She kicked at the ground with a booted toe.

I looked around. Whoever had fired the shot that killed Juarez could have done it from the cover of the tree line; or he could have done the killing and then gone back into cover. It had taken the agents thirty seconds or more to get to the body after they heard the shot being fired.

We headed back to her car. "Which way's their airstrip?"

She pointed back toward where we'd come from. "A couple hundred yards further. There's a road from the compound, but he wasn't on it, obviously."

"Were there any aircraft present?" I hadn't seen anything in the DEA summaries, but they might not have included that.

"No. The agents on the ground there had that buttoned up. They reported seeing and hearing nothing."

Why would he have run that way then? I thought. Instinct, probably, or sheer coincidence.

We arrived back at Nora's car. "Refresh my memory," I said as we got in. "How many were in the compound?"

"A dozen."

"All accounted for? Dead or captured?"

She fired up the Explorer. "That's one of the unanswered questions. We don't know."

"So people could've come and gone."

She headed up the gravel road toward the highway. "It would have been difficult to get in unobserved. The place was under surveillance from when Lopez cut out."

We bounced in a deep winter pothole. "Sorry." She gripped the steering wheel firmly. "He contacted Jerome from when he was still inside, so they had it buttoned down pretty tight." She gave me a quick glance. "You're thinking someone, or maybe more than one of them, came in after Lopez left? Someone unaccounted for?"

"It fits with the DEA's thesis. And it's possible."

She didn't like hearing that. "But it's so complicated, the way it happened. It could have fallen apart a million ways, there were dozens of variables that all had to work together. The DEA almost didn't find him, for instance, and how would someone other than an agent get access to Juarez when he was under guard?"

"I don't know anything, except what's in the summary you gave me. Let's say, for the sake of argument, there was an internal hit on, but they couldn't do it inside the compound. So when the raid came down, they took the opportunity."

She thought about that. "That almost sounds like a conspiracy between the inside and the outside." She slowed the car to a crawl. "That's the scariest theme I've heard yet. Do you really think that's possible?"

"No," I answered promptly. "It would mean the whole thing was premeditated, including the blown raid. But now that I've seen the location, it's obvious there are dozens of places to hide in the forest. Especially if you're familiar with the terrain. Which points to an insider."

"I doubt any of the bad boys were familiar with anything outside the compound and the airfield. They weren't your Paul Bunyan types." She was stubborn about this. "And what about the dogs? They found Juarez buried under a mountain of rubble; they easily would've found someone out in the open."

"Yeah," I admitted. I'd forgotten about the dogs.

Reaching the highway, she pointed the Explorer toward town. There wasn't a car or truck to be seen in either direction. "One more stop, then we'll go to my office and talk. And you can meet Sheriff Miller." She smiled. "I think you'll enjoy that."

The cemetery was on a knoll north of town. It was small, bordered by a low wrought-iron fence, similar to those you see in Civil War battlefield graveyards, particularly in the South. There were a few old, bent trees, and not much vegetation—grass around the graves, but dirt elsewhere. The modest gravestones and tombstones weren't arranged in an orderly fashion; they lay in loose angles to each other, as if each one had been placed without regard for any of the others.

Dennis's grave was near the top, toward the northeast corner. The small marble stone was set flush to the ground. I read the inscription:

DENNIS WAINWRIGHT RAY
1948–1995
BELOVED HUSBAND, FRIEND, SCHOLAR

And then, in Old English script:

A MAN FOR ALL SEASONS

Nora had a small bouquet with her. It had been on the backseat when she picked me up, although I hadn't noticed it. Ordinary flowers, the kind you buy in a supermarket. She watched me while I read the inscription, then she kneeled at the foot of the little marker and placed the flowers diagonally across it.

For a moment we were both still, me standing, her kneeling. She was bareheaded, and the breeze caught her hair and spiderwebbed some strands across her cheek. A finger moved them away, behind her ear. I assumed she was silently praying, or talking to him. I could feel my heart beating in my chest. This was a man I had known who had died before his time. Without the fulfillment of his promise.

Nora stood up, next to me.

"I come about once a week. It's on my way." She looked down at the stone. "It's only a marker. *He* isn't there, I know that, but I like to know that the only thing symbolizing him on this earth isn't being neglected." She shoved her hands into the pockets of her coat. "At the end, I was all he had. We were each all we had, for each other. So . . ."

Her voice trailed off. For a moment she was somewhere else. Then she came back. "You liked Dennis, didn't you, Luke?"

Her question caught me off-guard. "Of course I did," I said. "Everyone loved Dennis. He was our shining star."

"But for real," she persisted. "Not as an icon. Flesh-and-blood real."

"Yes, Nora, I liked Dennis a lot. You know that. I admired him tremendously."

That seemed to satisfy what she needed to hear. She took my arm. "We should be getting to my office." She looked at the grave again. " 'Bye, sweetie," she said. "See you."

We walked toward her car in silence. I thought about what she'd asked me—how I had felt about Dennis.

It wasn't as simple as the instinctive reaction that had come out of my mouth when she asked the question, I realized. Yes, I liked Dennis, as I'd told her. Everyone had, as far as I knew. Many of us virtually worshiped him. But as I thought about it more deeply, I tried to separate the man from the memory. Did we all love Dennis, or was it the image of Dennis, the dream he seemed to personify?

I could feel Nora's arm, resting lightly on mine as we made our way down the incline to the parking lot. She was flesh and blood, walking next to me. And I liked her, I felt I had liked her then and did now. But as I thought more deeply about her question, I couldn't be sure what my real feelings were toward her late husband; did I like him, too, as a man, a human being, or was it what he exemplified for all of us: the dream become attainable.

So we had thought then, twenty-some years ago.

The sheriff of Muir County looked like he had stepped out of a John Ford western. Small, wiry, tightly wound. Skin the texture of a tobacco leaf that has been hanging in the barn for a month. He was dressed Western-style, but not duded up—twill slacks, hand-tooled leather boots, crisp khaki shirt with snaps instead of buttons, corduroy sports coat with the county insignia over the lapel pocket. His handshake was firm, his gaze direct, almost confrontational. Thin lips that didn't promise smiles. He appeared fit for an older man—I pegged him in his late sixties. He had the physical demeanor of a high-country cowboy—I presumed he was native to the region—but he radiated the tough energy of a man who knows where the bodies are buried. He definitely looked like someone who didn't like to be fucked with.

After Nora introduced us, she said to me, "Sheriff Miller used to be a big shot with the FBI, before his retirement." She winked at him, almost daughterishly. "So he's familiar with how federal agencies work." As if to say, he shares my skepticism about their investigation.

Her thumbnail description changed my superficial take on the man. He was more sophisticated than I'd casually assumed. One thing it told me was he didn't like to be idle, regardless of his age.

"I'll leave you two," Nora said. "Come back to my office when you're finished here, Luke." Pausing at the door, she added, "The sheriff and I are the only people in town who know who you are. You can talk freely with him."

We were in Miller's office, down the hall from hers. Miller sat behind his desk. I took the chair facing him.

He immediately took charge of the conversation. "That was a hell of an ordeal you endured down in the desert there, being held hostage and then killing those two black-sheep police."

"I wouldn't want to go through anything like that again." I didn't want to talk about that. Not with a hard case I didn't know.

"Pretty heroic behavior."

"I had no choice."

"Most people, they'd do nothing and hope their guardian angel will rescue them."

"Doing nothing wasn't an option, not if I wanted to stay alive." I was talking about it despite myself. "And unfortunately, there weren't any angels around at the time."

"Never are when you need 'em, are there?"

I shrugged. Enough with the amenities already, I thought.

He picked up on my vibe. "Known our D.A. long?"

"We were in law school together. We were friends there. She and I and her late husband."

He frowned upon hearing me mention Dennis. Reaching into his center desk drawer, he took out a can of Bugler tobacco and a pack of Zig Zag cigarette papers.

"Mind if I smoke?"

"Feel free."

"Technically I shouldn't, this being a public space. You won't bust me, will you?"

"It's your office."

Deftly he tapped a line of tobacco down the center of a sheet, rolled a tight cylinder (not one-handed, mercifully), licked the paper, and lit up with a kitchen match he sparked off the sole of his boot.

He was showing off for me. I managed to refrain from applauding.

"Nora's a good woman." His blue-smoke exhale curled up toward the ceiling. "She's been through a lot." He sat back in his swivel chair, boots on the edge of his desk.

"Yes, I understand that."

He picked a loose piece of tobacco off his lower lip. "Why are you here?" he asked me.

He knew the answer, and he knew that I knew that he knew, but he wanted to hear it from me, not Nora.

"To consult with Nora about the murder that occurred up here. Be a sounding board."

He sucked on his cigarette. The dry paper crackled. "That's all?"

I wanted to ask him questions, not the other way around. He was conducting this meeting as an interview, an interrogation. His attitude put me on edge—he was playing the cop when the circumstances didn't call for it. "Do you think there's something else?"

One last drag on his smoke. He wet his thumb and second finger, snuffed it, deposited the stub in a Folgers can that was on the windowsill behind him. "Do you have questions you want to ask me?" he said, avoiding my question.

I jumped in. "Who do you think did it?"

"Killed him?" The abruptness of my question took him by surprise, threw him off-balance momentarily.

"Yes."

The boots swung off his desk. He sat up straight. "I don't know."

"Any ideas?"

He shook his head. "By the time I got to the body there were already a bunch of men around it. You couldn't tell. No one could."

"Do you think it was premeditated?"

He looked at me. "That's conjecture."

"I know. But do you think it was?"

He steepled his fingers. "Yes, I think it was."

"By one of Juarez's people? Like the DEA summary hypothesizes?"

He gave me a cold look. "That's pretty far-fetched, don't you think, Mr. Garrison?"

"So you think it was a DEA agent."

He didn't avoid my question anymore. "It had to be."

"When they interviewed you, did you tell them that?"

"In so many words."

"What was their reaction?"

"Thank you very much, we're investigating all the angles."

He couldn't gloss over his anger at what had happened and how he had been treated. We were sparring, for reasons I didn't understand, unless it was his normal personality, but we were on the same side regarding what we thought had happened out there.

"Do you think it's possible some of the men inside escaped?"

A vigorous head-shake. "Absolutely not. They were blind pigs in a shooting gallery, coming out of that house. If anybody got out, it was before the raid started, and we"—he caught himself—"*they* had the place surrounded."

"So the surveillance was solid? No one could've slipped through."

He nodded in agreement. "That part was done fine."

"Tell me about the raid."

"Amateur night in Dixie, start to finish."

"How's that?"

"Look at the results."

I leaned forward, my hands on his desk. "Okay, I'm with you there. But let's put the results aside for a minute. Why was it botched so badly?"

He canted forward, matching me. "I can give you two good reasons."

"What are they?"

He counted off on the fingers of his left hand. "One, they made all their decisions based on information from a snitch. A totally unreliable man, I know him from way back. He'd lie on his mother's name. All snitches stink, but he's really malodorous."

I've done some good work using snitches, but in principle I agreed with him. Using an informant who has his own motives is a bad way to build a foundation. You should have other planks to bolster your case.

"Okay, I'll buy that. What's number two?"

"You know the answer to that," he threw back at me.

He was cagey, this old man. Maybe he figured me for a spy. "Somebody tipped them off? They knew you were coming?"

He nodded.

"And no one except the members of the task force knew about the raid?"

"That's what they say."

Which meant somebody on that task force was dirty. I didn't have to say that out loud.

A thought had been gestating in my head, from when I was reading the summary. Now it crystallized. "Did you know that operation existed?" I asked Miller. "Before Lopez copped?"

Finally, a smile. More a grimace, but the lips did curl upward. "We knew there was something there. We had our eye on the place."

"For how long?"

A casual shrug. "Six months, a year."

How come this was just coming out? I thought. "How'd you know?"

"We knew there was an airstrip being built on the hush-hush by some out-of-state corporation, which we figured out quickly was a sham, we couldn't find them listed anywhere. This is a remote area, but our computers work as good as anybody else's. You mix one airstrip in a remote location together with a dummy corporation, you get bad news."

"So you suspected there was something going on out there. Something illegal."

"That's my job, being suspicious."

"Why didn't you do something about it?"

"Like what?"

"Tell the appropriate agencies."

"Oh, the DEA perhaps? You saw how well they handled it." He sat up, poker-up-his-ass straight. "I'll be direct with you, Garrison. I'm the law here, not some jerks who take their orders from three thousand miles away. I don't like these high-and-mighty dipshits coming into my backyard, throwing their weight around. They take all the glory if an operation's successful, and lay blame if they fuck it up." He spun back in his chair. "Which is exactly what happened."

I'd touched a nerve. Good. I didn't know how this would be helpful to Nora, since they were partners, but it needed to be known.

Then another thought arose. Did Nora know about this? She had to . . . didn't she? And if she did, why hadn't she told me?

I felt queasy. I'd come up here to do a favor for an old classmate in distress, and now I was finding that I wasn't playing with a full deck.

"Did Nora know about it?"

He nodded. "Yes."

"She didn't tell me."

He realized he'd committed a faux pas. He tried to make it right.

"There was nothing to tell, because we didn't do anything. You can't move in on someone because they build a place to land airplanes. We have to wait for complaints, we can't horn in on our own anytime we think something criminal might be going on."

He was right. Still, I would have liked to have known from Nora.

I was finished with him. "Is there anything else I need from you?"

"I've told you all I know. I wish I knew more, I'm damn frustrated by this. They shut me out in my own county, one of the biggest busts that's ever come down here, then it blows up in their faces, half a dozen people are dead, and a murder's committed fifty yards away from three dozen men, but no one knows who did it, and there aren't any suspects, just some blue-sky theory that exonerates everyone."

Our meeting was over. "Thanks for your help," I said. In truth, he hadn't given me much. The two details I'd gleaned from meeting with him were that he believed the same things Nora did, and he'd thought something dirty might be going on out there prior to the bust, but hadn't done anything about it.

More important to me, in the overall scheme of things, was Miller's conviction, even stronger than Nora's, that Juarez's shooting had the fingerprints of the task force all over it. The man had been in law enforcement his entire life, he knew the lay of the land. And being a former FBI agent, he had no illusions about the federal law-enforcement bureaucracy.

"Thank you for coming all the way up here," he said. "I know Nora appreciates it."

He escorted me the three steps to his door. "Nora's an exceptional woman. She's been through hell. I don't know what it is she wants you to help her with exactly, but I hope you can."

He cared about her. This was a man who didn't care about many people, I was sure of that.

"I'll do what I can," I told him. It was easy to promise that; that's what I was here for. Except I don't know what it is she wants from me, beyond someone from a better past to talk to for a few days, I thought, as I walked down the hallway to Nora's office.

*   *   *

"How come you didn't tell me you knew there was dirty business going on up there before the DEA got involved?" I asked Nora.

We were having lunch in Maize's Lunchroom, a coffee shop across the square from her office, an old-fashioned place that featured milk shakes and root beer floats and burgers on the grill. I was devouring a grilled-cheese sandwich—Kraft American slices on Wonder bread—one of the great bad-for-you sandwiches of my youth, and a cherry Coke served in a real old-fashioned Coke glass, the logo etched on the side. Fries to go with it. Nora, sensible female public servant that she was, had selected a Cobb salad and unsugared iced tea.

"Because I didn't want to tell you anything that might prejudge your perception of what happened that night," she said coolly, reaching over and spearing one of my fries. "And we didn't know what was going on up there, exactly, we just suspected there was something. Rightly, as it turned out."

"Why didn't you go in and check it out?"

"On what grounds?" she asked. "You were a prosecutor. Enlighten me. What would you tell a judge to get him to issue a search warrant?"

"I'd figure something out." The grilled-cheese sandwich was damn good, just the right amount of buttery grease on the bread.

"Like what? There were never any complaints filed, no obvious criminal activities."

"I'd figure out something," I said through a mouthful of sandwich. "My investigators would."

"My invest*igator,* singular, is Sheriff Miller, and he isn't about to walk into a lion's den without authorization and backup, plus he doesn't have the time to chase wild hares, he's stretched doing the basic stuff." She picked at her salad. "Anyway, that isn't the main reason. We could've come up with one, I don't deny it."

"So why didn't you?"

She rubbed the thumb that wasn't holding her fork against the tips of her fingers. "Money," she whispered throatily, like an old Sarah Vaughan record. "We don't have enough. We're the poor relations."

The plight of the county prosecutor. I'd faced it myself, in a rich county. You can only do so much. Your budget determines what you can and can't pursue, particularly when the situation is more a judgment call than bold facts in black and white.

"Miller wanted to try to slip someone in, deep cover, the kind of operation where your man goes in for a year or more," Nora said. "He fought for it like hell, but the cost didn't justify it. And we couldn't have gone all the way with it anyway, we're way too underfunded. We certainly couldn't have run the kind of operation the DEA did, even if they did screw it up. In the end, we'd have had to call them in anyway, so . . . we let nature take its course."

I nodded. We ate in silence for a minute. My straw made a loud sucking sound as I slurped the dregs of the Coke from the bottom of the glass.

"Are you finished?" Nora asked.

I looked down at my plate. It was so clean they wouldn't have to run it through the dishwasher.

"Guess so."

She signed the check, put down a dollar for the tip. The entire meal was under seven dollars, a cappuccino and a scone in Santa Barbara.

We walked back to her office. "Hold my calls, if I get any," she instructed her secretary, a June Allyson look-alike, complete with hairdo.

Nora closed the door behind us. "A murder was committed in my jurisdiction," she said. "I can't let that go unanswered, even if the federal government wants me to."

"Are you sure they don't want you to?"

She smiled. "They don't want us coming in and mucking up their investigation, such as it was." She looked at me steadfastly. "I've waited for them to come up with something. But they haven't. So now, I'm going to proceed."

"You're doing the right thing."

"I know. But I'm glad you agree with me."

I didn't know that what I'd done for her was very important. Listened, and agreed with her. She'd needed the reassurance, now she had it. Mission accomplished.

On a personal level, which was what this was about, she'd also needed *me* to be the one who did the listening. Not members of her staff, not others in the community. Me. I sat there a minute, thinking, *why?* Because I was a reminder of a better time in her life? Because I'd been in her shoes, figuratively speaking? Because I was now, in her eyes, an important figure, with the murder defense and the business in the desert under my belt?

She'd needed me to hold her hand. There was no one around to do that anymore. So she'd reached back into the past and pulled a name out of the headlines.

"You're going to have to turn over a lot of stones, most of which won't have anything under them. You know," I cautioned her, "at the end of the day you might not have enough credible evidence to bring charges against anyone."

"I know." She paused. "Money isn't going to be a problem, fortunately."

"The county's going to bite the bullet?"

She shook her head. "We don't have it. It could come to more than our entire budget for two years, easy. I've discussed this with Bill Fishell. The state's going to foot the bill."

Bill Fishell's the California attorney general. We've known each other for a couple of decades. He stayed in the system and moved to the top of the food chain. I didn't.

"Then you don't have a problem."

She frowned. "I have seven deputy D.A.s, Luke. Seven for everything. And none of them have the kind of experience a case this size needs. I'm going to have to go outside. Bill and I have been discussing this over the past month, in case I decided to go for it."

I knew what she was talking about. In situations like this, where a county D.A. lacks the resources to conduct an investigation and trial thoroughly, the state will appoint someone to do it, usually a member of the attorney general's staff. Once in a blue moon one of the big counties, L.A., San Francisco, San Jose, will rent out one of their aces, someone who knows his or her way around a capital murder case, because as sure as the sun is going to rise in the east tomorrow morning, if they did manage to obtain an indictment and go to trial, it would be a murder-one case with extenuating circumstances. A death-penalty case. You need a lawyer with experience to do that. Someone who can eat nails for breakfast.

"So you're going to bring in a gun."

"Yes, that's our plan."

"Have you been discussing candidates?"

"Dozens. We've narrowed it down to one person, a short time ago."

"When's he going to start?" I assumed it was a man; if it was a woman, she would have mentioned it.

"Soon, I hope. Bill and I haven't asked him yet." She stretched her long legs out. She had strong calves, I noticed. Living in this wild country, you could do a lot of outdoors stuff, hiking, things like that.

"In fact," she continued, "I was on the phone with Bill while you and Sheriff Miller were meeting. He gave me final authorization to make an offer."

"You'd better get on the stick, then," I counseled her. "The longer you wait, the colder the trail's going to get. And the quality of lawyer you want is booked way out in advance."

"I know." She gave me a tired smile. "I wanted to get your input before I made the conclusive decision to go ahead. The state of California is going to spend a fortune trying to find out who murdered an international drug dealer who was an unredeemable scumbag who would have spent the rest of his life in a federal maximum-security prison if he hadn't been killed. It won't be a popular move—especially if the shooter turns out to be a renegade federal agent."

I nodded in agreement. "Nora, I'm flattered that you wanted my opinion, although you could have come to this decision without me. You know what you're doing, I can see that from the short amount of time I've been here."

"I don't know if I could have or not, but thanks for the compliment. I feel more secure about it now, believe me."

"Then this trip was well worth it. Not only for the help, but to see you after all these years, still looking great and fighting the good fight." I smiled at her. "So when are you going to ask the lucky guy?"

The smile she sent back to me was tentative. She hesitated a moment, then stood up and walked over to me.

"Now."

Dinner was at her house again. Bad take-out Chinese. It didn't matter—I had no appetite anyway. The Scotch didn't help either, but I knocked it down and poured myself another.

"You had this planned before I came up here," I berated her. I'd been blindsided, and I was pissed off about it. I hate being manipulated.

"I didn't. I swear it."

"Bullshit." I was steaming. "You set me up."

"It's the truth, Luke, please believe me. I wouldn't run a con on you." She wasn't happy with my attitude. Which was too bad, because I was frosted from what felt like transparent duplicity.

"Well, what's this?"

"I didn't ask you to come up here so I could set you up. I didn't . . ." She tailed off.

"You didn't what?" I sounded like a jealous husband who's caught his wife in a sleazy affair.

I looked at my glass. It was almost empty. I put it down. I hadn't had anything to eat since lunch, and I didn't want whiskey fucking my head up. "You didn't what, Nora?" I said again.

"Want to use you." She was sitting across the room from me, looking miserable.

"Then what?"

"I . . . needed someone to talk to, and I'd been thinking about you, from the publicity last fall. Actually, I'd thought about calling you a couple years ago, after you won that big case. Seeing your name in the paper after all these years, I got a rush of pride. I know that sounds silly, but I did."

"A rush of pride? For what?"

"That someone I knew, who I'd shared an important part of my life with, was so successful. Reflected glory, you know what I mean?"

That's just what I needed. A woman whose own life hadn't turned out the way she'd envisioned it living vicariously through a man she didn't know, but had, superficially, in the distant past. As if the relationship in the past legitimized one in the present, even though the present for us had never existed.

"So this was a good excuse," she continued. "Then once we talked, I got to thinking about how right you'd be for this. Bill Fishell agreed with me, but I needed to know how you'd feel about it. The case, I mean," she said hurriedly, "not about taking it on."

"You should've been straight with me up front," I said. "It would've saved me time, you money, and you wouldn't have built your expectations up. I couldn't get into this for all the teabags in China."

She started crying. Softly, her head in her hands.

"Oh, shit, Nora, don't, come on." I walked over to her, put a hand on her shoulder. She was trembling. "Come on, don't."

She looked up at me. Her eyes were red. "I'm sorry."

"I'm happy to be here for you as a friend. But friendship and work are separate, and should stay separate."

"I know," she said, even more miserably than before.

I felt like a schmuck. Not because of what I'd said: it had to be said. But because she was so unhappy and wasn't keeping a stiff upper lip.

"Do you want something to drink?" I asked. When in doubt, apply booze.

"Yes, please."

"What do you want?"

"Whatever you're having."

I poured out a decent shot for her, refreshed my own glass. Then I sat down next to her.

"I'm not in the prosecutor business anymore. I left that a long time ago, and I've never looked back." I caught myself. "Actually, I did look back, for a number of years. But I got over it, and now I am over it. I don't want to go back to that."

She started to say something, but held her tongue and drank some Scotch instead.

"I'm married," I went on. "Fairly recently, after a traumatic divorce. We have a small son. I have a nice, easy practice. In the past three years I've almost been killed twice, and there've been other traumas, too. I've moved out of the fast lane, Nora. I'm not even on the superhighway anymore. I'm just a plain old country-road lawyer, doing the best he can."

"Which is very good. I know what you've been doing."

I let that pass. I'd already blown off all the steam I wanted to blow off.

"This is going to be an intense, time-consuming job. Too time-consuming. And I don't want to be away from my wife and child, not for the months this could take."

She nodded, agreeing with all my very good points.

"Also—if federal agents are involved, and I think they are, like you do and your sheriff and even Bill Fishell, I presume . . ."

She nodded her head again.

". . . this will get messy. You don't know where it's going to lead. These are rough and tough people, you get in their path at your peril."

"Physical danger?"

"It could happen. Anything could happen. None of it enjoyable. Which is why, my long-ago friend, the answer to your question is no. Listen, Nora, there are plenty of great lawyers who can do this job and will be happy to take it on. You won't have any problem getting one."

She'd stopped crying. She looked up at me. "They won't be you."

"They'll be better, believe me."

"You're a celebrity, Luke."

"That's really what I want to hear."

"Well, you are, whether you like it or not. You have a Teflon shield, Luke. You're unassailable, you're a hero because of what happened out in the desert. Your motives can't be attacked, unlike those of a career criminal defense lawyer, a Gerry Spence or Johnnie Cochran. You aren't political, and you've worked both sides of the aisle. I don't know another lawyer in the country with your qualifications, honestly."

I shook my head. "I don't want to be a celebrity. I hate it. All those interviews, they were awful. If I live the rest of my life in peaceful anonymity, I'll die a happy man. I'm really serious about that. And there are plenty of great lawyers who are as qualified as I am for this. Better lawyers than me, and you know that."

"Then I guess I'll have to take no for an answer," she said. "For now, anyway."

"Forever," I told her firmly.

She didn't reply to my objections. Instead, she walked over to the dining room table, picked up the cartons of Chinese food, and tossed them in the trash.

"There's a bar about twenty miles from here. It isn't too rowdy and they cook up decent Buffalo chicken wings. It's about as haute as our local cuisine gets. Let's not end our time together on a downer, okay?"

I put my hands on her shoulders. "Lady, that's the best idea you've had all day."

Long-necked Buds, spicy chicken wings, ranch dressing. When you're in the right mood, that's a combination that fell right out of heaven.

Hap's Happy Hour was another throwback joint, like the lunchroom. When Nora and I first walked in, I felt an unsettling déjà vu; it reminded me of the Brigadoon, the killing field out in the desert. I let the emotions roil around inside of me for a moment, then I sloughed them off. Lightning doesn't strike twice, not like that. And if it did, I'd be dead and it wouldn't matter.

Nora seemed to know most of the people here; she nodded and said hellos as we navigated the length of the room. There was no waitress service—we placed our orders at the take-out counter and settled into a back booth with a couple of cold beers.

"Quaint," I observed.

"Isn't it?" She drank her beer straight from the bottle. "It fits me . . . now. Who'd've thunk it?" She smiled at me and held up her bottle.

I clinked mine to hers. "To the good old days," I toasted. "And those to come."

"I'll drink to that. I hope that's a prophecy."

I inventoried the place. It was crowded—mostly men, although some wives and girlfriends were there, too. People that I assumed were typical for the area—cowboys, loggers, working-class men. The women had the same look in a feminine way. No one was dressed up, not a sports coat or tie in the crowd. Or skirt, for that matter, except for Nora, who was still in her district attorney clothes. Wood tables and booths, sawdust on the floor. Part of it had been sectioned off for dancing. Your basic shitkicker bar—a good place to get a load on, if one was so inclined.

"Come here often?" I asked her.

Nora shook her head. "I don't go anywhere often. I'm too tired after work to do anything except go home, eat, work, watch television, go to bed. I'm not a party girl, to put it mildly. Besides, I don't go to bars alone." She flashed a smile. "Bad for my image."

I wondered if she was dating, or had. My gut told me she wasn't and hadn't. She might have become acclimated to this region, but I didn't think there would be many men here she'd spark to. Even though Dennis had fallen, he'd been a star once. She'd savored caviar, hamburger wasn't ever going to taste the same.

"You're going to miss it around here, I'll bet," she teased me in a semimocking fashion. I had the feeling that was how she dealt with her world; with irony. Whatever it takes to keep you going. I've been there.

"I'll miss *you*." I said that to be nice, but I meant it, once the words were out of my mouth. She was a nice woman, attractive, and we'd had good times together back then, when we had all been young and the world had been full of promise, unlimited.

"Thank you, Luke. That's nice to hear from a man like you."

"What kind of man is that?" I enjoy being flattered as much as the next guy, but this was a mite uncomfortable.

"Successful. Purposeful. Has his life in order. And is cute." She took a quick swallow.

"If you only knew the truth," I bantered. This was our last night together, I'd turned down her proposal, I needed to keep the evening light.

"You say."

Our order was called. I walked over to the counter and got the baskets. It smelled good and there was plenty of it. I could tell, both from the clientele in here and people I'd seen on the street in town, that the locals took their eating seriously. What they lacked in quality they made up in quantity, and then some. Besides the wings, ranch dressing, biscuits, and fries, there were onion rings in bricks, an added bonus. Between lunch and this I was going to chow down more cholesterol than

I put into my system in a month at home, but no one from home was watching. I bought a couple more Buds and carried everything back to our booth.

We dug in, cleaning the grease off our fingers on paper napkins and Handi Wipes. "You're getting the knack," Nora said, watching me lick the last speck of skin off a wing.

"I'm a fast learner."

"Sure you don't want to—"

I put up a hand to stop her. "Look, Nora. You've got a righteous case, and it's good that you're pursuing it. With the state's money in your bank account you can do it the way it needs to be done. But I'm not your man. I'm just not."

"Okay." She bit into a piece of onion ring. "I had to give it one more shot."

"That's fine. But no more, all right?"

"Yes."

The jukebox was strictly country-western. A slow Randy Travis came on. A few couples got up and started to dance. For a fleeting moment I thought of asking Nora, but decided not to. The memory of our toes touching the night before, and my guilty-husband reaction to it, cautioned me against physically touching her.

She started on her second beer, put it down. "You haven't asked me about Dennis."

I don't know if I flushed—I definitely felt hot. "I didn't feel I should bring him up."

"Why not?"

"Embarrassed, I guess. I don't know."

"No one ever wants to talk about him. The people here, my parents, his former colleagues back in Denver and Washington. It's like he's the family retard you want to keep hidden in the attic."

"I wasn't thinking that way."

"Are you embarrassed for me, or yourself?"

"Both," I admitted.

"Well . . ." She took another pull from her beer. "*I'd* like to talk to you about him. Is that okay?"

"Sure."

"He killed himself."

So I'd been right about that.

"He blew his brains out, four years ago."

"Jesus, Nora, I'm sorry, I'm . . ."

"Uh-uh. Don't be. Nobody made him pull the trigger. And don't be sorry for me, I've had enough sorry to last me ten lifetimes. I'm sick to my stomach at people feeling sorry for me."

I was mute. I didn't know how to react, what to say.

She didn't need my complimentary voice. She needed to spew this out.

"It all turned bad so fast neither of us could understand it. And once it started going downhill, bam, it was an avalanche." She picked up a piece of chicken, started to eat it, dropped it back in the basket. "Which didn't help our sex life, either."

Oh, fuck. Where was this going to end?

"Sex between us was never good anyway, Dennis wasn't much of a performer. It wasn't important to him. He lived for work." She gave me a sideways, embarrassed look.

I didn't know what to say to that. I didn't think she was coming on to me, but it sure was awkward, sitting there and listening to this.

"Part of his lack of sexual interest was that he was sterile. We didn't know that until we tried having a family. I think that contributed to our sex life going bad—worse than it had been, I mean. I think it contributed to everything going bad, to tell you the truth. He wanted kids, more than me. He was devastated when we found out."

"You never thought about adopting?" The standard line; it sounded stupid.

She shook her head. "It would have been an admission to the world that he wasn't perfect. He couldn't deal with that."

I couldn't help it—I was too hungry not to eat, and I needed something to do beside sit like a bump on a log and listen to this. I shoved a dressing-laden wing in my mouth, washed it down.

"We talked about breaking up," she continued.

"Why didn't you?"

"More Protestant guilt. For better or worse, whatever. Because to leave him would have been to admit failure, my failure. It would have made our failures public, and that would have killed Dennis, before he killed himself. I couldn't do that to him." She gave me one of her intense looks. "I loved him, flaws and all. I really did love him, Luke. I'd followed him here out of old-fashioned wifely devotion and then I just stayed. To the bitter fucking end."

I reached over and touched her hand. She grabbed hold of mine like she was holding on to a life raft.

"A couple of years before Dennis died, I started working at the D.A.'s office. Then Turner Jenkins, the old D.A., retired and endorsed me. Forced me to run, truth be told. I ran unopposed and here I be." She let go of my hand. "It ain't the bright lights, big city, but it's home now. I can't explain why. My fate, karma, whatever they call it."

I wanted to say, *You aren't stuck here if you don't want to be. Not now.* But I didn't. It was none of my business. She'd already told me more than I wanted to hear.

"Hey, Miz Ray."

We both looked up. A hefty, good-looking Native American man in his late twenties was standing at the end of our booth, smiling at us.

Nora smiled back at him. "Hey, Wayne. Say hello to an old friend of mine, Luke Garrison. Luke, this is Wayne Bearpaw, one of Tom Miller's deputies."

Bearpaw. I remembered the name from the reading material: the deputy who had been with Miller on the DEA raid.

We shook hands, said hellos.

"I heard you were in town. You're the city lawyer's going to help our D.A. beat up the big boys from Washington," Bearpaw said, grinning at Nora.

"I put in my two cents, that's it," I corrected him.

"Luke won't be involved any further with our investigation. I'll fill you in later," Nora told him with a forced smile.

"Sorry to hear that. I've heard good things about you."

"You were there on that raid," I said, out of curiosity and to change the subject. I looked him over. He was big and strong. He could handle his end.

"Yeah, I was a warm body," he said derisively. "Like it mattered."

"Sounds like it was a real mess."

"Shit, and then some. Me and the sheriff, we were lucky we didn't get our asses blown to kingdom come when all that munitions blew inside. Stupid fuckers. They should've never stuck their damn selfs into it. Me and Sheriff Miller, we could've smoked those fuckers out. With enough time and money." He looked pointedly at Nora.

"Luke knows all about that," she said, placating him. "We're just having a friendly dinner now. Dinner among old friends."

"Yeah." He calmed down as fast as he'd heated up. "Didn't mean to come on salty there, but boy, that was a piss-poor operation. And then, after all that, they up and kill their own prisoner." He shook his head as if he still couldn't believe it had all happened the way it had.

"You think they did?" I was interested in his adamance over the killing.

"Who else was there? Nobody with a brain buys that shit about his own men doing him. I know how those people live. They don't operate that way."

"Wayne's our number one undercover narc," Nora said. "He's broken some big cases for us—big by our standards."

"Yeah, nobody suspects a dumb Injun," Bearpaw said, laughing.

"You weren't there, though?" I asked. "When Juarez was killed." Had I read that? I didn't remember.

A negative head-shake. "I went home once the survivors had been captured. We had nothing to do there, Jerome and them sure as hell didn't want us around. I was in bed sawing logs by the time the killing happened."

"But Miller stayed."

"He's an old warhorse. He's the best." The deputy gave Nora a good-bye salute. "Nice meeting you," he said to me. "Sorry you ain't coming aboard. I think it's going to be fun." He melded into the crowd.

"He sounds gung ho," I said, looking at his retreating back.

"We all are." She gave me a last-chance look.

"Well, I hope you get your man." I turned back to my dinner.

"I already didn't," she said directly. "But that's okay, I understand your reasons. I'll get the one who killed Juarez. If there's anyone to be getting."

We said our good-byes at my motel door.

"I'll keep in touch," I told her. "If I think of anything, or anyone who you should talk to, I'll call."

"Thanks."

It was after midnight, chilly out. I could have invited her in—I could tell she was reluctant to go back to her empty home, but I didn't have anything to drink, and it was time to close this chapter.

"It was great seeing you again, Nora, after all this time."

"You, too, Luke,"

"I can't tell you how sorry I feel about what happened to Dennis."

She nodded.

"This might seem like a shitty thing to say, but I'm glad I didn't know what had happened. My memories of him will always be good ones."

"I'm glad of that. I try to do that, too. Sometimes I can."

She was deflated, from my rejection and from bringing up the old wounds. I pulled her to me in a hug. She hugged back, her body pressing against mine. For a moment she laid her head on my shoulder. Then we separated.

"I hope you keep your promise," she said.

"About?"

"Keeping in touch."

"I will. Promise." I crossed my heart over my jacket.

We stood there in the dark. There was nothing more to say.

"Thanks for coming. You helped me a lot."

"I'm glad." I smiled at her. "Don't let the bastards grind you down."

"I've survived a lot worse than anything some stooges from Washington could ever do to me. I'll make it fine."

"Yeah," I said, "you will." She was one tough lady; she'd grown into it. A far cry from the young, idealistic, wealthy sheltered girl I'd known in school, who had the prince and the whole world on a string. "You have."

There was nothing left to say or do. She reached out and touched my sleeve for a second, then turned and walked to her car, got in, and drove away. I went into my room and called Riva and told her I was coming home.

A NEED FOR CLOSURE

I few from Reno to L.A., L.A. to Santa Barbara. It was early afternoon when my plane taxied in. Riva and Bucky were waiting for me at the gate. It was a good thirty degrees warmer here than it had been in Blue River—Riva was wearing shorts, sandals, a UCSB sweatshirt. She looked fetching and sexy and welcoming, and I grabbed her up in my arms as soon as I got to her.

"Missed you," I said into her hair.

"Me, too."

I swung Buck up onto my shoulders. We made like an airplane on our way to the parking lot.

"So how'd it go?" Riva quizzed me. "You didn't say much on the phone."

We were southbound on 101, heading for home. I was driving, she was in the front passenger seat, Bucky was in his car-seat in the back, half-dozing. I'd arrived when he normally takes his nap, but he wasn't going to miss out on seeing his daddy get off that big airplane.

"Different from what I'd expected."

"Different how?"

"For one thing, her husband didn't just die, he committed suicide."

Riva's mouth made a round, wordless O. "Jesus," she then said, "that's awful." She couldn't resist asking, "How?"

"Gun."

"Ugh." She turned and looked reflexively at Buck—a mother's protective instinct.

"Yeah. So there was that." I looked at my son in the rearview mirror—he'd fallen asleep. They look like angels at this age when they're sleeping. Mine does, anyway. He has curly blond hair, blue eyes, the works. Botticelli couldn't have created someone this perfect.

"And we talked about her work, this DEA case specifically. I need to talk to you about that, but it's going to take time, so let's get home, get me unpacked, have dinner, put Buck to bed, then I'll fill you in on everything."

She gave me one of her funny stares. "Is there something I need to know about?" Meaning, *Something wrong?*

"Not at all," I assured her. "It's complicated, that's all. And I want a break, okay?"

"Fine by me."

She had no cause to worry—and I had no intention of giving her any.

What with playing with Buck, feeding him his dinner, getting him ready for bed and then into bed—no small achievement, he was all keyed up from Daddy being home, tonight was a two-book, three-story bedtime—then the two of us having our dinner, candlelight, wine, the whole romantic trip, it was almost ten by the time we settled in for the story of my trip. My brief but interesting trip.

"Nora's going to do her own investigation of the fiasco up there. She isn't satisfied with the DEA's version of what happened. She thinks they're whitewashing it. Covering their tracks."

"Dirty tracks?"

"Looks that way."

"Crooked cops." She said the words with utter contempt, practically spat them out. "They're all over the place." She was referring to my episode in the desert.

"More than there ought to be, that's for sure." There ought to be none, zero.

"She wanted your expert advice."

"Yes."

"Which you freely gave."

"Yes."

We'd cracked a bottle of Taylor port, vintage 1985, a stellar year. It was warming me up nicely, after the coq au vin and the Santa Ynez Valley Syrah and the homemade oatmeal cookies. Nora was a nice cook, her venison stew had been excellent, but no chef on earth touches my wife's cooking, as far as I'm concerned.

"I read a yard of documents the DEA sent her on their investigation, interviewed a few local law-enforcement people. She was honed in already; she wanted someone like me, who'd been in the job, to confirm what she'd been thinking. Someone she knew and could trust. Thought she knew," I added. "Twenty years go by, you can't know that person. You know who they were, not who they are." Except for a decent resemblance physically to what she'd looked like at age twenty-three, Nora Ray was not the woman I'd known twenty-odd years ago—who is?

"So that's it? Do you get a certificate of commendation?"

"I'll put in for one." I stretched out on the sofa. Through the windows overlooking the harbor I watched the lights dancing.

"Her office can't handle the job internally. It's too small, and this case could be Godzilla. She's going to bring in an independent prosecutor. The state's backing her action—they're going to pay for it."

"This sounds like the big time." Riva was cuddled up to me, her head on my shoulder, her body against mine. Now she sat up. "It could be a nationally publicized case."

"It will be. Small county takes on big drug cartel and a major government agency. It's going to run into millions. Geraldo and Larry King will get plenty of airtime out of this one."

"Did she tell you who she's bringing in?"

I turned to her; I tried to smile, to make light of it, but I couldn't. "She asked me."

Riva stared at me in disbelief. "You've been holding this small, insignificant tidbit from me for what, seven hours? When does she want you to start? Your calendar's full for months. You could lay most of the work off, but . . ."

"I turned her down."

Her jaw dropped. "You what?"

"Turned her down. What would you think I'd do, take it?"

"I guess . . . yes."

"Why would I want that job? It's going to be a nest of hornets."

"I guess . . . because it's going to be a high-profile job, and you're a high-profile lawyer."

"Was. I don't want to be anymore." I shifted around so I could face her directly. "This could take up to a year. I'd have to live up there, most of the time. My entire practice here would go down the drain."

I'm a single practitioner; I don't have partners to cover me in cases like this.

"Your practice is never going to go away, even if you're gone," Riva said. "You're too good. And I know how those things work, you wouldn't be there all the time, there'll be slack periods. And you'd have a staff, wouldn't you?"

I couldn't believe what I was hearing. "You're talking like you *want* me to take this on."

"I want you to do what you want to do."

"What I want to do is not that." My glass was empty; I got up and refilled it; just a little, I don't drink that much port, it's too heavy. A little goes a long way for me now. Like a lot of things I used to indulge in. I sat down next to her again.

"I don't want to be away from you and Buck for a year. That's ridiculous."

"Who says we'd have to be away from each other?" She was knocking down every argument I threw at her. It was like she'd been offered the job and I was the one trying to dissuade her. "We'd come with you."

I literally broke into laughter. "You wouldn't last a week up there. Blue River would bore your tits off."

"I was living up-country when we met."

"That was different. That was sophisticated rural. This is nothing-to-do rural. And what about Bucky," I pressed on. "He's got playgroup, his ocean camp this summer . . ."

"Ocean camp?" She chortled. "He's two years old. He isn't going to ocean camp. He's with me." She reached over and softly touched my face with her hand; an intimate and provocative gesture. "And I'm with you."

"Which is why I'm staying right here in Santa Barbara, California, garden spot of the world."

She leaned back. "It's your decision. I want to make sure you're doing it because *you* want to, not because you're worried about me and the crown prince. Because we're like Paladin, except without the gun."

"I don't want to do it. I've had the spotlight. I don't need it anymore. I don't want it. I want to live a life of quiet bliss in the bosom of my family."

"I got your bosom, big daddy. Both of 'em."

On that note, we went to bed.

I woke up in the middle of the night. My mouth was dry, from the port. Quietly, so as not to wake Riva, I threw on my robe and went into the kitchen.

The clock on the kitchen wall read a quarter to four. I wasn't going to get back to sleep. We'd made love, and she had conked out almost immediately. I had tossed and turned before falling into a nightmarish sleep, where the little girl in the Brigadoon, the desert restaurant, was being blown away while I tried to fire the shotgun, which didn't go off, blowing up in my own face instead, women screaming, buildings like the compound in Blue River exploding, a woman who looked like Nora Ray floating down a river of blood, Nora turning to young Nora, Dennis was in there somewhere, too, a gun going off, his face flying away, literally flying away. Other fragments of gruesome shit like that.

Man, was I relieved when I woke up from that dream. I'd had similar ones, from about two weeks after the desert episode. At least Riva and Buck weren't in this one.

The *News-Press* hit the front door at five-thirty. I was already on my second cup of coffee. I brought it in and read it, back to front. The *L.A. Times* arrived at six. I was reading about how the Angels were going to be contenders and the Dodgers were going to be dismal when Riva came in and joined me. Buck was still asleep. He's been good to about seven-thirty for the past few months, a true blessing.

"You almost threw me out of bed, you were tossing so much."

"I'm sorry."

"It's okay. Another bad dream?"

I nodded. "That's another reason I wouldn't want that special-prosecutor job. I'd have to hire a live-in chiropractor."

She put on water for herb tea. She doesn't drink coffee anymore, not since she became pregnant. Buck's almost two and she's still nursing, at night. She's that kind of mother.

"I don't think taking that job would give you any more nightmares than you already have. You're a nightmare person, that's how you work out your anxieties." She dunked a tea bag in her cup. "It's not . . ." She stopped herself.

"Not what?"

"Not dealing with these anxieties, head-on."

"Thank you, Mrs. Freud." I didn't want to hear this, not at six-thirty in the morning.

"I'm sorry. You had a rough night."

"I don't want the job, Nora, I mean Riva . . ."

"Was she in your dream?" my wife asked archly.

"The whole world was in my dream." God, what a slip. "Al Gore was in my dream, for Christ's sake."

"Wow. That's serious."

"I don't need you mocking me first thing in the morning."

"Who said I'm mocking you?"

Bucky called from his bedroom. Riva headed that way, teacup in hand. She patted me on the back. "You'll be fine—as soon as you've gotten this bad-cop shit out of your psyche." Her parting shot as she slipped into our son's bedroom.

I drove down to my office. I practice alone, but I share a building with five other lawyers, an old, sprawling adobe near the center of town that dates back almost to Padre Serra. In previous incarnations this building was, among other things, a bar, before that a speakeasy; also, in the early years of the century, it was the city's leading whorehouse, and at various other times it's been a women's clothing store, office furniture store, etc. I'm told that my office, the largest in the building (I pay the most rent) was the star bedroom when the whores roosted here.

It's a good arrangement—we each have our own office and we share a law library, conference room, there are a couple paralegals we all use, receptionist, etc. The convenience and camaraderie of a firm without the necessary compromises. I headed up an eighty-person office when I was the county D.A.; being a lone wolf suits me now. I answer to no one, I come and go as I please, I don't have to take any cases I don't want just to keep the firm greased.

I'm different from my office mates in a few ways. My professional profile is considerably higher, so my hourly rate is, also—only a few lawyers in Santa Barbara bill four hundred dollars an hour, my going rate; not king of the hill in New York or Los Angeles, but big money in our smallish city. Also, I was the district attorney, and I've won a few highly publicized cases, so I've got considerable clout and experience.

A bunch of messages were waiting for me. Grabbing the phone slips, I ducked into my office. It was still early; no one else had made an appearance yet. Like me, most of the lawyers here do a good amount of litigation. Often they'll go straight to court before coming in.

Shortly after eight, people started drifting in. We exchanged greetings, filled each other in on what had transpired in my absence. Phil Sorkind, my closest friend in the bunch, stuck his head in around nine-thirty. He does mainly family cases—he'd been in court on a nasty custody one. He looked slightly agitated, but he often does—he attracts contentious clients, and he lets them get to him. You need to stay objective or you burn out. It's happened to all of us.

"How was the wild, wild West?" He had a Pete's latte in one hand, maple scone in the other. Phil's a solid forty pounds overweight, and he doesn't give a shit, he gave up that battle long ago. He can walk from the golf cart to his ball and back, that's enough exercise for him.

"Tame. All the rustlers were dead by the time I arrived."

He chuckled. "And your old classmate?" I'd given him a thumbnail sketch before I'd left.

"She's okay, but she's in a pickle." I filled him in on the botched raid, her desire to bring in a special prosecutor, my declining her offer; I didn't tell him about Dennis, his suicide, the personal stuff. He didn't know them, it was none of his business.

"High-visibility case," he said. "But you don't need any more of them, do you?"

"You've got that right, palsy."

We made lunch plans, and he split. The remainder of the morning purred along. A few clients came in, and we reviewed their situations. Nothing on my docket was going to court soon; I had a couple of big insurance cases I hoped I could settle, even though going to court would have paid me more. I hate going up against insurance company lawyers and their sleazebag hired-gun doctors—I always feel like I need a shower afterward.

My last morning appointment left. I sat for a short time with Louella, one of our paralegals, clearing up some paperwork, and was about to walk down to Phil's office and corral him to go to lunch when Don Schwartz, another of my office mates, stuck his head in the door.

"Check this out."

We followed him down the hallway to the conference room. Some of the others in the office who hadn't gone to lunch yet were clustered around the television set, which was tuned to CNN. The correspondent, a chic-looking woman wearing a trench coat (it wasn't raining but she looked good in it), was standing outside the gates of the California Men's Colony in San Luis Obispo, a hundred miles north of us. Behind her you could see squadrons of police ringing the structure.

"Riot or jailbreak?" I asked.

"Riot," one of the other lawyers answered without turning away from the screen.

"The California Men's Colony East prison is in a state of turmoil," the woman on the screen was saying. "Convicts have taken over one wing of the compound and have barricaded themselves against the authorities. It is rumored that they have taken some guards hostage, and that they have weapons, but those rumors have not yet been confirmed by prison authorities."

A series of mug shots were flashed on the screen. Different convicts, different races. Some white skinheads, some blacks, their heads shaved also, some Latinos. One ordinary-looking white man. Seven in all.

Phil, looking over my shoulder, did a quick running commentary as each shot went by. "Skinhead, another skinhead, coke dealer, somebody's chicken, L.A. Blood, Mexican Mafia." Then: "White guys shouldn't shave their heads. They look dorky, even if they have a million ugly tattoos and ninety-nine-inch necks. Black guys look good shaved. Like Michael Jordan."

I hadn't seen anyone in that lineup who even vaguely resembled His Airness. Then it hit me.

"Jesus Christ! That's William Lowenstein!"

"Who?" The other paralegal, Susan, who's only been in the office a few months.

"The plain-wrap white guy. The one with hair." Frizzy Jewish hair, receding rapidly. Prison can do that to you, especially if you aren't hardened before you go in.

"You sure?" Phil asked, alarmed.

"Yes, I'm sure. I saw him last month. We were working on his appeal, and I was trying to get him transferred out of there."

"This is trouble," Phil said. Others nodded in agreement.

"What's happening?" I asked.

The others looked at me sideways, as if they didn't want to stare at me directly. The kind of look people have when they've seen a really bad traffic accident, like a train hitting a school bus.

As if she'd heard me, the CNN lady began delivering more bad news: "A fight between two convicts in the yard last night escalated into a violent situation. Prison guards tried to dispel it with hoses and tear gas, but when that didn't work, they opened fire on the combatants. The seven men whose pictures we've shown are now confirmed to have been killed in the melee."

"What the fuck!" My knees started buckling.

"Most of the men who were killed were not involved in the actual fight that started the escalation," the announcer was continuing. "They were bystanders who were in the wrong place at the wrong time, according to informed sources."

The mug shots were shown again. The man who looked as if he didn't belong was definitely William Lowenstein.

"That's a bitch," Phil said sympathetically.

"It's murder," Rollie Lewis, another of the lawyers, chimed in. "These damn prison guards, they think they have a license to kill."

"No one's ever stopped them, that's the problem," Phil replied. "The goddamn institution's rotten at the core."

The California prison system is a disaster, everyone connected with law enforcement knows that. We're one of the few states that allows the use of live ammunition inside the walls, and the men who have died as a result of that corrupt policy are testimony to its failure.

"William Lowenstein," Phil said, putting a supportive hand on my shoulder. "What crummy luck. He shouldn't even have been in there."

William Lowenstein was a UCSB Ph.D. candidate in chemistry who decided he wanted to live higher on the hog than you can do off a graduate assistant's salary. So he started making LSD in the lab. Nothing big, enough pay for a decent apartment in town instead of having to live in shitty student housing in Isla Vista, buy a car (a used Audi wagon), eat out occasionally, outfit himself in some nice clothes. Trips with his girlfriend to Jamaica and Hawaii also got thrown into the mix. It was not a big drug deal, just one enterprising young man bettering his station in life. Only temporarily, until his dissertation was accepted and he could disappear in the diaspora of academia. A few years, maybe a hundred grand total in profits to him.

He thought he was a smart young man, and he was—a Ph.D. in science? You have to be smart. He was book-smart, all right, but he wasn't street-smart. He sold five hundred tabs of acid to an undercover narc. That is a felony in the state of California, and despite his otherwise sterling record he was sentenced to four years.

I was his lawyer. Having been a prosecutor, I'd seen the futility of heavy sentences for these kind of drug crimes. The guy wasn't a big dealer, part of a syndicate, like that one up in Blue River; he was selling to willing buyers, none of them children, he was a petty moke who got caught. I did the best I could for him; four years isn't the end of the world. His academic aspirations would have been shot, but some company in industry would have taken a chance on him. He might have had to leave the country to work, but his life wasn't ruined, just torn up temporarily.

He was sent to Chino, a minimum-security prison. That was appropriate—he had no prior record, and he wasn't a threat to society. But he had a problem: he was too smart for his own good. He fancied himself a jailhouse lawyer, to the point where he pissed off the warden so much that he was transferred. To a real tough joint. A rounding out of his book-learning education, so to speak.

He'd been in San Luis for two months. It was a horrible experience for him. His first night there he was gang-raped, and it didn't get better. I was working on having him assigned to another minimum-security facility—the transfer from Chino had been wrong, beyond the warden's jurisdiction, and I knew I could reverse it, given a little time.

Too late now. Time had run out on William.

I felt sick. "Poor bastard," I said to no one in particular.

"Yeah," Phil agreed. "You all right?"

"I'm okay. I wonder if his parents know yet?" His father was a doctor, his mother a school administrator. William was an only child. This would kill them.

I didn't want to watch anymore. "Let's get lunch," I told Phil.

We walked down the street to the Paradise, where I ordered a glass of chardonnay as soon as I sat down, and another with my grilled salmon. I don't drink at lunch, but this was a special occasion. A wake, in absentia.

"This has been a lousy year for the police," Riva said.

"How about the victims of the police?"

"That's what I meant. I meant public-relations-wise."

"If they stopped killing people and violating their civil rights, they wouldn't have that problem."

"You're sounding like Gloria Allred."

"Spare me."

I'm not one of those talk-show lawyers who think the police are corrupt as an institution. Nor am I a bleeding-heart liberal who cries for the killer behind bars and doesn't for his victims. I'm not a liberal at all when it comes to law enforcement, it was my life. But I do believe that the police have a special obligation, because it's their job and because they hold so much power, to uphold the law beyond that of an ordinary citizen. When police officers cross the line, they dishonor the ninety-nine percent who do it the right way. And they give the public the impression that the police are out of control.

Which they were in the Brigadoon bar. Even though Bill and Joe weren't cops anymore, in the public's eye, they were—once a cop, always a cop. The point is, people died as a result of law officers (and ex-officers) going beyond their mandate. When that starts to happen, and they aren't called to account for it, you're living in a police state.

It was night. I was back home. Over dinner I'd filled Riva in on the day's events up in San Luis Obispo. She doesn't watch TV during the day, except kids' stuff on PBS.

We watched some of the coverage, which our local affiliate was broadcasting live. The initial reporting had been wrong; the convicts didn't have guns, and they weren't holding any guards hostage. And you can't seal yourself in like in the old prisons, everything's controlled centrally. In a day or two, the reporter told us, everything would be back to normal.

"Normal?" I yelled at the screen. "You call seven men dead over a fight in the yard normal? One of them a Ph.D. candidate who shouldn't have been there in the first place? You call that normal?"

"I don't think the man in the little box can hear you, honey," Riva said softly. "You're going to wake Buck up."

"Ah, fuck it." I remoted the tube off. "Why don't they put happy shit on TV for a change?" I groused. "Boy Scouts helping old ladies across the street. Firemen rescuing cats from trees."

"Do you need a rocker or a walker?"

"Corrupt police, police brutality, malfeasance . . . murder, which is what happened to William Lowenstein, as far as I'm concerned, murder sanctioned by the state. I hope his family sues the shit out of those bastards, I'll do that one for free." I forced myself to calm down. "It sure seems like I'm attracting this stuff, doesn't it?"

"You're still thinking about what happened up in Blue River, aren't you?"

"I wasn't . . . I thought I wasn't . . . but this got me started again."

She'd gone into the kitchen, was putting the dinner dishes into the dishwasher. She turned the machine on, came back into the living room, settled down next to me on the couch.

"Let me ask you a question, husband of mine. Darling husband of mine."

"The Beatles, 1969. *Abbey Road*."

"How'd you know that's what I was going to ask?"

"Call me Carnac. What's the question?"

"If we weren't married, would you have taken that special prosecutor job?"

"We are married, so it's irrelevant."

She put her feet in my lap. I started massaging them through her socks.

"Oh, that's good. Right there." She stretched out like a cat. "But if we weren't. Theoretically."

"I don't know. I probably would have thought about it."

"You would've taken it, wouldn't you?"

I switched to her other foot. "Maybe. After what happened today, the odds would have gone up."

She pulled her feet away, sat up.

"Take that job, Luke."

"No way. It's going to be a mess. I'd be neglecting all my other clients, it's boring as hell up there, and I'm not going to be away from you, I've told you that."

"If you had a big lawsuit against Boeing and you had to go up to Seattle for three or six or nine months, you would, wouldn't you?"

"That's different."

"How?"

"It just is. I don't want to be a prosecutor anymore, for one thing."

She shook her head. "It wouldn't be about that. You've been railing about police acting wrongly, you don't like outside agencies coming into local territories, you've bitched about that for years, how that pissed you off when you were the D.A."

"That was then. Can we change the subject?"

"You've been having nightmares since you killed those two men."

That stopped me cold.

"So?" I finally said.

"They were rogue cops. The killer of the drug dealer in Blue River could be a rogue cop."

"Not the same."

This was an argument I wasn't going to win—these were my own words, coming back at me.

"Okay." I gave in to her. "After what happened today, added to what happened out in the desert, I would have taken the job. Thought seriously about it, at least. If we weren't married. And if a frog had wings, he wouldn't bump his ass on the ground so much. We're married, I'm staying right here."

"And keep having those nightmares? I'm not getting any sleep."

"I'll sleep on the couch for a few days."

"Uh-uh." She shook her head. "You're sleeping right next to me. That's the best part of being married, as far as I'm concerned—that big man-blanket I can snuggle up against. You ain't going nowhere, buster."

"Good. That's resolved." I got up, went toward the kitchen to make myself an Irish coffee.

"You ain't sleeping nowhere without me. Here or in a motel room in Blue River, end of nowheresville, California."

There was still coffee in the pot from this morning. I filled a cup, put it in the microwave to heat up, got down the bottle of Jameson from the liquor cabinet and the whipped cream from the refrigerator.

"It would be a bad decision, honey. You don't know what it would entail. A lot of important people will be mad at me, and at the end of the day I don't know if anything would ever come of it. That's a really serious accusation, accusing a government agent of killing his prisoner. That borders on assassination."

"All the more reason for you to get involved."

"You'd hate it up there, I promise you. You wouldn't last two weeks."

"If it came to that, we'd cross that bridge. We can handle this, Luke." She pulled my face around. "Look at me. This could be the most important case you're ever involved in. This could be big, huge," she went on. "You could uncover a pattern of killings like this, in other raids. Which is all the reason more for somebody to do it, and that somebody is you."

I made my Irish coffee with an extra shot of whiskey and went back into the living room. I wanted to go outside and take a walk; it was a beautiful night, clear, starry, full-mooned. Warm enough to be comfortable.

"We should get an au pair," I said. "We have that spare room. We could have some time to ourselves, like take a walk now."

She wasn't going to allow me to change the subject. "You haven't resolved those killings, Luke. This could help. You need to do something. It almost seems heaven-sent."

"In a perverse way, maybe."

"So be it. Who cares how salvation comes?"

"That's very poetic, Riva. Is that a quote?"

"It is now. Seriously, honey, there's bad stuff inside you that needs to be gotten out, looked at, disposed of. I think this could be the key."

I didn't want to argue anymore. "I'll think about it."

"Good." She took a sip of my Irish coffee. "That's too strong!"

"I'll sleep well tonight, after this," was my excuse.

I dream in color, which I'm told not many people do. It makes my dreams seem more real, not always an enjoyable experience.

This nightmare was particularly brutal and horrifying, and so literal there was no way I wouldn't think I was dreaming, even subconsciously. A task force was raiding Lompoc prison. I was running the operation along with Jerome, the DEA agent. We suffered heavy casualties but made it in, and then we started killing indiscriminately, anyone we saw. We fought our way to the wing where the prisoners had taken control. The prison wing turned into the Brigadoon bar. My client William Lowenstein was one of the men running the show for the prisoners, along with Joe and Bill, the men I'd already killed in the desert. I couldn't figure out how they were still alive, but it didn't matter, they were, and they were armed and aiming their guns at me. "Give it up," I told them, sounding like Humphrey Bogart. They laughed at me. I had no choice—I had to kill them. As I raised my gun, they started shooting at me. Then Jerome was shooting at me. I was hit by a fusillade of bullets.

I fell to the ground, dying . . .

Riva was shaking me. I woke up. I was sweating like a bandit. All the covers had been thrown off the bed.

PART

THREE

FALLING CHIPS

Nora was overjoyed to hear from me. She didn't ask why I'd changed my mind, and I didn't tell her. We set up a meeting with Bill Fishell at his office in Sacramento, to go over the conditions they'd have to agree to in order for me to take the job.

Luke Garrison, J.D.
Attorney-at-Law
106 E. De La Guerra St.
Suite 7
Santa Barbara, CA 93101
805-555-9876
805-555-6789 (fax)

March 10, 1999

Hon. William Fishell
Office of the Attorney General
Sacramento, CA

Nora Sherman Ray
District Attorney
Muir County, CA

Dear Bill and Nora,

Here is my list of what I'll need from the two of you in order to consider taking the job of special prosecutor for Muir County in the matter of the killing of Reynaldo Juarez:

(a) The investigation will be under Nora's jurisdiction, as she is the Muir County District Attorney, but I will have autonomy. I will report to her and consult with her, but it will be my show to run, the same way a federal special prosecutor works.

(b) I will hire the staff, and within reasonable limitations I will have free rein to do so.

(c) Although all investigations like this are inherently open-ended, I want to put a preliminary timetable on it; not to save the state money, that's your problem, not mine, but to give myself an exit, in case this looks like it could drag on for years. Basically, if after intensive investigation this situation doesn't start bearing fruit in six months, I reserve the right to walk away from it and let someone else take over, if you want to keep it going. I don't want to be stuck in Blue River the rest of my life.

(d) My billing rate will be $400 an hour, including travel, plus expenses. My normal workweek will be four days, Monday through Thursday. If my presence isn't needed, I won't be there, be it a day, a week, a month—I want to maintain my own practice, particularly with the cases already in the works.

(e) I will be provided with first-class accommodations, and given a comfortable living allowance. At my option, I will be flown home every weekend I am free, Blue River–Santa Barbara *direct*. Given the difficulty of getting in and out of Blue River, particularly during times of bad weather, this or similar transportation will be available to my staff when appropriate, and will also be used to bring in witnesses and/or suspects as is necessary. Time will be of the essence; it is also money.

(f) All travel and housing expenses for investigators and other staff working with me will be paid for by the state and/or county. We should assume that almost everyone on my staff will be from outside Muir County, some from outside the state, all top-of-the-line people. This is going to be a high-stakes game, only the best will do.

Sincerely,

Luke Garrison
Luke Garrison

I set my demands deliberately high. Going after a federal agent—or more than one, if there was a conspiracy—would be a rough piece of business, particularly since the man who was killed was a shitbag criminal who most people would think deserved killing. My team would be pilloried, possibly threatened. I had to protect them and see to it that everything but the actual work was smoother than silicon. The perks had to be premium, from housing to cars to family considerations to everything I could think of—whatever it would take to keep me and the professionals on my staff, who would be making sacrifices to live in Blue River for an extended period, happy and motivated.

A more personal reason for these stipulations was that a substantial part of me wanted no part of this. Playing God scares me, and special prosecutors have godlike power. It's hard to be humble under those circumstances. And Juarez was a piece of shit any way you cut it. I wasn't sorry he was dead; one less conduit for the drugs that would be out there for my son to buy someday.

Those were truths I had to acknowledge, and I felt okay about them. If Fishell tried to lowball me, I would walk away with a clear conscience and figure out another way to cure my nightmares.

I faxed copies of my stipulations to Nora and Fishell. Nora got back to me within an hour, agreeing to all my conditions. No surprise there, it wasn't her money I was going to spend. Fishell's more guarded reply came a day later; he'd do the best he could to satisfy me, but he couldn't promise everything at this moment. We'd discuss specifics at our meeting.

The following day I caught the milk-run United shuttle out of Santa Barbara to San Francisco, where I hung around a slow forty-five minutes, drinking airport coffee and reading the *New York Times,* before jumping on another small prop-job to the state capital. These planes are so sardine-cannish you can't stand erect in them, you Groucho Marx down the aisle to your seat. It's a pain-in-the-ass, time-consuming trip—commercial flights out of Santa Barbara are lousy, almost everything goes through L.A. or San Francisco. Having an airplane on call, to fly in and out of Blue River, would be a necessity for me, not a luxury.

An off-duty state trooper, an older guy with a flattop and an easy manner, met me at the airport and drove the Crown Victoria into the city, to Fishell's office in the state government complex. I went inside, passed through security, and rode the elevator up to the attorney general's complex.

Bill Fishell is a good guy, competent, hardworking. He was a good D.A. in Alameda County, he'll be a good A.G. The cops like him because of his strong opposition on the hot-button issue of private ownership of assault weapons, as grimly illustrated by this current disaster: If the druggies hadn't had their heavy artillery, especially the AK-47s (verboten to the police, God forbid they should have weapons on a par with the scumbags they're going after), good men would still be alive.

We sat around Bill's conference table. It was all informal, relaxed. Three friends with a common mission. Bill's legislative aide, a career assistant A.G. named Julius Schwartzman, also joined us for the record.

"You're asking for the moon," Bill said after we'd exchanged greetings, thumbing through my request memo.

"I'm being reasonable as hell," I countered. "But if that's how you feel, hire someone else. I hear Marcia Clark's getting bored with her television gig."

"If Luke doesn't come aboard," Nora said, jumping in, "it could take months getting someone else. Time is of the essence here."

Bill had to try to lowball me. If he didn't, some obscure civil service geek would discover these figures and throw a tizzy fit in the papers about them, and Fishell would have indigestion over it for a few days.

"I know, I know," he said, glancing at Schwartzman, who sported the bemused smile of one who'd seen a variation of this dance a million times, "but I've got duly-elected officials to answer to, most of them so green they can't find the bathrooms off the capital floor, let alone a piece of legislation. An on-call airplane?" He looked at the document in front of him. "That's what the bad guys do, Luke, they're the ones with the money. We're government flunkies here."

I was in the catbird seat, because although I did give a shit, it wasn't life-or-death with me. I didn't want him to call my hand, though, because you can't bluff in this game.

Nora reasoned with him. "Look at this." She pulled a newspaper clipping from her purse. "In Washington, D.C., it costs two hundred thousand dollars to clean the pigeon shit off one statue. One! And there's thousands of them. They're going to clean two this week, not even the Lincolns and Jeffersons, two nobodies. Three or four of those and that's the airplane, with lobster and Jack Daniel's thrown in on a daily basis, if that's what Luke wants."

"I prefer Johnnie Walker, but the gist of it sounds right to me. Given the work, and the caliber of person you have to have running this show, not blowing my own horn, just being realistic, this is cheap time you're buying, and quality work. Any other lawyer with the background and capability for this is going to charge you more, bring in unnecessary staff, go crazy with your money."

Fishell held up his hands in mock surrender. "Okay, okay. You're hired, you knew that before you came up here. At *three* hundred, not a dime more."

I smiled at him. I knew the state wouldn't go to four. "And the ancillaries, too, right?"

"Yes," he gave in. "You'll live as well as a major-league ballplayer."

Nora was beaming. "You won't regret this, Bill."

"As long as we bag a turkey."

"The DEA doesn't think their people are dirty," I reminded both of them.

"Somebody killed Juarez," Nora said. The entire operation had left a sour taste in every Muir County mouth, and Binaca wasn't getting rid of it.

"And everybody in the world thinks he deserved killing." The first words out of Schwartzman's mouth since the meeting started.

"Not by lynch mob," she shot back. "Cops aren't judges, not where I come from."

Fishell calmed everyone down. "Enough already. We all know this is going to be a test of the system." He looked to me. "How many people, Luke, and what's your timetable? Any more thoughts about it?"

I pulled some pages from my briefcase. "I want to wrap it up in six months. I'm thinking three or four detectives, plus support: secretaries, paralegals, runners. Quality people, the best I can get. It won't be cheap—we have to investigate everyone who was there, that takes time and talent. I'm assuming this wasn't an accidental killing, an agent losing his head and shooting Juarez in the confusion of the chase. Their OPR investigation would've smoked that out."

Fishell and Nora nodded in agreement.

"Almost sixty agents, eight of Juarez's bunch in prison. We may be going back as far as grade school, looking for connections, grudges, sneaky motives, money that can't be explained. A dirty cop, if he's smart, covers his tracks, and the men on this detail were capable agents. This is going to be a national case, Bill. Once we get started, we've got to drive hard to the finish, *and win*. We drill a dry well, we're the *Time* magazine cover of the year for assholes."

"Yes, I know," he said dolorously. Prosecutors hate getting involved in potential prosecutions they aren't assured they can slam-dunk; it fucks up the batting average.

"Agreed," Nora chimed in, nervous over the prospect of what might be coming, but clearly excited, too. Why shouldn't she be? This was going to be the biggest event in her life, a way for her to forget, or at least to begin to overcome, all her negative baggage and forge something positive.

"When do you want to start?" Bill asked. He glanced at Schwartzman, who was taking notes.

"As soon as possible. We're playing catch-up ball."

From across the room, Schwartzman kicked in, "Is there any kind of budget you can give us?" Schwartzman, as a career assistant A.G., had been there for half a dozen administrations. He knew how to deal with the power players, the state senators and assembly people who approved budgets.

"No," I answered, "I don't know who the players are going to be yet. I'll do the job as cost-consciously as I can, but you can't hold me to a figure. It's the nature of the beast."

Fishell nodded. In for a dime, in for a dollar. Millions of them, if it dragged out.

"This will be a political goodie," I told them, reading their minds, which were transparent on the subject. "We win, there'll be plenty of reflected glory for everyone to bask in."

There was nothing more to say. We stood up, shook hands all around.

"I've got about a week of cleanup to do at home," I said, "then I'll get going. I'll be making calls, see who's available and willing. I hope to be set up and running within a month."

"Whatever I can do," Fishell said.

"You'll be hearing from me plenty," I assured him. "But," I also reminded him one more time, "this investigation is mine to run. It has to not only look completely independent and neutral, it has to be, in fact."

Bill cuffed me on the shoulder. "Go get 'em, tiger."

Nora and I had lunch at Frank Fats, the downtown Sacramento restaurant where the power brokers break bread. All around us, men and women, the men in dark suits and white shirts, the women in the female equivalent, were chowing down on high-cholesterol mandarin food, virtually every table overflowing with platters. All on someone else's tab, the same as with Nora and me.

"This is going to be exciting!" She was giddy with anticipation.

I had to deliver the news; I wanted to be diplomatic about it, but it had to be said, in plain, clear, unadulterated English.

"This is my show."

What I'd said already, more than once. I took a bite of my Chinese chicken salad—I gave up the heavy lunch thing years ago. I want to dance at my son's wedding, when I'm old and sloppy.

She answered blithely, "I know." Like she heard me, but the words, not the portent.

"I'll tell you what I'm doing," I said, "I'll counsel with you every step of the way. But you don't get a vote. That's what *independent* counsel means. I answer to no one."

She looked up at me. She'd been concentrating on her plate.

"You're not happy hearing that."

"No. But I understand." She started to fork up a piece of fish, put her utensils down. "I can offer advice, can't I? If I have an idea, you'll listen to me, won't you?"

"Of course. But we've got to be purer than the driven snow. I've never seen snow being driven," I added, trying to lighten the moment. "What does it look like?"

Her response was flat. "White."

"You won't be shut out, Nora, I promise."

"Thanks."

She was glum now; she'd get over it. Those were the rules; I didn't write them, but when I'm in the game, I'll play by them. We all will.

"That applies to your staff as well."

"I understand that." She'd lost interest in her fish.

"And everyone else."

She stared at me: *Meaning?*

"Sheriff Miller and his deputies."

"Uhhh." She looked like I'd kidney-punched her. "That's hard."

"He's a tough old guy, I know. Excellent at what he does, too, I'm sure. He has more experience that the rest of us put together. But . . ."

"I know you have to conduct this in a prescribed way," she said, "and I can handle my end. But look, Luke—Tom was shut out of the raid, which shouldn't have happened. Jerome went against his own department's guidelines, which mandate local law enforcement has to be part of whatever they do. It's not supposed to be optional, and he messed Tom over, and it hurt things. Tom could have helped, if that egotistical shit had listened to him. Now you're telling me this." She shook her head sadly. "Tom's really going to be upset."

"And he'll have the right to be, and I still can't help it."

The waiter hovered over us with the bread basket. We both declined; he went away.

"I'll tell him," I said. "You don't have to. It's my job to."

She pushed her plate away. "He's going to be miserable. And angry."

"It's a potential conflict of interest. He was there."

Her head jerked around. "You're going to investigate *Tom Miller?*"

"He was there. I have to."

Now she really looked morose. "This isn't going the way I expected it to, Luke."

I reached over and covered her hand with mine. "It's a formality. We're together on this, every step of the way. But I have to do this by the numbers. I'm going to be under intense scrutiny. If it does turn out that any of the DEA guys have complicity in Juarez's murder, in any way, I don't want them or their lawyers to be able to shoot us down on a technicality."

"I guess."

"Trust me. We're partners."

Her eyes locked into mine. "You promise?"

"We're partners," I reiterated. "It's your jurisdiction. You won't be disappointed."

I had to say that; she was miserable. I hoped she wouldn't be for too long, but we were in the deep waters now. She was going to have to swim on her own.

She forced a smile. "I trust you, Luke." She paused. "Don't hurt me."

I winced; I prayed not visibly. I could feel the anguish in those three raw words all the way to my backbone.

"I won't."

Not only wouldn't I hurt her, I'd bend over backward to make good by her. For the first time in her life since law school, Nora Sherman Ray was going to have a positive experience. And it pleasured me that I was going to be the instrument to make that happen. Sometimes, I thought to myself, the past *can* be brought into the present. And washed clean.

I had a courtesy call to make—not one I wanted to make, but one I had to.

I drove the 101 south from Santa Barbara into downtown L.A., getting off at the Temple Street exit, heading south on Temple past the Music Center and through Little Tokyo until I got to my destination, the tall, salmon-pink granite Roybal Federal Building at Temple and Los Angeles Streets. I parked in the six-dollar all-day parking lot and crossed Temple on the green.

It was one-thirty, the end of lunchtime. A warm, clear L.A. day. There isn't as much smog in the basin as there used to be—the world makes cleaner cars than when I was a kid growing up in the San Fernando Valley, because the state of California and the U.S. government makes them. Which proves the government can work, even better than expected, when it's forced to. I strolled by pretty Latina secretaries in tight blouses and black heels, Asian businessmen in dark suits wearing wraparound shades, lawyers and bureaucrats and government employees, the downtown L.A. workforce. Hot dog and burrito vendors sold food from carts.

My first pass through the metal detector triggered the alarm, even though I'd deposited all the obvious stuff—money clip, keys, watch, briefcase—in the plastic tray. That didn't satisfy the machine, however, which has a hair trigger considerably more sensitive than the standard ones, at LAX for example. This one was set up like Tel Aviv's, with good reason: the Roybal Building, a nice piece of pork named after one of Los Angeles' old-time congressmen, whose district this was when he was alive, is the regional headquarters of the DEA, ATF, FBI, Secret Service, almost every federal law-enforcement agency. From their perspective, you can never have enough security. If it was up to them, no civilians would ever be allowed in the building.

My belt and wedding ring didn't stop the buzz, either. It was a loud, irritating sound; even though I half-anticipated it, I still clutched.

The line behind me was growing. That was their problem, although I was beginning to feel self-conscious.

The guard running the machine eyeballed my wardrobe, settling on my feet. "Take off your shoes."

I slipped out of my Cole-Haan loafers, sent them via the conveyor through the X-ray machine. Then I tried the detector again, almost flinching. If this didn't work, I'd be stripping down like Mike Tyson at a weigh-in.

The third time was the charm. "Your shoes have a steel last, to help keep the shape." The guard pointed to the X-ray screen. "They're good shoes."

I slipped my good shoes back on and gathered up my personal items. Then I walked down a long hallway and around a corner, past the magazine stand that also sells cigarettes, coffee, breath mints, prewrapped sandwiches, and other snacks, and took the elevator up to the twenty-fifth floor, where the DEA offices are located.

More security. I produced a photo ID—my driver's license—and signed in, stating whom I was seeing, the time of my arrival, and the purpose of my visit. I put "professional courtesy" in that space, although I didn't know how much I'd get.

"What time is your appointment?" the receptionist asked, not looking at me, too busy with important work. She was a middle-aged, light-skinned black woman with a no-nonsense visage. Another civil-servant gatekeeper who took her work and herself too damn seriously for my current taste. We were separated by a reinforced Plexiglas window, which I assumed was bulletproof. All the doors leading into the complex were locked from the other side.

I looked at my watch for her benefit. "Now."

She instructed me to take a seat and wait for Special Agent Kim to come out and escort me back to his office. Kim was the head of L.A. OPR, the Office of Professional Review, the DEA's version of Internal Affairs. He was in charge of the investigation into the Juarez killing.

He was pretty high up the food chain. I'd checked him out—his reputation was one of professionalism and incorruptibility. Which didn't mean he wasn't biased in favor of his own people. It's hard not to be.

"Agent Kim is in a meeting."

I didn't sit down, as she'd asked me to. She looked up at me, peeved.

"Please let him know Luke Garrison is here. Special Prosecutor Garrison. We have an appointment."

Kim didn't keep me long, less than five minutes. Early fortyish, slicked-back black hair, sharp shantung-silk suit. Tailored, from the way it draped him.

"How was the drive down from Santa Barbara?" he asked after we'd introduced ourselves and exchanged cards. His first name was Winston; his accent sounded East Coast, Philadelphia maybe. We'd never met, except over the phone, but he knew why I was here. Not a task to his liking.

"Easy. No hassle, as long as you aren't fighting rush hour."

"One of my favorite towns."

Santa Barbara's one of everyone's favorite towns.

"My wife and I drive up for a weekend and eat at Citronelle. Do you like that restaurant?"

"Yes," I said. "Great views."

He gave me a good look-over. "I saw you on TV, last fall. Hairy situation. You handled it brilliantly."

I didn't answer, there was no call.

He fingerprinted us in, the heavy metal-reinforced door shutting behind us. I followed him down a hallway that was decorated like a Bakersfield Sheraton. Pastel carpets, seascape prints on the walls. As we passed by various offices, I could see out the plate-glass windows to the city, the Hollywood Hills. To the west, the Pacific.

"Great views."

"Perk of the job. In lieu of better pay." He smiled, quick, tight. "I thought you were a defense lawyer now. You haven't been a prosecutor for what, four years now?"

He'd done his homework on me. "Five. I still am. This is a onetime thing."

He escorted me into his office, closed the door behind us. He had a cherry space, southeast corner, views clear to the ocean, without the direct heat of the afternoon sun. We sat facing each other across his desk, which was clean of paperwork. He didn't offer me a beverage.

"Your letter is disturbing," he said, getting down to business. He pulled it out of his middle desk drawer. "Uncalled for, unnecessary." He dropped it in the center of the desk. "Insulting, if you don't mind my saying so."

"I don't mind. I can understand your taking umbrage."

The letter was our initial calling card, sent by Nora, informing his agency that Muir County was going to investigate the Juarez killing, independent of the DEA and all federal agencies. That I'd been hired as a special prosecutor to run the case. I could have told Kim that it wasn't my call, this was the decision of the D.A. of Muir County, California, and the attorney general. But I didn't. I was the man now—all the light refracted toward me, for better or worse.

The letter was nonaccusatory, but the DEA wasn't going to take it that way, it was a shot across their bow. They'd done their investigation, their people had come across clean, who was this chickenshit county to question them? I would have felt the same way if our roles were reversed.

"You won't get anywhere. It's a waste of your time. And their money." His arm sweeping toward the grand view, the great people of the Golden State.

"We'll find out. It's my job, I'm taking it on, I'll do the best I can."

A distasteful look came across his face, which wasn't at all inscrutable. "You want to make us look bad. Pick on Washington. The national pastime."

I wasn't going to rise to his bait. I pulled the DEA investigation report from my briefcase, the one Nora had shown me in Blue River.

"Can we go over this? I have some questions."

"It's all there."

"I was a D.A. for ten years, Agent Kim," I said, the report dropping on his desk with a thud. "It isn't all there, it never is." He wanted to fire some high hard ones, fine by me. I'd start swinging for the fences. "I'm going to subpoena every agent who was there, if I have to. I'll subpoena you, if I have to."

"Try it."

The lines were being drawn fast, too fast. Neither of us wanted this; we weren't adversaries, just two men on opposite sides of the desk with difficult jobs to do and turf to protect.

I sat back, affecting conciliation. "You don't want that, and neither do I. Look, Kim . . . do you mind if we use first names?"

"No."

"Winston . . . a man was murdered."

"We don't know that."

"Okay. A man was *killed*. A federal prisoner who had been in the custody of your agents, who was supposed to be brought in alive. You know where the order came from. And you know she isn't happy about the way it turned out."

He was listening—reluctantly.

"Somebody *may* have broken him free, and somebody *definitely* killed him. The same person, maybe, or persons? Juarez was a federal prisoner at that moment in time, but he was also a California citizen."

"He was a piece of shit. Worse than shit. You know that, Garrison."

"That's not the issue. Someone killed him, probably murdered him, that's one thing I hope to find out, and who did it, and why. And how did he get loose, and why? How does this all tie together?"

I put the documents back in my briefcase. "We're not working together, and I'm not asking for your cooperation. I don't even want it, it would cloud the issue. But if you have raw information, I'd like to see it."

I stood up. "I'm not looking to hang anyone. But when an agency investigates itself, it leaves them open to disturbing questions. Nothing to do with anyone's personal honesty, it's institutional—you know that."

He gave me a blank stare—the old bureaucratic stoneface. Screw this, I thought.

I turned to leave. "I can find my way out."

He put up a hand to stop me, as I'd hoped he would.

"Sit down, Garrison."

"Luke."

"Luke. Come on, sit down."

I sat down.

"You want a Coke?"

"Sure."

He took two cans out of a small refrigerator, handed me one. I popped the top. He did the same. Then he went to his filing cabinet and took out several thick file-folders, carried them back to his desk, set them down.

"All our interviews. Everyone who was there that night. They're complete."

"Can I see them?"

"Not on the record. Invasion of privacy, the laws are strict."

I knew that. I thought maybe he'd bend them, in the spirit of cooperation. If I wanted to see them, I'd have to get warrants. I might have to, I thought, somewhere down the line.

"I can summarize them for you."

I didn't know how much good that would do without seeing the raw data. "What about the Shooting Incident Team report?"

"That I can give you. I don't have a copy here, it's back in D.C., but I'll get one for you. The bullet went right through Juarez's head and lodged three inches into a tree. The impact from that stripped the casings. We couldn't get a ballistics match."

"If there had been," I said, "we probably wouldn't be having this discussion."

"It's a bitch." He shook his head at the incredibleness of it all. "We're still working at it, though."

That was a surprise to me. "You have people up there currently?" Nora hadn't said anything about that.

He shook his head. "Not officially."

"But unofficially?" An agent prowling around up there could foul up my investigation. Not that I could stop them.

"This isn't a dead case, not by any means. We have some irons in the fire. Which is another reason I wish you wouldn't do this."

"Give me a reason not to," I said. "Give me a name."

"I can't. But we'll have something, sooner or later. I can't say more now. In the meantime, you could mess us up badly. I really wish you'd reconsider this."

He wasn't going to give me a name, or anything else. Shutting the state and Muir County out, once again.

"Sorry," I said. "We're moving ahead."

"None of our people did it," Kim said. Not defensively; with certainty, and anger.

I hate it when people insist on their rightness. "What makes you so sure?"

"Because it would have been too hard to contain." He hefted the interviews, a heavy bundle. "Every agent there was questioned, each one individually. We really grilled them, this wasn't patty-cake. The questionnaires alone took a couple hours to fill out. We had to do this right, we don't want to cover anything up." He pointed to the report Nora had given me. "You know what we think."

"One of his own? I can't buy that, it's preposterous."

"You don't live in that world. It's totally dog-eat-dog, cutthroat. Don't forget, Juarez had a huge bounty on his head. That supersedes any loyalty, not that there is any, nada, zero."

He finished his Coke, three-pointed it into a trash can near the door. Nothing but net.

"But we've given that one up," he admitted.

"Oh?"

"It didn't pan out. But something else came up that was much more plausible." He took another file out of the case, handed it to me. A thin document, half a dozen pages. "This you can look at, but you don't have to now, you can take it with you, examine it later. I'll tell you what it is."

He opened it. "Somebody infiltrated his gang. Someone from another gang, probably another Mexican gang. He was waiting for the big buy to go down, but when we kiboshed that, he took Juarez out instead."

So that was their case; I'd figured we'd get there eventually. "Did you get anyone in your raid who fits that description?"

"Not that we know of. But we don't know if we got everybody."

I shook my head. "You don't believe that, so don't expect me to. You'd find that out. You'd have it on the front page of every newspaper in the country. TV, the works. You're not an agency to hide their light under a bushel, not with the crap publicity you've been getting."

He didn't have a comeback to that.

"Has anyone claimed the reward?" I asked.

He laughed. "And get snuffed within twenty-four hours? The informant, Lopez, he's getting a taste, but shit, no. Two million's chump change for the size deals they're doing. We're talking huge, man. Nine figures. Enough snow to float the world."

Anything's possible, I thought, but I wasn't buying this.

Kim was reading my mind. "There's only one way, in my opinion, that someone on that task force could've done this."

"What way is that?" Now this was worth listening to, even if I decided it was bullshit or con. It would point me toward the direction they wanted me to go, which would be a strong sign not to. Or watch out for.

"It couldn't have been one agent. They were too clustered, no one man could've pulled it off without someone seeing a piece of it happening, or figuring it out."

"Two men, then?"

"No. For something like this to work, they all would have to be dirty. Or many of them, most of them. It would have been a major conspiracy, not some spur-of-the-moment rump action. And that could not have happened. There aren't that many dishonest agents in the DEA, let alone on one strike force. These agents came from different jurisdictions, all over the West. Some barely knew each other. It doesn't fly, any way you look at it. And . . ."

Here he paused, too dramatically, I thought, but he wanted me to really get it.

"If somehow, some one-in-a-trillion chance, there had been a conspiracy? It wouldn't have held. It would've been too big. Someone would've cracked. Think of the prestige, not to mention the reward—two million. If one of ours had killed Juarez, and another agent fingered him, we'd have paid that reward to the informant."

That didn't sound right to me. An agency encouraging agents to rat out each other? Great for morale, not to mention one's physical well-being. That would've been a quick frag, no questions asked. "Why?" I asked.

"Because we can't tolerate a dishonest, dirty agent," Kim said, his voice rising. "If I thought one of ours did this, I'd draw and quarter the motherhumper personally. I mean that. So this idea that we covered up something, or didn't investigate it as fully as we could, put that notion out of your head."

"Okay. I hear you." I was impressed; not at his utter candor, necessarily, but at his conviction.

"But you're going to pursue your investigation anyway."

"Of course. No matter what your reports say, someone killed the guy. So what if he deserved it, we're not the jury, right?" I took the report about the gang wars off his desk, held it in my hand. "Maybe this is how it happened. And maybe I'll find it out." I dropped it back on his desk. "We want a suspect, Winston. A living, breathing person. Someone we can prosecute, or at least point to. Not a report, not conjecture."

He leaned back. "Well, Luke, I hope you find one. But it won't be one of mine, I can assure you of that."

If he'd been a friend, I'd have bet him a steak dinner. But we weren't friends, now or in the future.

"I hope not," I said truthfully. "I hope it's a bad guy. A real bad guy, not a dirty agent." I gathered my stuff. "We'll be talking again, I imagine."

"You know where to find me."

"Thanks for your time." I got up. "And for seeing me, and for getting me that shooting report you said you'd send. You can mail it to my Santa Barbara office."

He escorted me out. We said good-bye and shook hands. It wasn't a warm parting.

MY KIND OF PEOPLE

I met with my team of investigators at what was left of Juarez's house, which had been confiscated by the DEA after the raid. They'd flown in from various parts of the country the day before. All of them—two men, one woman—were experienced investigators from various counties in California. I could have brought in people from anywhere, but after giving the matter some thought, I decided to go this way. It would save some money, and it would keep the case where we wanted it—in the hands of Muir County, and the state.

This was a quickie trip, for us to get a feel for each other and check out the lay of the land. The real work, forming a special grand jury, beginning to interview the participants and to investigate everything, would start in the following weeks.

Kate Blanchard, the lone female in the bunch, would be my lead shamus. She's the only female private eye in Santa Barbara, and the best of either sex, for my money. I use her on everything. She was a cop in Oakland before she moved to S.B. and fell into her present occupation, which she's been doing for about six years now. I trust her explicitly—she's an extension of my own eyes and ears out there.

Louis Alvarez is from L.A. His specialties are big actions—murders and such—and investigating police brutality cases, which makes him a logical, albeit controversial, fit for my team. He's outspoken, sometimes provocative, the kind of guy who likes to throw oil onto the flames.

The obvious qualification Louis brings to this particular case (besides ability) is that he's Latino, second-generation Mexican-American. He grew up in the barrio, he knows the players. If it turns out that Juarez's murder involved his own people, or a traitor in his midst, Louis will be our best hope for finding that out.

Keith Green's another big-city detective. If you've heard of any of us, he's the likely candidate; he played defensive end for the Raiders for a couple of years in the early eighties, before he blew out his knees. Being a prosecution investigator is a way station for him; he's a semester shy of getting his law degree, after which he'll move into either prosecution or criminal defense.

A black man working on the side of the police can be held suspect by his own people, but he handles his situation with aplomb. He's straight, everyone always knows where he stands with him. He will play the reverse race card if he has to. He has strong connections with the big black gangs up and down the state, which could be important to our cause, because of the various associations they have with the Mexican, Central American, and South American gangs, including Juarez's people, those who survived the raid.

One thing about Keith—he doesn't run from his roots. He doesn't let the police give him one ounce of shit, he'll come down on a bad cop, white or black, faster than a white man will. Nobody's an angel in his book, nobody's untouchable. He was the lead investigator for a commission a few years back that wound up bringing significant indictments against a dozen crooked cops, some of whom were black, men he'd known growing up in the hood. He's like me in his strong belief that bad policemen, or bad anythings in the law community, are worse than regular scumbags, because they have so much unbridled power.

The rooms in the compound's main house were large (those still standing), on a baronial scale, high ceilings with redwood cross-beams, sparsely furnished in big Spanish-style pieces. The government had partially refurbished the parts that had been burnt and shot up. Once their investigation, and now ours, was finished, the compound would be sold to the highest bidder.

The place was sealed off—it was still a federal crime scene. They'd let us in, reluctantly. A call from Fishell's office to the Justice Department in Washington took care of the access, but it was made clear to me that my colleagues and I were being tolerated, not welcomed.

Before we got down to business, I led the others on a quick tour. The compound was impressive, even in its current shape. The way rock stars or pro basketball players live, I imagine.

The coolest rooms were the VIP bedroom suites—half a dozen of them, decorated in Playboy Mansion style, circa 1970: king-sized beds (one shaped like a Whitman's chocolate-box valentine), all covered with velvet or fake animal-skin covers. Every room featured large gold-flocked mirrors, some of them on the ceilings. The bathrooms were equally ornate, big Jacuzzi tubs, gold-plated faucets. Nicely arrayed in the drawers of each bedside table were ample supplies of condoms, along with an assortment of sex toys—vibrators, dildos, leather bindings, french ticklers. Topping off this hedonistic potpourri, there were about a hundred porno videos in the TV room, featuring almost every variety of sexual activity the human mind can conjure, with the notable exception of male homosexuality. Most of the videos had melted in the fire—only the charred covers remained.

It hit me, looking at this stuff, that nothing had been touched (except to be inventoried, I supposed). Normally, items like these are taken like booty, a perk of the job. In this case, because of the circumstances surrounding Juarez's killing, the DEA was playing everything scrupulously straight.

The kitchen was huge—the occupants ate like lords (according to their taste, which ran to Mexican food, red meat, anything microwaveable). The industrial freezer, where they'd found Juarez, was stocked with frozen pizzas, tamales, other such items, as well as haunches of beef and venison, sides of bacon, legs of lamb. In the large pantry, dozens of bottles of expensive tequila, vodka, cognac, Scotch, bourbon, and cases of Coors, Heineken, and Corona beer were jammed in the big refrigerators.

Leaving the house, we circumnavigated the property. I showed them where the DEA task force had set up its principal bivouac, where the various players were when the house was raided, the location of the trailer in which Juarez had been sequestered, the direction he ran when he escaped, where his body was found. I pointed out the stakes where the body had been found, the bullet hole in the tree.

We ended our tour by walking to the airstrip. It wasn't fancy, a single runway long enough to take about any size jet made, and a tin-roof shack off to one side that had the bare-bones equipment needed to get the planes in and out. Looking east, you could see for a hundred miles, and nothing was there, except for some carrion-seeking buzzards circling high up in the bleached-out sky.

"Great hideaway altogether," Keith commented. "Almost impenetrable."

We stood at the edge of the runway, bracing ourselves against the dry wind coming off the high-plains desert. The stark solitude invited reflection. I didn't know what the others were thinking, but I was pondering the aborted raid.

In my mind's eye, Juarez and his men are emerging from the compound into the night, the sky dark and starry, driving the narrow access road to the strip, all of them eager, anticipating, Juarez cool, emotionless, waiting to do the business he came here for, then flying out on the money plane. They watch as two airplanes come out of the southern sky, backlit by the pre-dawn false sunrise, one after the other flying in low, touching down. There are some quick introductions, perfunctory greetings. Juarez checks out the money—one hundred million dollars in cash. No bills larger than hundreds, a cornucopia of cash, it would have weighed hundreds of pounds. Taxpayers' money, bait to snag a killer whale. His counterpart, the moneyman, Jerome's man, would have checked out the drugs and found them satisfactory. He would have been jumping out of his skin in excitement and nervousness. Meanwhile, shadowing Juarez's movements, Jerome and his band of sixty have made their way to the strip under the cover of darkness and are in place, waiting for the exchange. And then, at the precise, perfect moment, they swoop in, the arrests are made, and heroes have been created. Now Juarez is picking lint out of his belly button in an isolation cell in the toughest federal prison in the country, as are his men. The ripples from the arrest have traveled the length of the country, the entire hemisphere. And Juarez is still alive, and Jerome's career is in the ascendancy, he's riding high.

And I'm not here. I'm home with my family, enjoying my life.

But it didn't happen that way. Even if it had, Juarez would still be dead. Because that was the plan—whoever's it was who killed him. This drug lord wasn't leaving here alive, and the entire Justice Department could kiss somebody's ass. Whoever pulled the trigger had his own agenda, and that meant Reynaldo Juarez was a dead man.

The DEA had satisfied itself that the killer wasn't one of theirs. Perhaps that would turn out to be true. I was dubious, but I hoped so. Better that Juarez was killed by one of his own than by a cop. But however it fell, somebody had killed him.

*   *   *

Back in Blue River, my team and I gathered at the motel bar. They were taking off in the morning, going home to tie up loose ends. I'd commandeered a plane to fly them to Reno, where they would catch commercial flights to wherever they were going.

After having a drink and a short discussion about methodology with them, I went back to my room, called home, spoke to Riva and Bucky. She was about to get him into the bathtub, no easy feat, so it was a short conversation.

"I'll see you in a couple days," I said. I was flying home Friday night.

"We'll be waiting."

We kissed over the phone. I showered and changed and headed out into the night.

Nora had prepared an elaborate dinner—roast chicken, wild rice, green beans with almonds, a fresh tossed salad, a chilled bottle of white wine. I hadn't expected that—I'd told her I'd come over at the end of the day and informally fill her in on where we were going. After that I figured a pizza back at the motel and a movie on cable TV. Now here was this fancy dinner, which she'd obviously put her time and energy into, much more so than the first meal I'd had here with her. She'd taken time to pretty herself up, too; she had a discreet amount of makeup on, something I hadn't seen before, had pulled her thick hair back into a French braid, and was wearing a nice outfit, a dusty rose silk blouse and matching slacks that highlighted her good features and downplayed the others.

"I hope you're hungry," she said gaily as she led me into her house. "I rarely get to cook for someone who has good taste." She blushed. "Actually, never. I hope you didn't make other plans," she added coyly/expectantly.

She was flirting with me; friendly like, but the scent of it wafted off her like a mysterious and vaguely disturbing perfume. At the same time, it was a posture she was unfamiliar with, so there was a nervous edge to it.

"No," I said. "No plans."

I sipped some wine and glanced at the evening news on CNN while she set the table and put the finishing touches on the meal. Her house was cozy; a fire was going in the hearth. All very homey, very domestic. The little lady getting dinner on the table at the end of the day. Except she wasn't my little lady, and I wasn't her old man.

"Soup's on."

The meal was excellent, like the previous one my last trip here. I knew she was eager to know about what had gone on with me and my team, but she restrained herself from bombarding me with questions, allowing me to wind down and enjoy our dinner together.

"You can cook, lady," I complimented her, pushing my plate away after the second helping. "You are very talented in that area."

"I'm talented in many ways, Luke."

Was she being sensitive, or was this more flirting? "I know, Nora."

"Have room for dessert?"

"I don't . . ."

"Chocolate cake. Homemade. My grandmother's recipe."

"Twist my arm." Shit, if I kept eating at her table, I'd be a blimp by the time this investigation and trial, if things went that far, were over. "Small piece."

It wasn't a small piece. I ate it all.

We sat in the living room, on the two small couches that faced each other across the glowing fireplace. She tucked her bare feet under her.

"How's your family?" she asked, making small talk.

"They're fine." I didn't want to bring my personal life into my relationship with her; if she chose to let me into her life, that was all right—she needed someone to talk to. I didn't.

"Do you talk with them on a daily basis?"

I nodded. "We talk in the evening. Before my son goes to bed."

"Did you talk to them tonight?"

"Un-huh."

"They must miss you."

"Yes, but I'll be going home most weekends, so it's not too bad. Riva's used to a lawyer's schedule."

"You must be a wonderful father . . . and husband."

"I try."

She leaned forward. "How did it go today?"

I explained that I'd shown the others the crime scene. "I'm convening the grand jury next week. That's when we'll get into it for real."

"Will I be able to sit in?"

I hesitated in answering.

"Not all the time," she added swiftly. "Just here and there. I should be present at the outset, to introduce you and explain what you intend to do. People up here are suspicious of outsiders. I want to make sure they cooperate with you fully."

I thought for a moment. I didn't want this to be a case of letting the camel stick its nose into the tent and waking up in the morning to find the entire animal inside. But that didn't have to happen—I was in control of the circumstances. I didn't want to exclude her, I'd made that promise to her, and to myself. And her reasoning made sense: the DEA investigators had been cold-shouldered by the locals, and that lack of cooperation had undoubtedly hampered their effort.

"Sure, why not?" I decided. "Certainly, an introduction's in order. After that, we'll play it by ear, okay?"

"That's all I ask."

She got up to pour us a couple snifters of cognac, then she sat back down, but next to me this time. Her soft hip grazed my leg; it was a disconcerting feeling.

"Cheers," she said.

"Back." I touched her glass with mine, at the same time shifting my weight so we were no longer touching. Be careful, I cautioned myself. Don't give her reason to expect there's something here that isn't.

The real caution was for me, not her. Obviously, I wasn't going to get involved with her sexually, but I didn't want an emotional attachment of any kind. It would be an easy trap to fall into, because she was lonely; I had to resist falling into that emotion, which can be draining. Nora and I could be friends—but not the kind of tight confidants she wished we could be, of that I was pretty certain.

She needed a good girlfriend. Better, a man to call her own. Neither of which she was going to find in Blue River, where there are more deer than people. I thought that when this was over, I could try to find a way, psychologically and emotionally, to help her leave the ghosts behind and move on to a larger, more satisfying, more hopeful arena. She was still a relatively young woman, attractive, smart, competent. There were men out there for her. Out there in the bigger world, not in this one.

She walked me to the front door. We stood at the threshold, her in, me out.

"Good night, Nora. Thanks for dinner."

"Thanks for coming. And for not shutting me out."

"I'll stop by your office tomorrow, in the morning, before I take off." I was flying home that afternoon.

"See you then."

She leaned forward and kissed me, on the lips. A quick brush, but it was on the lips.

"You're a good man, Luke."

"Thanks, Nora. You're a good woman."

"A good man is hard to find."

"So's a good woman."

"A good man is harder. Much harder."

I didn't reply.

"Good night, Luke."

She stepped back inside and closed the door. I walked to my car. I was going to have to keep my distance from Nora. Actually, the reverse was true—I was going to have to make sure that she kept hers from me.

FORMING THE NOOSE

L adies and gentlemen of the grand jury, good morning . . ."
    The Muir County grand jury meets in what used to be the old
high school, which no longer functions in that capacity since the new regional one was built two blocks away, a decade ago. Now the facility is
utilized for various civic purposes—adult ed, dance classes, senior-
citizen workshops, teen drug and alcohol programs. As the grand jury
in this sparsely populated county meets sporadically, it wasn't fiscally
prudent to give them their own, permanent space.

I was seated on a folding chair on the stage of the auditorium. It was
a large, dark room, old wood wainscoting, peeling paint of that ubiquitous washed-out puke-green color that always seems to cover the walls
of public institutions such as schools, jails, and mental asylums. Half the
overhead lightbulbs were out, left unreplaced, which compounded the
dreariness of the place.

Nora stood at the podium. She was dressed in one of her professional
ensembles—dark gray skirt and jacket, starched white blouse buttoned
to the neck, opaque white hose, low heels. Almost no makeup, hair
done plain. The grand jurors, eleven men and women, most of them retirement age, sat in the first two rows of the center section, facing us, in
seats that had fold-down arms for student note-taking. A few of the old
ladies, the ones with permed hair and makeup on straight, had pens and
notebooks in hand. The others didn't. They knew their duty: do what
the D.A. tells you to do. You don't need to take notes for that.

"It's nice to see all these familiar faces," Nora said, smiling.

Some of them smiled back. Others looked like they needed a caffeine jump-start.

"I've appeared before you several times over the past fourteen months, since you were sworn in," Nora continued. "Today, however, I'm not here in my normal capacity. This is a unique occasion. I want to introduce all of you to an old friend and colleague of mine. Luke Garrison"—she turned and pointed—"is the distinguished former district attorney of Santa Barbara County. He has been appointed a special independent prosecutor by the state of California to investigate a crime that occurred here."

I listened with bemusement; I liked the "distinguished" bit, although it made me feel like a relic up on a shelf, something of importance one's grandfather saved from his youth, dusting it off and bringing it down once a year for a special show-and-tell.

"Mr. Garrison is here because this situation is too expensive and time-consuming for my office to handle," she told them candidly, feeling the need to explain why she wasn't doing this herself—that my coming in and taking over didn't mean Muir County was second-rate; or by inference, that they were.

"This happens sometimes, in counties all over the country, big ones as well as small. It doesn't mean we can't do the job ourselves—it enhances the possibility of doing it better. It's actually a star on our chart," she continued, "that the state thinks this situation is so important they're willing to spend money to help one particular county."

She looked out at her people. None of them seemed to be in a snit about my being here.

"Mr. Garrison is going to investigate the shooting that occurred six months ago, out at the area we used to call Remington's Woods, before it was bought up and turned into what we later found out was a haven for drug dealers. You know the place I'm talking about."

Most of those facing us nodded; the others were too lethargic.

"As you recall, there was an aborted drug raid there last fall, which resulted in the tragic deaths of three federal agents from the Drug Enforcement Administration, as well as the deaths of four men who were in that compound at the time. Four criminals, I must say, whose activities, and those of similar men, poison our children across the county. They were not nice men. But it would have been better if they had not been killed. It would have been better if no one had been killed."

She was laying it on thick, so they'd understand that they were going to be sitting in judgment of the killer or killers of people who, in a just world, deserved to be killed.

"One of the men who was killed, whose name was Reynaldo Juarez—in this case, we may find out the word *murdered* is the correct word—is going to be the subject of Mr. Garrison and his team's investigation, which if successful may result in indictments in one form or another—first-degree murder, second-degree murder, manslaughter, so forth. You're all familiar with those terms, I've asked you for such indictments before. The object is to find out who killed Juarez, and perhaps why, although that is a separate issue from what Mr. Garrison will be addressing today."

She glanced back at me again. I nodded in agreement.

Continuing on, she said, "I'm sure you know the Drug Enforcement Administration has been conducting their own investigation of this killing—they've been all over Blue River and Muir County the past months. Some of you may have talked to agents, formally or informally. So far, I'm sad to say, they haven't come up with any suspects, or any leads towards developing a suspect or suspects. And for now, they don't seem to be able to."

She paused to make sure they were still with her. They seemed to be.

"Reynaldo Juarez was a rotten human being," Nora said, "but at the time of his killing, he was in federal custody. He was a prisoner, with all the rights our system accords people who have been arrested but not yet convicted of anything. He was in the custody of agents of the federal government, but he was killed in Muir County."

Another quick pause, a glance back at me, then she pressed on.

"As Muir County D.A., I am mandated to investigate all crimes that take place in this county. That's why you elected me. Not to pick and choose, not to decide whether I like, or have any sympathy for, the victim of a particular crime—which, as I've said, I didn't, in this case. My feelings are irrelevant, as should yours be. We're a nation of laws, not emotions, and although that can be a pain in the neck sometimes, in the long run it's good, it protects our freedoms."

This is eloquent, I thought as I listened. She's good at this; it sounds as if she really believes it, too. Maybe she could run for state assembly someday, or Congress. It would get her out of here while allowing her to keep some roots, some connection to Dennis. Perhaps that mental compromise could assuage the guilt feelings she has that have kept her, all these years, in what has to be an alien, not desirable place.

"So," she concluded, "that's all I have to say, for now. I'm going to turn you over to Mr. Garrison, who will explain what he is going to do, and what he expects from you."

I got up, buttoned my jacket, walked to the podium, shook Nora's hand, turned to face the small group.

"As Mrs. Ray has told you," I began, "my name is Luke Garrison. I am a lawyer, a member of the California bar, a former district attorney in this state. Also, as she told you, I have been appointed to be a special independent counselor to investigate and, if proper evidence is forthcoming, to bring forth indictments against the person or persons who killed Reynaldo Juarez in this county in September of last year."

Their stares were blank. I took that to mean they'd be compliant, as grand juries normally are. Nora hadn't given me reason to think otherwise.

"The investigation we're about to embark on, ladies and gentlemen, will require the same things you've done in every case that's come to you during your time serving on this grand jury. You will, at our request, be issuing subpoenas and warrants, taking testimony of witnesses, suspects, and so forth."

I cleared my throat. "The difference in this case is that for openers, we *think* we had a crime committed, but we're not sure—how this man Juarez was killed may turn out not to have been prosecutable. I doubt that, but it's a possibility. What is different here is that we don't have a suspect; or to put it more precisely, we have dozens of possible suspects, and what we're going to do is try to develop a few of them, or maybe only one, from these dozens.

"We're going to be pushing kind of far afield to do that, and you're going to have to help us. You're going to have to trust us, and know that we're doing this for the right reason: to find guilt. Not to punish innocent men, or in any way be vindictive."

I waited to make sure they were still paying attention, then I proceeded, "We have about thirty-six legitimate suspects in this killing. They are agents of the federal Drug Enforcement Administration. There may be more suspects we'll want to investigate, down the line. We'll find that out as we develop this case. But there are at least thirty-six suspects out there."

There was a faint stirring down below me; the first animation of any kind I'd seen.

"Why so many?" asked one of them, an old lady, one of the old ladies who had brought a notebook and pen.

"Because that's how many people were there and fit certain general criteria," I answered.

Arriving at who was a suspect was simple arithmetic: subtraction. None of the prisoners could have killed Juarez, because they were all in secure custody. When the chase ended and the agents had staggered back to their base, the other prisoners were as they had been left—handcuffed; which meant they weren't suspects, they couldn't be. Secondly, while most of the agents had discharged their side arms during the assault on the compound, a minority hadn't. Ballistics proved that some guns had not been fired that night. So those agents were cleared up front.

Which left everyone else. Head nods told me they understood.

I had carved away the fat and the gristle. Now I moved on to the protein.

"I want this grand jury to authorize almost unlimited investigative authority to me. I am going to want warrants that will let us go into their private records. We need to look at bank accounts, phone logs, travel schedules, marital problems, anything suspicious. The same for their wives, close relatives, close friends. We are going to get into some real private places, places you and I wouldn't want the government looking. But you have to give me that power if I'm going to have any chance of getting at the truth."

This was heavy stuff, the prosecutor as bully-inquisitor. But I saw no other way to do it.

"We aren't going to go fishing in every ocean in the world. But in the waters we will be trolling, I need to be able to throw out as many lines as I can, even if no one thinks there's any fish out there."

I looked at each of them one more time.

"This is a tough job, for you and for us. We're going to be investigating who killed a career criminal, an unregenerate bastard, excuse my language. If that man had been properly arrested and brought to trial, Mrs. Ray or a state or federal prosecutor would be throwing the book at him—life imprisonment without parole, maybe even the death penalty. That's what makes this situation so difficult, so unique. And so necessary."

Sheriff Miller poured me a cup of coffee. "How do you take it?" he asked.

"Black's fine."

He passed the cup across the desk to me, poured one for himself. "Watch it," he cautioned. "It's hot."

I took a careful sip. "This is good," I said, surprised. I hadn't had coffee of this caliber in Blue River. I didn't know you could find it.

"It's Pete's," he informed me, stirring a dollop of two percent into his. "I prefer it to Starbucks."

"I didn't know you could get those here." I hadn't seen designer shops of any kind in Blue River. Maybe in the Ralph's, the only chain supermarket in the county. I had yet to pay it a visit.

He smiled, shook his head. "You can't. I get it mail order. You want anything of decent quality here, you get it sent in. I've got every upscale mail-order catalogue there is. You want, I'll lend 'em to you. Man of your tastes isn't going to be satisfied with what's on the local shelves."

"Thanks. I'll take you up on that."

He took out his tobacco and cigarette papers and rolled a thin, tight smoke, lighting it with his signature match to boot sole, his exhale of blue-gray smoke lazily drifting above his head.

As I watched him perform his brief ritual, I was reminded that this was no hick I was dealing with. He might be the small-town sheriff with mud-caked rough-out Western boots up on the desk and the roll-your-own cigarettes, but he was a former FBI agent, a graduate from a quality law school, a man who had lived in Washington and other big cities, had rubbed elbows with powerful people.

"So what was it like out there that night?" I'd covered some of this with him before, but that had been informal. This was official.

He shook his head in doleful remembrance. "Unadulterated hell. Classic bad news. Everything that could go wrong, did." Another headshake. "Jerome got anxious and . . ." He trailed off, watching his smoke plume curl up to the ceiling.

"Did you have a good, clear feel for what was going on, when it was going on?"

He shook his head.

"I had a good feeling for it—good if you mean did I know what was happening. I've been in law enforcement my entire life, nothing much gets by me."

"Of course," I said deferentially.

"What you're asking is, was I part of it, physically, did I have input?" The question was rhetorical—he answered it himself. "No. I was excluded. Me and my deputy. We were there strictly for show. So that later on Jerome could say we were, by the book." Another head-shake. "But no, we were relegated to the sidelines."

He picked his coffee up, took a sip. "It's cool enough now."

I drank from my own cup.

Miller squinted at me through the haze of his cigarette smoke. "This is official, right? You're debriefing me. Everyone that was there that night is technically suspect. Which has to include me, doesn't it?"

"Technically."

"I understand, I've been in your position. Of course, I had nothing to do with Juarez's death or anything up there that night." He frowned, remembering a bad memory. "Jerome didn't want to consult with me in the slightest. He would've been much happier if I had taken a pass, gone home to bed." He dragged down a third of his smoke. "Which was too damn bad for him," he said, the anger showing. "I could have helped him."

"Give me a for instance."

"I would have counseled him not to go in. The operation had been turned off, because the planes couldn't land." One last drag, then he stubbed out his smoke in a Harrah's ashtray. "He wanted Juarez come hell or high water, and that's all she wrote."

"You weren't where you could have influenced the outcome at all?"

"I thought going in after Juarez was a stupid idea, like I said. But once Jerome decided he was going to, I accepted it. I follow the chain of command." He emptied his ashtray into the wastebasket under his desk. "I asked in on the action. I wanted to go in there with him. It is my county, after all," he said, the memory of the snub still an annoyance.

I could picture the scene. The stubborn old lion, the equally stubborn young turk.

"What was Jerome's response?"

"Thanks but no thanks."

"So you were cut out."

"Completely. You've been out there."

I nodded.

"The hill that overlooks the compound. My deputy and I watched it from there."

I visualized the hill he was talking about. It was at least two or three hundred yards from the compound interior. They had been exiled to Siberia, no question.

"You were up there the whole time?"

This time he shook his head no. "When all hell broke loose and the shooting started, my deputy and I ran down towards the compound. There were men trapped down there. We had to try to help them, at least provide some cover." Anticipating my next question, he went on, "But we didn't get far, because the DEA fired their shells into the house, and it started blowing up." Another derisive head-shake. "Now that really was a dumb move. You had to figure something like that could happen. First explosion, I looked at my deputy, he looked at me, we turned tail and ran like hell."

He finished his cup of coffee, refilled it halfway, added his drop of milk to it. "I'm as brave as the next man, but I'm not a fool." He refilled my cup without my asking. "What can I do to help out here? I want to help, as much as I can."

"I don't know," I told him candidly. "You won't be part of the official investigation—I need to maintain my independent stance, and besides, none of the players live here, most of my investigating will be handled outside Muir County."

He didn't show any emotion, one way or the other. He merely nodded in understanding.

"But if I can think of a way to use you informally, I will. I value your experience, and you were there, you can provide us with an objective, first-person point of view."

He nodded again. "Thank you. Although I should say, I don't think anyone can be objective about this kind of incident."

There wasn't much more for me to do with him.

"A couple more questions, Sheriff."

"Shoot."

"What kind of gun do you use?"

"Side arm?"

"Yes."

"S and W .38. The old policeman's revolver. I've had it since my days on the Bureau."

"Did you fire it that night?"

He shook his head. "No." He stared at me. "It was checked out by a member of the investigating team. It's in one of your reports."

"Right." I didn't remember that, but I didn't doubt him. Anyway, a .38 wouldn't have the velocity to power a bullet clear through a man's head. And the bullet that had killed Juarez had been a 9mm., not a .38.

I reached for my briefcase. "I'll be in touch."

"I'm here, I'm not going anywhere."

I stood, offered my hand across the desk. He stood with me. "Can I ask you a question, Mr. Garrison?"

"Luke. Sure."

"How are you approaching this?"

His question threw me off balance. "How do you mean?"

"Here's my question."

He'd been building to this, but he hadn't found the right opportunity. When I got up to leave, he couldn't wait any longer.

"Here's what I think. If I were investigating this. Which I'm not," he hastened to add.

"Fire away anyway."

He pulled his tobacco can out again. "I'd ask myself, who profits from Juarez's being murdered?" He started rolling another toothpick-thin cigarette. "The reason I think that is, it isn't enough that the sole motive for this killing was in eliminating a bad human being. Somebody had a reason to kill Juarez, other than self-righteous anger. Otherwise, whoever killed him would have simply apprehended him once he found him out there in the woods. Juarez was unarmed." He lit his fresh smoke. "There was no reason to kill him just because he'd escaped."

I knew that. It was important. I liked how the man was thinking.

"What else?" I asked, encouraging him to finish his thoughts.

"Well . . . why did Juarez try to escape in the first place?"

"Good question." I'd thought it myself.

"Panic would be my guess. Those handcuffs aren't too difficult to get out of if you know what you're doing, which he surely would have. He finds himself free, takes a chance. It was scary out there, real warfare. That can screw up your head if you're not used to it, which I don't think Juarez was, he was one of those clever fellows who's never in the direct line of action. He only came this time because the stakes were so high."

"Yes, I know."

"Anyway, he gets loose and bolts. Don't forget, he'd been hiding in that meat locker, half-frozen to death, his senses wouldn't have been as sharp as normal. If he'd had a clearer head, he would have stayed put. He'd have known the odds of escaping that way were the usual, slim or none. He would have waited until he was in jail and then his fancy lawyers would have sprung him. Remember, the reason for the bust evaporated. It was very dubious, as a former district attorney you know that. So Juarez could have shown good cause that he should never have been arrested."

I was listening intently. This old man was on top of the game.

"What about the bounty on his head?" I countered.

"That's legitimate," he agreed. "But it's an allegation. It would have to be proven in a court of law. Witnesses in cases like those often don't show up. Sometimes they die mysteriously. Regardless, it could have been a difficult case to prosecute. Don't you agree?"

"I don't know," I answered. "I haven't looked at that case closely."

"Perhaps . . ." He checked himself.

Perhaps you should, was what he was going to say. But he didn't want to step on my toes. He wanted to be my ally, to be brought in.

"Anyway, that's all I have to say. I don't want to waste any more of your time."

He walked me to the door. "This is a crappy case, isn't it?"

"Because of the players and the circumstances."

He nodded in agreement. "I have my own grudge with Sterling Jerome. I think the man loves himself too damn much. But he's a quality agent. They all are. They're fighting the good fight."

"I know."

"Can you imagine what would have happened if the planes had landed, the deal had gone through, and those drugs would have gone out into the streets of America?"

"If the moneyman wasn't Jerome's man?" I asked. "If it was a real drug deal?"

"Yes. Which is how it works ninety-nine percent of the time. They ruin people's lives. Now one of those pricks is dead, and the entire team of men who were there are under a cloud. No matter what happens, many of their careers are going to be destroyed."

"Yes, I know."

"Sometimes the bad guys win, and the good guys lose. I hate it when that happens," he said.

I nodded silently.

"So that's why I say, someone had a motive for killing Juarez. A sinister motive. Pursue that line. That way lies justice."

Outside the office, I thought about what Miller had postulated. He was a smart man, a thoughtful man. Way above the caliber of a normal county sheriff, whose chief job is getting himself elected. This man was a true pro.

I was going to make use of him. I didn't know exactly how, but he was too good a resource not to use.

Luis Lopez, Jerome's informant, was being held in a tightly guarded, quarantined cell in Reno, the closest federal prison to Blue River. He had zero contact with any other inmates. He showered alone, exercised alone, ate in his cell. Always under the watchful eyes of guards. No one was allowed near him except for his lawyer; Juanita Montoya, his common-law wife; select members of the prison staff, such as the warden; and the team from the Federal Witness Relocation Program that had been assigned to his case.

Lopez's new existence was almost completely established. In a couple of weeks he was going to be whisked from the prison and sent halfway across the country with his family to a destination known only to Jerome and a select few in the federal system, who could monitor his comings and goings and offer protection. Once that happened, Lopez would disappear into the fog, and anyone looking for him would be hard-pressed to locate him. Jerome would be zealous about that.

———————

Louis Alvarez passed through prison security and waited for Lopez in a small holding room adjacent to the cellblock where the prisoner was being kept under tight watch. A few minutes later Lopez was escorted into the room. He sat down across the table from the detective.

"I'll be right outside if you need me," the guard told Lopez.

"I won't be needing you," Lopez answered curtly.

The guard left them. Lopez turned his attention to Alvarez. "I don't have anything to say to you."

"You don't know that," Alvarez rejoined unflappably.

"Yeah, I do."

Alvarez stared at the prisoner. "I could fuck you up good, *ese.*"

"The hell you could. I got protection. Pretty damn soon, I fly this cage, Columbo couldn't find me then."

Alvarez leaned back in the metal chair. This was going to be fun. He loved fucking with the heads of assholes who had attitude.

"That so?" He reached into his briefcase and pulled out a thin document. "You know what this is, shitbird?"

"The addresses of the motels in Bakersfield where your mother sucks cock."

Alvarez grinned. "That's in Fresno, and she's the madam, not one of the working girls. You're confusing her with your own mother, and your wife and your sisters."

Lopez snorted through his nose. "I'm deeply hurt. In other words, fuck you."

"My asshole's too tight, even for your skinny two-inch dick."

Lopez pushed back from the table.

"Where you going?" Alvarez asked, fighting not to laugh in the prisoner's face.

"Out of here." Lopez turned to the door.

Alvarez shook his head. "Our meeting isn't over until *I* terminate it." He gestured toward the door. "Go ahead. See if they'll let you out."

Lopez hesitated.

"In the meantime, let me acquaint you with this." Alvarez donned his half-frame tortoiseshell reading glasses, started scanning the document. "The DEA is setting you up in the Federal Witness Relocation Program. You're going to be relocated to Chicago, the north side. Nice neighborhood, good schools for your kids, about twenty-five percent upwardly mobile Latino, you'll fit right in. The exact address is 12237 West Arlington Street, unit number eighteen. A three-bedroom condo, you own it, the deed is in your new name, which is Jaime Moreno. Your wife's name is Julia. Your telephone number is 555-7387, area code 773. You have a job as a head line inspector with the Chicago Transit Authority, pulling down $52,500 a year plus benefits: health insurance, pension plan, sick leave, four weeks paid vacation a year. Not to mention the untraceable and untaxable half million you have in an offshore bank account, as a reward for your endeavors, courtesy of Uncle Sam. You drive a dark green, three-year-old Nissan Pathfinder, Illinois license plate number ACD498." Alvarez dropped the document on the table. "And so forth."

Lopez sank back into his chair. "How did you find all that out?" he croaked.

"Doesn't matter. Point is, I know. And if I know, somebody else could, too." Alvarez smiled at the prisoner. "You still have nothing to say to me?"

Lopez shook his head. Fucking federal bastards. Like they could really offer him protection. He should have known better.

"Ask away," he said dully.

"Thank you," Alvarez said crisply. He withdrew a few four-by-six index cards from his briefcase, put Lopez's dossier back inside.

"When did you start soldiering for Reynaldo Juarez?"

"Forever. We grew up together. We were like brothers."

"Cain and Abel?"

Lopez flushed. "I only turned against him because I had no choice. It was that or life without parole. He would have done the same thing if it had been reversed. And I would have understood."

Alvarez didn't comment on that lame justification. "How long were you in Jerome's pocket?"

"About a year. Little more."

"How often did you meet with him? In person, on the phone, whatever."

"It was irregular. Whenever I had something I had to pass on, I'd leave him a signal and we'd get together. Usually it was over the phone."

Alvarez looked at another card. "You gave Juarez's entire operation to Jerome? Players, shipments, locations, buyers, the works?"

"I answered what he asked me," Lopez said defensively. "I didn't volunteer nothing."

"You were paid. Handsomely."

"It was risky business, man. One slipup . . ." He drew his finger across his throat.

Alvarez dropped the index cards on the table. He leaned forward on his elbows. "Somebody inside knew that raid was coming down, didn't they? Somebody besides you."

Lopez shook his head. "No. No one knew."

"You sure?"

"Absolutely."

"How can you be so sure?"

" 'Cause I am. I was there. No one inside knew it was going to happen. Hell, right before I cut out we were all laughing and joking about how invisible we were. Believe me, nobody knew."

Alvarez leaned back. "You can tell me, you know. It doesn't matter now. Your brother is dead. Because of you," he added weightily.

Lopez held his ground. "No," he protested firmly. "I did not kill him. They were going to take him alive. I wouldn't have done what I did if I thought they were going to kill him."

"On whose word?"

"Jerome's, of course. He wanted Juarez alive more than anyone. He was running the show. It was a done deal."

"Then how come the DEA ran into a firestorm? If Juarez and the others thought they were invisible, how come they were so prepared for an attack? Like they knew it was coming?"

Lopez shook his head. "That's what I'd like to know," he said, greatly agitated. "All I know is, it wasn't one of us. Anyway, when the planes weren't coming, I figured the raid was going to be canceled. Jerome pulled a fast one on me."

Alvarez looked at the prisoner with contempt. "So you were working both ends of the street, weren't you?"

"I had no choice. You get in that position, let's see how you'd do."

"Better than you did, I can guarantee you that." Alvarez despised this piece of shit sitting in front of him. Not only a criminal, a dealer of suffering to innocents, but a squealer to boot.

Lopez slumped in his chair. "Are we finished now?" he asked plaintively.

"After you answer me this: Who told the people inside that compound that they were going to be attacked? Who could that have been? It would've been a lot better if that raid hadn't been answered, you've got to know that. Those men who died, on both sides, they'd be alive."

"Shit, you think I don't know that? I was sick when that happened. Those men who died were my brothers, man. I went against them, but they were still my brothers."

"So now I'm back to my main question—who did it?"

"One of the attackers, of course." Lopez looked at his inquisitor like he was crazy not to understand that.

"But when?" This was a key question that was bewildering to the prosecution.

Again, a head shake no. "It had to be after I left. But exactly when, I couldn't tell you."

Alvarez thought for a moment. He started to ask the next question; then he thought better of it and didn't.

"Thank you for your cooperation," was what he said to Lopez. He pressed the signal to the outside. The guard opened the door immediately.

"We're done here," Alvarez said.

The guard pulled Lopez to his feet.

"I don't think I'll need to see you again," Alvarez told Lopez.

Lopez looked at Alvarez's briefcase. "What about that?"

"It's going in the shredder. No one's ever going to know. You have my word."

Lopez nodded. "Thanks."

"Okay."

Lopez was taken away. Alvarez sat down in the empty room. He thought of the question he hadn't asked Lopez: *If the men inside were warned, why didn't Juarez make his escape before the raid?*

The answer, of course, was that they didn't know until it was too late. So the next question would be, *Why didn't they?*

He knew that answer, too: *Because whoever tipped them off waited until it was too late for Juarez to get out.* And the second part of the answer was: *Because that person wanted Juarez to be killed. Because if fire was answered with fire, that would be the perfect cover to do it.*

At the same time Alvarez was meeting with Lopez, Keith Green was being driven in a Range Rover 4.6 to a clandestine meeting with Curtis Jackson, the head of the 94th St. Terrors, one of the major black gangs in Los Angeles. The word *gang* is a misnomer, a trivialization; they're a conglomerate that moves tens of millions of dollars of drugs a year, plus weapons, stolen cars, other ill-gotten items; that sometimes does deals with Mexican gangs such as Juarez's, as well as with Asian gangs, especially Vietnamese ones based in Orange County, and Chinese tongs in San Francisco.

Keith didn't know where they were going, precisely. Somewhere in south-central L.A. Jackson's people—two men in their twenties—had picked him up in the parking lot of Musso & Frank's restaurant on Hollywood Boulevard, where he'd gone to have chicken potpie for lunch after flying in to Burbank Airport from Oakland on Southwest Airlines. The rendezvous had been arranged under a blanket pledge of immunity—nothing that came out of the meeting would be used in any criminal proceeding. It was tacitly acknowledged by both parties that a meeting between brothers, especially when one of them flashes a world-championship ring (Raiders 38, Redskins 9, Super Bowl XVIII, 1984), would be the most likely to bear fruit. The Raiders may now be a shadow of their former selves, but their badass reputation and bygone glory (long bygone) still hold a mysterious, if unexplainable, cachet among their loyal fans, which includes black gang members, outlaw bikers, other citizens of dubious character, and some die-hard Los Angeles politicians.

Keith harbored no such illusions. His season tickets were for the 49ers—he runs with the winners, unapologetically. Although he doesn't broadcast that tidbit; if his former glory opens doors, that's fine.

It was rush hour, which in Los Angeles is about twenty hours a day. Traffic crawled bumper to bumper down the Harbor Freeway. The tinted windows were up, the air-conditioning cooled the interior to a consistent, crisp sixty-eight degrees. A rap group Keith didn't know blew out of the CD, eight speakers, better than being there in person. Keith stared out the window. Some small talk about the Raiders, why have they been down for so long now? Why don't they have a black coach, Art Snell was better than the current chump. That played out, the conversation drifted to the recent NBA contract. It was agreed by all aboard that the players were chumps who caved in. You don't put a ceiling on your profits, profits are unlimited, whatever the market will bear. If that ain't the American way, what the fuck is? They should know, Keith mused. He sure doesn't drive a Range Rover that goes out the door at seventy thousand dollars.

They got off the freeway at Ninety-sixth Street, cruised over to Central, headed south a few blocks, pulling into a parking lot in a shabby strip mall behind a nondescript two-story office building, which was flanked by a barbershop, a beauty parlor, a Pioneer Chicken take-out joint, other small businesses, none of which looked to be thriving. Same old same old, Keith thought. Two riots and thirty-five years and nothing's changed.

Not his problem. Not today.

He followed the two men up a back set of stairs and entered a small reception area, which was empty. The sign on the door read WILLIAM PIERCE, ATTORNEY-AT-LAW. An interior door that led to the office proper was closed. Keith Green knew the office's tenant by reputation. Pierce was a well-known Los Angeles criminal lawyer, a middle-aged black man with a client list that consisted mainly of people like Curtis Jackson, who needed a crackerjack mouthpiece. Pierce's main office was in Beverly Hills. This was a satellite facility for when he needed to meet with the ordinary folk in an appropriate setting.

One of Keith's escorts knocked on the inner door. A muffled voice spoke a few words from the other side. The escort opened the door and stood aside as Keith entered.

Diplomas and testimonials on the walls. Pictures of Pierce with celebrities—jocks, entertainers, politicians. And an old blown-up photoposter from the sixties of Huey Newton and Bobby Seale. Seated behind the pressed-wood, oak-laminate desk was a man who bore a resemblance to Spike Lee, the film director, except he didn't wear glasses and was about fifty pounds heavier, all muscle. Curtis Jackson. He stared at Keith, unblinking.

"You ain't wearing a wire by any chance, are you?" Jackson started out.

"No," Keith answered, standing inside the doorway. "You want to check me out?"

"I trust you," Jackson said. "This time. We're not wired here, either. Whatever we say, it stays in this room."

"That works for me."

Jackson smiled at Keith. "You were one of my idols, when I was a little kid."

Keith walked into the room and sat across the desk from Jackson, who looked past him to his men who were hovering in the doorway. Jackson nodded, and the door closed. Keith glanced over his shoulder. They were alone, Jackson and him. Jackson picked up a softball-sized Nerf basketball off the desk, started playing with it.

"You play ball?" Keith asked. He knew the man wasn't a jock, but it was an easy icebreaker. "You got the physique."

Jackson shrugged, a shade too nonchalantly. "Playground, shit like that. College wasn't never in my future. Hoops, no football. I was a decent point guard," he went on, elaborating on his lie, unable to stop himself in the company of this famous athlete, whose manhood, by virtue of his sports background, was beyond questioning. "I didn't go for the rough stuff. Big-ass rhinoceros like you lay a hit on me, I'd be maimed for life, could be." He smiled.

"Basketball's cool. Where it's at now, far as the real money's at. We all gotta go our own direction," he added, staring at Jackson noncommittally.

"This is true." Jackson tossed the Nerf basketball between his hands. "You're part of the team investigating Reynaldo Juarez getting killed," he said levelly. "Which is why you want to see me."

Keith nodded.

"What do you want to see me about, then? I don't know who killed him, if that's what you want to know."

"I didn't think so. And if you did, you wouldn't be meeting with me. You'd be running from me as hard as you could."

Jackson looked at Keith behind half-shaded eyelids. "I don't run from no one." He leaned forward. "You flew down here to see me, and I took time out of my busy schedule to accommodate you, so let's get to it, all right?"

"You called me."

Jackson stared hard. "Sorry, my man," he said dismissively. "You've been fed false information. I've never talked to you, met you, been in your eyesight."

Keith was having no truck with this. He hadn't flown down here and taken time out of *his* busy schedule to get jerked around, even if the jerker was a multimillionaire who purportedly hung out with such luminaries as Puff Daddy and Eddie Murphy.

"You got word to Luke Garrison, my boss, that you had some stuff to talk about that we might be interested in."

Jackson stared at Keith. He flipped the soft basketball at a coffee-can-sized basket that was suction-cupped against the back wall. It bounced off the rim and fell to the floor.

"Your lawyer tells us you have something that might help us," Keith said. "What would that be? Information, some kind of physical evidence, rumors floating around, what?"

Jackson leaned back. "Reynaldo Juarez. You're trying to find out who did him."

"That's no secret."

"Well, the thing is, him and us were rivals. His organization still is, though when they kill the jefe, the organization don't survive too good. But anyways, I can't say I'm sorry he's dead, you play the game, you gotta accept the consequences." His eyelids narrowed further, thin slits. "Like getting killed."

"High risk, high reward."

"I ain't weeping no tears over him or nothing, somebody takes out a rival, that's good for my business. Strictly business, man. Nothing personal."

Like a drive-by shooting is business, nothing personal, Keith thought. Tell that "nothing personal" bullshit to your victims, motherfucker.

"You're out to nail the DEA for it," Jackson went on.

Keith shook his head. "We want to find out who did it. Whoever that was. We're not out to get any particular person or organization."

Jackson shook his head. "You want a DEA scalp."

"Where'd you hear that?"

"All over," Jackson answered. "You want to send a shot across their arrogant bow, that they can't dis the local authorities."

"What?" Keith's surprise wasn't feigned. This was new. He hadn't heard this wrinkle—Luke Garrison had not mentioned anything on this aspect of the investigation. And he would have, Keith knew, if it was in the mix. Luke wouldn't hold anything back from his team.

"The lead agent on that raid. Jerome." Jackson said the name like he was saying the word *turd*. "You know who I'm talking about."

Keith nodded.

"He disrespected the D.A. up there. Some woman, dyke probably. And the sheriff. That old sheriff up there, he don't like being fucked over, even if he is an old fart who ought to be dead already. He used to be an important person, back in the prehistoric days. You know that?"

"He was an FBI agent." That was all Keith knew about Tom Miller. He had never met the man, not yet.

"He got a memory like an elephant, this old sheriff. And he don't like Jerome. Those DEA agents, they're good at pissing people off. Not just dealers. Straight people. FBI and DEA, they don't get along," Jackson continued. "FBI, CIA, DEA, none of 'em gets along with the others. Bad shit between them all. They all want to hog all the gravy."

Keith didn't reply. This was Jackson's party.

"Here's the other thing got people's mouths moving," Jackson said, cutting into Keith's train of thought. "Why was this Jerome such a hard-ass about keeping the local sheriff off the case, away from everything?"

"Where did you hear that?" Keith asked, alarmed. That wasn't common knowledge; not that he knew of.

"It's all over," Jackson said dismissively. "The walls have ears, how do you think I survive out in that jungle?"

"I have no knowledge of that," Keith lied.

"Check it out."

"I will. But so what?"

"So why would they do that? That's against their own protocol. You work with the locals, they know the lay of the land better than outsiders."

Jackson was right, again. Jerome had gone against the book by excluding Miller. One of the main reasons this task force had been formed—because the DEA had shut the Muir County authorities out. They had to conduct their own investigation, they'd been forced into it.

"Unless . . ." Jackson stopped.

"Unless what?"

"The DEA planned something ugly and didn't want any outside witnesses."

Keith shook his head. "That doesn't make sense. Juarez was no good to them dead, except as a trophy. Alive, he could have given them the skinny on his whole organization, every gang in the country, yours included."

"You fucking right."

Keith was perplexed. Jackson was contradicting himself from one sentence to the next.

"Unless," Jackson said again, "the DEA was mixed up with Juarez. If he stayed alive, he could fuck them up good. Remember that talk about how the DEA and CIA was working with the anti-Sandinistas to sell drugs in the ghettos?"

"That turned out to be bullshit."

"The government is in the drug business, that isn't bullshit. What do you think goes down in the fucking Golden Triangle, man? You think those Burmese and Thais and Vietnamese and whoever lives out there could move all their shit if our government really wanted to stop them?"

DEA ops and drug dealers working together? It was done all the time—witness Jerome's use of Lopez. But in this specific situation, that Juarez was somehow connected? That would blow this case into the stratosphere.

"But that ain't logical," Jackson said, turning the discussion around again.

"No, it isn't."

"So what is? Out there that night?" Jackson leaned back. "Want to hear my opinion?"

It was obvious to Keith that Jackson had been thinking about this. Heavily.

"Sure."

"Who benefits the most, Juarez being offed?"

"You."

Jackson laughed. "I wasn't there." He pointed at Keith. "Dead men tell no tales. Juarez is alive, the feds turn him, he could fuck up his own people, half the shit moving up and down the West Coast. Not to mention me and lots of others."

"One of his own." Keith said it.

Jackson nodded. "It makes *sense*," he said forcefully. "*Business* sense. Which is the only kind of sense I'm interested in, you dig? The DEA wanted Juarez alive, correct? His people knew where that could lead, correct? The rest of it—DEA hotheads, pissed-off sheriffs, that's speculation." He leveled his heavy-lidded stare at Keith. "I'm a *busi-ness*man, Mr. Oakland-old-football-player. I don't deal in speculation."

Keith stared at him. What the fuck was this all about? "Why are you telling me this?" he asked. "The DEA is your enemy, their mission in life is to shut you down and put you in jail past forever, and my ears are hearing that you're saying they didn't do it? Wouldn't have, couldn't have?"

"*Wouldn't* have, I think not, *couldn't* have, fuck yes. Somebody there shot the man, and they were the ones that were there. But what's the motive? I just told you who had one and who didn't. That's what you should be looking for. That's why people kill other people, usually. 'Cause they got a reason."

Keith felt like a character out of *Alice in Wonderland*. "I missed something, I think. Tell me again, why are you laying this on me?"

"Because I don't deal in speculation, and neither should you. Somebody out there setting up businessmen like myself and then *offing* them for no good reason and plenty of wrong ones? That makes me nervous, you understand? Like, who can I trust if I can't trust the government to play by their own rules? I mean, they're fucked up, but they got rules. I know they broke a lot of 'em just going in like they did, but they did take him prisoner; if they'd wanted him dead so bad, they would've concocted some bullshit on the spot. Happens all the time—you know that as good as me. So *if* they killed Reynaldo Juarez when he was their prisoner, then they're just gonna walk in my crib and shoot my head off. On the street, my mother's house, wherever."

"You're overlooking one thing, aren't you?" This was a worrisome conversation.

A disturbing thought came to Keith's head—was this meeting a setup? Had the DEA sunk their hooks in Curtis Jackson and were now using him to try to discredit, muddle, screw up, the investigation?

"What's that one thing?" Jackson asked Keith.

"Juarez was in the custody of the DEA agents on the scene when he broke out. How did that happen if someone there didn't help him?"

Jackson shook his head in exasperation. "People escape custody all the time, my man. You never heard of that? Everyone there was so juiced and pumped they didn't know shit from what was happening. I been in those situations, it's ground-level warfare. You ain't thinking, you're barely reacting. It's all confusing, everybody's running around like crazy, Juarez sees his opening, boom, he's the Roadrunner."

"That sounds like speculation to me," Keith said dryly.

Jackson showed his disagreement. "That's *presumption,* not speculation. One's about what you know, one's about what you *think* you know." He leaned back in his lawyer's chair. "Like I said, I'm a businessman. I can't afford to deal in speculation. That's for women and children." A brief pause, a tight smile. "And dead men."

And investigators chasing a wild goose? Keith wondered.

I deposed Sheriff Miller and his deputy, Bearpaw, in front of the grand jury. It was pro forma—it had been clearly established that Bearpaw was miles away from the compound by the time of Juarez's escape and killing, and that Miller was among the last of the pursuers to arrive on the scene. Then I walked down the street to our office and sat with Keith and Louis while they briefed me. Kate sat in with us.

"We can't believe anything out of Lopez's mouth," Kate said tartly. "Snitches are liars until proven otherwise, and everything about him points the opposite direction from what he said."

We all agreed.

"But that still leaves the question open as to whether Juarez knew an attack was coming," Louis observed. "Or if it was good security, and Lopez was sandbagging Jerome? Egging him on, even."

"To what purpose?" Kate asked.

"So there'd be a raid," Keith theorized. "No raid, Juarez escapes uncaptured, no big reward for Lopez."

"And no trophy for Jerome," Louis added. "It was his best chance to nail Juarez, which was his mission in life. He might not have had another opportunity that good."

"Or lost him to another agent," Kate kicked in.

"Or agency," Louis added.

"Let's take Lopez at his word this one time, for the sake of conjecture," I said, wanting to look at this angle a bit more before we moved on. "That they didn't know there was going to be a raid, and that their security was lax. Doesn't that point to an informant from the outside? And wouldn't that have to be someone on the task force? No one else knew."

"Which leads us back to a suspect from within the task force," Louis said. "Where we've been from the beginning."

"For the raid," I pointed out, "not the killing. There's cross-purposes working there. Especially for Sterling Jerome." I was thinking out loud. "Jerome doesn't go in if he thinks there's going to be resistance, because

Juarez could be killed and that fucks him up. He was emphatic about that. We knew about his impassioned statements to his people before the raid—'Take Juarez alive, that's the reason we're doing this.' So maybe it does fall on Lopez—that he lied to Jerome about that."

"Like I said, a snitch is a snitch," Kate proclaimed.

"Let's table Lopez for now," I said. "What Curtis Jackson told Keith is more disturbing to me. With deeper implications as to how we're going to conduct our investigation, I think."

The others concurred.

Keith turned to me. "How do you feel about the possibility that our local D.A. and sheriff *are* orchestrating this because of the shabby way they were treated?" he asked. "She's your friend. Could she be using you?"

"I can't imagine it," I said. "But anything's possible."

I had to say that. I didn't believe it, but I couldn't deny the possibility, however remote.

"I don't believe it," Kate averred. "It's Jackson shooting off his mouth, trying to influence this. The more muddled it all gets, the more suspicion is spread around. Which is good for criminals. It's like taking sides with the Iraqis against the Iranians. You get in bed with wrongos because you think you'll get something out of an unholy alliance, and in the end you get screwed regardless."

"Jackson had a point, though." Keith tapped a ballpoint pen against his palm. "The DEA was damaged by Juarez's being killed. And Juarez's people were saved the possibility of being ruined by their boss turning evidence. They're still out there, and now the government has to be a hell of a lot more cautious in going after them."

"What about the notion of Juarez being mixed up with the DEA? If he'd been turned, that would be cause for killing him, wouldn't it?" Louis asked.

"I think it's the opposite," I said. "He can't help them if he's dead."

"But he could rat out that DEA agent. Or the whole agency," Keith reminded us. "If his handler thought that was going to happen, killing him makes sense." He paused. "You think Juarez could've been on the DEA's payroll?"

"That would be wild," I said. "We can try to check it out. I don't think we'll get anywhere, seeing as how we're on their shit list. But I'll see if we can find anything out." I went on, "About Juarez's own people snuffing him. Does anyone buy into that?"

I looked at them. It wasn't a popular proposal.

"No," Keith said, speaking for everyone. "If that's the case, then they don't wait until *after* the bust to kill him. They do it *during*. We've been through that already." You could hear the frustration in his voice; and we were just getting started.

"It doesn't hurt to repeat it," I said. "Sometimes the circumstances change your thinking. Or fresh evidence." I paused. "There's one situation where it's possible, though."

"What's that?" Kate asked.

"When all hell broke loose, Juarez hid out in that freezer without his people knowing it. He knows he's in jeopardy, so he hides and hopes either that the DEA will find him first, or no one will."

"Jesus, Luke, that's really pushing it," Kate said. "Besides, he would have come out when the shooting stopped. What's he going to do, wait in there until he freezes to death?"

"He wouldn't have known it was over," Louis pointed out. "You can't hear in there. Anyway, even if he could, how would he know his side lost? They had superior firepower, or thought they did, they usually do. What does it look like if he does come out and all his guys are waiting right by the door? What's he gonna say, 'I was looking for a Popsicle'?"

Everyone laughed; hollowly.

"I know it's a lame notion," I said, "but we have to examine all the possibilities, even if they're foolish and stupid. This is a bizarre case. We shouldn't assume anything is the way it ought to be, or normally is."

Louis interjected another wrinkle. "Did you hear they might file a lawsuit against the DEA for illegally raiding them?" he asked, his voice rising in weary indignation—this would not be the first time the bad guys sued the good guys for doing what their job description says they must do. "The warrants were issued for a drug deal, which there wasn't one, technically. Their lawyers are going to marshal a strong argument that the raid had no standing."

"Too bad the scumbags get the same rights as the good people, ain't it?" Keith said. "Better. They have better lawyers."

I nodded; I'd heard about that lawsuit. Why shouldn't they? They had nothing to lose. If some misguided judge let a motion like that in the door, there'd be more egg on the government's face. The bad guys become the good guys. Ruby Ridge all over again, with even less justification. Which were potentially the circumstances here. It was the reason Nora had brought me in, after all. We were still, essentially, at ground zero.

"If a DEA agent killed Juarez and we find evidence to support that, then we'll go to trial," I said, concluding the meeting. "Regardless of our personal feelings. If it was someone else, we'll prosecute that. Whoever we can find to prosecute," I said, spreading my arms wide, "we're going for it!"

They tried to muster laughter. It wasn't easy.

"Listen, people," I said. "If the Supreme Court, in its infinite wisdom, says a president of the United States can be criminally indicted for lying about getting a blow job, then a DEA agent sure as hell can be held to the same standards for killing an unarmed drug dealer. Even if he deserved it."

That evening Nora and I had dinner at her place. She asked; having kept her out of my loop I couldn't say no, even though I wanted to.

"How's your investigation going?" she asked. "Or shouldn't I ask?"

"Too early to tell anything. You know how that goes."

"Tom Miller told me you took his deposition and his deputy's."

I nodded.

"Does that mean they're in the clear?" She caught herself. "You're not supposed to discuss the case with me, are you?"

"You're right," I said, trying not to let her hound-dog look of supplication bother me. "But to answer you anyway, we did, and they are. I have to go by the book."

"Like talking to me? Or not? You're not going by the book now." She tried out a smile. It didn't work very well.

"We're friends, Nora. Friends are allowed to talk to friends."

"I agree. They should."

I sipped some wine. I was buying time, to try to figure out how to respond to this conversation.

Nora and I were old friends. We'd been in school together, an important time in people's lives. Having dinner, talking about work that was important to both of us, should have been not only allowable but natural, candid. And she was the lead player in this; she'd hired me. We should be talking about this case as much as she wanted to.

But I was holding back.

If Nora was Norman, a male friend from law-school days, it would be different. I'd be telling him whatever came to mind, even using him as a confidant, a partner. With Nora, I wasn't doing that. It wasn't that she was a woman and I was a man—many women lawyers are my friends, and I have easy, comfortable relationships with them when it comes to work, values, so forth.

My uneasiness was about need—her emotional need. The musk of it was in the air, nothing you could define or give an identity to, something ethereal out there, like air, unseeable, untouchable, but you know it's there, you breathe it in and out. I don't like the word *vibe*, it seems sixties antiquated, but that's what came to mind—there was a vibe between us.

The problem was that it was one way, from her to me. Under any circumstances that wouldn't have been good; in these, it wasn't only bad, it was dangerous. She was physically horny, I'm sure, but that wasn't the main ingredient. She was looking for warmth, closeness, and validation. And there was no one around to give it to her. Her husband was dead, a failure as a lawyer, non-father of children, almost everything. All her eggs had been in their little basket, and none of them had hatched. They were long gone now, withered and cracked and blown away in pieces. But her essence, her feminine drive, that was still alive.

She hadn't overtly said or done anything to confirm that my instincts were true, of course. She wasn't that foolish, or bold. But I knew they were. Which was why I was keeping her at arm's length, professionally as well as personally.

And yet here I was. I didn't know why I was doing this, except that she needed me. She needed my friendship, and I couldn't refuse it. Not back when she had phoned me out of the blue and asked me to come see her, not when she had inveigled me into her scheme to investigate this mess, not when she had done just about everything in her power to be a part of my life, if only tangentially, and not when she had come at me sexually; subconsciously, maybe, I didn't know, but it was there.

She was needy, and I was guilt-ridden. I had been up and down, but I had a great life now, and she had a crummy one. We had started out evenly, more or less. In fact, she'd had the advantage then, she was from a privileged background, she was a brighter star, she was associated with the brightest star, and together she and Dennis had the potential and clout to go further than any of her classmates. Instead, I, and most of the others in our class, had surged ahead of her; so that now, when she had this chance to regain some ground, I felt obligated to help her. To say no to her, to dash any slim hope she had of recapturing the dream, would have been an act of cruelty.

So I told her what we were doing. The interviews with Agent Kim and Lopez the informant and Curtis Jackson the rival drug kingpin, the concern among members of the team that this could be more complex and unsettling than any of us had initially thought.

By the time I was finished reciting my litany, we had finished dinner and were having what had become our ritual postprandial cognac in the living room. This time our bodies weren't touching, not even close. It was as if she sensed my uneasiness at that kind of proximity and was being careful not to violate my space.

"Do you still think there's a possibility someone other than a DEA agent could have shot Juarez?" she finally asked.

"I don't see how, but there must be. I'm worried," I told her, finally admitting it to myself.

"About what?"

"A conspiracy, what else?"

She nodded. "Yes," she agreed softly. "It's what I've always thought, Luke. Or at least felt was a possibility."

I sighed; I was tried. "I'm feeling the prosecutor blues. I haven't felt them in a long time—I haven't been a prosecutor in a long time, it's a hard switch to throw, it's like you have to flip your brain one hundred eighty degrees. You do defense lawyering, you develop a mentality against the system. Now I'm the system again, and I'm investigating the system."

"But if someone in the system commits a crime, haven't they forfeited their position in the system?"

The angels-dancing-on-the-head-of-a-pin argument was spinning inside my head: If the good guys do something bad while fighting the bad guys, is that at the same level of badness as the bad guys doing something bad? Is crime all black-and-white, or are there gray areas? Absolutist or situational?

"Of course. But if I wind up indicting a DEA agent for killing a man who everyone in the world knows was an evil bastard who deserved to die, I'm not going to be dancing in the streets."

"But what if it *was* premeditated? If there's something conspiratorial going down, then isn't that as bad as anything Juarez or any other criminal could do?"

She leaned over and touched me, her hand on mine. There was no sexual energy in the touch; it was one of a friend reassuring another friend. "You got into this because of those rogue cops you killed out in the desert, isn't that right?"

I nodded, my mind flashing back, the fear, rage, the blood pumping so hard I thought my heart would burst out of my chest.

"It's a good thing you did kill them. Because if you hadn't, *you'd* be dead," she declared bluntly. "Which supersedes any anxiety about going after rogues. So if this turns out like that, then isn't prosecuting and convicting the bastards the right thing to do? The only thing to do?"

What could I say? She was right. And she understood how I felt, trying to balance the tightrope-walking nexus of objective justice and subjective righteous retribution.

I hadn't been looking at her for real. I'd only seen the superficial trappings, some false front in my mind, not the person behind it. I had been thinking that the emotional protection was one-sided, me toward her. But it wasn't.

"You've got a great head on you for seeing through the bullshit, Nora." I almost felt like apologizing, but I didn't want to get into emotion, there was already too much of that. "I shouldn't try to fight that, because of some legalistic protocol. You definitely can help me."

"Thank you." Another quick touch, fingers to back of hand. "We can help each other, Luke. Whatever justice there is in this, we can find it, together."

She held out her hand. I shook it.

"Partners," she said. "To the end."

"Yes," I agreed with relief. "Partners."

IF YOU BUILD IT, THEY WILL COME

Wayne Bearpaw's mother, Louisa, was one of the elders of their tribe, the White Horse Nation. The term *nation* is a generous characterization of the tribe—there are less than five hundred members, for over a century there haven't been more than that, and they have never occupied more territory than they do at present, a thousand square miles situated in the most rugged, desolate part of the county.

Unlike her son and most of his generation, Louisa had never moved off the reservation. She'd traveled to various parts of the country, mostly on tribal business; she also enjoyed her vacations, primarily to Vegas and Reno, where she was an aficionado of the one-armed bandits and crap tables. But she had always made her home on the barren piece of land where she was born.

This was not to say Louisa was content with her life. About to turn sixty (she could easily pass for fifty; her long hair was still black, her figure strong and tight), she had fought long and hard for a better life for the members of her tribe. Better housing, better schooling, better medical care, programs to combat alcoholism and drug abuse, more jobs. She had been successful in all these endeavors, but to a degree that fell short of what she wanted, conditions that would make life on the reservation comfortable and enjoyable, rather than the past and still-current situation, which was having to work your ass off just to maintain the basics of life.

More than anything, they needed jobs, industry on the reservation, so the young people wouldn't have to leave it to have a decent life. Some money was available, from mineral-rights royalties, but that wasn't work. Having money's only half the struggle—jobs provide value, self-worth. She wanted jobs for her people, full employment within their own boundaries. Only then would they feel complete.

The infrastructure, as on most poor reservations, was derelict. The roads were terrible, even by Muir County standards; the public buildings, such as schools, fire stations, and so forth, were old firetraps. Reservation housing was crummy, but at least the structures had plumbing, electricity, natural gas, the basic amenities that have long been taken for granted in the rest of the country but hadn't been available on many reservations, including this one, until recently.

Many of these improvements had come about as a result of Louisa's tireless lobbying for them at the county, state, and most importantly, federal level. There's money out there and she works hard to get as much as she can for the tribe. Sylvan Furness, the regional BIA director in Sacramento, has her phone number on his speed-dial, that's how much they talk.

Which was where she was on a midweek spring morning, sitting in Furness's office with three other tribal leaders, two men and another woman, Mary Redfeather. They had driven down the night before in Louisa's Dodge Caravan, bunking with a member of the tribe who works here in the state capital as a field rep for State Fish & Game. Sometimes they stay in a cheap motel, but if they can save money, they do. The tribe's paying for this trip, which means it's their own money they're spending. Dinner had been takeout from Taco Bell and a six-pack of Tecate.

"Hey, you guys," Furness said, greeting the delegation in his outer office. He hadn't kept them waiting for more than a few minutes; Louisa gets on his case if she has to cool her heels. He's known her a long time now. Staying in her good graces makes life a lot easier and less complicated. Louisa has no qualms about firing off a fax or an E-mail to Washington, to the congressional committees on Native American affairs, to anyone she thinks can help.

"Hey, Sylvan," Louisa greeted him back, speaking for the group. She's a forceful speaker, she usually takes charge. "You got any good coffee around here?"

"How many?" he asked.

They all raised their hands. He took a twenty out of his wallet, handed it to his secretary.

"Get four coffees from Starbucks and some croissants," he instructed her. "Come on in." He waved his guests into his office.

A short while later, coffee and pastries in hand, they sat around his conference table. A letter on tribal stationery was in front of Furness.

"So," Furness said, initiating the conversation, "you want to buy that property adjacent to yours." He thumbed through the letter. "The one that belonged to that drug syndicate."

"We'd rather you outright gave it to us," Louisa said with a smile. Her compatriots smiled along with her. She tried the coffee—tasty. It's what she drinks at home, brewed up in a Krups coffeemaker. None of this supermarket-house-brand cowboy coffee crap for her, like her mother used to drink.

"What a stellar idea," Furness responded jovially. "Would you like us to throw in the California Water Project along with it?"

He liked bantering with Louisa. She was sharp and had a good sense of humor. For an older woman she was damn attractive, too. She was wearing a Mexican-style blouse and a skirt that showed off her bottom nicely, had her hair coiled up in a braid. Some turquoise and silver jewelry around her neck and wrists. None of the dumb squaw about this woman, she could make it anywhere.

"That's state," she joked back. "You don't control that. But that property we want is federal. That's yours."

"Technically," he explained, "the Justice Department's taken receivership of it, since the DEA confiscated it. Interior isn't involved. Seizing property isn't allowable for us. Wish it was."

She made a brushing-aside motion with her hand. "It all gets thrown into the same big pot. But anyways, you're right, we know no one's going to give it away, even though it doesn't have much value, being isolated up there in Muir County, which ain't nothin' but rednecks and redskins. We want to buy it, like our letter says."

"Where're you going to come up with the money, Louisa? The location might not be as great as some others, but it's a formidable piece of property. Some rich hunting type might want to buy it for a lodge type of scene."

"The money's for us to worry about. As far as some rich Anglo buying it, I don't see that. All the good hunting surrounding it is our property, reservation land. We're the logical party to buy it, Sylvan. You've got to agree with that."

He bobbed his head neutrally, but didn't say anything that could be construed as a commitment or even an endorsement.

Louisa pressed on. "What we want now is to know is this something we can talk about seriously? 'Cause we're serious, and I can't see anyone else being serious about it. Like I said, it's too far and gone."

Furness thought for a moment.

"It's a white elephant, Sylvan," Louisa continued. "Every month it sits out there unused, it costs the taxpayers money in upkeep. If it was me back there in Washington in charge of handling it, I'd want to get it off my hands as soon as possible. To the first serious bidder," she emphasized. "I'm sure the bean counters would agree with me." She made a mental note to fax her congressman when she got back to her office.

"Well . . . I'll have to find out what kind of price we're putting on it. *They're* putting on it," Furness amended quickly.

"Okay," she said, stealing a glance to the rest of the delegation. The tribe had gotten its foot in the door. That was the hardest part. Now it would be a question of negotiation.

"So getting back to my question," he said. "How is your tribe going to come up with the money to buy it? White elephant or not, it's pricey."

"Float a BIA loan, is what we'll try first. Cheap money."

The Bureau of Indian Affairs offered low-interest loans to tribes for capital investments. The more self-sufficient a tribe was, the less money the government had to shell out to keep them afloat. The tenet "the end of welfare as we know it" applied to reservations as well as the inner cities.

"You'd have to have a commercial use for it," Furness reminded them. "If it's so isolated up there as you claim—and I agree with you— how can you make money off it?"

Louisa leaned toward him, flashing a conspiratorial smile. "Gambling."

Furness rocked back in his chair. "Pretty far off the beaten track for gambling, isn't it?" he said tentatively.

"For a white man's hunting lodge it's isolated, that's true. But gamblers go where the action is. It already has the airfield, big enough to land jets."

"What if Prop. Five is declared unconstitutional?" Furness fretted. "You know there's going to be a constitutional challenge."

"So what?" Louisa said with an air of dismissal. "We'll go back on the ballot and change the constitution. People want gambling, Sylvan. And they want the Indians to have their shot—finally. Anyway, Governor Davis is on our side. He'll figure something out." She leaned toward him. "Don't worry, it's our problem. You take care of your end."

Furness was buffaloed. He didn't think a gambling casino would qualify for a BIA loan. On the other hand, if it was successful, it would take the tribe off the dole. Anytime a tribe could be weaned from the government's teat, Washington was happy, especially the congressional subcommittees that had to authorize the money, which always came grudgingly. "I don't know . . ."

"If they don't," Louisa told him with authority, "we'll find it. Maybe we can talk some of the rich tribes into kicking in. Indian power."

She smiled. Where they'd get the money from was none of nosy Uncle Sam's business. He'd been dictating to the original Americans for two hundred years now. Now they were fighting back, and winning.

"You really think you can make a go of gambling up there?"

She nodded. "It wouldn't only be gambling. Some of the best hunting in the country's on our reservation. We control that—no one can hunt our land without our permission. We could put together gambling and hunting junkets. Like going on safari in the Serengeti. It could be the new chic thing, Sylvan. And it would provide employment to our people on their land. That's the most important thing."

The tribe planned to bring another wrinkle into the mix, but Louisa wasn't going to mention it to any government official, even one she had an easy relationship with. The drug compound, and several miles of the reservation north of it, were flush up against the California/Nevada border. The corresponding Nevada county on the other side of the line, Bison County, offered legalized prostitution. She had surreptitiously discussed leasing a sliver of that land with some members of the Bison County supervisors' board and adding it onto the existing compound. A big hotel on the Nevada side of the border. A big whorehouse. Gambling and hunting in California, fucking in Nevada, all on private or Indian land, where neither the federal or state governments could touch them.

Furness thought about her proposal. Maybe it could work. He'd listened to wilder schemes. This woman was a powerhouse. If anyone could make it work, she could.

"Okay," he said. "Why not give it a try? I'll start getting the paperwork together."

Louisa leaned over and gave him a peck on the cheek. "Thanks, Sylvan. You're a good friend."

The others got up to leave. They all shook hands with Furness.

"This is a long shot," Furness cautioned as he walked them to his door. "Don't get your hopes up."

"We're Indians." Mary Redfeather said. She hadn't spoken a word until that moment. "We never get our hopes up."

"I didn't mean to imply it was hopeless," Furness corrected himself. "You have to try, right?"

They nodded in agreement.

"So." He had taken them as far as he could for now. "Why do you think this will work?"

Louisa Bearpaw gave him a sage, knowing look. "If we build it," she said, "they will come."

Juarez's former chief lieutenant, Filipe Portillo, a thin, pock-faced man in his late twenties, sat across from Kate Blanchard and me in a booth in El Sombrero, one of the stellar old Mexican restaurants in the heart of the east L.A. barrio. His lawyer had appealed the trial judge's denial of bail on the Muir County bust and had been successful. So Portillo was out now, awaiting his trial.

It was a warm day, dry, the sky light blue, cloudless. Two-thirty in the afternoon, the end of the lunch cycle. We were sitting on the patio behind the restaurant. Traffic from Whittier Boulevard could be heard cruising by, whomp-whomp mufflers. Portillo was wearing a white T-shirt, baggy khakis, Kobe Bryant high-tops. His sinewy arms sported numerous jail-house tattoos as well as a few legitimate ones, the most conspicuous a monstrous snake curling around his right biceps. A raven's bright black tailfeathers protruded from the snake's mouth, as if the rest of the hapless bird had already been devoured. There were some letters and numbers high up on his shoulder, gang ID, I presumed. A gold cross dangled from his left ear. A large plate of food—enchiladas, tacos, rice and beans, salad—sat in front of him. Portillo ate with gusto, rolling the beans up in tortillas, washing the food down with a Corona out of the bottle.

I drank iced tea; Kate was toying with her Coke straw. She had done a preliminary interview with Portillo and had set up this meeting. Neither of us had an appetite, either for the food or for the man sitting across the table from us. I was hoping he could shed some new light for me. He had been there alongside Juarez, the prisoner Sterling Jerome had questioned after the raid.

I could have brought Portillo up in front of the Muir County grand jury, but it would have been a waste of time and money. He didn't kill his boss—he'd been in handcuffs when Juarez had made his break. I was hoping to get something else from him: motive.

"The word on the street is you're the man now," I started out. I'd heard that from Kate, who had good sources.

He shrugged nonchalantly as if to convey through body language that what I'd said was true.

"My old lady thinks I'm the man," he said in a lightly accented voice. "You talking about something else, I don't know what that is."

"Your organization."

"I'm a carpenter, so you must mean my union. That's the only organization I belong to." Another shrug, followed by a tight smile.

I returned his smile with one of my own that was equally insincere. "You're sitting on two priors, ace. Another fall, you're buying twenty-five to life. That was me, I wouldn't be taking it lightly."

He shook his head slowly, almost mockingly. "Even the judge knows that bust was crap. He practically said so in open court. I had to cover my mouth to keep from laughing." He scooped up a forkful of enchilada, chewed with his mouth open. I noticed he needed dental work.

"What a judge thinks and what a good prosecutor can convince a jury of are two different things. Keep that in mind."

"I've got a good lawyer. I ain't worried."

"Whatever." I didn't want to engage him in a spitting contest. "There's another word on the street."

He waited for me to continue. I glanced over at Kate. She was enjoying the repartee.

"Your man Juarez was done in by one of his own."

"No fucking way." He took a long hit from his beer, wiped his mouth with the back of his hand.

"That's the skinny. And you know what that means."

"It ain't true, and I don't know what it means."

"Somebody's trying to pin the tail on the donkey." I smiled. "Guess who the donkey is."

He shook his head. "None of us killed Reynaldo, certainly not me." Another hit from his Corona. "You trying to play games with my head? Don't. It ain't gonna work, and you're gonna piss me off." He leaned in toward me. "You're gonna be needing me down the line, man. You're gonna need witnesses to what went down there. I'm happy to cooperate, 'cause I want whoever did that to pay for it. But you've got to treat me with respect. And talking a bunch of shit don't do that."

"Maybe. But I'm looking at this, I have to think, who benefits from

Juarez not being on the scene anymore? Who gets a bigger piece of the action? There's only one candidate, Filipe. That's you."

"No."

"Who else?"

"It don't work that way."

"Oh? How does it work?"

"First off, I'm not involved in whatever bullshit you think I'm involved in. Like I said, I'm a carpenter, journeyman union. That's all."

"All you're going to talk about."

"All, period."

I sat back. "All right. You're a journeyman carpenter, period. Let's talk theoretical, okay?"

He gestured at his plate. "You're buying my lunch. Talk theoretical all you want."

"Let's say—we're just hypothesizing here—there's an organization. Any organization. It makes a ton of money. And there's no taxes paid on it. It has a boss. He makes the most money. Maybe as much as thirty, forty percent of the profits. Everyone else gets the crumbs, the leftovers. You with me so far?"

"Uh-huh." He continued with his eating.

"The boss kicks off. Has a heart attack, gets hit by a truck, stops a nine-millimeter bullet at close range. However it happens, he's dead. What happens to that thirty or forty percent?" I smiled. "The ones that're left split it up. Isn't that how it would work? Hypothetically, of course."

"Maybe. I don't know."

"Or maybe a new boss would take over and rake it all in. You're Juarez's successor. You're the logical candidate."

He started to take another hit from his beer, then paused, his arm frozen in midlift. "You're trying to set me up, you motherfucker!" He slammed his bottle on the table.

"Like how?"

"You're trying to set me up for Reynaldo's killing, aren't you? What are you, trying to get *me* killed? You start spreading shit like that around, that is not healthy, man." He glowered at me. "And if I ain't healthy, I could think of other people who could get sick real easy. Terminal. You know?"

I glanced at Kate. She was listening intently. Later we'd play this back on the tape recorder she had hidden in her purse. Portillo had neglected to ask us if we were wired, and we hadn't mentioned it.

"How am I setting you up?" I asked. "We're talking hypothetically here, Filipe, aren't we? You're a journeyman carpenter, you're not involved with any drug organization. So what's the concern?"

He pushed his plate away—he'd lost his appetite. He was fidgeting now, and I was enjoying watching it. I knew Kate was, too.

"Rumors have a way of becoming facts," he said. "Especially in what I do."

"Pounding nails and sawing lumber?"

He turned away in disgust. Pointing at Kate, he said, "She told me anything we talked about here was between us. That it wouldn't be used against me."

"Like immunity?"

"Yes, like immunity."

I could feel the sun heating up on my back. I drank some of my iced tea.

"I can't offer you anything on that bust." I paused to let him twist a bit. "Although I could talk to the prosecutor. If you were cooperating with me on this one."

He snorted. "I ain't worried about that one. Like I said, it's crap, and I'm gonna beat it. I ain't worried about that."

"Then what?"

He started to answer me, then stopped.

"The rumors," I said. "That become facts."

He nodded. "The word starts circulating I set Reynaldo up, which I didn't do, I'm exposed. We were partners, I loved him like a brother. Help set him up? That's the last thing I'd ever do."

"I heard someone else say the same thing," I told him.

"Who?"

"Luis Lopez. Another one of your . . . carpenter friends."

He spat on the floor. "Fuck Luis Lopez and his family for ten generations," he growled. "That piece of dogshit is a dead man."

"If you can find him." The conversation was heading in the right direction now. "He's gone underground, what I hear."

"What am I, stupid? He's in the slam, where he's been since we were arrested. They're watching his bones like a hawk. But they can't watch him forever."

"He has too many enemies?"

Portillo nodded. "The world's his enemy."

"Inside as well as out."

"Definitely."

"I believe you," I said. "But you know what's interesting about that?" I glanced at Kate again. We were getting somewhere now. I'd opened the trapdoor, and he had accommodated us by entering.

"What?"

"That Lopez and all the rest of your people are inside, but you aren't."

He looked at me with a funny look, like he was starting to get the picture, but couldn't see all of it. Yet.

"I have a good lawyer. He got me out."

"What about the rest of your friends that didn't get out? Don't they have good lawyers?"

He could feel the door close behind him.

"They have good lawyers. They . . . didn't take care of their business, like I did."

"Do you know how lame that sounds?" I challenged him.

"I don't know and I don't give a fuck," he said. "What's that supposed to mean?"

"Nothing to me. But if I were one of your friends still locked up inside, eating bologna sandwiches and drinking Kool-Aid instead of sitting out in the sunlight in the free world chowing down on good food and beer, I'd think about my man Filipe making bail, when everyone else is denied . . . I'd be wondering about that." I clapped my hands together loudly. He jumped. "I'd be thinking really hard about that, Filipe!"

He slumped back. "Those DEA fuckers are setting me up, aren't they? They killed Reynaldo and they've got to have a scapegoat."

I cocked a finger at him. "Could be. Wouldn't be the first time they set someone up, would it?"

He shook his head. "It ain't gonna work."

I laughed. I didn't have to fake it. "You don't sound like you're convinced."

"I wasn't involved. That's fucking ludicrous." He was heavily on the defensive now.

"Does that matter? When rumors have a habit of becoming facts?"

He stalled for time by pulling a pack of Marlboros out of his pants pocket, fishing one out, lighting up. "I didn't set Reynaldo up." He exhaled. "Anybody that knows me and him knows that."

"Oh? And how do they know that, Filipe?"

He looked away for a moment. Lunchtime was over now; we were the only ones left on the patio. He tilted his beer bottle back, but it was empty.

"How?"

"Reynaldo was the leader," he said, finally admitting the truth. "You don't kill your main man and survive very good."

I flashed to Keith's interview with Curtis Jackson. Jackson had said the same thing.

"Reynaldo was our meal ticket. Why would we want to do in the man who was making us all rich?"

"You wouldn't, if that's how it worked." I turned to Kate, who nodded. We were in agreement. "So what they're saying on the street is wrong."

He looked at me.

"You're not the man. You're just a foot soldier."

"I'm more than a foot soldier," he said, unable to not show his wounded pride.

"You're not the man."

"No," he finally admitted. "The man is dead."

Portillo's burgundy Infiniti Q45 was parked in front of the restaurant in a handicapped space, a parking ticket on the windshield. He extracted it from under the wiper blade, ripped it up, dropped the pieces in the gutter.

"You'd better watch your ass, Filipe," I cautioned him.

He looked up and down the street, trying to play it casual. "What do you give a shit for?"

"I don't care if you live or die, ace," I told him candidly. "The more scumbags like you aren't on the street, the safer it is for the decent people. But I may need you as a witness later on. So until then, don't be careless."

"Hire a bodyguard," Kate advised him. "If you haven't already."

He shook his head. "My people know I'm clean." He didn't sound convincing—to us or, I was sure, to himself. He got into his chariot and drove off into traffic.

Kate and I walked down the block to her car. We were driving back to Santa Barbara. We wanted to get going to avoid the heavy rush-hour traffic on the westbound Ventura Freeway.

"What did we learn?" I asked her, as she pointed us toward the northbound Interstate 5. "That we didn't know already?"

She shook her head. "Nothing, really."

"We need to know more about Juarez. He's the key, not his minions. What his life was, who he was connected to. Maybe we can find a common thread through all this."

"I'm already on it," she assured me.

I relaxed in the passenger seat. It was nice having someone else drive. "Portillo didn't kill Juarez, we know that." I was thinking out loud. "And I don't believe he was part of a setup to do it. It was humiliating for him to admit to us that Juarez was the cock of the walk and he was just another chicken in the barnyard. A man like him doesn't fess up to that unless there's no way around the truth of it."

"Or else he's way smarter than I think he is, and he's trying to fake us out."

We were inching up the freeway ramp. It was going to be a long trip home. At least I wasn't driving. Even when L.A. traffic isn't at its worst, it's terrible.

"He isn't."

Portillo may have been a good lieutenant, but he was no leader, he had no imagination and not enough ruthlessness in him, one meeting with him told me that.

"He's being used. Which he knows, and he's scared about it. We need to keep an eye on him, for his own good as well as ours." I looked out at the sea of cars surrounding us. It felt like every vehicle in America was on this freeway. "I'm getting the feeling we're all being used."

"By who?"

"I don't have a clue. Whoever would benefit, and I don't know where that goes, yet. Maybe I'm overly suspicious—you can get paranoid real easy when you're dealing with characters like these."

I pulled out my cell phone to call Riva and tell her I'd be late for dinner—we weren't going to beat the traffic, it was going to beat us, which was too bad, since this was one of the few weekday nights I'd be home for the next several months. Riva would understand, but she wouldn't be happy. Me, neither.

"But if we are being manipulated," I continued, "whoever's orchestrating it is connected to Reynaldo Juarez's killer."

Wheeling, West Virginia, has never been on my must-visit list of American cities. But when you take on an investigation like this one, you get to go to places you never imagined you would (and don't care if you never did). Nothing against Wheeling, or West Virginia as a whole, but it's down the list, after China, Tahiti, Prague, and about everywhere else I can think of, even Disney World.

Unfortunately for me, Sterling Jerome hadn't been posted to any of those exotic locales. He had been exiled to Siberia, or the closest equivalent the Justice Department could send him to. A one-man office, with nothing to do and all the time in the world to do it in.

I sat in Jerome's office, which wasn't even in a federal complex; the DEA had rented the office from the state—they didn't have a regular presence in the region. There are drugs available in the area, of course, there are drugs everywhere in America, but not at the level that is worth spending government money on.

This was a newly created office, an artificial post, because regulations prohibited them from firing Jerome—there's something to be said for civil service protection, by those protected by it. The twelve-by-twelve cubicle, four windowless walls, was in the basement. Above ground was the Department of Motor Vehicles. I doubted that any of those people, busy issuing driver's licenses and vehicle registrations, knew they had a DEA big shot in their midst. Former big shot.

It was a dismal spot, a little rabbit warren stuck in a big Dilbert-like maze.

Jerome was on the phone. It sounded to me, listening to his end of the conversation, that he was talking to a woman, probably his wife, who, I knew, had not forayed to this remote spot with him, but had remained in Los Angeles. It wasn't a happy conversation. Apologetic, wheedling, angry. As I watched him, I thought of Sheriff Miller, almost a continent away in Blue River. Like Jerome, he had been exiled to nowheresville when he was in his prime. Each was the other's shadow nemesis now, but the parallelism of their unfortunate circumstances, although separated by almost four decades, was almost karmic.

I couldn't imagine Jerome seeing his circumstances that way, should I point them out to him—which I wouldn't, of course. Being compared to Miller would be the straw to break his back, if it hadn't been already.

He ended the discussion by slamming the phone down on his battleship-gray, government-issue metal desk, whose paint was peeling. The desk, and the other few pieces of furniture in the room—bookshelves, file cabinets, coatrack—looked as if they'd been requisitioned from storage, where they'd been buried under a thick layer of dust for years. Then he looked up at me.

"Thanks for seeing me," I said, trying to be pleasant. I sipped at my cardboard container of take-out coffee from the commissary. It was tepid.

"I didn't have a choice," he said not curtly but forthrightly. "Orders from above." He meant Washington, not the first floor of this building. "You would've dragged me back to Blue River otherwise."

"Thanks anyway." I didn't want to be this man's enemy. He already had enough of them.

"So," he said, staring at me, "what do you want?"

"I want to know who murdered Reynaldo Juarez, of course."

"How the hell should I know?"

I had decided before interviewing Jerome that I'd be as civil and agreeable as possible. Given his fall from grace, and the stories of his arrogance and ill-temper, returning his wrathful attitude with one of my own would subvert my goal. Besides, that kind of short-fused behavior turns me off, especially in myself. Calm is a potent weapon.

"Because you were there, you were in charge, it was your operation, Juarez was in your custody, he escaped from your custody, and he was killed by someone who was out there that night, most probably under your command, regardless of the spin your agency's putting on it. So logically, I think you should have some ideas about it."

Curtly he replied, "Read the DEA material. The Shooting Incident Report and the OPR summary. It's all in there."

"I have. It doesn't answer my questions. I wouldn't have trekked across the country otherwise."

"It's all the answers I have, pal. I can't make any up."

"I'm not asking you to do that."

"Then what do you want?" he threw at me a second time, his tone insinuating that I was either hard of hearing or feebleminded.

"Maybe you can remember some things you didn't before," I suggested. "Now that you've had time to think about it." I looked around his space—with only two of us occupying it, it felt cramped. Add another body and it would have been downright uncomfortable.

He shook his head. "No, I can't."

"Or won't?"

He looked like he wanted to come over the desk at me. He restrained himself, but I could see how his hot temper and impetuousness got him into trouble. He was an act-before-you-think kind of guy. Which was why he was rotting here in purgatory.

"Can't," he repeated, spitting out the word.

I placed my hands on his desk. "You've dug a grave for yourself, Mr. Jerome." I kept my voice low, evenly modulated, unthreatening. "But the dirt hasn't been thrown over you yet. You still have a chance for redemption."

He shook his head. "No," he said flatly. "I don't."

"You sure?"

He nodded. "Absolutely."

"Why?"

He indicated his cramped space. "Look around you. If this isn't a coffin, I don't know what is."

I didn't have to look around. I was in it, I could feel it. Certainly spending eight hours a day cooped up in here would offer one a powerful preview of eternity in a box.

"Look," I started over, "if you didn't kill Juarez—"

"I didn't," he shot back at me.

I leaned forward, toward him.

"Look, man," I beseeched him, "I'm trying to help you, okay? Not for you, for me. I want to get to the bottom of this. An important government witness was murdered. That didn't help you. You know that better than me or anyone else. There's two keys to this—you and Juarez. He's dead, so he's no good to me. But you're not. You help me, Jerome, you're helping yourself."

I didn't know if what I'd said was true. Regardless if I indicted, brought to trail, and convicted Juarez's killer, it might not help Jerome at all. He had been in charge, he had authorized a raid he shouldn't have, it had turned to shit on his watch. He was responsible for the government's losing someone they didn't want to lose, as well as some of his own. Still, I figured his vanity, pride, or anger toward his bosses could be appealed to and used.

He sat back, as if the effort of remonstrating with me had drained him.

"I wish I could," he said, his voice calmer now, washed of the bile he'd been spewing. "But I don't know how. I'm fucked, that's all there is to it."

He got up, started pacing the tiny confines. He couldn't go more than three steps in any direction, but he was full of pent-up energy, he couldn't sit still—I'd unleashed him from physical dormancy. "If you knew how much thought I've put into this . . ."

He hesitated a moment. It was hot in the small room; there was no thermostat, he had no control on the temperature. I stood, took off my jacket, loosened my tie, sat back down again. He was primed now, ready to let out whatever he'd been holding in the past six months.

"What happened that night destroyed my career. I was doing really well, I'm sure you know that. But that was an anchor, I'm dead now, dead in the water. All of us who participated that night are. Our careers are finished, none of us will ever move up. If we're lucky, we'll ride it out in places like this until we qualify for our pensions." He grimaced. "They can't fire all of us. It would make them look like shit. They just do this instead." He indicated his cubicle.

"You were all cleared."

He waved my disclaimer off. "Yeah, we were cleared. Technically. But not in the minds of the wheels up high. We disgraced the organization. After all the other fuckups of the past decade, this was the final straw. There's a stench to this that is not going to go away. We can't be cleared of that." He gripped the top of his desk chair, his fingers turning white with the pressure. "I should resign, it's what they want, but I don't want to give the bastards the satisfaction." He let go his death grip on the chair, walked the three steps to the other end of the room behind his desk, turned back to me.

"I lost good men that night. They died because I led them into dubious battle. That's a sword that's going to hang over my head the rest of my life. As it should," he added quickly. "I was responsible, and I take full responsibility."

Another pause—he was thinking of how to say what he wanted me to hear, clearly.

"I don't know who killed Juarez. But believe me, I want to find out as badly as you do, Mr. Garrison. Worse. To you, this is another case. But to me it's my life, my career. I owe it to my friends who died that night to find out. That's the most important thing."

I hadn't said anything during this explosion of emotion. Now I asked the question, the same one I'd asked earlier, putting it differently this time. "Thinking back. Are you positive none of your men were involved in this murder?"

He started to say something, didn't, turned away, tuned back to me. "No."

The air went out of the balloon with an audible whoosh.

"No, I'm not."

As if purged by this admission, he sat back down.

"I'm not positive. I don't think so, I can't imagine one was, but I couldn't swear to it." He leaned forward. "But—saying I'm not a hundred percent positive one of my people didn't do it doesn't mean I think that one of them did. I don't. I'm saying it isn't impossible."

"Then you must agree with the findings of the investigation. That someone associated with Juarez or his gang killed him."

"Or more likely, a rival."

"Someone who infiltrated his group?"

"It's very possible. We did it."

"Lopez. I know."

"If we could, a rival gang could, too."

More than one turncoat among Juarez's close inner circle? Others had voiced that theory, but it still felt far-fetched to me. Maybe I needed to look at it more closely.

"You *want* to find out," he said again. "I *have* to."

"I'm going to." I stood and put my coat back on. I'd gotten as much as I wanted, for now. The next time we talked it would be in Blue River, in front of my grand jury.

"Can I help?"

His question caught me by surprise. "How?"

"With your investigation. I want to help."

I shook my head. "You're the one who's being investigated, remember?"

"You think I did it?" he asked incredulously.

"It doesn't matter what I think. You're still under investigation. Everyone who was there that night is under investigation." I waited a beat. "*My* investigation."

He nodded, stealing a glance around the enclosure like the walls had ears. They might have; I hoped not.

"Don't worry," he said, reading my mind. "I have this place swept weekly. I still have buddies in D.C. who want to see me weather this shit-storm. It's only a three-hour drive. Although it might as well be a million, as far as the power train goes." He plucked at his starched white dress shirt, sticking to his body. "What I was going to say was, I know that technically I'm under investigation, by you. But I can help you. You're going to come across names of people and organizations I'll know more about than you ever can. You could wind up stumbling over the killer and not knowing it—but I would. If I knew what you were doing."

I didn't want to deal with this. Not now. "I'll think about it," I told him. "We'll see."

He came around the side of the desk, so that we were face-to-face, inches apart.

"This is my life, Garrison," he implored me. "Don't cut me out like the pricks in Washington did. I didn't want Juarez dead. That night ruined my career. My marriage, everything."

I backed away from him—this was too intense, too personal. That call from his wife that I'd eavesdropped on could have been her telling him she had hired a divorce lawyer. That's one of the worst calls a man can get; I know, I got one myself once.

"You want this," he beseeched me again. "But man—this is my life. I *need* it."

The Streets of East L.A.

Reynaldo Juarez entered the United States under the wire east of San Diego when he was two years old. He was the baby; he came with his mother, father, five older brothers and sisters. His father carried him wrapped up in a shawl, pressed close to his body, the two tied together with clothesline. The smell of his father's body, combined with that of the dirt they crawled over for hours too many to count, the stomach-wrenching stench of rotting food left behind by previous groups combined with that of human excrement that clung to them like a second skin, plus the fear sweat from the dozens of Mexican men, women, and children who were in their group, was one of his first and most indelible memories. That and the gleaming red eyes of the thousands of rats who inhabited their dark passage and took bites out of some of them. One of his sisters died from rat-bite poisoning less than forty-eight hours after they had reached the promised land; for the rest of his life, Reynaldo Juarez lived in deathly fear of rats.

At least they hadn't been robbed, murdered, or raped, the fate of many wetbacks he later met when he was growing up in east L.A., some of whom became lifelong friends and members of his gang. That his own people would prey on others when they were in a hopeless situation was also part of his memory bank. After he was grown, and rich, he helped bring many Mexicans to the United States, especially those from his home region high in the central mountains, and he made sure they were treated decently on their journey.

The first man he killed, when he was in his midteens and already an established dealer and supplier, rich enough at sixteen to buy his parents a nice house in Tustin and himself a Jaguar convertible, suites in Vegas, and expensive hookers, was a coyote who had savagely raped two young girls during a crossing, while their parents and others who were with them had to stand by helplessly and watch. The girls were not even old enough yet to have started their monthly bleeding. One of Juarez's closest friends, a cousin of the girls', went crazy with anger and vengefulness when he was informed of the atrocity. The cousin and Juarez had crossed the border to Tijuana, tracked the coyote down, abducted him from his house, and brutally tortured him for hours, before slitting his throat with a dull knife and leaving the body to rot within sight of the border, a clear signal to other smugglers who were disrespectful of their less fortunate brothers and sisters that they must behave around Reynaldo Juarez's family and friends, a large and extended group, or face a similarly grisly demise.

That was an honorable killing, as murders go; others he committed or authorized—of opposing gang leaders, members of rival drug cartels, cops who got in his path—were not. He was a ruthless businessman who did whatever he had to do to sell his product, an outlaw known and feared in his subculture, his community, and by law officers of every stripe. In the end, nobody wept when he died, except for his family and the others in his organization. His family cried because he was blood; the others, because he was money.

From the time the investigation started, Kate had been trying to trace Juarez's life, from his distant past to his recent death. She had learned that the boy who had entered his adopted country tied to his father's chest, stinking of human shit and Big Macs, had made it big, a modern version, in the barrios and ghettos, of a success story: he was a multimillionaire, paid taxes on almost none of his earnings, lived like a rajah, and had never been convicted of a major crime. That he had never spent a night in jail as an adult was part of his legend, because his nefarious exploits were no secret to anyone—his slipperiness in avoiding the arm of the law was a huge thorn in law-enforcement agencies' sides nationwide. Accordingly, what had happened in Muir County was a source of great, if clandestinely acknowledged, satisfaction to the police; Sterling Jerome was a hero to them, fuck the bureaucrats and the horses—make them asses—they rode in on.

All these elements, the fear and adulation in the barrio, along with the hate toward Juarez in the police forces, were making Kate's task more difficult than it already was, which was plenty difficult by itself. Jaurez was like a Latino Howard Hughes. He had houses scattered all over—besides the lodge in Blue River, he owned lavish estates in Los Angeles, Las Vegas, even a villa on the coast of Spain—but hardly anyone ever knew where he was at any particular time, whether he was sleeping in one of his own beds or was on the move, living in hotels under assumed names. His official residence was his L.A. home on St. Cloud Drive in Bel Air, close to the Bel Air Hotel and Bel Air Golf Club. The proximity to those elite establishments seemed to mean nothing to him; to the best of anyone's knowledge, he had never played golf and had not taken a meal in the hotel restaurant or used any of their facilities.

Which is not to say he didn't; it's that there wasn't anything on record to substantiate that. He kept a low profile, he didn't hobnob with movie stars or famous jocks, like gangsters of an earlier era. It was rumored that welterweight boxing champ Oscar De La Hoya was a friend, that the two had hung out at Juarez's home to shoot pool, sweat in the Jacuzzi, and screw beautiful women by the carload, but that was one more rumor that couldn't be confirmed, and De La Hoya's people flatly denied it.

There was one gaping hole in his personal history. From the ages of eighteen to twenty-one, it was a complete blank. It was rumored—another rumor, there were hundreds of rumors about Juarez, many more rumors than known facts—that he had lived in Europe or the Middle East. That he had studied Tibetan Buddhism in a remote mountaintop monastery in northern India. That he had tried to go straight and bought a Honda dealership in Houston. That he was married to a WASP socialite from New England and had children with her.

All, some, or none of these stories might have been true. No one had been able to track any of them down—it was as if Juarez had dropped off the face of the earth for that period. What was known was that after living under the radar for several years he had surfaced in his hometown, Los Angeles, and almost immediately thereafter became the leader of a major drug organization, moving millions of dollars of product a month into the streets. And that he'd done this, overcoming all opposition, for the rest of his life, almost two decades.

Kate was looking for connections. People who had known Juarez and could be linked to his most recent drug operations; competitors who wanted him gone; confederates who felt they had been fucked over and wanted to bring him down; people in law enforcement, like Jerome and countless others, who were sick of Juarez getting away with murder, literally, and who might have gotten to someone close to him, either through bribery, threats, or appeals to masculine pride, which runs deep in Latino culture. She was also trying to reach out to family members and close friends who wanted to know who had killed their shining light. So they could take revenge.

It had been difficult getting people to talk. No one in law enforcement would, for the record. They were all glad the bastard had been taken out, but they didn't know anyone who had tried to do it or tried to recruit someone with access to Juarez. All the cops knew about the DEA investigation and its conclusions and were loath to publicly criticize a sister agency, even if it was one they often feuded with. The best anyone would say, strictly not for attribution, was that Jerome, more than almost anyone else in the entire world, had a raging hard-on for Juarez, that he had consecrated his life to capturing him. Everyone Kate talked to, from LAPD beat cops and sheriff's deputies up to captains and chiefs, as well as several FBI agents, believed that Jerome would gladly have killed Juarez and thrown his remains to the buzzards if he hadn't been under orders not to; it was also sworn to, emphatically, that Jerome was honorable, that he would not place himself above the law and above his orders.

Not one gang member—Latino, black, Aryan, Asian—would talk to her. The only person who had spoken for attribution was Curtis Jackson, to Keith Green. That had been brother to brother, and it had been for a purpose, to confuse and fuck with the investigators' heads; so Luke thought, and she was inclined to go along with that, having known and dealt with a lot of Curtis Jacksons.

Louis, being Latino, talked to members of the family and a few close friends, those who dared talk to him. Wary conversations, almost no meat on the bones. Although Louis was an *hermano*, he was also a cop. They wanted to know who did it, but they had no idea who, so they said. They all swore that his "associates," as they characterized the other members of his inner circle, would never have betrayed him. He was good to them, like a father, even though he was not an old man, younger than some of them. These associates were all rich because of Reynaldo's industriousness (no one admitted that his organization was a criminal gang that brutalized people, murdered opponents and innocents alike, and caused massive hardship) and would not speak against their leader.

"They're scared to talk," Kate said.

It was the end of what had been a long and basically fruitless day for Kate and Louis. They sat in a rear booth in El Coyote on Beverly Boulevard in Hollywood, drinking tall margaritas and eating chips with salsa and guacamole. Kate loaded up a blue-corn tortilla chip with guacamole and ingested the whole affair in one big bite.

"Yummy." She looked around. "This is a great place, Louis."

"They've been here forever," Louis told her. "My dad used to take me as a kid. Across the river, the great divide."

When Louis was a boy, growing up in the fifties, east L.A. had been home. Crossing the L.A. River was a big deal then. Now Los Angeles is Hispanic all over, from the desert to the sea.

"You want to eat dinner here?" he asked, reaching for a menu. "Or do you have to drive home tonight?"

He wasn't hitting on Kate; they're friends, colleagues, even though, in her early forties, she's a very attractive woman. He knows that she's long been divorced from a former cop up in Oakland who was tossed off the force for abusing her, a real prick. She won't try marriage again, not in the foreseeable future, anyway.

He's divorced, too. It goes with being a cop, he guesses, so many of his friends who were on the force with him are, but he has a nice girlfriend his age, a paralegal with one of the big downtown firms. He's too old to stray, not when he has a good thing going. Male cops have been partnered up with female cops for so long now, because of affirmative action and similar minority-supporting programs, that the male/female arrangement is taken for granted. You can do the job or you can't, sex doesn't come into play that much. A good thing, Louis thought. In the old days, office romances killed a lot of marriages that weren't that bad.

"I'm staying over. I booked a room in Santa Monica."

"You like the beach?" He signaled for a waitress.

"Yep. It's cooler down there, and I can get up in the morning and run before starting up work."

The waitress took their orders. Kate ordered a combo plate—after a tough day in the field, she was ravenous. Louis, a big man with a waistline problem, opted for a fish dinner, hold the beans.

"Are we getting anywhere?" Louis asked. He liked this job; the pay was good, ditto the players, but it was frustrating not knowing exactly what you were looking for. This wasn't like regular detective work, interviewing witnesses, taking depositions, tracking down husbands or wives who had flown the coop, etc. Reynaldo Juarez was a spook, a phantom. Trying to find out who he was connected to in relation to this case, if in fact there was any connection, a dubious prospect, was turning out to be a study in exasperation.

His not to wonder why, not at 125 dollars an hour plus full expenses. Still, he liked to produce results. He knew Kate felt the same.

The waitress put their plates down in front of them. "Everything okay?" she asked pleasantly.

"Smells great," Kate told her with a smile.

She turned back to Louis. "We're eliminating all the blind alleys and dead ends," she said, attacking her food with gusto. Catching the waitress before the woman was out of earshot: "Can I have a beer, please? Bohemia, if you've got it."

"Make it two," Louis said. He tried a bite of his fish—delicious, sautéed in garlic and oil, just the way he liked it. "We're going to eliminate until there's nothing left to eliminate and we'll be left with a cloud of smoke and a hearty 'Hi-yo, Silver.' "

"If so, then we'll have done our best. If the needle isn't in the haystack, you can't find it, can you?"

"I never have."

They finished their meal. Kate paid the check, tucking the receipt into her purse, next to her Glock 17.

Outside in the parking lot, they discussed plans for tomorrow. Louis was heading back to east L.A., to try to mine for nuggets among the few friends of Juarez's they hadn't contacted yet. He didn't expect he'd have much luck—the Chicano community had closed their doors to the investigation.

"What about you?" he asked Kate, getting into his Seville. He was an American-car man, always had been. The Caddy suited him—big, smooth, comfy on the freeways.

"Keep looking for connections. See if there's something out there we've missed."

"Good luck."

"See you."

"See you."

Louis headed east on Beverly. Kate drove the opposite direction, toward the ocean.

I was going to have dinner with Nora to tell her about my trip to West Virginia, Jerome's anguish over the disaster and its effect on his career and life, fill her in on what my detectives were pursuing, which wasn't encouraging, so far.

She met me at the door to her house in a terry-cloth robe. "You're early," she said.

"I knocked off early. I'm in a holding pattern."

"I was going to take a swim," she said. "Care to join me?"

It had been a sweltering spring day, muggy for the area. I was in my normal working clothes, feeling hot and clammy. There was still plenty of light in the sky at seven in the evening.

"A swim would be nice, but I don't have a suit with me."

She squinted against the low late-afternoon sun over my shoulder, appraising my physique. "One of Dennis's old ones ought to fit you," she declared. "I'll forage for it. It's stuck away somewhere. Come on in."

I followed her into the house. It was nice and cool—the air-conditioning was on, humming low.

"All this and a pool, too?"

She smiled. "The pool, the Jacuzzi, the whole shooting match."

She led me out onto her rear patio. I'd never seen her property before, I'd always been here after dark.

Before the tree line, there was an impressive yard. A hundred yards square, at least. Most of it was grass, freshly mowed, almost as manicured as a putting green. Flower beds were strategically placed, giving the area a smart, sophisticated feeling, as nice as many of the fancy properties I'd been on in Montecito. Closer to the house there was a long, narrow lap pool with a beautiful tile deck, a large barbecue area, and off to the side, a Jacuzzi, built into a fieldstone deck.

She turned to me. "Let me get that suit of Dennis's for you. Be right back."

Kate lounged on her queen-size bed at the Shangri-La in Santa Monica, browsing through the latest edition of *People* magazine. She liked the old art deco hotel. The rates were half those of the Miramar up the street, and it was right on Ocean Avenue, a good location. She could walk along the bluff overlooking the ocean at night, run it in the morning.

The missing years of Reynaldo Juarez. Where were they?

She'd already checked on the military and the prisons. As far as she could find out, he hadn't been in the service, and he hadn't served time in any jail—county, state, or federal. He had a passport—she'd checked that out, too. Foreign travel before he turned eighteen, to central and South America. Then lots of forays outside the country after he was twenty-two, dozens of trips to Colombia, Equador, and Honduras alone, plus other South American countries, as well as Europe, the Far East, Australia, Egypt, Israel. He seemed to love to travel; often he went by private plane. Planes used to transport drugs, she surmised, but there wasn't any product on those planes when he was. That was one of his survival secrets: he was never directly involved in a transaction, never in immediate contact with anything illegal. There were always buffers between him and his deals, multiple screens. The deal up in Blue River would have been one of the few exceptions.

What do people do between the ages of eighteen and twenty-one? She had been working then, a young mother trying to make ends meet. She had been the exception in that regard; most of her friends, like her daughters, went to college. Of course, where Juarez came from, college wouldn't be commonplace. A kid would have to be motivated to go to college from one of the east L.A. high schools.

Restless, she put her magazine aside and perused the *TV Guide*. Nothing worth watching.

College. That would be a long shot. How many colleges are there in the state of California alone, a hundred? Juarez was already a money-making machine by the time he was in his midteens. By then he knew what his path was, and it didn't include learning about Plato or calculus or going to Friday-night fraternity parties. Still, the ages when he was off the charts are when people go to college.

He had actually graduated from high school—Garfield, one of the biggest high schools in the country, almost one hundred percent Latino. She wondered what the percentage was of kids going to college from Garfield High, twenty years ago. That would be a place to start. It would be tedious, time-consuming work, but she might as well give it a try, she had no other leads to chase.

She checked the movie listings for the Third Street Promenade theaters. There were a couple playing she thought she could tolerate. If not, she'd have a drink in one of the restaurant bars. Or two. She could use a bracer, in anticipation of what faced her as soon as she got up in the morning—driving all the way over to east L.A. at the height of rush-hour traffic, then starting to slog through old college records (if that hunch had any legs), then driving home, again facing rush hour.

Tomorrow was going to be a long, long day. Screw the movies—she was going to treat herself to a tall, cold drink.

I emerged from Nora's house wearing one of Dennis's baggy old swimsuits. He had put on weight in the years after he left law school; I remembered him as a thin man, but the waist on this baggy old suit was at least a forty. Although I had the drawstrings pulled as tight as I could, it still hung loose around my waist.

Nora, wearing a dark blue tank suit, was already in the pool, swimming laps. She had good form. I remembered she'd been a swimmer in college, as I'd been—one of the first things we'd found out about each other those initial weeks in law school, something in common to grow a friendship on.

I joined her, essaying an easy crawl. I missed the ocean; I made a mental note to take Buck down to Butterfly Beach when I went home over the weekend.

We swam for fifteen or twenty minutes, then we climbed out and toweled off. The sun was almost down now. Nora went inside and came back with an open bottle of wine in an ice bucket, two glasses, and a plate of cheese and crackers. We sat in lounge chairs by the pool, sipping the wine. It was still hot out—our suits were dry in less than ten minutes. I told her what was happening with my investigation, which wasn't much.

"We're not getting anywhere." She sounded depressed.

"It's early in the game. We have to be patient."

"Maybe the DEA was right after all." She didn't sound happy voicing that.

"Isn't our objective finding out who the killer is? We're not looking to pin it on the agency, are we? Wouldn't you be happier if it *wasn't* a DEA agent?"

"Why should I be?" She almost snapped at me.

"Because they're the good guys."

"They weren't the good guys that night."

"Look, Nora. Don't let bad experiences you've had with them or other big agencies cloud your judgment. People make mistakes. In that job, it's a given."

"They make too many damn mistakes."

"How long are you and Sheriff Miller going to carry this grudge against them?"

"Tom isn't carrying a grudge anymore. He lets bygones be bygones."

"But you don't."

She nodded. "I can't help it. I don't like being treated like the village idiot in my own backyard. I know that's childish and vindictive, but . . ."

"I can understand that. No one does. But you're going to have to get over it, starting now. This can't be a grudge match, some Hatfield-McCoy wingding."

She sighed. "You're right. As usual."

We went inside and had dinner—steak, potatoes, salad. She'd scrounged up an old bathrobe of Dennis's for me—we were still in our now-dry bathing suits. It felt kind of funny, wearing her dead husband's clothes, but I didn't dwell on it. We finished off the white wine with the salad and had a bottle of red with the steak.

After we were done eating, she stacked the dishwasher and turned it on. "I'm going to have a hot tub. Care to join me?"

I turned to her with an uneasy look. She laughed, as if reading my mind.

"I'm not stripping down in front of you, Luke Garrison. Not with this middle-aged body. I'm keeping my bathing suit on. And so are you, guy," she said, almost giggling schoolgirlishly.

"Sounds . . . okay." My earlier concerns about her intentions toward me seemed silly, unfounded. "I have to use the john, then I'll join you."

It was dark when I came back outside. Nora had turned on a few outdoor lights. She was already lounging in the hot tub up to her neck, her hair pulled up over her head in a casual bun. "Come on in slow-poke," she called to me merrily as I tentatively approached the edge. "The water's steaming. I hope you like it hot."

"Hot's good."

I stuck a toe in. Hot it was. We'd be lobsters in a few minutes. I eased into the tub, bit by bit. Then, submerged to the bottom of my chin, the bubbles foaming around my chest, I looked up at the dark sky, the countless stars in the firmament that you only see in outlying areas like up here. Man's light can't compete with these, I thought contentedly.

I closed my eyes, laid my head against the wall of the tub, and let the evening take me away: the steamy, bubbling water, the infinity of stars overhead—I was becoming spacey, my mind drifting off, not sleeping, but as in a half-wakening dream state.

Her hand was on my cock, under the baggy trunks.

This was not a dream. My eyes popped open.

She was naked. Her abundant breasts, the nipples fat and pink like a baby's fingers, grazed my arm, which rapidly began forming goose bumps despite the heat of the water. She was kneeling next to me, perched on the seat, her leg touching my thigh, her hand caressing my penis, which was, to my consternation, becoming erect.

"Nora . . ." I tried to move; she held onto me.

"Luke . . . please . . ."

It was as if I were under water—not how I actually was, in a hot tub with my feet able to touch the bottom, but in a vast, viscous ocean, deep below the surface, trying to swim to the surface, but unable to. I felt like I was trapped in molasses, my muscles exhausted from the heat, the alcohol, and the shock of her unbelievable action.

"Nora, you can't . . ."

Still holding onto my penis, which was now fully erect despite my fervent desire that it not be, she placed her free hand across my mouth, hushing me.

"Let me. Please. Just for a moment."

I didn't know whether to shit or go blind. Yet my reaction, unbelievably to me, was not to push her away, or in any way be harsh with her, although I felt I should be, as she had broken a basic trust; it was, for reasons not completely known to me, that I didn't want to hurt her feelings. A stupid impulse, of course, but that's what was there: I didn't want to hurt her.

I didn't want her hand on my cock, either. That could only lead to all kinds of tragedies.

"Look, Nora . . ." I reached down to try to pry her hand off me.

"Dennis was impotent at the end. It wasn't that our sex life was bad, it was nonexistent."

"Nora, don't. That's . . ." Jesus, that was the last thing I wanted to hear, about her sex life with her dead husband. I didn't want to hear anything, really, I wanted to get the hell out of there as fast as I could.

She wouldn't let go. Her grip tightened; not painfully, but snugly.

I wasn't just erect now; I was becoming aroused.

"Not always, not completely. But most of the time, even before we moved here. Then once we did, he could never . . ."

Her eyes bored into me. She was crying.

"I haven't held a man's erect penis in ten years. Or had one inside me for fifteen. I never knew a man besides Dennis, I'm practically a virgin. So please," she implored, "let me. Just for a little while longer. Please, Luke."

"Oh, Nora." I was begging her. "I'm not the right one for this. Find someone else to . . . do this with. I'm not the one."

"There is no one else."

She was stroking me. "I'm the goddamn district attorney. Being normal isn't good enough, I'm held to standards above the law." She was almost laughing, bitterly, through her tears. "I have to be as chaste as a fucking nun."

I finally managed to pry her hand off my erection. Leaping out of the hot tub, I ran into the house.

Nora stood in the hallway, wrapped in her robe, her hair still wet. I was closer to the door. I was dressed, sort of—I had my shirt and pants on. My shoes and socks were in my hand; my jacket was slung over my arm.

I was shaking from the incident—anger, regret, remorse. The anger was at her, on the surface, but it was really at myself. What was I thinking when I got into that hot tub with her? That we'd relax with a glass of wine and sing the Stanford fight song? This wasn't like some repressed sexual desire that I let out, in the guise of rationalizing to myself that she'd seduced me when I was looking the other way. This was flat-out dumbness, lack of awareness of how needy and desperate she was.

I wasn't born yesterday. All the signs were there, clearly visible.

The best I could do, in my defense, was to plead pity. I hadn't wanted to hurt her feelings, so I wound up screwing everything up royally.

"What are you going to do?" she asked, her voice a low, husky whisper.

"Go home. What else?"

"To Santa Barbara?"

I looked at her then. "What?"

"Are you going to quit?"

That stopped me. I hadn't thought about that.

"I'd understand if you wanted to." She wasn't remorseful in her attitude.

"Well, I'd like to, now that you mention it." I'd had trepidations from the start about this. Now I had a reason to bail out.

"What would you tell people?" She stared at me, one hand holding her robe closed. "What would you tell the attorney general?"

That was a good question.

"You can't tell them you're quitting because I gave you a hand job in my hot tub, Luke. That's one thing you can't do."

I faced her. "Is this some kind of not-so-subtle blackmail, Nora?" Now I was truly angry. "Some sword you're going to hold over my head? If I wanted to quit, I could come up with dozens of legitimate reasons." I paused. "And no one would believe you if you told about this."

"Sure they would." She said it calmly. "After Monica Lewinsky, people are never going to believe the man again." She looked me in the eye. "Because they know men lie about these things, and women don't. Even if it isn't true."

That stopped me cold. Pulling a cigarette and a lighter from the pocket of her robe, she lit up, blew smoke toward the ceiling.

"I didn't know you smoked." That was an inane thing to say; I didn't know why I said it, except my mind wasn't firing on all cyliders. Hardly on any.

"There's a lot of things about me you don't know, Luke." She walked toward me, stopping a few feet away. "Tonight was one of them, but there are others."

"I don't want to know what they are, Nora." I had to get out of here, and quick.

"No, you don't," she agreed. "Look," she said, exhaling a plume of smoke in my direction, "what do you want, an apology? I'm sorry I fondled your cock? That I didn't respect your marriage vows, to a woman I've never met and means nothing to me? Well, I'm not." Another inhale, exhale. "If I'm sorry for anything, it's that we didn't have intercourse. After all these years, I still haven't gotten laid."

"Which is never going to happen with me."

She took a step toward me. I took one back.

"Look, Luke. It's not the end of the world, okay? I'm not going to bust you with your wife. No one's going to know that you got into my hot tub with me—voluntarily—and that as soon as I touched your precious penis, it got hard, and that as upset as you were over my behavior, you didn't stop me . . . immediately."

My cheeks were burning—what she'd said was true, all of it.

She stubbed her cigarette out in her empty wineglass.

"If you want to feel guilty over this, that's for you to decide. I don't think it's that big a deal, we didn't shack up for the weekend and profess undying love to each other. You turn me on, okay? After all those years, when you came up here and I laid my eyes on you, I thought, 'This could be nice.' But you weren't interested, and that's okay." She paused. "Actually, it's not okay, but that's the way it has to be, and I can live with that. I've lived with a lot worse."

"I have to leave, Nora." I was trying to stay calm, but I was shaking like hell inside. "I'll talk to you tomorrow."

"So you're not quitting."

"No," I answered with resignation, "I'm not quitting."

"I'm glad. We need you."

I nodded. I wasn't quitting. I couldn't quit, I had no intention of quitting. We both knew that, from the start.

"Luke . . ."

I was at the door. I turned back to her.

"Don't guilt-trip me, okay?"

I didn't answer; because I was.

"Think of it as a mercy . . . well, it wasn't a fuck. You could've done that, you know. A couple minutes of good old-fashioned screwing wouldn't have been the end of the world, not even a pimple." She sighed. "But it sure would've been nice for me."

"You're wrong, Nora. It would have mattered. To both of us."

I knew it was a mercy whatever; that was my rationale for not thinking of myself as a complete bastard. It was a feeble rationale, though. Riva would never accept it, because that's all it was—a crappy rationale. I also knew she'd never know, unless Nora busted me, and she wasn't going to do that.

Nora nodded. "Yeah, I guess it would've." She gestured at the open door. "You'd better get going. I'll see you tomorrow. I've got stuff to do. A day or two to cool this off wouldn't be a bad idea."

"Your decision," she said. "You know where to find me."

I started to leave. She stopped me one last time.

"Don't take it so seriously, Luke. It really is not that a big a deal." She fished another cigarette out of her robe pocket. "And Luke—don't make me feel guilty, okay? I'm glad I did what I did. I'm glad there's still a woman inside this." She tapped her chest.

"Good-bye, Nora." All I wanted was to get the hell out of there.

"Good-bye, Luke. Take care driving. We need you safe up here in Blue River."

Kate went through half a dozen administrators, office registrars, and faculty members before she found one who had been at Garfield for twenty years and remembered Reynaldo Juarez. A woman, Mrs. Escuela, who taught college-prep math. They sat together in the faculty lounge.

Mrs. Escuela was middle-aged, a few years older than Kate, so Kate guessed. Not in the best of shape—plump, her hair graying, which she wasn't dyeing, a wisp of a mustache on her upper lip. Kate sized her up as a down-to-earth woman who had seen it all in her decades at this sprawling public high school. She was now the dean of the math department; back then, when Reynaldo Juarez was a student, she was a young teacher, not many years out of college, teaching the fundamentals to students who were woefully unprepared to go into the world and get a job, let alone go to college.

"Do you remember him?" Kate asked. "They were peering at the yearbook of Juarez's senior year. His face, youthful but already purposeful and intense, stared out at them.

Mrs. Escuela nodded. "Oh, yes. I remember Reynaldo. Very well."

"Why was that?" Kate asked, curious. This woman had witnessed thousands of students passing through her classrooms. How many did she remember "very well"? And how come Juarez was one of them?

"Because he was one of my brightest. One of the best students I ever had. He could have done anything with his life," she added sorrowfully.

"You know about how he turned out."

"Oh, yes." Mrs. Escuela shook her head. "He was into that world even then. He drove a fancy school to car and wore designer clothes. And always a pager. One of the first at the school." She leafed through some pages in the yearbook. "They're banned now, of course. Or they'd be going off incessantly. Back then, it was kind of a novelty. That was before crack was such an epidemic." She looked at the photo of teenage Reynaldo again. "He didn't sell drugs here. He was careful about that. He was never in trouble here. But everyone knew."

"Did he have many friends?"

"He was a figure of admiration because he was a big drug person, which is like being a big sports or entertainment figure to so many of these misguided kids. But he kept to himself. He didn't let many people get close to him. He was a very private individual."

He didn't change in that regard, Kate thought.

"Do you know what happened to him after high school?" she asked. "No one I've talked to seems to know."

Mrs. Escuela thought for a moment. "Perhaps he went to college, although I tend to doubt it. It wasn't his vision of himself. Like I said, though, he was very bright. Some of the faculty here encouraged him to apply not merely to college, but to elite schools, like Yale, Princeton, Stanford."

"He was that bright?" Kate asked, not so surprised.

"Yes, he was." Mrs. Escuela nodded. "And he could have afforded it. With the money he had made from his unlawful activities."

"So did he? Apply to those schools?"

Mrs. Escuela shook her head. "I don't think so, but I don't know for sure. I wasn't his adviser. That was . . ."

She turned some pages in the yearbook, coming to pictures of faculty members. She put her finger on one, a mousy-looking man of indeterminate age—the prototypical public school teacher of cartoons. "Mr. Winkowski. He was Reynaldo's adviser. He might be able to tell you."

Kate took out her #651 Reporter's notebook. She always carried one with her; it fit in the back pocket of jeans, or in a side jacket pocket. "Does he still teach here?" She was starting to get excited.

A shake of the head. "No. He retired some years ago." Mrs. Escuela sighed. "Burnt out. That happens all the time. It's been building in me for years. I don't know if I'm going to make it to my full retirement. Or still caring, if I do. That's what happens when teachers stay on—they lose their zest, their love for teaching." She turned back to Juarez's picture in the yearbook. "It's too much about discipline now. There isn't enough teaching. Too many of them want to be like Reynaldo turned out, it's glamorized in music, sports, movies, television. Get it now. And even for the ones who don't think like that, who go to college, it's an uphill struggle." She closed the yearbook. "Everyone knows that California used to have the best schools in the country, and now we're ranked at the bottom. It isn't going to change soon. Not while I'm still a teacher, I'm afraid. Despite what the politicians promise."

This is all important, Kate thought, but she wasn't here to discuss the entire weight of the world, just the potential whereabouts of one student who became one of the country's major drug dealers. That was enough weight for her at the moment.

"This Mr. Winkowski. How do I get in touch with him?"

"They have his home phone number in the office. I'll walk you there. It's time for my next class."

Ten minutes later, Kate was on her cell phone, driving her car toward Interstate 5, making her way back to Santa Barbara. She was talking to Miklos Winkowski, Juarez's high school adviser. She had called him in southwestern Michigan, where he was living in retirement.

"It's cheap living here," he explained over the line, as if divulging classified secrets, before she even asked why, which she wouldn't have; she didn't know the man, she wasn't interested, all she cared about was finding whatever links she could to his former advisee, Reynaldo Juarez. But he was bound to tell her—the same spiel, she knew, that he gave everyone from California who called him.

"Half the price of L.A. I've got family here, it's where I came from originally, so I fit right in, even after thirty-five years being away. A teacher's pension and social security doesn't cut it there in L.A.; here, I'm living good."

Having presented his case, he was ready to answer questions.

"Yep, he was college material. Any college."

"Did he go?"

"Um-hum." He had a Midwesterner's nasal inflection, coupled with a slight foreign accent. First-generation, she thought. It was second nature for her to guess where people came from and what they looked like, merely from their voices—always sleuthing, a detective's work is never done.

She had her notebook out, pen ready. "Where?"

"Stanford."

So that was it. The missing years. Jesus, she thought, I wonder if he was an undergrad there when Luke was in law school. And Nora Ray, too. Kate decided he wasn't, Luke was too much older; but it was intriguing as hell.

"So he went to Stanford. Do you know anything about his life there?" She didn't have to ask that question. She could do that research, now that she knew.

The old schoolteacher threw a bucket of cold water on her, long distance two thousand miles.

"He didn't have one. He dropped out, end of his freshman year."

She sagged. "You know that for a fact?"

"Sure do. He came by, summer after his freshman year. Told me he wasn't going back."

"Did he say why?" Fuck; right when she thought she'd made a breakthrough, she was right back at go, and she hadn't collected her two hundred dollars.

"He didn't fit in. He got homesick. He looked it, too. Like a whipped dog."

Juarez insecure? So the guy was human after all.

"He never went back. You're sure?"

"You can check it out, but from what I know, he didn't. There weren't many Latinos there in those days. He'd been king of the hill down here, up there he was just another beaner, pardon the expression. I'm not racially prejudiced, it's the word they use."

"It sounds like he was feeling sorry for himself."

"Could be. Ray was strong, even as a young man. But he didn't pull it off up there in Palo Alto. I think that was tough on him; he'd never felt overwhelmed before."

"So what happened to him after that?" Please, give me something.

"Don't know. I never saw him again, talked to him, anything. He vanished from my radar screen."

"Did he go to another college?"

"Might have. He'd qualified to the state universities. So maybe he went to a public college. Where he wouldn't be a novelty, if you understand me."

The traffic was zipping by her at a good clip.

"Yes," she said, ending the conversation, "I understand you."

SECRET LIVES

I got home late Friday night; later than I wanted, but there was work on the table I had to clear before I left. That's always been a problem with me—I can't let things go until tomorrow.

There was another reason I'd delayed my trip—I felt guilty, and ashamed. I have been through the hell of a bad divorce, the loss of what I'd thought would be a marriage that would last forever. Then I'd met Riva, and she'd pulled me out of the doldrums. We're going to be together for the rest of our lives if I have anything to do with it, and I know she feels the same way, having had her own share of screwed-up relationships.

I'd seen it coming with Nora, and I let it happen anyway. I didn't want it; it wasn't about a quickie with someone from the past, a scratch of a sexual itch to see what it was like, nor was it some middle-aged affirmation of my own sexuality, which I don't need to affirm. Nora had never been a woman on my sexual radar—she was already taken when I met her, and I wouldn't have gone for her anyway, I'd never felt that kind of pull toward her.

I tried to con myself about the feeling-bad-for-her part, how I was performing some psychological service in letting her get close to me, that my actions had been passive, I hadn't made a play for her, I just hadn't reacted fast enough to stop her. But those rationales didn't work, because they were bullshit. I knew she was hot for me, I knew it the minute I walked in the door the first day I hit Blue River. And there had been all that talk about how bad her sex life had been with Dennis, the impotency, the sterility, how it had been forever since she'd been laid.

She couldn't have sent a stronger signal if she'd strapped flashing lights to her forehead.

I hadn't taken strong enough steps to stop her. Not even close.

When I was a teenager, and later, as a young man in college, I had the usual guy fantasies about getting it on with every woman who caught my eye, not just regular fucking but some kind of emotional preening, a cock-of-the-walk thing: the best piece of male ass ever—the guy *she,* whoever the imaginary *she* was in those immature, feel-good fantasies, would remember for the rest of her life.

Yeah, right. That ain't the way it works, which is why it's a fantasy. When you grow up and get into a stable, loving relationship, you realize that how things work in the real world is much richer than any fantasy you could concoct. And that your cock isn't independent of your heart.

The truth is that Riva's the best lover I've ever had, because I love her the most.

They met me at the airport, of course. Buck was asleep on his feet, but he gamely trotted to me, falling into my arms like a sack of cement as soon as I reached down for him. I sat in the backseat on the drive home, cradling him in my arms, the seat belt around both of us. Not the legal way to protect him, but the right way, tonight. His warm body was pressed up against me, his little boy's breath warm on my neck. I couldn't remember the last time I'd felt this good; or this contrite.

I put him to bed while Riva put the finishing touches on our late dinner, a favorite of mine, crab cakes, fries, slaw, beer. God, it was good to be home. I knew I was missing them, but it had taken the incident with Nora to make me realize how badly.

"It's getting pretty up in Blue River now," I said. We were in bed together. We'd just made love. There had been a desperation to it on my part that I'd tried not to show. If she felt anything different, she didn't say anything about it. Probably figured I was horny from being away from her.

"Uh-huh." She was half-asleep, cuddled up against me, the way we do it.

"Maybe you should come up for a while, now that the weather's nice."

"Uh-huh. Okay."

"You will?"

"Sure. I've been missing you, too. So's your son. We could use some new scenery."

"So—you're coming back up with me on Monday?"

"Yeah."

She rolled over. "I was wondering how long it would be before you couldn't stand not being with us," she said, smiling at me.

"Why didn't you say something?"

"I didn't want to interfere with your work, honey. I know how it goes."

"You won't be interfering." She was coming up—I couldn't believe it.

"I'm sure we'll find plenty to do."

"Definitely. There's great hiking, you could start horseback riding again, I could find some cabin way out where we could—"

She put her lips on mine, shutting me up. Then she pulled back, running her fingernails along my back, which she knows I love.

"We'll find plenty to do. You don't have to do it for us. Now let's go to sleep, Luke. I only sleep well when I'm lying next to you like this."

She was asleep in less than five minutes. I lay there, feeling her warmth, her presence. Her.

Sometimes it takes a bolt of lightning to get your attention. What had happened that night with Nora had done that for me. Maybe that was a blessing in disguise, to remind me that you can never take the important stuff for granted, you have to keep working at it, all the time.

No, pal, I thought, talking to myself. That was not a blessing. The blessing will be that you escape it without ruining your life.

Tom Miller sat in the study of his house, spinning through his ancient, massive Rolodex while eating a ham and Swiss cheese sandwich on rye. Fifty years of names were in that old card file, thousands of them, going back to his beginning days with the Bureau. The majority were yellowed and curled with age, the precise fountain-pen handwriting faded with the passing of time. Rarely did he get rid of a card; even if someone died, which over the past decade had become the norm rather than the exception, he generally kept the card in the file. Sometimes he did so out of nostalgia, an old friend's name he didn't want to cast into the trash can. More commonly it was because a particular name, while no longer relevant in and of itself, would trigger a mental connection in his head that would lead to something useful in the present.

Scores of the names on the small four-by-two cards were FBI agents, mostly past, but some current. They had their own section in the *F*'s, cross-referenced alphabetically by assignment, location, hierarchy in the Bureau, and reliability—how useful they were to him, and how trustworthy: could he talk to them freely about sensitive issues and know they'd keep their mouth shut about dealing with him. Quite a few were in that category—the old man was still respected, even after all this time of not being on the official roster. Besides names, addresses, and phone numbers, there were spouses' names, children's and grandchildren's, and something special about the person—he played tennis or golf or hunted, his wife raised roses or bred golden retrievers, was a gourmet cook or painted still lifes. Their kids were doctors, lawyers, in other solid professions. The personal touch was important, even if it was faked.

Over the years Tom had diligently kept up with the agents he'd served with, and they had in turn passed him on to the newer generations, informing people who had never met Tom Miller that he had been a quality agent and would always be a good man, so that even now, almost into this ninth decade, he had a strong network of people inside the Bureau who helped him when he needed it.

Like now.

He needed to be part of this case. There were many reasons—professional, ego, personal. Jerome had cut him out deliberately, maliciously. Garrison, Nora's friend, was doing it because he wanted his own people, who had no personal stake in the matter and would be objective. Miller understood that, but it didn't mean he had to like having to sit on his hands and watch the show pass him by.

The truth was that it was killing him to have to remain on the sidelines and watch. He couldn't handle it, not a second time.

He hit the Touch-Tone buttons on his phone.

"Hello?" It was a middle-aged woman's voice, sounding impatient.

"Florence Turpin?"

"Yes?"

"It's Tom Miller. How are you?"

The answer was hesitant. "How did you get this number? Who are you?"

"We've spoken before," he said, projecting an assuring tone into his voice—FBI agents have unlisted phone numbers, for security reasons. Their families, particularly, can be paranoid about having their privacy and safety invaded. "I'm a friend of Bruce's."

Bruce was her husband. As an upper-echelon player in the Bureau, he'd had his share of death threats over the years.

"Oh?" She still didn't sound convinced.

"I'm a former agent. Now I'm a county sheriff out here in California. Bruce has assisted me on matters in the past."

"Oh . . . yes." Her voice lost its suspicious edge. "Yes, I remember you now, Mr. . . ."

"Miller," he said again. "Tom."

"Right. Tom."

"Right. Tom."

"How are your tulips?" he asked, glancing at the card in front of him. "Are they up yet? It must be getting on that time now back there in Virginia."

He'd hit the right button. She began gushing on about how well her bulbs had done this year. He listened long enough to make her feel good, and appreciated, then he asked her to please put her husband on the line.

"Bruce Turpin." The male voice was flat, military-brisk.

"Tom Miller, Bruce. From Muir County, California. I was a close friend of Reed Chalmers. I hope you remember me."

Reed Chalmers and Miller had joined the Bureau at the same, after the war. Chalmers had stayed on, rising high—he had been Turpin's boss at the Bureau. He was dead five years now. Chalmers had been a good friend and resolute supporter of Miller's, when being so wasn't easy or expedient.

Miller had flown East for the funeral. More importantly than the paying of last respects, which cost almost a thousand dollars, with the airfare, car rental, hotel room, meals, etc., the act of showing the colors had been a smart way for Miller to stay in the good graces of those currently in the Bureau, such as Turpin, who had been mentored and supported by Chalmers. Money well spent.

The voice brightened. "Sure. I remember. How are you, Tom?"

"Fine, Bruce. You?"

"Can't complain." Taking on a tone of surprise, he asked, "You're still the sheriff out there? You haven't retired yet?"

"Almost. I'm finishing my last term. Passing on the torch."

"Well, good for you. It's good to keep active. I don't know what I'm going to do when my mandatory comes up."

"Do you hunt?" Miller asked, looking at the man's card, which stated he was an avid hunter.

"Was J. Edgar Hoover . . . ? Never mind—yes, I hunt."

"Well, you can come out here and go hunting with me. We've got all the big game you can handle."

"You're a hunter, too, Tom?"

"Bow and arrow."

There was a low whistle of appreciation from the other end of the line. "That's a man's work. You do that . . . at your age?"

"Oh, sure. I took down a six-hundred-pound elk this past February. Put a hundred-grain broadhead straight through his heart at fifty yards."

This wasn't a boast; Miller didn't embroider, he didn't have to.

Turpin was warm to the conversation now. "What kind of bow did you use? The reason I'm asking, I've been thinking of starting to hunt that way. More sporting, more challenging."

"I agree," Miller said. "Evens the odds. I have a Golden Eagle single-cam bow, seventy-pound draw weight. It's a good instrument."

"Listen, I may take you up on that offer."

"Anytime, Bruce. I'm the sheriff, so hunting season's always open up here. Particularly on the reservations, where the state laws don't apply."

"You're tight with the redskins, huh?"

Miller didn't care for the implied slur, but he let it roll off his back. "I'm friendly with everyone, Bruce. My job." He paused. "Except certain agents in the DEA whose heads are too swollen for their hatbands."

"I know all about that situation," Turpin said sympathetically. "We've talked about it in our shop. Those agents are not well thought of in the Justice Department these days, to put it mildly."

Miller smiled, hearing that. This wasn't hunting talk now, what he was doing; this was fishing, for real. He had cast his line and the protégé of his dearly departed friend had taken the bait, as he'd figured he would.

"Or here, either," he said. "I assume you know that we're conducting our own investigation into the matter."

"Yes, I do. I wish you good luck with it."

Turpin's voice had an edge to it; the FBI hadn't been brought into the investigation—the DEA had kept them at arm's length.

"Thanks. If there's anything to be found," Miller said, "we'll find it. I'll find it," he said with conviction.

"I'll bet you will," the other responded. "I'll bet you'll pin their ears back." There was a moment's hesitation. Then: "Any way I can help you, Tom?"

"As a matter of fact, Bruce, there is."

* * *

My investigators finished interviewing the DEA agents who could have been Juarez's killer, or involved in it. Criteria included guns having been fired, being part of the chase after Juarez when he escaped from custody, several other factors. Now it was time to bring them before the grand jury for questioning, and hope that one of them would crack. They were all long shots, but there was no other way of doing this: to find the needle in the haystack, *if it was there,* we had to methodically start pulling off straws, one by one, until the needle was found.

The subpoenas went out. We would be in session four days a week, Monday morning through Thursday afternoon. No more than two agents a day could be questioned because of the amount of detail I needed to get into, so we were going to be at it for over a month, unless something broke sooner. I wasn't going to work five-day weeks; I would need the long weekends to collate my thoughts and notes with my team, and more importantly, I wanted to spend as much time with Riva and Buck as I could steal.

I was avoiding Nora, of course. When we saw each other, we were cordial, polite. She was friendlier than I was; she had nothing to lose. I did. The change in our situation meant that I wouldn't be including her in the process.

She knew Riva had come up north with me; I mentioned it the first time I saw her after the hot-tub incident, mid-morning the following Monday when I returned. I hadn't introduced them yet, although I would. Riva had talked about having Nora over for dinner, but I was stalling on that.

I had more pressing things going: the core of the investigation. So it was that on the following Monday morning, a warm, breezy day, we got started on the direct testimony of the DEA agents who could be considered suspects. The school's former cafeteria had been set up as the grand jury room. I had scheduled the witnesses in order of their importance in the raid, from bottom to top, which meant Jerome and the heavy hitters would come in last. We had prepared an elaborate questionnaire for each witness, to be completed in advance of his appearance. Most of the questions were identical—their background, education, time spent in the DEA, other operations like this one they'd been part of, what their role was in this specific action.

When they took the stand I elicited that information verbally, for the jurors' benefit—I believe that repetition helps memory. That boilerplate questioning alone took over an hour. Large maps and diagrams of the entire area were pasted to the walls, with flags and pins stuck in them denoting various places where elements of the raid had taken place—where they'd waited, who had been next to them, in front, how the attack went, what each did when the raid got under way, the same for when the shootings started inside the compound, afterward. I made each one walk me through his specific role, step by step, minute by minute.

Besides having the maps, I had commissioned a large three-dimensional model of the area to scale, which was set up on a ten-foot-by-ten-foot table, placed in the center of the room. There were also blowups of the scene, where the body had been found, the tree where the killing bullet lodged. The grand jurors' chairs, elevated on risers so they could see down onto the exhibits, ringed the table. I also had each man's weapons brought in: his personal automatics, any rifle or other long-barreled gun that had been deployed, plus any other piece of equipment he had used—binoculars, night-vision glasses, his uniform, radio, watch, the works. Everything and anything that had been physically at that compound that night.

Getting responses out of these men was like pulling teeth on a battlefield with a pair of pliers. They answered each question precisely, giving me no more information than what I specifically asked for, volunteering nothing. They were angry at being here—they felt disrespected and were scornful. They had been through this already, with their own agency—but not in such detail, which pissed them off even more, that we would be delving more deeply, as if we did really think one of them did it. They were also scared, although they wouldn't admit it. What if it had been one of them? What if something they said incriminated a fellow agent?

That was my main purpose—to discover conflicts in testimony that would lead to something significant, help make a case.

One thing became obvious, from the first witness. Once the raid started, and didn't go exactly to plan, the situation on the ground turned to shit, a complete snafu. People were running around in the dark, not knowing where they were going, where shots were coming from, who was shooting back. Some of the casualties had almost certainly come from friendly fire. For a few minutes, before the backup artillery started, and they were able to retreat to some half-assed safety, the rain of fire was incredibly intense. They were exposed, out in the open. Men had panicked—they had never been trained for this, this was like fighting an unseen enemy in some unknown jungle.

"Tell me who were the half dozen men closest to you when the firing started," I asked the first witness.

"I . . ." He stammered, then clammed up.

Patiently, I showed him the list of agents who had been there that night. He looked at it like he was reading Chinese, or Martian. He didn't have a clue—they hadn't known each other long enough, having been brought in from different places.

I walked over to the model. "Where were you?"

He got up from his chair and used the pointer to place himself, tentatively.

"Not here?" I asked, moving the pointer a few inches, which translated to about twenty feet away from where he'd pointed.

"Maybe," he conceded. "It was dark. None of us had ever been inside the place." He was flustered; and he had been a peripheral player, he wasn't one of the bunch going in the door with Jerome, and he had escaped the closest direct fire.

If this man was disoriented, I thought, how had it been for the others, closer to the center? They were lucky more of them hadn't been killed—they hadn't planned for a counterattack of the ferocity they had faced. It wasn't *The Red Badge of Courage,* but it wasn't Iwo Jima, either.

What I also realized, which gave me a real jolt, was that they'd all been in denial for the past six months. Buried deep down, they all thought, and feared, that one of them might really have done the killing, despite their uniform denials to the contrary. And that denial and fear had to be tearing them up.

I needed to figure out how to use that emotion.

Near the end of the second week's questioning, I tried a gambit. The witness was one of the men who had been at center of the action, both during the raid and after, when Juarez was being held prisoner, before his escape. This man had been near the trailer, close enough to walk in without attracting undue attention.

"Agent Wilkes," I said, "you went in the trailer when the prisoner was inside, isn't that true?"

"No," he corrected me, "I didn't."

I frowned, as if something wasn't right, suddenly.

"Of course you did." I picked up a document from my desk, looked it over. The document had nothing to do with this line of questioning, but he didn't know that; nor did the members of the grand jury, who perked up at this.

"No, I never did," he protested.

"Well, that's strange. That's very strange. Other agents who were there, right by you, have testified in their sworn written statements that you did."

"No," he said, starting to get nervous, "they couldn't have. I didn't."

"Are you saying they're lying?"

He was flustered now. "No, I'm not saying that."

"Then you're lying."

"No!"

"Well, someone is."

"No."

"Then what?"

"I . . . I was never in that trailer, so I'm not lying. I swear it, I was never in there."

"So these men who said you were, they're the ones that're lying."

"I . . ."

"Or maybe they were mistaken," I said, giving him a little slack.

"Yes," he said, jumping on it, "they must've been. Because I never was inside the trailer."

"Okay," I told him. "I'll accept that."

He exhaled like a man coming up from fifty feet below the surface.

"For now. But let me caution you—if others come into this room and reiterate that you did go inside there, I'm going to have to indict you for perjury. You understand that, Agent Wilkes, don't you?"

He went white. "Perjury?"

"Lying under oath."

"But I haven't."

"That's why we have trials, and juries. To find out who's lying, and who isn't."

"I'm not lying. I swear it."

"I hope not. You're already in enough trouble." I gathered up my papers. "You're excused—for now."

He started to get up from the witness chair, but I put a hand up to detain him.

"Don't forget, Agent Wilkes. You're still under oath, and under subpoena. You are not to speak about this to anyone, do you understand?"

"Yes, sir."

"*Anyone.* Not your wife, not any of your fellow agents. Especially not any of your fellow agents. That would be a very serious offense. You do understand the seriousness of what I'm saying, don't you, Agent Wilkes?"

"Yes, I do."

"Okay, then. You can go."

He hesitated before getting up again. I didn't do anything to impede him this time, so he did.

"Agent Wilkes," I called out. He was almost to the door.

He turned. He was scared now. No more of the badass swagger he'd brought in with him.

"If you do remember anything that happened that night, that you haven't yet remembered, you're going to call me right away, aren't you?"

"Yes," he said with alacrity.

"Good." I smiled. "And once again—these proceedings are secret. What we say here, stays here. You've got that straight, don't you, Agent Wilkes?"

He nodded. "I hear you."

Kate strolled across the Stanford campus. God, what a life, she thought, looking at the kids in their T-shirts and shorts, riding bikes, tossing Frisbees, congregating in small groups to talk, share coffee, flirt. How great it would be to come here as a young person. They all looked so comfortable, so confident.

She hadn't been to college. Hers was the stereotypical working-class background of the previous generation—married right out of high school, kids shortly after. She'd had the spunk to quit that marriage before she got in too deep, join the Oakland police department, then again when she felt compelled to leave that, to move on to what she was doing now. She had a better than okay life, after years of floundering around; she made damn good money, the work was exciting, she met interesting people. No relationship, at the moment. That would come, when she was ready again—she'd been in one a few years back, a nice guy who made wine in the Santa Ynez valley, but it hadn't gone all the way—one of those things. After two failed marriages, the last one a blistering disaster, even worse than the first, she was going to be super-cautious before making that kind of commitment again. For now she was happy living on her own.

Her daughters would have appreciated going to a college like this. She didn't have the kind of money to send them here, and although they were smart, they weren't of the caliber that could win a scholarship to a Stanford. That was okay—they'd make it anyway. Still, it would be heaven to spend four years in these cloistered surroundings.

One thing she noticed as she walked along—the racial mix. The majority of the faces were white. A goodly amount of Asians, too. Far fewer blacks and Latinos. Things had changed, but not enough.

She thought about the object of her investigation. What was it like, twenty-some years ago, to be a minority kid on this campus? You'd definitely feel different. Especially if you came from a place like east L.A., and you weren't the star of the basketball or football team.

Reynaldo Juarez had great self-assurance, from the cradle, apparently. But in this kind of environment, would that have held up? Would he have been prepared to not be the center of attention, because of things over which he had no control, his background and his ethnicity? A proud young boy, already self-made (through illegal means, but still self-made), might hate a place like this. It could remind him that no matter how well he did, he would always be looked at in a certain way.

That brought up another interesting question: Had Juarez been selling drugs while he was a student? By the time he started here as a freshman he'd been doing it for years; would he have stopped, tried to be straight, a regular college student? Dealing would have brought him popularity. It could also have gotten him into trouble.

Maybe he'd been kicked out. That would be a plausible reason for his not coming back after the one year.

The registrar's office had his records ready; she'd called ahead. His grades were better than decent, mostly B's, one A, in Spanish Lit., one C. Certainly good enough to keep him in school; flunking out wasn't the reason he left, and he had not been expelled—he had no negative marks on his record.

He had lived in a dorm, hadn't joined a fraternity. They had the names of the other students in his dorm. Kate stuffed the list in her pocket—she'd check them out later. If she wanted to find out more about his life on campus, the clerk told her, she should check the library, the old yearbooks, and other publications. The woman suggested that perhaps he had joined a Latino club, or some other extracurricular activity, where he might have met someone whose path he crossed later on down the line, someone who'd kept up with him and could help her with her investigation. The registrar's office didn't know about things like that, they didn't keep those records. Reynaldo Juarez had left without a trace—there had been no requests for transfer of credits to another school.

She sat in the library, the yearbook for Juarez's freshman (and only) year opened in front of her. She flipped through the pages, looking at the pictures. What a time. All that ugly disco stuff, the makeup, hair, clothes. She'd looked like that, she thought, smiling. An ugly decade.

First thing, she'd gone to the pages with the freshman pictures, tiny shots of faces looking into the camera—the bulk of the yearbook was for the senior class. There he was, in the middle of the page, surrounded by other *J* surnames. He was a cocky bastard. And young. Only eighteen. But already a killer, and a drug dealer. Unlike the others in the pictures surrounding him. Those were the real kids. He was only their contemporary chronologically.

There was a Latino club, a pretty big one, most of the Hispanic students in the school were members, but he wasn't. He wasn't on any sports teams, he wasn't in the school band, debating society, mountaineering club, he wasn't in any class plays, anything athletic or social. He had been a student, nothing more.

How do you track someone who doesn't leave footprints?

She turned back to the single picture of him again, his class photo. He did have a different look from the other students'. His hair was long, as was theirs, too, most of them, but his was slicked back, out-of-fashion style, Elvis, not Lennon. You could almost reach out and touch the grease on that hairdo. Glancing through the adjacent pages, tracing her finger down the rows, she noticed that other Spanish-surnamed students, Jaramillo, Javier, Jiminez, didn't wear their hair the way he did—they wore it shorter, preppier. They were trying to fit in. He wasn't.

Wait. A name she passed triggered something. What was it?

She went back to the top of the *J*'s, started again. Jaramillo, Javier, a first name of Jesus, a common Latino boy's name . . .

A girl's face stared out at her. A defiant look to it, like she was saying, "I don't buy it." Her hair was long and wavy, deep auburn, because this was an Irish face, with one of those lovely peaches-and-cream complexions. The face reminded Kate of a young Maureen O'Hara, one of her favorite actresses from the old movies. The pretty face was made more attractive because it wasn't ordinary, there was character to it, not common in an eighteen-year-old. You could see it, even in this tiny little photograph.

The girl was not Latina. She was Anglo, through and through.

Her name was Diane. Diane Jerome Richards.

Nora was kneeling on the living-room floor of my condo, playing with my son. They were building a fort with his blocks. She looked up as I came through the door.

"Hi." Her voice was bright, cheery.

"Hello," I said slowly, bending down and giving Buck a hug. What was she doing here?

Riva came in from the kitchen, wiping her hands on her apron, a picture of domesticity. "Nora's staying for dinner."

"Oh?"

"We thought it would be nice for us to get to know each other, since she's your old friend. And your boss." Riva smiled, winking at Nora.

"I'm not Luke's boss." Nora got to her feet. She was dressed casually—she had changed before coming over. "He answers to no man—or woman."

"He answers to me. Don't you, darling?" Riva gave Nora another wink, like Lucy and Ethel. Two women, already ganging up against the guy.

"Always."

I shucked my jacket and made myself a vodka tonic. I needed it, and not because my workday had been hard. Sipping my drink, I walked over to Riva, put an arm around her shoulder, gave her a kiss on the cheek. Nora watched, smiling like a dear old friend.

"Your son's adorable," she said. "Anytime you need a baby-sitter . . ."

The middle-aged childless woman's promise, and desire.

"Not that there's much to do around here at night. But you know, a movie or something." Nora smiled. "Bowling's popular."

"I'm sure we'll take you up on that." I was playing it casual, but my nerves were jingling inside. "So you invited Nora over," I said to Riva. "That was . . . nice."

"Actually, I invited myself." Nora turned her smile on Riva. "I wanted to meet the lucky woman who snared Luke Garrison."

"It's the other way around," I told her. "I'm the lucky one."

"We're both lucky," Riva said, "so let's drop it, okay? We don't need to prattle on in front of Nora, she'll think we're stuck-in-the-mud fogies."

"I wouldn't think that," Nora said brightly. "I think you are lucky—both of you."

Riva clutched my hand, hearing that. She was remembering what I'd told her about Nora's life with Dennis. I knew that wasn't what Nora was thinking about, but I kept that opinion to myself.

Nora turned to me. "So—how goes the battle?" To Riva: "I only know what he deigns to tell me. Talk about your independent counselor." She was preternaturally chipper.

"Nothing new to report. Nobody knows anything, the party line. But I'm rattling them. Someone might break, if they think I'm going to bring a blanket indictment and take a bunch of them to trial."

"Except you're not going to do that. We're not chasing wild geese. Your words."

"I know that, and you know that. But they don't."

"Well, let's hope we catch a break. And soon. I'm getting awfully nervous about this. There's a ton of pressure coming down from Washington. Bill Fishell calls every other day, asking what's going on."

"Tell him to hold the fort."

"I do." Nora turned to Riva. "Can I help you with dinner? I don't want to talk shop anymore, it's boring. And I never get to cook for anyone, besides myself," she said straight-faced, not looking at me.

"I've got the kid covered," I said quickly, scooping him up and swinging him to the ceiling, which brought the usual shrieks of laughter. "We're going to play with the horsies. Right, Buckaroo?"

"Right, Daddy!" he screamed joyfully.

While the women went about getting dinner ready, I cored and sliced an apple, tucked the pieces into my pocket, and carried my son outside on my shoulders, horsy-back style. The condo development had been built on the edge of a working ranch—the ranch fence came up to the edge of where we were living. Real horses grazing in the field on the other side would amble over to us and let Bucky rub their noses and give them sugar and the apple slices. Riva was taking riding lessons over there, western-style. She was getting good at it. I figured the other shoe would drop when we got home—she'd want a horse. And all the expensive crap that goes with it.

If that's what she wanted, she could have it. She can have anything she wants. A faithful husband, for openers.

I did have new information about the investigation, but I wasn't about to share it with Nora; not yet, anyway. Kate Blanchard had called and delivered the jolt about the girl named Jerome. That a girl in Juarez's class at Stanford, more than twenty years ago, had the same uncommon last name as the leader of the group I was investigating didn't mean anything in and of itself—there might be no connection. But the coincidence was intriguing. Kate was going to follow it up and get back to me, if there was anything to it.

Buck and I stood at the fence and fed the apple to the horses, an old mare and an old gelding, the one Riva rides. Maude and Big Red, two good horse names. Buck giggled as they slobbered over his tiny hand, their big horse lips sucking up the fruit.

"Pretty soon you'll be riding, Buck, like Mommy," I told him, hoisting him closer to the horse's face.

He smiled and nodded at that. With a name like Buck, you ought to be able to ride a horse, not that he knows that yet.

All those things he's going to be learning to do over the years. I'll be there, cheering him on, watching, helping, being a part of it. I'm old for a new dad, it means more when you've been waiting this long. I want to make sure I'm always there for him. One guaranteed way to do that is to keep my cock and the rest of myself out of single ladies' hot tubs. And everything else of theirs as well.

Dinner was casual and unstressful, given the circumstances. Nora left shortly after, citing fatigue. After putting our son to bed, Riva and I lounged around in the living room. It was great, having them there, although the digs weren't up to our usual. No porch to sit on at night, no view of the ocean. But we were together, that was the important thing.

"She seems like a nice lady," Riva commented. "Not as uptight as I'd imagined."

"She's in control of herself," I said. "Most of the time. She has to be, she's highly visible; in her job being in control or looking like you are is half the battle."

"It must be frustrating for her, having to stand outside and look in the window in her own jurisdiction," Riva said. "Can't you confide in her more?"

"Did she say something to you about that?" I asked, irritated.

"Not in so many words. But I could tell. You wouldn't like it, if you were in her position."

"I wouldn't let myself be."

"She didn't have a choice, Luke."

"You always have a choice." I didn't want to get into this with her; and I didn't like Nora trying to use Riva to get to me.

"I'm doing the best I can for the case. It isn't about personalities. She has to remember that. We all do."

"I'm sure you're right." Riva got up. "I'm tired. Let's go to bed. That's why we came up here, isn't it?"

"One of the main reasons."

As we were falling asleep, she said one last thing about Nora.

"She's lonely. It's so apparent, the way she was with Bucky. I don't even know the woman and my heart went out to her, all the heartbreak she's had. She needs a man in her life. You ought to help her out."

The hairs stood up on the back of my neck. "Like how?"

"Find somebody for her. We could have her down to S.B. for a weekend. You must know some nice eligible men, don't you?"

"I'll think on it," I said, feeling my body quivering. "When this is done. Can we not talk about Nora anymore tonight? I'm with you. I don't want anyone else in our space."

"No one is."

She fell asleep on her side. No one is, I thought, except Nora's shadow.

"I've got good news and bad news," Sylvan Furness said. "Which do you want to hear first?"

"The good news, I guess," Louisa Bearpaw answered with unease. Was this going to be yet another screwing-over by the BIA?

"The Justice Department has agreed to turn jurisdiction of that compound over to Interior, and Interior is willing to sell it to you."

She smiled—that was a surprise. "Great. How much?"

He hesitated, then timidly told her, "Two million."

She stared at him, her jaw dropping. "Are you shitting me?"

He shook his head. "No. That's what they want."

"Jesus Christ, Sylvan, that's outrageous. It isn't worth half that."

"We have all the construction bills. It cost almost that much to build."

"It didn't cost the government one thin dime," she replied hotly. "No one ever pays full price for a government seizure. You'll be lucky to get fifty cents on the dollar."

"Not this time." He shifted uncomfortably in his chair. "I told them it was going to be too much money, but they don't care."

"They'd rather just sit on it."

He nodded. "For the time being."

"Jesus, what morons." She sipped her take-out coffee, which tasted like metal in her mouth. "Okay, so that's the good news. Some good news. What's the bad news? You're going to nuke the reservation?"

"The department's turning down your loan request."

Louisa Bearpaw shrugged her shoulders. "Why not?" It was a rhetorical question. "When have they ever done anything for us?"

"It's because you want to use the property for gambling," he explained nervously. "They don't want to be in the gaming business."

"They wouldn't be, Sylvan, we would, but obviously the great-white-father attitude is still alive after all."

"Come on, Louisa, you know it's not like that."

"No, I don't," she said, "but I don't care. I can't worry about what I can't do anything about. Changing two hundred years of screwing the Indian is something I can't do anything about, so I'm not going to try."

He threw up his hands. "Sorry."

"No big deal. We expected it."

Louisa was again in Furness's office in Sacramento. Just her this time. The others who had come down with her from the reservation, Mary Redfeather and one of the men who had been at the previous meeting were nervously waiting for her over coffee in an IHOP down the street. She'd wanted this to be a one-on-one meeting, her and the BIA man. She figured she could work him better if it was just the two of them alone.

"I'm sorry you drove all the way down here to hear that," he said apologetically. "I could have told you over the phone. I told you that."

She shook her head. "I know. That's not why we came."

He was perplexed. "Why did you?"

"Remember how I told you if you couldn't get us the loan, we'd come up with the money some other way?"

"Yes," he said slowly.

"Well, we've got it," she said, flashing him a smile. "We want to get started negotiating right away."

"Oh." He was taken aback; he hadn't expected this. "Where'd you get it?"

"What does the BIA care, as long as it's legitimate?"

He was on the defensive, she had him on the run. "It doesn't . . . I guess."

"Good." She leaned forward. "Let's get down to business. Are you authorized to negotiate for the department? Can you make a deal on your own?"

He pursed his lips. "I can negotiate . . ."

She bored in on him. "Can you say yes or no?"

He hated feeling weak in front of this woman. "No," he admitted. "I have to get department approval on any deal we'd make."

She nodded. "Okay. Now I know the lay of the land." She reached into her purse and took out a pad and pencil. "Two million's bullshit, it's way too high, you know that and I know that and the dweebs in Washington know that. It's no reflection on you, Sylvan," she said, smiling at him, "I know you're there for me, as much as you can be. And I appreciate it, believe me. I know you'll do as right by me as you can. Won't you?"

He swallowed, nodded. "Yes, Louisa. I will."

"That's what I want to hear. So let's start talking turkey for real, okay?"

"What did you offer?" a nervous Mary Redfeather asked Louisa.

They were in the IHOP, working on their second big carafe of coffee. With the laws in California now they couldn't smoke at the table, they had to go outside. Mary had been outside half a dozen times already this morning, waiting for Louisa to come back from the meeting.

"Eight hundred and fifty grand."

"Did he take it?"

"He's getting back to me. You know how that works." She opened three sugars into her coffee, to give it some flavor. "It'll take months, but we'll hear from them."

"Two million's way too much," the man, whose name was John, said with sour pessimism. "We can't pay that."

"We could if we had to," Louisa corrected him, looking over her shoulder to make sure they weren't being eavesdropped on, "but we're not going to have to. They'll come around."

"How much do you think they'll settle for?" Mary asked.

Louisa sipped her coffee. Not very good. She needed to remember to make a pit stop before they started the drive home, all this bad coffee she'd been drinking.

"About a million. Maybe a million one. They can't do anything with it, they can't get more than that. No other drug dealer's going to buy it, that's for sure. So who else would want it, except us?"

"That's still a lot of money," John fretted. "We don't have that kind of money."

"We'll get it," Louisa said confidently. She signaled for the waitress. She needed to put something solid in her stomach, to soak up the coffee bile.

"Where?" Mary asked dubiously.

"I've been talking with a group of investors," Louisa said. "People who can see the possibilities."

"I didn't know you were talking to anyone," Mary said slowly. "How come you haven't come to the council with it?"

"Because I didn't want to waste everyone else's time," Louisa explained impatiently. "I wanted to wait until we knew Interior would sell us the property. I'm going to come to the council, believe me."

"Are these investors of yours Vegas people?" John asked. "Can we trust them? They're opposed to Indian gambling. They'd try to take it out from under us."

She shook her head. "No, these aren't established gambling interests." She turned to the waitress. "A bran muffin, please, butter on the side." To her friends: "You going to eat anything?"

They weren't; they'd eaten while she was meeting with Furness.

"Trust me," she assured John and Mary after the waitress left to get her order. "The money's there." She smiled. "And this time it's the Indian who's going to win, instead of the white man."

Kate flew into O'Hare on United, picked up her rental Saturn at Avis, then headed south on I-94, which took her to I-90 east, into northern Indiana. Once she got through the snarl of Chicago and Gary, it was easy driving, mostly farmland, dotted with small towns along the way.

By the time she reached the outskirts of South Bend, twilight was coming on, an especially brilliant meltdown of burnished oranges, silvers, vermilions, purples. Detouring by Notre Dame, she witnessed the reflection of the dying sun as it shimmered off the Golden Dome. She'd seen the famous landmark on television, watching football games, but she had never been in the heartland of the country before. She'd lived her entire life in California.

She let her mind journey, conjuring images formed from secondhand experience, of burning leaves in the fall, golden retrievers running across soccer fields, swimming in quarries, tailgate parties at football games, snowmen in the winter.

She found the address she was looking for without much difficulty.

A substantial brick-and-wood split-level on a shady, tree-lined street. A Diamond Back mountain bike, similar to the one her younger daughter had, was lying where its owner, probably also a teenager, had dropped it on its side, midway up the flagstone walkway that bisected the lawn from the curb to the front door. A mud-splattered 4Runner was parked in the driveway in front of the open garage doors that revealed a lawn mower, shop tools, the accoutrements of the comfortable upper-middle-class suburban life.

Home sweet home. Would it be as sweet an hour from now?

She pressed the doorbell, shifting her soft briefcase from one shoulder to the other. Sounds of footsteps galloping down a hallway, the door flung open. A tall, gawky teenage boy loomed over her. Without a word he turned and called over his shoulder.

"Mom, it's for you."

They sat in the pine-paneled family room. From behind a door somewhere else in the house Kate heard the muffled sounds of a computer game. Her younger daughter was a computer freak, she had all the latest games, Kate knew the sound. Diane Jerome Richards, the boy's mother, sat across from her. A tall, athletic-looking woman, wearing jeans and a sweatshirt. Her red hair was short now, utilitarian in cut. They were drinking iced tea. A plate of homemade cookies sat on the coffee table between them.

"Thank you for seeing me, Diane," Kate said. "May I call you Diane?"

The woman smiled. "Of course, Ms. . . . ." She scrounged in her jeans for a card.

"Blanchard. Please, call me Kate."

The woman nodded, glancing at the business card she'd put in her pocket, the card that had come with the letter. "Kate." She wasn't ill at ease, but her expression was solemn. "Your telephone call came as a shock, I have to admit," she said. "I'd buried that part of my life. I'd hoped it would never be resurrected."

"I'm sorry. But I have to do this."

"I understand."

"Have you lived here long?"

Kate didn't want to plunge right in to the point of her trip halfway across the country. Her desire was to help Diane Richards, the former Diane Jerome, feel comfortable with her; or at least not uptight, the normal condition people have with strangers who suddenly drop into their world and turn it upside down.

"Ten years. My husband's a professor at Notre Dame. Economics. We came when he was finishing up his thesis and stayed on when they offered him tenure."

"You have a lovely home. Do you work, also?"

"Thank you. Yes. I teach. Fourth grade."

The doorbell rang again. Without moving from her chair, Diane called out, "Kenny, your pizza's here!" She explained, "Ron, my husband, is teaching tonight. Kenny has evening spring basketball practice at the high school. I'm not going to cook just for me."

Kate smiled. "I have two teenagers of my own. Rusty's Pizza's the first number on our speed-dial."

The tall boy barged into the room. Diane handed him some bills from her purse. He took them and left without acknowledging Kate.

Time to do what she had come for. Kate reached into her bag and pulled out the yearbook she'd taken out of the Stanford library. Opening it to a Post-it-marked page, she showed it to her hostess.

"This is you?" Kate pointed to the woman's picture from two decades past.

Diane barely glanced at it. "Yes, it's me."

Kate flipped the page. "And you know him." Her finger hovered under the tiny photograph of Reynaldo Juarez.

"Yes. I knew him."

"He was . . ."

"My boyfriend."

"And Sterling Jerome is your brother?"

A curt nod of the head. "One of them. By two years. He's the closest in age to me." She broke off her look from Kate. "That was so long ago. I used to have wishful fantasies that it didn't happen, that it was all a dream."

Turning to Kate again, she said, "It did happen. I can't will it away." She hesitated for a moment. "Not that I want to. It's part of me, who I am." Her voice was suddenly sorrowful. "Who I've become."

They met the first semester of freshman year. They were in the same dorm, segregated boy-girl by floor, but the traffic flowed up and down the stairwells like water out of a faucet. They were as opposite as two eighteen-year-old kids could be, which was the initial attraction. A clas-

sic pairing: he the barrio hood with a brain, an attitude, and a reputation, driving a fancy car and spending piles of money in San Francisco on the weekends, she the protected daughter, the only girl, the baby of a hard-drinking Chicago Irish clan, her big, red-knuckled fireman father and big, hardheaded brothers full of old-fashioned Irish prejudice, ready to stomp any boy who would look sideways at her, especially if his skin was brown and his name was Juarez. As lazy and shiftless as niggers, her father would say, and as smelly, her mother, no stranger to bigotry herself, would add.

This was when she was younger, going to parochial school all the way through high school, when black and Latino kids started infiltrating the Irish-Polish-Italian closed circle. She heard her parents and didn't say otherwise, although she had secret girlfriends she knew her family would disapprove of, a black girl and one from El Salvador.

No boyfriends, she traveled with her friends in a safe pack, all the parents and families knowing and approving of each other. She finally began dating her senior year, acceptable boys, from acceptable families. Nothing serious, no going steady, no staying out past midnight. Irish, like her family, and one Polack boy whose father was an important alderman and drank with her father and uncles. But that was where the line was drawn.

They didn't want her to go to Stanford, all the way out there, De Paul and Loyola were good enough for her brothers, what was wrong with those fine Catholic colleges, but the priest who was the principal of the high school, a scholarly Jesuit, convinced them it was all right. She was a smart girl, it was in her interests to broaden her education. Stanford was no hotbed of radicalism like Berkeley, up the road. And it was a great school, they should be proud that one of their children was so smart, so qualified.

They gave in, and she went.

Reynaldo was full of swagger, but he was shy around her. Her pale beauty, the purity of it, overwhelmed him. They looked at each other and away from each other for months, finding excuses to be in the common rooms at the same time. By the luck of the draw they had two classes together, chemistry and calculus, so they found themselves in the same lab at night, or studying in the same small group with the graduate assistant math tutor.

Finally, he asked her out. For coffee. She said she wouldn't mind a cup of coffee.

A week later, they were lovers.

They were cool about it. Their friends knew they were hot for each other, but they didn't know how deep the feeling was. He lavished money on her, took her out to dinner, to restaurants of a caliber she'd never stepped foot into in her life, first locally, in Palo Alto, then up to San Francisco, to fancy establishments where the waiters handed them leatherbound wine lists and unfolded their napkins onto their laps. Driving his Porsche Carrera, the Eagles and the Police blasting from the speakers.

She exposed him to movies, plays, to the symphony. Growing up, she had been to movies, to plays, to the symphony and the Chicago Art Institute with her friends. He had never been to any of those things, but he had a new life now, and a new woman, who could show him the ropes. He loved the symphony, the big romantic pieces, Tchaikovsky and Rachmaninoff, and he loved the art, too, especially the Impressionists. An entire new life was unfolding for both of them, and they savored it, they devoured it. And the sex was fantastic, they couldn't get enough of each other.

He bought her clothes, so she'd be properly dressed when they went to these fancy places. Expensive designer clothes, on the flashy side, he was Latino, he had colorful tastes. Her mother would have ripped the dresses off her body. She felt self-conscious when first she wore the new dresses and blouses and skirts, but she quickly got used to them. She loved the way she looked in them, how the silks and cashmeres and fine cottons felt on her. After being in drab Catholic school uniforms her entire life, this was like being a movie star.

He drove her to the airport to catch her flight home for Christmas. Standing in the stale air of the terminal, waiting for her plane to board, he told her, for the first time, that he loved her. She told him that she loved him, too.

Her family knew how to celebrate the holidays. They ate too much, they got drunk, they had a wonderful time. They were all together, the boys, the oldest with their wives, and Diane, the baby, home again, in the bosom of her family.

Her mother confronted her between Christmas and New Year's.

"You're pregnant."

"What're you, nuts?" Her heart was pounding like there was a sledgehammer slamming way inside her chest.

"Who is he?"

"You're crazy, Mom. I'm not sleeping with anybody."

"We'll see what Dr. Schwartz has to say."

She didn't want to see the gynecologist, her mother had to practically tie her up and drag her.

"Don't tell Dad we're going, Mom," she pleaded.

"Don't worry. I'm not gonna. Because I don't want to see him kill you. My baby. My littlest angel, who's gonna ruin my life."

"Don't talk like that, Mom. For God's sakes."

"Mother Mary of God, pray for us sinners."

The test came back positive.

"I'll ask you again, once," her mother said. They were in a bar a few blocks away from the clinic. Her mother was on her third 7&7. She was drinking a Coke. "Who's the son of a bitch?"

She broke down. "A boy from school."

Her mother slammed her fist onto the table. "I knew it! We never should've sent you away. Fucking Jesuits! Fucking Jesuit bastards who said it would be good for you! Since when is getting knocked up good for you!" she shouted.

"Mom, please." She looked around wildly. People were watching them, but nobody here knew them, thank God. "It's not the end of the world."

"For me it is. And your father . . ."

"You don't have to tell him. Please, Mom. Don't tell him."

"He's your father. He has to know."

"Mom." She was fighting to stay calm, because her mother was off the wall. "We can keep this between us."

Her mother looked at her over the rim of her whiskey glass. "Are we talking about an abortion here? Taking the life of an unborn innocent?" She sighed, finished her drink.

"I . . ." She loved Reynaldo, but she couldn't have his child. She couldn't have a child, period. She was a freshman in college, she was going to go to law school or med school. She was going to have a career. Having a baby at eighteen wasn't part of the great plan.

"You're gonna have to," her mother said, signaling the bar waitress for another round, holding up two fingers to signify she wanted a double. "You can't have some . . . who's the father?"

"Just . . . just a boy. From school."

"A boy from school. Does this boy have a name?"

"Oh, God, Mom, does it matter? If I get rid of it, who cares who the father is?"

"Because I want to know who you're fucking," her mother said, ice-cold. "What is he, a kike? A nigger?"

"No, Mom."

Her mother exhaled a massive sigh of relief. "At least it's a white man's baby you're carrying. So who is he already? Is he rich? What's his father, some bank president or something? All those kids out at Stanford, they're all blue bloods, aren't they?"

The waitress brought her mother's drink. She slammed down half in one gulp. "Maybe you should keep the little bastard." She chuckled. "The little bastard. That's a good one. So, all right, I'm calming down now. Maybe it isn't the end of the world. The name, Diane. What is this boy's name?"

She told her mother Reynaldo's name. Her mother fainted, right onto the floor.

"What happened then?" Kate asked. It was dark outside now. She was breathless, listening to this. They were alone in the house.

"We have to tell your father." Her mother was revived now, slumped against the back of the booth, a drink in one hand, filtered Camel in the other, the ashtray in front of her overflowing.

"For God's sakes, Mom, no! You promised."

"I didn't know it was a spic."

"Don't use that word, Mom. He's Mexican, not Puerto Rican."

"They're all the same."

It was as if a sea change had come over her. From girl to woman. She got up from the booth.

"They're not all the same, Mom."

She walked out, took a cab home, packed her clothes, took another cab to the airport, and flew back to Stanford calling Reynaldo's house in Los Angeles from the airport to tell him when her plane was arriving.

He was there to meet her. Of course.

There was only one solution. They would get married, at the end of the spring term. The baby wouldn't be born yet, their child would not be a bastard. It was fine that they had to get married, they were in love, they would have gotten married sooner or later anyway.

Her mother told. Not right away, she wrestled with it for some time. She knew that to tell Diane's father, her brothers, would be tantamount to issuing a license to kill. But she did, over Easter Sunday dinner, when *the celebration of the Resurrection and its message about everlasting life was more than she could bear. Plus she and all the clan, gathered from all over into the bosom of the family, had consumed copious amounts of whiskey and Guinness, especially her husband and her boys, Sterling foremost among them. The horrible truth spilled out.*

Diane wasn't home with them. She'd stayed in Palo Alto. She got the news over the phone from her brother Mike.

"We're coming out."

She didn't run from them, she didn't hide. Nor did Reynaldo, he wasn't about to back off from anyone, he was a man, he was only nine-teen but he'd been a man for years. If he could survive and flourish on the mean streets of East L.A., doing what he did, he could handle these prejudiced assholes. And she was his woman, protecting her was his job. He arranged, through her, to meet her brothers, the three who had come out to deal with this. The meeting would take place in the library. A public place, where they would all have to act civilized.

Diane wasn't going to come to the meeting. After Reynaldo and her brothers talked, she would join them, if he told her things were okay. She was reluctant to do even that. She didn't want to see her brothers at all, her pregnancy was beginning to show. That would inflame them, even more than they already were. She didn't care if she never saw them again. She had cast her lot in a different direction. Reynaldo convinced her they had to do this—they couldn't run from her family.

He shaved, showered, put on some good clothes, left his room to meet them, to show them that he was worthy of their sister's love. But her brothers didn't deal honorably with Reynaldo. They laid in wait outside his dorm, until he emerged, alone, to go to the library. Catching him by surprise, they jumped him, tied him up, took his gun, which he had hidden tucked into the back of his pants under his shirt (he was from the street, he always carried when a situation might be dangerous), threw him in the trunk of the car they'd rented at the airport, a big Buick with a big trunk, plenty big enough to hold a body, and drove to a deserted area near the beach, twenty miles away.

Waiting in her dorm room to hear, Diane knew something had gone wrong. She was petrified.

At the beach, the Jerome brothers, Mike, Joe Jr., and Sterling, hauled Reynaldo out of the car trunk, where they proceeded to beat the living shit out of him, teaching him a lesson, so that he'd never come near their sister again. Beating him unconscious.

After they'd finished administering their punishment, they left him for dead on the beach, drove back to the campus, abducted Diane from her room kicking and screaming, and drove her to San Francisco, where a doctor performed the abortion they had already arranged, in a hospital, under a false name. They paid the bill in cash.

They stayed overnight, making sure she would survive okay (the operation, not the emotional trauma, they didn't care about that), and to ensure that her spic lover wouldn't find out where she was and try to join her. Then they went home, having done the job they had come out to do, leaving her with a warning: Never see him again, or we'll kill him.

She did see him again. Two days later, when she went back to the campus, feeling hollow inside, and found him in the university hospital, recovering from the vicious beating her brothers had inflicted on him. He was too tough for them to kill. He had crawled to the highway and flagged down a car, the driver called an ambulance.

He didn't tell the police who had done it. He said he didn't know who it was. The police, after their inquiry revealed his background, concluded it was a gang thing, like a drive-by shooting. They weren't inclined to put energy into investigating it—he was a former drug dealer. Case closed.

It took him a month to recover. She came to the hospital every day. It was hard for them to be with each other. She wasn't carrying their child anymore, and he had almost died, both at the hands of her family. Who didn't know any other way to show their love.

They finished up the school year after he got of the hospital and resumed classes. Neither of them was interested in schoolwork, but they both struggled through, maintaining their grades by sheer force of will.

The semester ended. They were going home for the summer. They would see each other again, in the fall. They would start over fresh.

It was hard to stay in touch, she had to call him from friends' houses. As the summer wore on, they communicated less and less with each other.

Love can survive almost anything, but not everything. Theirs didn't survive this battering of their hearts, bodies, and souls. When the fall semester began, neither of them was there to begin sophomore classes. She transferred to Northwestern. He didn't transfer anywhere, as far as she knew.

And then she stopped hearing from him altogether.

*　　*　　*

Diane Richards made a vodka martini for Kate and one for herself. She talked briefly to her husband over the phone from the kitchen, then rejoined Kate where they were sitting.

"He'll be home in about forty-five minutes," she told Kate.

"Would you like me to be gone by then?"

"I'd prefer it."

"Sure. We can be finished by then."

They drank their martinis in silence for a few minutes. Then Diane finished her story.

"I lost contact with him altogether. I called his family, but they didn't know where he was, or at least they wouldn't tell me. I could tell they didn't approve of him seeing me. I was the reason for his dropping out. I could understand that." She sipped her drink. "So after a while, I stopped trying."

"And you never heard from him again?"

"Once. Towards the end of my junior year at Northwestern. I had readjusted—slowly. I'd met Ron by then, he was there in graduate school, we were dating. My family approved of him, not that I gave a damn, I cut off all communication with them, paid my own way through school on partial scholarship, student loans, work."

Diane nibbled on her cocktail olive.

"But it was good with Ron, he was solid. There for me. It wasn't like it had been with Reynaldo, that fire we had. But you can only have that when you're young. I wasn't looking for that anymore." She paused. "I didn't want that."

Kate watched and listened, sipping her own drink. It was as if, for a moment, the woman went somewhere else. Then she returned from wherever she'd gone.

"There was a postcard in my mailbox. It was a picture of Machu Picchu, in Peru, those famous ruins. Just one line—'You would love seeing this with me.' No signature, no return address."

"It was from him."

"Oh, yes. I'm sure."

"And that was all."

Diane nodded. "That was all. I never heard his name again . . . until last fall, when I heard it on the news."

"You knew it was him."

"Yes." She nodded.

"And you knew your brother had led the raid."

Another nod.

Kate hesitated before asking the next question. "When you were at Stanford—when you were seeing Reynaldo—did you know he was dealing drugs?"

"Yes. Not there, he wasn't selling them there while he was a student, he promised me he wasn't, but I knew he had."

"What did you think about that?"

"Honestly?" Diane smiled. "That it was glamorous. I knew it was wrong, but you know, a young girl practically out of the convent, the edginess of it, being with someone who lived in an illegal world, it was exciting. Vicariously, not for real," she added hastily.

Kate pondered on that. "What would have happened if you had stayed together? If you hadn't gotten pregnant, say, and your family hadn't found out? How would you have dealt with being married to a drug dealer? A menace to society? Someone whose life would always be in jeopardy?"

"I wouldn't have."

Kate looked at her, the skepticism clearly showing on her face.

"He would have gotten out of the life."

"You know that for sure? That sounds more like a young lover's dream than a reality."

Diane nodded emphatically. "We talked about it, extensively. He knew how I felt. Not only about the immorality of it, but the danger. To him, to us as a family in the future."

A sudden thought flashed through Kate's mind. "I just had a weird hit. Sad, really."

"What's that?"

"Your brother, who wound up being a crusader in the war against drugs, helped push Juarez into going back to being a seller when he was really on the way out."

Diane nodded somberly. "Yes, I know. I've thought of that, many times."

Another thought came to Kate. Much heavier, chilling. "Do you think your brother Sterling knew that that boy he almost killed, and Reynaldo Juarez, the legendary drug lord, was the same person?"

"Yes. He had to know."

Jesus, Kate thought. Wait until Luke hears about all this.

"What about the people your brother worked with over the years at the DEA? Do you think any of them had knowledge about what happened between Sterling and Reynaldo? The vendetta your brother was carrying against him all those years?"

Diane shook her head. "I'm sure they didn't. I don't think anyone ever knew, outside of our immediate family. We never talked about it after that. It was one of those terrible family secrets everyone takes to their graves."

"No one except Reynaldo Juarez," Kate corrected her. "Who took it to his."

"Yes." Diane was on the verge of tears, finally.

It was time to go—Kate had what she needed. She put the Stanford yearbook back into her briefcase. "One last question, Diane."

"Yes?"

"Do you think your brother Sterling might have killed Reynaldo Juarez? Do you think he was capable of it?"

The former Diane Jerome stared down at the floor, her elbows on her knees. She was spent, this evening had taken a heavy toll on her. She looked up at Kate.

"I don't know if Sterling killed Reynaldo. I hope he didn't. But I do know that Reynaldo was a lifelong obsession with Sterling, ever since going back to that time at Stanford." She sat up straighter. "*Did* he kill him? Like I said, I don't know. Did he want to? I'm sure he did. Was he *capable* of doing it, emotionally?" Her eyes bored in on Kate.

"Absolutely."

DAMNING EVIDENCE

Kate's news hit me like a bombshell, since it was one.

We were sitting in my temp office, after hours. I'd had a grueling day with my grand jury witnesses. She had called as soon as she left the Richards house, but she hadn't reached me with her news until the following morning. She'd flown back to Blue River from Chicago via San Francisco, arriving shortly after I was finishing up with the grand jury for the day. My head hadn't been in the testimony I was taking—I was anxiously waiting on her.

On the airplane she had made copious notes about their meeting. I skimmed through them while she helped herself to a Beck's from the office refrigerator.

I dropped her information on my desk. "This changes . . . I don't know what this changes. A lot of things. Holy shit! Good work, Kate!" I congratulated her.

"Thanks, boss." She chugged some beer. "What do you think you can do with this information?"

"Keep it to the immediate team, for openers," I said, meaning the two of us and my other investigators. "I don't want this getting out prematurely."

"Do you think anyone at his agency knows?"

"I can't imagine they do, or they wouldn't have allowed Jerome to be the agent in charge of busting Juarez. They never would've let him near Juarez. They're sticklers on that kind of stuff." I got a brew for myself. "Kim's going to shit marbles when he finds this out. The whole Justice Department will. This is going to drive a hole right through that agency." I took a long, sweaty hit. It went down good. At this moment, I was a happy man. "If . . ." I held a finger in the air.

"If . . . ?"

"We get an indictment on Jerome."

"Do you think there's a chance you won't?" she asked, surprised.

"I think there's a good chance we will, but it's not a lock," I cautioned her. "Let's not break out the champagne yet, beer'll do for now." I leaned back in my swivel chair, the kind lawyers and newspaper editors favored fifty years ago. I like them, too, but they're hard on your back. It was what had been available up here when we decorated.

"In and of itself this is not enough proof that Jerome killed Juarez. He had plenty of other reasons for hating the guy, legitimate ones. And we know that he was ferocious on the subject of bringing Juarez in alive."

"Talking the talk and walking the walk are *muy* different," Kate rebutted me. "You don't think if Jerome had brought Juarez back alive, Juarez's lawyers wouldn't have used what happened back then against Jerome?"

"How could they have?" I like sparring with people who think, it keeps me on my toes. "If anything, that's confirmation that Jerome was zealous against Juarez even back then. Don't forget, Juarez was already an established drug dealer when he hit the Stanford campus. What brother is going to sit by idly while his innocent little sister gets involved with a death merchant? They'd give him a medal."

"Jerome didn't know anything about Juarez's background," Kate snapped derisively. "All that thickheaded mick knew was that Juarez was a greaser who'd knocked up his holier-than-thou sister, the family virgin. The war on drugs had nothing to do with it."

"You know that, and I know that," I told her. "But Jerome could plead otherwise, that he had found out about who Juarez was, and that was his reason for beating his ass to a pulp and leaving him for the vultures to feed on. Not because he knocked her up and disgraced the family." I laughed. "From what you've told me, that's a hard family to disgrace."

Kate drank some beer. "I thought you'd be more excited."

"Hey, don't get me wrong," I told her, "I am incredibly excited. This absolutely points us in Jerome's direction as the prime suspect." I held up my hands like a crossing guard. "What I'm saying, though, is that this information, in and of itself, isn't enough to go for an indictment. We might be able to get one, but it would be weak, and we probably couldn't get a conviction. An indictment's only a way station, Kate. I want a conviction."

I finished my beer, tossed the bottle into the trash can. "I want an airtight case. No leakage." I grabbed up her notes. "Make copies of these. Just us for now."

"What's my next step?"

"Start looking at Sterling Jerome. Let's find out what else there is in his ugly past. A couple more of these"—I handed her the notes—"and we're off to the races."

Sheriff Miller poked his head into my office, carrying a manila folder in his hand. It was a few days after Kate had brought me her exciting news.

"Got a minute?"

"For you, Tom, anytime." I was feeling expansive. Breaking a case can do that for you, and we were definitely onto something. "How's it going?"

"Can't complain. Mind if I sit down?"

"Be my guest."

He took the chair across the desk from me, turning the folder over in his hands.

"I know I'm not part of your investigation, but this is important to me, too. More important than it is to you, Luke. To you, it's a job. To me, it's . . ." He hesitated. "More than that. It's a stain on my record that has to be wiped off."

"What happened out there that night was no reflection on you, Sheriff. You did everything you could to avert it."

"I don't know. Maybe I should've been more assertive." He was fighting for self-control, thinking back to the incident. His old weatherlined face was reddening. "It was my jurisdiction. Jerome had no right to shut me out like he did."

"Yes, I agree." Then I asked, "Are you feeling the same way about me not including you in my investigation?" I knew he was, but I felt obligated to ask.

"I'd be happier if I was part of it," he admitted freely, "but like I've told you, I can understand why it has to be this way. Not being a part of it—officially."

The way he said "officially" perked my ears up. He was working toward something.

"I have been nosing around," he said. "Checking things on my own. Not getting in your way, Luke," he added quickly, "I wouldn't do anything unprofessional like that. But I have friends in law enforcement who lend a helping hand if I need one. Here in California—and back in Washington, too."

He opened the manila folder, took out a sheet of paper, handed it across the desk to me. "Follow up on this."

I glanced at what he'd handed me. It had been faxed from FBI headquarters.

"We haven't asked the FBI to come in on this."

I was peeved—I didn't want my investigation going off the tracks. People out of the loop, freelancing on their own, no matter how well-intentioned, usually cause trouble.

"I know you haven't, and I apologize in advance for stepping on your toes, if I have," he said. "But we're all pulling on the same oars, aren't we?"

"I hope we are."

"Then take that and follow up on it." He pointed to the document in my hand.

I looked more closely at the page. It appeared to be a bank statement, from the Miami branch of a Colombian bank. Most Central and South American banks have big divisions in Miami. It's the de facto financial capital of South America—many rich South Americans don't want their money in banks in their own countries, their economies are too unstable.

There were no names on the statement, just numbers: ID numbers and what might have been financial numbers, dollars most likely.

"What is this?" I looked more closely at it.

"Somebody's bank account."

"I can see that," I said with exasperation. "What about it?"

"It might be worth your looking into." He calmly sat across from me like an owl perched on a limb, scanning the ground below for his next meal.

"Does this have anything to do with our investigation?" It had to, why else would he be giving it to me?

"Check it out and then you'll know," he said, deliberately being enigmatic.

"Tom." I dropped the document on the desk in front of me. "Let's not play games with each other, okay? If you've got something to tell me, tell me."

He got up. "I accept that I can't work on this officially—I don't like it, you know that—but you can't stop me from nosing around on my own. I'm the sheriff, that's my job. And I have friendships going back decades, friends in high places who believe in me." He looked at me, to make sure I was getting the drift. "Who knows? If I do it good, you might sign me on as part of the team. Officially. I prefer walking in the front door instead of the back, Luke."

He leaned down to me. "You're missing a bet not using me, son. I've got a wealth of information stored in this old head, and contacts going back decades. If you truly want to solve this crime and bring who did it to trial, you ought to take advantage of me. I only want to help, that's all."

He stood tall. "And I'm going to. Officially or unofficially."

The senior judge of the Muir County Superior Court, Cyrus McBee, had been assigned to our case. The local counsel for the big lumber companies before he was appointed to the bench, he was a team player who knew what side his bread was buttered on. He found a friendly judge in Florida who issued a search warrant for the bank account, and I was on my way to Miami. I could have sent one of my investigators, but I had a feeling this was going to be big, and I wanted to see what was in that account as soon I could.

I sat in a secure viewing room in the bank, reading the printouts the senior vice president had given me. My hands were shaking.

I read the papers several times. Then I placed them in a manila folder, sealed it, put it in my briefcase. The vice president was mailing me a duplicate, certified mail, for protection. Exiting the room, I thanked him for his help and his time, went outside into the piercing Florida afternoon sunshine, got into the taxi the bank had called for me, and went directly to the airport, where I flew nonstop to Los Angeles, hugging the briefcase firmly to my chest the entire trip.

My state airplane took me to Blue River. I drove to the condo. Bucky was already in bed, asleep. I gave him a soft kiss on his warm forehead, then joined Riva.

"Did you have a productive day?" she asked.

I told her what I'd found. I tell her everything, we're not one of those marriages that separates work from the rest of my life.

"That's incredible. What are you going to do now?"

"Bring Jerome into the grand jury. See if he has an explanation for this."

"What explanation could he have?"

"His mother died, he won the lottery. I don't know. I can't prejudge the man, I've got to give him a chance to explain it.

She laughed. "And then you're going to hang him."

"No, honey. He's going to hang himself."

"Did my information help you?" Sheriff Miller asked.

"Immeasurably."

We were in my office again. He always came to my office. He was a stickler for protocol; I was senior to him in this, even though he was almost twice my age and had more experience.

"Here's something else for you." He gave me the name of a business owner in the county who'd had transactions with some of the DEA agents around the time of the raid.

"I'll talk to him. This sounds good."

"That's another reason you should be using me," he said, pleading his case forcefully. "Local knowledge. None of your people know anyone here. Folks here aren't going to talk to you, you're outsiders, like the DEA was. But they talk to me, because I'm one of them. They seek me out. I listen to them, and I take them seriously."

He got up to go.

"These people here are unsophisticated, I'll be the first to say so. I know; I've lived in both worlds. But they aren't stupid. Me, either," he zinged me.

"I don't think you're stupid, Tom. You're smarter than I've been on this. You're making my case for me."

"Then make it official."

What could I say to that? He was right on.

"You're on the payroll. Officially."

We shook hands.

"Is it too late to offer an apology for cutting you out?"

His old face creased with an ear-to-ear smile. "It's never too late for that. Besides, you don't owe me one. You don't owe me anything. I have to earn my stripes, like any other man."

"You've earned them, Sheriff. You've more than earned them."

                    *   *   *

"State your name for the members of the grand jury, please."

"Ralph Harrison."

Harrison was sworn in, took his seat. He was of medium height, built like a beer keg. I'd heard he was a committed iron-pumper. He looked like one; he had severe acne, one of the bad side effects of heavy steroid use. His truck, festooned with NRA bumper stickers, was parked outside. Someone had pointed it out to me as I entered the building. It was a massive old Ford, with three gun-racks mounted behind the seat, each supporting a powerful hunting rifle.

I ambled over to him. He was a friendly witness, this wasn't going to take much time. But it was another brick, an important one, in the wall I was building.

"Would you tell us what line of work you're in, Mr. Harrison?" I began.

"I'm the owner of Harrison's Gun and Supply, in Southridge."

Southridge is a one-block town in the northern part of the county. Once you get past Southridge, you're in national forest and wilderness area. Some of the reservations are located nearby, also. If you're going hunting, you go through Southridge. And you buy your ammunition and other supplies from Harrison's.

"Are you the largest gun and supply store in Muir County?"

"One of them. Blue River Gun and Supply, in town here, is pretty big, too. We both do good business."

"Do you recall an incident in the area of Muir County known as the compound in the fall of last year?"

"You mean that shoot-out?"

"Yes."

"Sure, I do. Everybody round here knows about that. That was big news, for us."

"And later, did you meet any members of the DEA Internal Affairs team that was investigating that incident?"

"Uh-huh."

"What were the circumstances of your meeting them?"

"A bunch of 'em were going hunting up in the Fremont National Forest. They stopped in the store to buy their licenses and some other stuff."

"What kind of stuff?"

"Ammo for their rifles. One of 'em bought a pair of boots. Knives and some other equipment for field-dressing their deer, if they got any. Hats, sunscreen. The usual stuff hunters buy."

"Any guns? Rifles?"

"No. You can't buy guns over the counter in California. There's a ten-day waiting period."

"Even for federal agents?"

He shook his head. "The law applies to everybody. No exceptions."

"But not to ammunition. Bullets."

"No. You can buy them right off."

I assumed everybody in the room knew this; hunting and fishing are the biggest recreational sports in the area. I was laying my groundwork, for the record.

"Were you in the store when they came in?" I asked.

"Yes, I was."

"Did you sell them their goods?"

"Yes."

"So you got to know them."

"They introduced themselves. We talked about how the hunting was going. A good salesman is polite and attentive to his customers."

"Did they ask you about that incident at the compound?"

"No."

"Nothing about it?"

"I knew they were investigating it. I asked 'em if they'd come up with any leads."

"What did they say?"

"They were working on it, but they couldn't talk about it."

"Did you draw any conclusions from that, Mr. Harrison?"

"That they hadn't found anything." He paused. "Let me put it another way. They weren't going to tell me anything, was the way it seemed."

"You didn't think that was out of the ordinary, though, did you? The police don't normally talk to civilians about investigations in process, do they?"

"Around here they will sometimes, but that's 'cause everybody knows everybody, small towns don't hold secrets. But I wouldn't expect some federal agent who'd never met me before to walk into my gun shop and start blabbing off the top of his head."

"So as far as you were concerned, they were acting normally."

"Yeah. They were going after their deer and they were looking forward to it."

"You said you sold them any ammunition for their rifles."

"Yes, sir."

"Did you sell them ammunition for their handguns?"

He laughed. "You don't use a pistol to kill an elk. Least not around here. Maybe in the movies."

"Okay. I want to make sure I'm clear on this. They didn't talk to you about the investigation they were in the middle of."

"No. They did not."

"Did they ask any questions?"

"About their investigation?"

"Yes."

"No. They didn't ask me anything."

"They didn't ask if you'd seen, or noticed, or heard anything out of the ordinary, or suspicious, around the time of that raid?"

"No, sir."

"Okay."

I walked back to my desk, consulted my notes for a moment, returned to the witness chair.

"Well, Mr. Harrison, I'm going to. I have some questions for you about certain things you observed during that time."

"Fire away," he said with no consciousness of irony.

"Did you meet, or get to know in any fashion, any of the agents of the Drug Enforcement Administration who were on that raid?"

"Yes. I met one of them."

"Do you remember when that was?"

He nodded with certainty. "Yes, I do."

"When was that?"

"Four days before that raid."

"Four days. Are you sure?"

"Yes."

"You remember the date that well."

"Yes, sir, I do."

"Why is that?"

"Because what he asked for was . . . kind of unusual."

"Unusual how? Did he want to buy something?"

"Yes."

"What?"

"Ammunition."

"What's unusual about buying ammunition in a gun shop?" I turned to the grand jurors. They were paying attention and seemed puzzled, like me.

"He wanted to buy ammunition for an automatic pistol. Nine-millimeter. Full-metal jackets."

"So?"

"Well, there were a few things that seemed weird to me. I had him pegged for a law officer of some kind. I didn't know federal, state, whatever, but I figured federal, state cops don't have the broomstick so far up their . . ." He glanced over at the women in the grand jury box. "Up their behinds. In my business you gotta know these things, 'cause sometimes they'll set you up. You know, like send somebody in underage, or try to talk you into selling them a gun on the spot, without waiting the ten days the state requires, things like that. You learn how to read people. And I read him to be a cop."

"Okay," I said. "I still don't understand what's unusual about a law enforcement official buying ammunition for an automatic pistol. They carry them. Why wouldn't they want to buy bullets for them?"

He sat up straight, ready to take me to school on the subject. I didn't need the lecture, I knew the reasons he'd felt the way he did, because we'd gone over them. But this was the heart of this testimony, I wanted it dead-on, straight, clear, and strong.

"First of all, officers don't buy ammunition for their handguns. It's provided to them. Buying ammunition would be a waste of their money. And they don't like to waste money. They're the worst freeloaders in the world."

"Okay. Why else was this a strange request?"

"He wanted a box of full-metal jackets."

"So?"

"Federal cops don't use full-metal jackets. They use hollow points."

"Could you explain the difference to us?" I checked my jury. They were still with me.

"A hollow-point bullet explodes on impact. The police use them because they do more damage, they don't pass clean through. You get hit with a nine-millimeter hollow point, you're down. Maybe not dead, but down."

"And a full-metal-jacket bullet?"

"It doesn't explode on impact. It cuts a clear target path, which makes it a less disabling bullet, which is why the police don't use them, they want the best odds, which makes sense. Don't get me wrong, a full-metal jacket, especially a high caliber like a nine-millimeter or a .45, is going to do serious damage."

"Kill someone?"

"Absolutely, it hits the right place."

"Like in the brain?"

He smiled broadly. "You get shot in the brain with any bullet, you're dead."

"Okay, I understand," I said. "Now, Mr. Harrison—if someone wanted to shoot another person in the brain, let's say from almost point-blank range, and they *didn't* want the bullet to be identified, what type of bullet would they use? A hollow point or a full-metal jacket?"

"You mean so the bullet couldn't be traced back to a particular gun?"

"Yes."

"You'd use a full-metal jacket, no question."

"Because . . . ?"

"Because at point-blank range, with a weapon that powerful, the odds are it would be an in-and-out shooting."

"Meaning?"

"The bullet goes into the target and comes out. It doesn't stay in the body—the head, in this case, if it's to the brain."

I only had a few more questions—he had answered the important ones.

"Did you sell this man the bullets?"

"Yes. I sold him a box."

"Did he say what he was going to use them for?"

"Target practice."

"Okay." I paused, then went on, "Later on, you found out who this man was, is that correct?"

"Yes."

"Was his name Sterling Jerome?"

"Yes."

"And you learned that he was in charge of the task force?"

"It was common knowledge around here."

"After you learned his identity, did anything else about him strike you as being strange?"

"Yes, something did."

"What was that?"

"The task force was set up on the other side of the county. That's a hundred and fifty miles away. I thought, why would anybody drive three hundred miles round-trip to buy bullets for target practice when they could've bought them right there in Blue River, where they were staying?"

I smiled. "And why do you think he did?"

"The only reason I can figure is, he didn't want anybody to know."

One down, two to go. My next witness was coming in tomorrow, under tight security. To guarantee his protection, I didn't tell anyone his name other than the members of my immediate team; not Tom Miller, my new ally, and certainly not Nora, who I was keeping as much at arm's distance as I could.

I briefed her on Harrison's testimony, as a courtesy. She bugged me like crazy for details, but I was deliberately vague; I didn't trust her. I wasn't worried about her divulging anything, she wouldn't—but she might try to work me over, psychologically or emotionally. Staying away from her was the safest course of action I could take.

I did speak to Bill Fishell, over the phone. He was excited—we were getting somewhere, my investigation might have a real payoff. This was extremely important to him. He was getting heavy flak—from the federals, who for many reasons wanted to scotch our investigation, from congressmen who were being pressured by the federals, by state officials who felt that if the U.S. government had conducted an extensive investigation and found nothing prosecutable, why were we wasting state money on one of our own?

"This conversation is confidential, between you and me, Bill," I warned him in advance.

"Fine." He paused. "Is there a problem with Nora?"

"No," I lied. "It's my policy, blanket. The fewer people who know what's going on, the fewer the chances for leaks, even if they're only accidentally."

"Well, I'd include her in, if I was running the show, it's hers, she brought you in. But since I'm not running the show, I'll leave her involvement to your discretion."

"Thanks. For now, that's how it has to be."

I hung up, knowing I'd planted seeds of doubt in his mind about Nora. They were for the wrong reasons, but I couldn't help it. She had initiated our sexual encounter, she was going to have to pay the price for that. After I got an indictment, assuming I did, I could bring her back into the loop before the trial, which would be months away, if I was comfortable with her by then. For the present, I couldn't do it any other way.

It was a shame, and ironic. I hadn't known or cared about this. She had, deeply. And now she was on the sidelines, not even being allowed to watch.

"This next witness is here under a grant of immunity," I told the grand jurors. "That means nothing he says here can be used against him in a criminal proceeding."

I motioned to Keith Green, who was standing by the door. He went out and came back a moment later escorting Curtis Jackson.

Getting Jackson to testify was a real coup on Keith's part. He had been working Jackson for a long time. The gang leader's contradictory testimony had been troubling to Keith; to me, too, but particularly to Keith, who kept looking for hidden meanings in it. Why had Jackson wanted to talk to him in the first place? He had nothing to gain, ostensibly, except to show off, and that wasn't a good enough reason, Keith thought, not to the point where he would jeopardize himself by shooting his mouth off. That could get him into real trouble, as much with his own as with us.

He hadn't softened his wardrobe or persona for the upstate white hicks. His outfit was almost caricature pimp. Chartreuse suit, purple shirt. Gold chains around his neck, crosses dangling from his ears, a nose ring in his right nostril. Jordanesque head shave.

I swore him in and started right up. I wanted to get him on and off as quickly as I could. He was not a good witness; his demeanor, his entire being, was threatening. And he was an outlaw, he was like Juarez, a true menace to society.

But he could help us. We were strange bedfellows, but you can't always pick your allies. Curtis Jackson was yet another example of the upside-down nature of this case, the scumbags helping to bring down what were usually the white knights.

I elicited his biography, his particulars, including his ranking in the California drug hierarchy, which he embellished, of course, he couldn't resist making himself look good. Perversely, that worked, in this case. Importance equated credibility.

"You knew Reynaldo Juarez," I noted.

"I knew him by reputation," Jackson answered. "I never met him, face-to-face."

"Is that normal? That you wouldn't have met? Since you're in the same line of work? Close competitors, so to speak."

"Of course it's normal. Where're you from, man, the dark side of the moon? We were enemies. You don't associate with your enemies. That's a good way to wind up dead. Or them dead. Kill or be killed. That's how it goes. I know—I've been there." He turned and glared at the jury, to make sure they got his message.

My jurors, listening to Jackson's ravings, were fascinated with him in the same way they would have been if I'd brought in E.T.—he was alien to their existence. Seeing a man like Jackson, a career criminal who was openly boasting about killing people, isn't the same up close and personal as it is on TV or at the movies. It's much scarier.

"You do know that Juarez was killed during a Drug Enforcement Administration raid, don't you?"

"Of course I know. Everybody knows that."

"How did you feel about that?"

"Good. I felt good."

"Because he was a rival."

"That's right."

"Did you have any other feelings?"

He nodded. "I felt bad, too."

"Bad?" I asked in surprise.

He drew in a deep breath. "Not bad. Scared. I don't mean I'm scared or anything, but getting shot down in cold blood like he was, that's cold, man."

I stepped back. "Where did you hear Juarez was killed in cold blood?"

"It was all over the street. Soon as it happened."

"News travels fast."

"That kind does."

"What else was on the street?" I continued. "About that killing."

"That it was a contract hit."

I turned to look at the jurors. They looked as if they'd been zapped with a cattle prod.

"Would you repeat that?" I asked slowly and deliberately.

"Man who capped Juarez was paid to."

"You're saying the person who shot Juarez was paid to shoot him?"

"Isn't that what I just told you?" Jackson asked indignantly. He wasn't, really, I'd prepped him, but he was acting it well.

"Yes. I want to be very clear on this point," I stressed. "According to your grapevine, the assassination of Reynaldo Juarez was a murder for hire."

"Yes."

Talk about sucking air out of a chamber.

"What was the reason? Did the grapevine say anything about that as well?"

I turned to the jurors again. They were watching intently. They had not paid this much attention to any previous witness I'd brought in.

This was a delicate line I was walking. Nothing Jackson had said would stand up in a courtroom; it wouldn't even be allowed. It was all hearsay. I couldn't use it in a trial. But in the grand jury room, it's permissible. Moreover, it's necessary. Sometimes you have to use hearsay and other indirect kinds of evidence to get your indictment. Then you work on substantiating it, and more often than not, you do. The rationale is that the ends justify the means. The danger is that sometimes they don't.

"Yeah," Jackson said. "There was a reason."

"What was it?"

"The word was, a DEA agent crossed over."

"Crossed over."

"This other drug gang bought this agent, like you buy a car, a house, a woman, anything. Everything's for sale in this world, it's just about how much. That is one true thing I have learned."

"Who were they rumored to be?"

"Another big east L.A. Mexican gang, who wanted to eliminate Juarez, take over his business, own it all. They made this agent an offer he couldn't refuse."

"What was the offer?"

"Money. Lots of it."

"Was there talk about how much?"

Jackson shook his head. "Not a number I heard exactly. But heavy. Maybe up to seven figures."

"A million dollars."

"Up to."

"This agent was offered up to a million dollars to murder Reynaldo Juarez."

"That was what I heard, yeah."

I looked at the others in the room. Rapt attention. Back to Jackson: "And the agent took the deal?"

Jackson looked at me like I was brain-damaged. "Juarez is dead, ain't he?"

"Yes, he's dead, all right. Do you have any idea why this particular agent was selected? Or did they go from one agent to the next, until they found one who'd get in bed with them?"

He chortled. "Like they're gonna go to a bunch of 'em, find out if one was down with 'em. Why not take out an ad in the *L.A. Times*? Shit, get real."

"So it was one specific agent who was targeted from the beginning."

"Yes."

"Why this particular agent?"

" 'Cause he had a hard-on for Juarez a mile long."

I glanced at the grand jurors, particularly the women. They were so caught up in what Jackson was saying the obscenity went right by them.

"That was known?"

He nodded. "In our business, you know who's after who. You have to, to survive. This one had his crosshairs on Juarez, forever."

He grinned, showing a diamond in one of his front teeth.

"What had been frustrating this guy was that Juarez could never be pinned down. He was more of a ghost than the Holy Ghost, nobody knew where he was, except his own tight circle. Sometimes even they didn't know. He knew how *not* to be there, you know what I mean? This one time, it was about the only time he ever did get pinned down. One time too many for him, it turned out."

I nodded. "But if Juarez was so elusive, why did this rival group think this particular agent could get to him? That anyone could?"

"It was his mission in life," Jackson said simply. "Man on a mission, he'll hunt until he dies. Or he kills."

I stepped away from the witness chair and glanced over at Keith, who gave me a silent thumbs-up—Jackson had come through. For his own selfish, egotistical reasons, of course; he didn't give a shit about helping us, we were the law, the enemy. But to be involved in getting an indictment against a prominent DEA agent who'd been a major warrior in the fight against drugs? He'd crawl a mile over broken glass on his hands and knees to do that.

I turned back to him. "You know this agent's name, don't you."

"I know what I heard," he said precisely.

I leaned in close to him. "Would you tell us the name that you heard?"

He faced the grand jurors. It was a time-warp tableau, Ice Cube meets Tommy Dorsey.

"The name I heard was Sterling Jerome."

"Thank you, Mr. Jackson." I turned to my jurors. "For the record, Sterling Jerome was the special agent in charge of the Western States Task Force that stormed the compound the night Reynaldo Juarez was shot to death."

Evening. Our office. Major strategy powwow. Myself, my investigators, Tom Miller, and Nora.

I'd engaged in a strong internal debate about whether to include her. I was uncomfortable in her presence, naturally. But after a lot of soul-searching, I relented.

Sheriff Miller convinced me.

"She's miserable, being left out," he told me.

That's what I needed—to be guilt-tripped. But the old campaigner knew what buttons to push. He was carrying water for her; they were a team, that was his job. Even so, his logic was irrefutable.

"You want to use every ounce of brainpower available, Luke. The fact that you *can* legally exclude her doesn't mean you *have* to. Good God, you've brought this beat-up old relic of a small county sheriff into the circle," he said in his ironic self-deprecating way, "which you didn't have to do, so why not her? It's a slap to her pride if you don't afford her the same courtesy. Besides"—he nudged me in a joking fashion—"people are going to wonder why you aren't."

Having tossed off that remark, he then paused and gave me a peculiar look, as if he suspected things no one other than Nora and I should ever know. "Is there personal animosity between the two of you?" he asked with concern.

"No," I replied quickly, wanting to stay clear of anything of that nature about Nora and me. "I don't want interference with what I'm doing, that's all. It was the strongest condition of my taking this job."

"She's not going to interfere, you know that full well," he said with easy assurance. "She believes in you, Luke, she's your biggest supporter. That woman would do about anything for you."

I didn't know if she'd put him up to pressuring me or not, but I knew he was right—I couldn't let my personal problems with Nora override my professional obligation, which was to do the best job I could.

Her input could help.

The consensus was strong that Jerome was Juarez's killer, or part of a conspiracy. It's what everyone wanted. We needed a killer, and he fit the bill.

I was the only demurrer, partly out of caution, partly because you have to look at both sides as carefully as you can—someone has to play devil's advocate. Otherwise you can get caught up in emotion, which then takes on a life of its own. Emotion is fine as long as it's grounded in fact. If it isn't, you can be prosecuting a case that isn't airtight after all, and you can wind up losing when you should have won.

But the evidence was powerful. Nora, being the other lawyer in the room, summed up the arguments, with buttressing from the others. Kate, standing at the blackboard, wrote the points down as Nora enumerated them. I sat back, listening.

"Jerome had a personal, intimate vendetta against Juarez, going back decades," Nora said, ticking the items off on her fingers. "Not only DEA agent against drug lord, but brother avenging his sister."

"Which he never told his superiors," Keith put in. "A strong breach of professional ethics. He should never have been part of the operation, let alone being in charge."

"That's super-heavy," Kate kicked in. "This was a blood feud, on the cosmic level of the Capulets and Montagues, with an overlay of ethnic bigotry and racial prejudice."

"He violated administration guidelines by conducting the raid, without the drugs being on the scene," Nora continued with her mock presentation. "He shouldn't have gone in at all. And his information was false, which further aggravated the disaster. He relied on an unreliable snitch who had his own cross-motives, rather than having hard, irrefutable information."

"Which resulted in the deaths of his own people, and others in the compound for whom there was no reason for arrest, under their warrant," Louis said.

"All of which we knew about," Nora said, "but we didn't know the context. The personal issue gives his actions a completely different context, which I think is chilling."

I nodded, listening.

"Now the three killer items," she continued. "Jerome buying the full-metal-jacket bullets on the sly, Jackson's testimony that a rival gang bought Jerome, and the Miami bank account. Those are huge; you put all that together, it's a raging fire under the smoke. Especially the bank account, that's the most damning piece of evidence to me. That is concrete, there's no maybes about that. Jerome deposits half a million dollars in a bank account a week after Juarez is killed? That's too coincidental for me. Put that together with Jackson's testimony, to me that is a smoking gun."

She turned to me as if we really were rivals in a courtroom. "If this was a normal case that I was prosecuting, I'd take it to court in a heartbeat. You would've, too, Luke, when you were a D.A. And I can't imagine you not doing it here . . . can I?"

Everyone turned to me. It was my decision. I got up.

"First of all," I said, "I'm not doing anything until I bring Jerome in front of my grand jury tomorrow and hear what he has to say. Every single one of these issues you've brought up are legitimate and could be building blocks for us. Or not, depending."

I started laying out the counterargument. "Buying ammunition for target shooting is not evidence of guilt. The type of bullet he bought bothers me, but not if it's for target shooting. So by itself, I wouldn't go on with that. That's number one. The thing with the sister is complex as hell. That worries the shit out of me. But is it really that bad, from the DEA's point of view? I'm not advocating that Jerome shouldn't have divulged his family's history with Juarez, of course he should have—but in the real world these guys live in, which is ugly and brutal, it could be seen as a good thing. If I've got a sister that's running with a drug lord, don't I want to break that up?"

"Except he didn't know that then," Kate clarified.

"You don't know that," I rebutted. "The fact that his sister says so doesn't make it so. Maybe the family did know, or found out. Yeah, I know racism was a motive. Maybe the only one. But maybe drugs were, too. And . . ."

I paused, to make sure they really got this next point.

"Jerome's going against department regs is the weakest link in this argument against him. He accomplished what he set out to do. He captured Juarez. How he did it happens in police work all the time. Sometimes you have to strike when the iron is hot, even if all your ducks aren't lined up. That raid resulted in the capture of one of America's most wanted criminals. If Juarez hadn't escaped and been killed, we would not be having this discussion or investigation, and Jerome would be a hero. Jerome didn't need to kill Juarez, killing him wasn't as satisfying as parading him in front of the world, humiliating him, and throwing him in jail for the rest of his life. The Justice Department was already cranking up the press releases, until Juarez got away. Now Juarez is a martyr to a lot of people, and we may be indicting a career DEA agent. Shit, talk about a clusterfuck."

Mutters and groans. I was raining on the parade. But I had to.

"The keys for me are this rumor going around that Jerome had crossed over, and the bank account. He's not only a murderer for hire then, he's a traitor to his country. But you don't convict a man on the hearsay testimony of a criminal who has every motive in the world to lie. We can't trust Jackson, he's a crook. He's a liar by definition."

"Even liars tell the truth sometimes," Keith said. Jackson was his key contribution to the investigation, he wanted that to be solid.

"Sure they can. And maybe he is. But we don't take it on faith, agreed?"

Everyone agreed; reluctantly.

"So now the bank account. I agree that's a biggie. But what if there's an honest, legitimate explanation for it? He won the lottery. His mother died and the estate was settled. He hit it big in the stock market. There could be dozens of valid explanations. If he has one, we're on shaky ground."

I sat down. We'd gone as far as we could go, we'd covered the bases.

"If he doesn't, then all those other things we've talked about carry much more weight. Tomorrow will tell."

———

Nora caught me alone in the office. I was packing my briefcase, about to leave. Everyone else had gone home for the day.

"One minute of your time?" She took one step inside.

"Sure. As long as it's about business. We don't talk about anything personal anymore. And I don't want to be alone with you, so make it quick. My wife and kid are waiting for me."

"I understand," she said, keeping her distance. "I just wanted to thank you for letting me in."

"You've got a smart head, you can certainly help. As long as that's all it is."

"I can control myself. I promise."

"You'll have to. Anything else like what happened, the curtain goes down."

"I know."

"Good night, Nora." I stuffed the remainder of my homework into my briefcase.

"Good luck tomorrow, Luke."

I waited until I was sure she was gone, then I locked up and left.

INDICTMENT

As opposed to the angry, depressed, defensive man I'd met in West Virginia, the Sterling Jerome who entered the grand jury room and swore to tell the truth was calm and assured. We had ended our previous meeting as allies, so he thought—edgy and situational, but on the same page, two soldiers in the quest for the truth. He had no reason to believe this encounter would be any different.

I greeted Jerome cordially. Ran through his background, his credentials as a federal agent, awards he'd won, citations he'd received, the usual crap. His résumé was impressive—he had done a lot of good work. In a small way, the world was safer because of his efforts. He believed strongly in his work, in the cause. He was all-American, apple pie, motherhood. Unfortunately, he also was a man who made up the rules according to his own code, which didn't always fit with the oath he'd taken. But shit happens, and in the end, good triumphs in the big-picture scheme of things.

That was his take on himself.

It was clear from his demeanor that he didn't know about his sister's meeting with Kate Blanchard. That was critical. If he had, he wouldn't be sauntering in like this. He might not even have come, or at least he would have tried to throw a legal roadblock at me. That was a big part of my scheme—to try to catch him off-guard.

"I'm going to start out by asking you some questions about the raid on the compound that night," I began my interrogation.

He nodded. "Fine. It's all in the public record. My actions are an open book."

He turned to the grand jurors, giving them a confident look. He was a professional, he was going to tell it like it was.

We'll see, I thought.

"You spent a great amount of time setting up that operation, didn't you?"

"Yes, I did."

"How much time?"

"I had been on the trail of Reynaldo Juarez for the better part of a decade. This particular operation was over a year in the making."

"You were going to catch him red-handed, making a megabucks drug deal. Money and drugs were going to be exchanged, and you were going to catch him and the others in the act."

"Yes."

"But that didn't happen."

He shook his head sorrowfully. "No, it didn't, unfortunately."

"When that sting went south, why did you proceed anyway? Didn't you need to have that happen?"

"Technically, yes. Practically, no."

"Would you explain for us what you mean by that?"

"Reynaldo Juarez was one of the most important and lethal drug lords in the United States. We needed to apprehend him."

"So you decided to go ahead with your raid, even though the pretext had vanished."

"We had no choice. It was that or let him flee." Another look at the jury. "This man was quicksilver. He was impossible to pin down, locate. If we hadn't tried to catch him that night, we might not have had another chance. This was our best, and most likely our only, opportunity to get him."

"I see." I glanced at my notes. "Did you inform your superiors about the change, and how you were going to deal with it?"

He shook his head emphatically. "No, I did not."

"Why didn't you?"

"There wasn't time to go through the bureaucracy. I was the agent in charge, on the scene. There are times when you have to make decisions based on your experience and what the alternatives are."

"So you took it upon yourself to try and capture him, regardless of the conditions of the arrest warrant."

"Yes," he answered defiantly.

"Is that a commonplace occurrence? To go against the book, so to speak?"

"No. It isn't commonplace. But it isn't unknown, either. You do the best you can, given the circumstances."

"Okay." Another look at the notes. "So you decided to raid the place and catch them."

"Yes."

"Unawares. You were going to surprise-attack them."

"Yes."

"And did you?"

"Yes, we did."

"You conferred with the other members of your team?"

He hesitated a moment. "We did. This was the decision we decided upon."

The first lie. He had acted autonomously. The others on his team took his lead.

"When you went in, did you encounter resistance?"

"Yes."

"Heavy resistance?"

"Very heavy."

"Did you expect that would happen?"

"No. We didn't."

"Why not? This was an armed camp, wasn't it? Why wouldn't they be ready to resist such an attack?"

He sighed heavily. "Because we had been given to believe that they were unprepared. That we could take them by surprise without encountering much resistance."

"Who gave you that information?"

"We had an informant inside their camp."

"One of your agents?"

"No."

"Who was this informant? Someone you trusted, I assume."

His countenance darkened. He was beginning to lose his cool; just a bit, but I could see the change. I wondered if the jurors could. Maybe not yet; but they would, of that I was sure.

"He was one of them."

"A member of the drug ring?"

"Yes."

"In common parlance, was he what is commonly known as a snitch? A turncoat, stool pigeon, to use an outmoded word?"

"Yes. Our informant was a snitch."

"Then you're saying that his information turned out to be bogus. He was wrong."

"Very wrong."

"Why was that, do you think?"

"He lied to me." Jerome looked at the jurors yet again. "It's an occupational hazard of the trade, unfortunately. Snitches aren't always as reliable as you wish they were." He gathered himself. "But they're vital to solving crimes. It isn't a pretty world out there. You take what you can get." Amplifying, he continued, "They can get a big head. Think they know more than they do. These are immature, violent men. They think with their sexual organs instead of their brains."

He had obviously rehearsed that reply. Expected the question and was ready with the best answer possible. "Let me say it again. It's an ugly world we live in. If you wait for the perfect moment, the perfect informants, you can blow important arrests. I couldn't wait. Juarez was too dangerous to be at large one day longer. I made a decision, and I went with it."

"You didn't feel you were being overzealous? Not cautious enough? Men were killed in that raid. In hindsight, don't you wish you had waited for a more propitious moment to try and nab your quarry?"

He shook his head in disagreement. "Hindsight is for armchair historians. I had to go."

I pushed my offensive. "That's part of your MO, isn't it, Agent Jerome? To charge in headfirst, without testing the waters? To bend the rules and hope the results will get you out of hot water?"

He flushed. "What's that supposed to mean?"

"You disobeyed a direct order that came from the top of the Justice Department, didn't you?"

"No," he answered defiantly.

"You didn't?"

"No one ordered me *not* to raid that compound."

"If you had checked with your superiors, wouldn't they have told you not to, given the change in circumstances? The change in the entire operation? You were supposed to bust a multimillion-dollar drug transaction, and in the process apprehend Reynaldo Juarez and the others involved. Wasn't that how it was supposed to be? No drug deal, no arrests. Yes or no, agent."

"Fuck," he muttered under his breath. I heard him; the jurors, sitting farther away, didn't.

"The drug deal was the back end, okay?" he tried to explain. "Of course we wanted to make that. But getting Juarez was the primary objective."

"Of yours or your agency's?"

"Everyone's."

"So the drug deal was a pretext."

"It was a sting. We wanted the drugs *and* Juarez."

"So when you couldn't get one, you figured at least you'd get the other."

"Yes." He sat up straight, obstinate, uncompromising in his conviction.

"Okay." I felt I'd made that point. "I can understand how the means are supposed to justify the ends. Although I must tell you"—now I turned to the grand jurors—"that would be a very difficult case to prosecute and get a conviction on. Unless your prisoner never gets to go to trial."

"What is that supposed to mean?" he bristled.

"Whatever you want it to mean."

We glared at each other for a moment. This was not the lovefest he'd thought it would be.

I move on. "So you finished your raid and found Juarez."

"Yes." He smiled. "We found him. Hiding behind a wall of Popsicles."

"He behaved in a cowardly fashion."

"Very. He was a coward, deep down."

"You arrested him. You interrogated him."

"Yes."

"About how long?"

"An hour. I wanted to get the show on the road. Get them into jail. Having them in custody out there wasn't doing us any good."

"But he escaped."

Jerome closed his eyes. "Yes. He escaped."

"Wasn't he secured? In handcuffs?"

"Yes, he was handcuffed."

"You cuffed him yourself."

"One of the other agents did," he admitted , showing some uneasiness.

"Do you remember who?"

He shook his head. "No, I don't."

"But he was definitely handcuffed. Secured."

"Definitely."

"You checked that personally."

He started to reply, then stopped.

"Did you check that out yourself?"

"I assumed they were secured. He wasn't going anywhere."

"He wasn't?"

"At the time."

"Maybe they weren't locked at all?"

"They had to be."

"You don't know how he got out of his handcuffs, do you, Agent Jerome?" I was motoring, asking my questions fast, not giving him time to think about his answers. I wanted spontaneity.

"I wish to God I did."

A thought occurred to me. "Would your key open another agent's handcuffs?"

"Yes, they would."

"Why? Aren't they unique, like the lock on my door?"

"They can't be—for the security of the prisoner." He explained to the jurors, "If you have to unlock an arrestee quickly, let's say there's a fire or an explosion, and you have to release him so he can be safely moved, my keys have to fit your handcuffs, and vice versa."

"In other words, anyone who was there that night could have unlocked his handcuffs and freed him."

A vigorous head nod.

"But no one else. None of his own gang."

"Not necessarily," Jerome replied carefully.

I gave him an incredulous look. "What's that supposed to mean?"

"It was chaotic out there. Dark. We didn't know the terrain as well as I would have liked. Someone could have snuck into the trailer where we were holding him and released him."

I stepped back, looked at the grand jurors with a now-I've-heard-it-all expression on my face. "You serious?"

"It's far-fetched," he admitted, "but that was a strange and crazy night. Many things happened, that were so different from what usually happens, that I wouldn't rule anything out."

"But following that line, wouldn't it be much more logical to assume that a DEA agent unlocked those handcuffs rather than one of Juarez's gang members sneaking past three or four dozen agents, getting into a guarded trailer, releasing Juarez, then getting away? Listen to yourself, man," I said derisively, "you sound ridiculous."

He reddened again—humiliation was unbearable to him. But he couldn't do anything to stop me, not in here.

"I said it was far-fetched, okay?"

I threw down a trump card. "So you're admitting it was one of your agents who did it."

"Not at all."

"Then how did he get loose?"

He slumped in his chair. "The only thing I can think is, the cuffs weren't secure after all."

"That's . . . incredible," I finally said. This was a new one on me.

"I know."

"Deliberately?"

"I think . . . accidentally."

"He was never secured properly?"

"That's the only conclusion I can come to."

"That's a damaging conclusion."

"I know it is." He turned to the jurors. "We're human. We make mistakes."

"That's a lalapalooza."

He had no comeback for that.

I waited a moment to let that sink in—they hadn't only disobeyed orders. They were the gang who couldn't shoot straight. Unless Juarez had deliberately been released, which is what happened; these guys don't make mistakes like that.

"Let's change subjects. You're a good shot, aren't you, Agent Jerome?"

"Pretty good," he said modestly.

I looked at one of my notes. "You have excellent marks on the range."

"Like I said, I do okay."

"You like to shoot?"

"It's part of my job."

"You go out to the range, what, once a month?"

"About that much."

"These are scheduled? It's part of being proficient?"

He nodded. "It's a requirement of the job."

"And when you go out to the range and fire your weapon . . . do you use your own weapon when you go to the range?" I interrupted my own train of thought.

"Yes. You want to make sure your weapons are in good working order."

"Right. Now when you go to the range, who supplies the ammunition? Do you bring your own?"

"No. It's given to us."

"The agency does that."

"Yes."

"So you don't buy your ammunition."

"No."

"What kind of ammunition do you fire at the range, Agent? Whatever they have on hand?"

"We fire the ammunition we would use in the field, it if were to ever come to that. You want the range work to approximate what could happen in the real world as closely as possible."

"And those would be hollow-point bullets?"

"Yes. We always use hollow points."

"In the field and on the range."

"Yes."

I walked over to my table, picked up the testimony of Harrison, the gun shop owner, and the sales receipt he'd given me. Crossing back to Jerome, I handed the receipt to him. "What is this?"

He read it over. "A receipt for bullets for a nine-millimeter automatic pistol."

"Is that the caliber of bullet you use in your personal weapon?"

"Yes. That's standard in the department."

"What kind of bullets are these?"

He looked at the receipt again. "These would be full-metal jackets."

"That's a different kind of bullet from what you use?"

"Yes."

I took the receipt from him. "You purchased these bullets for your weapon." I handed the receipt back to him, pointing out his name over the line "purchaser."

He stared at it, realizing the implications. "Yes. I bought them."

"A few days before your botched raid on the compound."

Very slowly: "The raid was successful. We nailed our quarry. The aftermath was the problem. But the raid itself was successful."

"You consider losing three men a successful raid?" I asked, my voice rising.

"We're in a war against drugs," he answered, equally heated. "There are casualties in a war. That's regrettable. No one is more unhappy than I am that those men died. I sent them to their deaths, I take responsibility for that, and it'll be with me until the end of my life. But our raid was successful. We captured one of the most despicable criminals this country has produced."

"You could've captured him without the loss of lives, Mr. Jerome. If you hadn't gone cowboying out there on your lonesome. Disregarding orders is normal for you. With tragic results, as we saw in this case."

"Fuck you." He said it under his breath, but loud enough for me to hear, which he wanted.

I wheeled on him. "What did you say?"

He glared at me. "Nothing."

"That's what I thought. You have nothing to say."

We were into our own private war now. I regained the receipt and walked away from him, so that I was standing near the grand jury box. Them and me, together, against him, alone. "Why would you buy bullets if they're given to you free of charge, Agent Jerome? A type of bullet that's different from what you use."

"I—"

"And why would you go a hundred and fifty miles away to buy them?" I pressed on, not letting him finish. "You were in Blue River. This gun shop is at the opposite end of the county."

"I wanted to get away."

"You wanted what?"

"This raid was about to happen. Finally. I'd spent ten years of my life chasing after Juarez. This was going to be the most important bust of my entire life. I needed to get away and clear my head. To mentally and emotionally prepare myself."

"And buy bullets." I didn't try to hide my derisiveness.

"I had pent-up energy. Shooting my weapon is a way of releasing that."

"So why didn't you buy the kind you would use if you used your weapon?"

"When I'm shooting on my own, I prefer full-metal jackets."

"And why is that, pray tell?"

He disregarded my sarcasm, although I knew it was enflaming him. "They're cleaner. They give you a better feel of how accurate you are. Hollow points obliterate everything. I wanted to see if my aim was as true as it could be."

I looked at the jurors to see if they were buying this. They looked dubious.

"You're aware, I know, that a full-metal jacket killed Juarez, not a hollow-point bullet."

Jerome stared hard at me. "I didn't kill him, if that's what you're insinuating."

I turned my back on him for a good, long beat, rummaging through papers on my table, letting him hang, letting the jurors look at him. Then I turned back.

"You have brothers and sisters, don't you, Agent Jerome?"

He gave me a strange look. Haunted, almost; certainly surprised.

"Yes."

"One of your sisters is named Diane Jerome? Diane Jerome Richards?"

I'd blindsided him. "Yes," he answered, his voice barely audible.

"Would you repeat your answer so everyone can hear you. You have a sister named Diane Jerome Richards, that is correct?"

"Yes." His voice was firmer—he was trying to recover. "Diane Richards is my sister."

"She attended Stanford University for one year. Her freshman year. Is that also correct?"

He stared straight ahead. Not looking at the jurors, not looking at me. "Yes."

"And while she was there, she had a romantic relationship with another freshman student, is that right? A male student?"

"I . . . guess she did."

"You know she did. Don't you?"

Very slowly he answered, "Yes."

I asked my next question while facing the grand jurors. "What was the name of the boy your sister fell in love with, Mr. Jerome?"

A deep breath, from the bottom of his gut. "Reynaldo Juarez."

His breath was reverberated by the dozen and a half from behind me.

"Is that the same Reynaldo Juarez who was killed after the raid that you led on the compound here in Muir County?"

"Yes."

"The same Reynaldo Juarez you had relentlessly pursued for over a decade."

"Yes."

"When you found out that your sister was dating Reynaldo Juarez, back there at Stanford, did you do anything about that?"

"How do you mean?" he asked cagily, trying to figure a way out.

"Did you and some of your brothers go to Stanford, kidnap Mr.

Juarez, drive him to a deserted area, and beat him within an inch of his life?"

He took his time before answering. "No."

"You didn't?" I asked incredulously, the tone of my voice clearly telling the jurors I knew he was lying.

"We went out there to talk to him."

"Talk to him. What about?"

"We didn't want him seeing our sister."

"Because he was a drug dealer? You didn't want your sister having a love affair with a drug dealer?"

"Yes," he answered firmly.

I took a moment to let all this sink in; we'd been moving at breakneck speed, on a subject for which the jurors hadn't been prepped.

"How did you know he was a dealer?" I challenged him. "You weren't with the DEA then. You were barely into your twenties, isn't that true?"

"I was not yet working for the Drug Enforcement Administration."

I moved closer to him. "You had no idea of any of that at the time, did you? All you knew was that your sister was in love with a Mexican boy, isn't that the truth of it? You didn't want a Chicano for a possible future brother-in-law, did you. That's why you and your brothers went to Palo Alto—to stop him from ever seeing your sister. Isn't it, Agent Jerome!"

He was holding steady—it was a struggle, but he was managing to stand up to my fusillade. So far.

"We felt they were wrong for each other. It had nothing to do with him being Mexican. I've got plenty of friends who are Mexican-Americans."

"Bully for you," I complimented him sarcastically. "How very tolerant. So his being Mexican had nothing to do with your beating him half to death? It was simply the wrong choice for Diane, is that what you're telling us?"

"We didn't do that. I've told you that."

"You're under oath, Mr. Jerome. You know what the penalty for perjuring yourself before a grand jury is, don't you? You've appeared before grand juries before."

"I'm not lying."

"What if I produced hospital records?"

"They wouldn't say who messed him up."

"If you didn't beat him up, how did you know he was?"

"You're trying to trick me," he complained. "I'm not here as a hostile witness."

"You're acting hostile, as far as I'm concerned. Please answer the question."

"I know it because you just told me. I didn't know it otherwise."

"Even if I produced an affidavit from your sister that says you did beat him, you and your brothers? How would you respond to that?"

"I'd have to say she was mistaken." He was fighting hard, not giving an inch. "We never beat up on the guy."

"But you were obsessed with him, weren't you? You were so obsessed with him that for the rest of your life you conducted a personal vendetta against him, didn't you?"

"No."

"You hated him so much you even took money to kill him, didn't you?"

He almost came out of his chair. "What are you talking about?" he screamed. "I never took money from anybody. That's outrageous!" He was fighting for self-control, and losing. "All right. I did hate him. Why shouldn't I? The man was a cowardly bastard. He was a murderer, a drug dealer. I'm proud to hate someone like that. Everyone should be." He was really spewing now. "So what if he had known my sister? That makes my going after the son of a bitch better, not worse." He turned now and stared at the jurors. "Okay. I knew him, I admit it. I didn't want my sister seeing this scumbag, I admit it. I'm glad as hell he's dead. I'm suffering no remorse about that whatsoever. But I didn't kill him. I had orders not to, and I obeyed them."

"Like you obeyed the orders not to raid the compound unless the drug deal you set up went down," I shot back.

He shook his head; but he didn't answer.

"You wanted Juarez dead. You'd wanted him dead forever. You were in a position to make that happen—for all we know, the reason you joined the DEA was to have proximity to him. You set that raid up to look legitimate, then after you couldn't murder him during the raid and had to take him prisoner, you snuck in and unshackled him and told him you'd give him one last chance to get out of your life, out of this country. He could take his chance and run, or you'd kill him there, on the spot. Didn't you—Agent Jerome?"

"You're crazy." He turned to the jurors, beseeching them. "This is insane, all of it. I'm a federal agent, I would never do what he's saying. I'm not a murderer!"

"And then you went after him, didn't you? You tracked him down and you killed him with the full-metal jackets you had secretly bought a few days before, one hundred fifty miles away. Didn't you?"

"No!"

I retreated to my table, picked up my last group of documents.

"Do you know what these are?" I asked him from twenty feet away.

"I can't see them from here, so, no."

I walked to him. "Can you see them now?"

He looked at the papers in my hand. "Yes, I can see them now," he said venomously.

"Do you know what they are now?"

"No, I still don't know what they are." He was trying to give it back as good as I was throwing it at him.

I showed the documents to the jurors. "They're bank statements." Back to Jerome: "From Mr. Jerome's bank account in Miami, Florida."

"My what? I don't have a bank account in Miami."

I paused, looked at the papers in my hand. "That's interesting." Handing him one of the papers, I asked, "Isn't that your Visa card number at the bottom of the page? Your Social Security number? Your birth-date?"

He read the page carefully. Looked up at me, his face registering sheer bewilderment. "Yes, they're mine. But I don't have a bank account in Miami," he protested. "I don't have a bank account anywhere in Florida."

"This document says you do."

"It's wrong. I don't." He was in panic mode now, worse than when I'd hit him with his sister's relationship with Juarez.

"This document says you opened this account by wire five days after Reynaldo Juarez was murdered." I ran my finger down the pertinent lines. "Take a look for yourself. Five hundred thousand dollars was wired into this account upon opening. Look at it, man! Tell me if that isn't what's on the page!"

He looked at it, his hands shaking as he held it.

"I don't have a clue as to what any of this is," he said, his voice shaking uncontrollably. "But I swear to you, this is not my bank account. I don't have anything like five hundred thousand dollars."

I turned my back on him. It had come down to this. If he had admitted to the bank account and had a plausible reason for the money, I would still have asked for an indictment; I think. But he hadn't. He was flat-out lying.

I had no choice.

"Okay," I told him, my voice flat, as drained of emotion as he was emotional. "I'm done with you—for now. You're excused."

He got up to leave. His legs were shaking, he had a difficult time with the mere act of standing.

"Make sure my office knows where you are," I instructed him sternly. "At all times."

He nodded. He was numb. He walked out.

At the end of the day we celebrated, the team and I. Champagne all around. Okay, so it was domestic California sparkling, but who's reading the label?

When I awoke the following morning, I had come back down to earth. We had our man. The grand jury had indicted Jerome on a count of murder in the first degree. So we'd done our job, the first part.

The unfortunate thing was, he had killed a man far worse than he. But my business is about the rule of law, which has to stand equally for everyone, tarnished white knights and scumbags alike. I believed that last year, last month, last week, last night. I believe it now. That doesn't make applying it sweet or easy, in every circumstance.

PART

FOUR

GIRDING FOR BATTLE

We took a family vacation to Hawaii, Kauai, up near Hanalei Bay, a condo above the beach. It was Buck's first time in warm ocean water—he took to it like a dolphin. We swam, made sand castles, flew kites. When he napped, Riva and I hired one of the local kids to watch him while we took walks along the beach, grateful and happy to have some intimate time together. It was a peaceful, restful week, a good bonding for us as a family and a time of reenergizing for me, after the tensions and pressures of the investigation.

Unfortunately, it had to end and I had to go back to work, preparing for the trial. Jerome's arrest and indictment had been a front-page story on every newspaper, magazine, and television show across the country. I was duly lionized: the hero of the desert, the fearless prosecutor representing the tiny county that took on big government and brought it to its knees—all that bullshit. I hated it, both the public ass-kissing and the invasion of my privacy. I had done my job. I had no vendetta against anyone, including the DEA. They hadn't handled their investigation satisfactorily, but they hadn't been trying to overtly cover up, they simply couldn't force themselves to look hard enough into that abyss. It's tough judging your own, men you work with, live and die with.

Winston Kim and I had lunch in L.A. shortly after the indictment was handed down. He wasn't apologetic, but he did offer congratulations. The agency was having a hard time over this. Their procedures had been attacked in newspaper editorials, the television talking heads had castigated them, and some congressional committees launched punitive, publicity-seeking inquiries.

None of that lasted very long; after the shouting and posturing died down, it became clear that Jerome was an aberration, a man so hellbent on personal revenge that he had crossed the line. The *man* was at fault, not the organization. Now that I wasn't locking horns with them, I, too, felt that was as it should be.

Things were dormant while I prepared my case. Jerome's lawyer, John Q. Jones, one of the best defense lawyers in the country, an old warhorse from time immemorial, had tried unsuccessfully for a change of venue from Muir County, since its jury pool was small, and everyone knew about the case. As I expected, Judge McBee dismissed the motion— Jerome was going to stand trial where the crime had been committed. He also denied Jerome bail. This was a capital offense, and there was concern that Jerome would try to leave the country. He was held in the Muir County jail under tight security, overseen by Sheriff Miller and his staff.

McBee set a trial date—five months. This wasn't going to drag out with delays and appeals if he could help it. Justice delayed would be justice denied in this case. He wanted us to move ahead as quickly as possible.

John Q. objected to the trial date, as I'd know he would, claiming he wouldn't have enough time to mount a proper defense. Judge McBee denied that motion as he'd done the others. The trial was going to happen—the sooner the better.

As I had expected, Jerome was forceful and aggressive about maintaining his innocence, insisting he'd been set up, a victim of a conspiracy—by whom, he didn't say. Several tabloid television shows, *Geraldo, Larry King,* etc., interviewed him from his cell. Finally, Judge McBee got annoyed with all the publicity and the aggravation and put a halt to it.

That Jerome had hired John Q. Jones as his attorney was a powerful indication of the seriousness of this trial, and that it was going to be fought to the bitter end. (It was unstated but understood, certainly by me at least, that friends of Jerome's inside the DEA were paying the legal bills, which would be high, well into six figures.) John Quincy Jones (John Q., as everyone in the legal world addresses him) is an old man now, over seventy, but still formidable as hell. The grand old man is semi-retired now, but he'll let himself get pulled into a case if the merits stir his blood. Defending a man like Jerome is classic John Q.: he's as polar opposite from supporting government agencies such as the DEA as any man in the country. But he's a staunch believer that every man, no matter how vile, must have the best defense he can. I knew John Q. would give me everything I could handle.

My preparation was done at my office in Santa Barbara. There was no reason for me to physically be in Muir County; I could work more comfortably and efficiently in my own space. My investigators drifted in and out as I needed them. On the few occasions I had to be in Blue River, I flew in, took care of business, and flew out. I only spent a few nights, none in Nora's company. I was cordial with her, but distant—I had no further need for her, it was up to me now.

I had a strong case to prosecute. True, everything was circumstantial; we didn't have an eyewitness to the killing, nor did we have a ballistics match to the bullet that had killed Juarez. But the evidence was overwhelming, nonetheless. In my days as Santa Barbara D.A. I had prosecuted many cases that didn't have nearly as much evidence, and I'd gotten easy convictions in almost all of them. This one was a winner—my instincts told me so, and my instincts are rarely wrong.

A month before the trial was to start we moved back to Blue River. Riva and Buck were coming, which was great. I needed the ballast she provides, and her being there would keep Nora off my back. I estimated that the trial would take no more than two or three weeks, after which I could return to my everyday practice and my normal, easy life. My fervent wish was that this would be my last brush with celebrity. I'd had enough of the limelight.

Louisa Bearpaw E-mailed Sylvan Furness and told him they'd be down in the morning with the deposit money. He hadn't expected that; for all her confident talk, he had thought the tribe's crazy scheme—which was how he saw it—would fall flat. Where was the poor tribe going to come up with that kind of money? But there was the message, on his computer screen: They would be in his office tomorrow morning, ten o'clock sharp. Check in hand. Have the papers ready for signing.

Louisa breezed in, her entourage in tow, including the tribe's lawyer-accountant, a middle-aged Chinese-American man from a prominent San Francisco firm. She was wearing a sharp-looking dress in a silklike fabric that accentuated her good features. Her thick hair flowed down her back in a long braid, her dark eyes were bright, fiery. A warrior princess, ready to count coup. Metaphorically, that is.

"You got the paperwork ready?" she asked peremptorily, skipping the amenities. The tribe had been waiting months for this day.

"Nice to see you, too, Louisa," Furness said. He was nervous; his palms were sweaty. He wasn't used to dealing with this tribe in this fashion, equal to equal.

"Sylvan." Louisa leaned forward on his desk, bracing her weight on her hands, which were splayed out on the surface. "We can chitchat later. Okay?"

"Sure, Louisa." She was in his office ten seconds and he was on the defensive already; she was a manipulator, a good one.

"So, Sylvan. The documents. May we?" Her hand was outstretched, practically in his face.

He handed her the thick, ten-by-fourteen-inch manila envelope. She passed it behind her to the accountant without cracking the clasp. They had already seen the preliminary draft; this shouldn't have any surprises. Still, she asked, "Do we have to read this telephone book?"

"You know you can trust me," Furness assured her with a friendly smile.

"We have to read it," the lawyer-accountant said firmly.

Furness flushed. He was offended; not that the accountant should want to read it, of course he should—it was his tone of voice, simultaneously accusatory and condescending.

"Do you have the money?" Furness asked curtly, fighting for equilibrium.

She opened her purse and withdrew a legal-sized envelope. White, with a window in it for the recipient's name and address: *U.S. Department of the Interior.* He could read the words through the cellophane. She handed it to him across the desk.

"You don't have to read it," she said, grinning mischievously.

He couldn't help himself—he opened it.

The check was made out on the tribe's account. One hundred fifty thousand dollars.

"It's good," she said dryly. She was smiling, feeling her oats.

Furness wasn't. "I'm sure it is," he responded stiffly.

The lawyer was perusing the document, flipping the pages rapidly.

"How does it look, Julian?" she asked. "Can we trust the white man this time?"

"You never can trust the white man," the lawyer replied humorlessly, not lifting his eyes from the pages. "That's why you hired me."

Furness wanted to say something about her trusting him, but decided it would sound wimpish.

They all waited in silence while the lawyer took this time. He turned over the last page and looked up. "It's okay," he pronounced.

Furness, who had been standing rigidly without realizing it, sat down behind his desk, using it as a psychological barricade.

"Let's go over the basics, so we're clear with each other," he said. She wanted business? Fine, he'd give her business. Official, formal business.

"Let's," Louisa came back at him, still smiling, as if to say, *We're friends, Sylvan.* It was another way of trumping him, he thought, looking at her seated across the desk, one leg insouciantly crossed over the other.

"This is a six-month option to buy the property," he said, referring to his own copy of the document. "That's clearly understood?"

"Yes." She nodded.

"If the transaction goes through, we'll transfer title to your tribe, and you'll annex it. Washington's okay with that, since the land's contiguous. The full purchase price is one million, three hundred thousand dollars. All cash, no bank contingencies, no second trust deeds, no notes of any kind. Cash on the barrelhead."

"Correct," she said firmly. She didn't look back at her lawyer—she was in charge.

"If you don't pay the remainder within the prescribed time, you lose ten percent of your down payment, fifteen thousand dollars. No extensions. Agreed?"

"It's your property, you hold the cards. As usual," she added caustically.

"As you'll notice," he continued, ignoring her sarcasm, "it's been signed by the secretary of the interior. You'll sign as representative of the White Horse Nation. You're authorized to do this?"

This time, she glanced behind her, at the others in her party. They nodded their approval.

"Yes, I have authorization." She reached into her purse and took out an old-fashioned fountain pen. Her lawyer handed her the papers, placing his finger on the proper line for her to sign.

"Remember, Louisa," Furness said in a last cautionary note, "if you don't make the rest of the payment, you lose this opportunity. There won't be any extensions. The property will go on the auction block. We're giving you a first look here, so that's how it has to be."

"I understand all that," she said impatiently. "Can we sign now, please?" She was holding her pen, her hand poised above the document.

"Yes," he said, feeling a sadness he didn't fully understand. He wasn't going to see her much anymore, he knew.

She inscribed her signature in the appropriate places, both on the tribe's copy and the Interior Department's. Furness placed his in the top desk drawer; it would be pouched to Washington in the morning. The tribe's copy went back into the manila folder, the lawyer tucking it protectively under his arm.

"You have one hundred eighty days to raise over a million dollars, Louisa," Furness lectured her, unable not to be a bureaucrat. He gave her and the others what he hoped was a stern look. "If you don't, you lose your chance. And your money."

He was dubious about their ability to raise the remainder of the funds in so short a time; as the BIA representative, he knew how much was in their kitty for speculative ventures—not much, nothing near the million-plus dollars this agreement required. It wasn't coming from other tribes, the department had checked that out. Nor was it Nevada gambling money—the casinos were fiercely opposed to Indian-reservation gaming, it took money out of their pockets. They'd spent millions fighting various state ballot initiatives permitting expanded reservation gambling—they weren't going to subsidize their competition.

Louisa stood up, her smile fixed on her face.

"Don't worry," she assured him. "The white man will get his money. And the Indian will get the land. Finally."

Riva had a surprise for me when I came back to our home away from home at the end of my workday.

"Honey, meet Joan Canyada," she said, angling her head in the direction of the dining area, which we'd set up as a play station for Buck, with his toys scattered about the floor and a portable crib pushed up against a corner, in eyesight of the kitchen, from where she could keep an eye on him.

As I looked over, a young Indian girl jumped to her feet, scooped our son onto her hip with a practiced gesture, and came forward. She'd been down on the floor on her hands and knees, playing with him. He clung to her like a little monkey.

"Hello, Mr. Garrison," she said, extending her free hand.

"Hello," I replied, shaking her hand. I leaned over and took him from her. He snuggled up against me.

The girl looked to be in her late teens or early twenties, although I'm not good at guessing the ages of Native Americans—living up here was my first experience with them as regular people you see on the street. She was wearing jeans and a halter top, her thick black hair pulled back off her face. Pleasant-looking girl, flat features, on the solid side.

"Joan's going to work for us as an au pair while we're here," Riva explained. "It'll free me up to get out occasionally, or if you and I want to have an evening out."

"Sounds good." I was glad Riva had done this; I didn't want her going stir-crazy up here. And having someone like this girl was much better than having Nora baby-sitting for us, as she'd volunteered to do. The last thing I wanted was Nora and Riva spending time together, especially without me around.

"Joan goes to community college," Riva said, wanted me to feel comfortable about this, figuring I couldn't object to a college kid. "She is taking this semester off."

I nodded. "Where do you live?" I asked, making conversation.

"The White Horse reservation," the girl answered, making a face. "North of here."

I knew of the White Horse reservation, although I'd never been there. It was the largest reservation in the area. I remembered that Bearpaw, Tom Miller's main deputy, was from the same reservation.

I mentioned that to her: "Do you know Wayne Bearpaw?"

Her dark complexion reddened visibly. "Everybody knows Wayne," she answered with a girlish titter.

The way she blushed and answered confirmed my intuition, when I'd first met him, that he was one of the local heartthrobs.

"My girlfriend Maria goes with him," she added. "I see him around a lot."

"He's a deputy sheriff," I explained to Riva. "He was there that night, with Miller."

Riva cocked an eye—that was new news.

"He's on my witness list," I told her. "He and Miller are helping me out now, also."

I turned to the girl. "So you're off college for a while?"

"Yes, sir."

"Were you working somewhere else?"

She shook her head. "There aren't many good jobs around here for kids my age." She paused. "There aren't many good jobs for anyone around here. Especially my people."

The reservation had a high unemployment rate, that I knew. "Well, glad to have you with us," I told her, hoping my tone of voice would put her at ease.

"Joan's going to be living here with us," Riva said. "She'll sleep in Buck's room with him. They're getting along great already."

As if in confirmation, Buck reached out to Joan. She took him from me.

"He likes you," I said. "He doesn't do that with everybody." He is gregarious, but he has his likes and dislikes, like all of us.

"He's a sweetheart," she cooed, nuzzling her lips against his neck, which brought forth a giggle. "We're already good friends. Aren't we, Buckaroo?"

"Yes," he squealed.

I shrugged out of my coat and loosened my tie. "I'm going to make myself a drink. You want one?" I asked Riva.

"There's a bottle of white wine open in the fridge. We're having trout for dinner. Fresh caught. Joan brought it."

"My uncle fishes about every day," the girl said. "Hunts in the winter. How he puts food on the table."

I remembered Nora telling me about the venison she had in her freezer. It was a common thing, obviously. Especially in a region where hard cash was scarce.

"Now that you're home, I'll get dinner started," Riva said. "It won't take long."

After pouring a couple of glasses of wine and handing Riva hers, I looked through the mail. Most of it comes to me at the office—this was flyers and a few magazines, forwarded from Santa Barbara. I leafed through a week-old *Sports Illustrated*.

"I want to thank you for letting me live here with you."

I looked up. Joan had come up behind me, Buck in tow.

"This is much nicer than . . . where I live. Way nicer."

"Glad to have you."

She shifted from one foot to the other. "You're going to be trying that case soon, aren't you?"

"Do you know about it?"

"Everybody around here knows about the trial," she said energetically. "It's the biggest thing to hit this county in years. Nothing ever happens around here," she added, as if implying, *This is a dull and boring place and I can't wait to get out.* "But that's going to change."

"How so?"

"That fancy spread? The one the dope dealers owned, where the raid took place?"

"Yes?" I sipped my wine.

"We're going to buy it."

I looked over at her. "You're what?"

"My tribe. We're going to buy it."

"Oh?" I hadn't heard anything about that. Something like that was outside my purview, so it wasn't my affair, but in a small community like Blue River there aren't any secrets. Not that this was a secret, obviously. What it meant was, I wasn't part of this community. I put my blinders on and did my job and that was it. It was an interesting development, though.

"Does the tribe have plans for it?" I really didn't care, but she was standing right there, I had to say something.

"We're going to set it up as a casino."

"A casino? Way out here?"

"If you build it," she informed me boastfully, "they will come."

Where had I heard that line before? "I guess so. People like to gamble, that I know."

Like most prosecutors—or ex-prosecutors—I'm not in favor of widespread gambling. It's a vice, and vices attract undesirable elements. Vegas and the other multibillion-dollar meccas notwithstanding, nothing good comes of it, except to those running the show, and the shadowy figures who operate behind the scenes.

"It'll be a way for our tribe to become self-sufficient," she said, sensing my disapprobation. "We're not sitting on oil wells or mineral rights." She was almost defiant in her attitude.

"Well, that's a good thing," I said as mildly as I could. I didn't want to get in an argument with this kid, right off the bat.

She, too, was happy to retreat. "Would you like me to give Bucky a bath? Or is that something you and Mrs. Garrison do?"

I looked at my son, nestled in her arms. "Do you want Joan to give you a bath, Buckaroo?"

"Yes!" he said happily.

"Go for it," I told her.

She carried him into the bathroom, started the water running. I changed into a T-shirt and shorts and joined Riva in the kitchen.

Three weeks to go before the trial began, John Q. Jones paid me a visit. We sat in my office, the door closed.

"I can't believe a lawyer as smart and experienced as you is going ahead with this meshuga case," he said, immediately going on the offensive.

I laughed. "You can do better than that, John Q."

"It's crazy," he said, persisting. "You don't have a case."

"You're grasping, big fella." I grinned at him. "You wouldn't be here if you really believed that."

"I'm here because I like and respect you, Luke, and I don't want to see you make a fool of yourself."

I learned back, still smiling, not wanting to laugh in a legend's face, but unable to restrain myself. "That's damn nice of you to consider me, but I can take care of myself."

"Not if you take this all the way," he said, stubborn as an ox.

"I'll take my chances."

"I've gone through your evidence. It's all circumstantial."

"So what? Circumstantial evidence is often better than so-called hard evidence, you know that."

"Not this time."

He was starting to annoy me. I don't mind sparring with opponents this way, but you say your piece and then you drop it, at least until the actual trial.

"Like I said, I'll take my chances. I've got a great case, and you know that," I said, pushing him.

"No eyewitnesses. No murder weapon."

I threw up my hands. "Save it for trial, okay?"

"You'll be sorry."

I had to answer that. "Your client placed himself above the law. I'm not dropping that. I'm surprised you're in here like this, John Q. I'm surprised you took this case on, to tell you the truth."

"He's innocent, Luke."

"Oh, shit. Spare me."

"He is."

"How do you explain his actions that night, then? He took the law into his own hands, he went in with an improper warrant, *the prisoner was murdered on his watch*!"

"That makes him the killer? There were sixty people there that night. More that you don't know about."

"Like who? You going to produce some surprise witness at trial? I've seen your discovery, John Q., your witness list. Don't jerk me off, okay? Not for this."

"Luke . . ." He looked at me with a pitiable expression, like I was about to do something terrible to myself and he was trying as hard as he could to stop me.

"What about the sister's testimony?" I barked at him. "That means nothing to you, right?"

He sat back, momentarily deflated. "That's not good."

At least he was admitting that.

"Not good? It's terrible. It's prime motive."

Even as I was saying that, I cautioned myself to be careful not to let him suck me into a trial before the trial. I was holding all the aces. Showing him my hand, even one card, was foolish. He was baiting me—I had to hold back from taking the hook.

"Let me ask you a question," he said in a more conciliatory tone.

"What is it?"

"If Jerome was the murderer—he wasn't, but I'm saying if—why in God's name would he open a bank account for half a million dollars right after the killing? Why would he expose himself that way? You've met the man. He's not an idiot."

I shrugged. "Maybe he is an idiot. Or maybe he's just an arrogant fuck, okay? There's lots of evidence pointing to that. The laws don't apply to him, that's how he thinks, how he operates. So why not open an account? He's got the money, what's he going to do, stick it under his mattress? He's a walking, raging ego, John Q., he thought he was untouchable."

"He's too bright. He would have covered himself."

"He never thought he was going to be a suspect. That's what he is. And it's not like he deposited the money where he lives, he went to considerable pains to conceal that money."

"You found it easily enough."

"It was hard work." I wasn't going to tell him I hadn't found it at all, that my off-the-books sheriff had done it for me, with his deep FBI contacts. I was lucky Tom Miller had been so inquisitive, so dogged. Otherwise, I wouldn't have that vital evidence.

"You've never considered that maybe he set up? That this bank account's a setup?"

"No," I answered stiffly. "I've never considered that. And I'm never going to."

"Maybe you should."

"No," I said, "and I'll tell you why. If I'm setting somebody up, I'm not going to drop half a million dollars to do it. It could have been done for fifty K, a tenth of what went into that account. Look at it realistically, pal. You owe it to your client to do that. Nobody would've done it that way." I engaged him, eyes to eyes. "It's not a setup. It's the real deal."

"I don't agree," he said, still digging his heels in.

"Then you prove it at trial," I challenged him. "Because if you're going to raise that as a defense, you're going to have to carry the burden of proof, not me. Which I would be happy for you to do."

He was fishing. I'd thought that's why he'd come in—now I knew it.

"What're you really here for, John Q.? You looking to cop a plea? Knock it down to second degree?"

"No, that's not why I'm here."

"I couldn't go for that myself," I said. "Because this was premeditated, going on two decades. But I could talk to Bill Fishell about it. Save the state some money. He did kill a piece of shit, that's the only redeeming value you've got."

"No, I don't want to plea him out."

"I didn't think so. And we wouldn't have, either."

He got to his feet heavily. He was an old man, he was showing his age. "I know you wouldn't."

I walked him to the door. "See you in court."

"See you," he said back to me in a leaden voice.

I closed the door on him.

He shouldn't have taken this case. It was a loser for him, not the way a lawyer of his stature should be finishing off an illustrious career. The desperation had shown through, like looking into a clear pane of window glass. He was going to come back to me with a plea. I could feel it in my bones. I wouldn't take it, of course; I'd been testing the waters with my offer, to see where he stood. And he'd shown me. He was standing on shaky ground, his footing uncertain, tenuous.

I knew where I stood. I stood tall.

* * *

Saturday morning arose sunny and warm. We were going out for the day, all of us, including Joan, who had settled in nicely. She was going to take us to the White Horse reservation and show us where she lived. Riva, who's interested in everything, especially other people, their lives, their families, and so forth, had asked her to. Joan had agreed, although her enthusiasm for the trip was lukewarm at best.

"There's nothing to see up there," she'd protested, "just a bunch of old shacks. And old people."

"I'm sure we'll find something to make it worth our while," Riva had assured her. "We're not fancy. Besides, you need to get home, and it'll be easier if we take you."

Joan had mentioned that she needed to pick up some items, clothing and the like. She had planned on hitching a ride with some friends, but when she could do that, she wasn't sure. Riva, being the considerate person that she is, was doing the girl a favor, in her mind. And we wanted to get out of Blue River and see other parts of Muir County.

"Okay," Joan had reluctantly acquiesced, not wanting to offend her new employer. "But you're wasting your time. You'll see."

We drove out of town, Riva and I in the front seat, Joan and Bucky in the back. An hour's easy driving brought us to the White Horse Reservation entrance, a narrow scar that angled off the highway.

"Here it is." Joan pointed as we approached the turnoff. Her voice was flat, her eyes averted, as if this was the last thing in the world she wanted to see. Or wanted us to see.

No signs indicated this was anything other than a road to nowhere—if Joan hadn't been with us, I would have driven right by. I turned in, and we raised a big cloud of dust as we bounced down the rutted roadway.

We passed by cinder-block houses standing in isolation, decrepit house trailers, other remote, battered dwellings. They did have electricity—the proliferation of pizza-sized television satellite dishes on the roofs testified to that—and I didn't see too many outhouses, but this was bad poverty.

Now I knew why Joan had been reluctant to bring us here.

I glanced over at Riva as we bounced along the rough, potholed road. She was feeling the same thing I was: embarrassment for Joan. Not that we cared where or how she lived, but that she would think that we did. That we'd judge her.

Too late to do anything about that now. We were here. To try to ameliorate the situation, bring it out in the open, would make her discomfort more acute. We'd stop at her house long enough for her to get what she needed, then leave.

The reservation center, such as it was, consisted of a cluster of low buildings on either side of the road about a mile in from the highway: a small elementary school, a firehouse, a few stores, a church. A handful of older people were clustered about, conversing with each other, going in and out of the stores. We didn't see any kids. They glanced at our car with curiosity as we drove by.

"My house is about a mile further," Joan instructed us. She was scrunched down in her seat, her head barely above the bottom of the window.

"Will your parents be home?" Riva asked solicitously.

"I guess." From the tone of Joan's voice she was hoping the place would be empty, she could run in, get her stuff, and get away without having to introduce us. "My father's gone. Maybe my mom."

"What about your brothers and sisters?"

She shrugged. We knew that Joan had two older sisters and a younger brother, she'd told us about them. I wasn't clear how many were living at home, or on the reservation. She didn't talk much about her family; her conversation with us, when it was about her, was her future, her dreams. She wanted to go to four-year college, become a teacher, a nurse, a dental hygienist. A professional. Her plans didn't include living on the reservation as an adult.

Her house was wood-frame, in need of paint. Small, not much space for two adults and four kids. We parked in front and got out to stretch.

"I'll just be a minute." Joan didn't want us to come in, that was clear.

"Potty."

We looked down.

Bucky held his arms up to Joan. "Potty, Joan."

He's only been toilet-trained a few months—Riva isn't pushy about that stuff. He won't wear diapers during the day and prides himself on being able to hold it in. Now he was squirming.

"Okay, Bucky," Joan sighed. "Come on." She scooped him up, turned to us, and said, "You can come in, too, if you want to."

A woman opened the door as we approached. Joan's mother—she looked like her daughter, except she was shorter and squatter. A tentative smile creased her face, which was deeply etched with sun lines. She was Riva's age or younger, I assumed, but she looked at least a decade older.

"Hello, honey," she said warmly, giving Joan a bear hug.

"Hi, Mama," Joan replied, hugging her back in the perfunctory way teenagers do when others are around.

"Are you Mr. and Mrs. Garrison?" the woman asked us.

"Yes," Riva answered. "And you're Mrs. Canyada. It's a pleasure to meet you. You have a lovely daughter. She's been a lifesaver."

Hyperbole, but it did the job—the woman's smile expanded all the way across her face.

"And this is your little boy," Joan's mother said, cooing at Buck. "Isn't he so cute!"

"Potty," Buck said.

She laughed. "Right inside. Come in, all of you."

The interior was tiny, but neat. One room for living, eating, cooking. A few doors let off to the back.

"Come on, Buck. Let's go potty," Joan said, leading him into the bathroom.

Riva and I stood in the middle of the small room with Joan's mother. "Can I get you something to drink?" she asked.

"No, thanks," I started to say, but Riva, right on top of me, jumped in. "I'd love something cold. Wouldn't you, Luke?"

"Sure," I regrouped quickly, realizing I'd offend the woman's offer of hospitality if I didn't.

Mrs. Canyada got a couple Cokes out of the refrigerator.

"I needed this," Riva said, taking a swallow. "It's dry, out in that car."

I drank from my can. The cold soda felt good, going down.

"Thank you for hiring Joan," the woman told us gratefully. "She likes working for you."

"We're happy to have her," Riva said, smiling warmly as Mrs. Canyada beamed. She's great with people, my wife, she can put anyone at ease. Looking around, she walked over to a battered chest of drawers that was pushed up against a corner wall, on which there were some framed family photos.

"Is this Joan?" she asked, picking one up. The picture was of a girl about ten, staring intently into the camera.

Mrs. Canyada nodded. "Her confirmation picture. She wasn't happy. She didn't like her dress. It was a hand-me-down, from her sister Betty."

"Nothing wrong with hand-me-downs," Riva said. "I wore plenty myself from my older sisters."

I was about to say, *I didn't know you had any sisters*, but I caught myself in time.

"Well, tell her that," Mrs. Canyada said. "If she heard it from you, she'd listen."

"Isn't it always like that?" Riva said, mother to mother.

"Ain't that the truth."

One minute in each other's presence, and they were already friends and allies-in-arms.

Joan led Buck out of the bathroom.

"All finished?" Riva asked him.

"He did a real good job," Joan said. "I'll get my stuff." She disappeared into the rear of the house again. A minute later she was back, a duffel bag slung over her shoulder. "Okay, we can go now," she said, moving toward the door.

"Good-bye, Joan," Mrs. Canyada called out to her.

Joan turned, came back to her mother with a guilty expression on her face. "Bye, Mama."

"Don't be a stranger, honey," her mother implored, her eyes searching her daughter's face.

"I'll call you."

We said our good-byes outside, by the car. Out back behind the house I noticed clothes hanging on a line, a hand-crank washing machine near it.

"You be good, you hear?" the mother told the daughter.

"Yes, Mama."

"She's in good hands," Mrs. Canyada said to Riva. "I can tell that."

"Thank you."

As we were getting into the car, the woman looked around at her bleak surroundings. "This is going to be different soon around here. It'll be too late for me, but life here's going to be better for my kids. A lot better." She looked at her daughter.

"They know about us buying that place, Mama," Joan said. "I told them. It's not a secret."

I remembered Joan telling us about the tribe buying the drug compound and turning it into a casino. "Good luck to you with it," I said. "I hope you can get people to come up here." I didn't need to explain my feelings about gambling. And in this situation, I could be flexible in my attitude. Anything legal that could help them pull themselves out of this kind of poverty couldn't be all bad.

"Thank you. We're keeping our fingers crossed." Then she repeated her daughter's earlier statement to me: "If you build it, they will come."

It was their mantra. If they said it enough, and believed it enough, it would come true.

We took a different route back to Blue River. It led us on a loop out the back side of the reservation, skirting the state line, heading down toward the area where the compound was located. It was more scenic—there were scattered trees, a variety of high-country tall pines, firs, and spruces.

"This isn't bad," Riva remarked.

"It's pretty," I agreed. In a rugged sort of way.

We drove for several miles. Rounding a blind curve, we saw, to our left, a barbwire fence running along the side of the road for several hundred yards—someone's private property. Signs were posted at intervals: NO TRESPASSING. NO HUNTING. VIOLATORS WILL BE PROSECUTED TO THE FULL EXTENT OF THE LAW.

"Whoever lives in there likes their privacy," I commented.

"That's Sheriff Miller's spread," Joan informed us. "And he does like his privacy, that's for sure. He runs people off there all the time. The locals all know to stay away, but we get these hunters coming through that think the signs don't apply to them, you know? Or they're not going to get caught? They find out fast not to mess with old Sheriff Miller. He'll take a shotgun to your car, or something more personal if you know what I mean. He's got motion detectors and video cameras and all kinds of high-tech equipment in there. You sneak in there, you are noticed, I kid you not." She laughed. "Kids'll go under the wire on a dare, you know? They come flying out of there like they've got an M 80 up their behinds."

"Were you one of them?" I teased.

"Not on your life," she swore resolutely. "Sheriff Miller, he means business."

Riva was checking it out through the windshield. "Have you ever been there?" she asked me.

I shook my head. "We don't have that kind of relationship. Whatever business I do with Miller is in the office."

Looking through the fence to the wooded property behind, I wondered how large the place was. It looked big.

"Potty, Mommy."

Riva swiveled around to him. "Again? You just went."

"Potty," Buck said firmly.

When he has to go, he has to go—we've learned that lesson. And we hadn't brought a change of clothes for him with us.

"You'd better pull over," Riva cautioned. "As soon as you can."

Up ahead I saw a break in the fence, where a driveway intersected the highway. A gate blocked access into the property.

"Is that the entrance to Sheriff Miller's place?" Riva asked Joan.

"Uh-huh."

"I could use a bathroom myself," Riva said. "Why don't you pull in? He isn't going to run you off."

I felt uneasy about that—not about Miller "running us off," or anything hostile, but about us encroaching on his evident desire for privacy.

"Let me call first," I said. "We don't even know if he's home."

I pulled off the highway onto the shoulder, in front of Miller's entrance, and reached into the glove compartment for my cell phone. I'd called him at home a few times, so I had the number in my notebook.

The phone was picked up on the second ring.

"Hello?"

It was Miller.

"It's Luke Garrison, Tom."

"Oh." A pause. "How are you, Luke? Are you working today? I was in earlier, I didn't see your car."

"No I'm not at the office. Actually, Tom, I'm at the entrance to your property."

"You are?" He was surprised; I'd caught him off-guard.

"Yes. We've been out sight-seeing, Riva and me and our kid and a girl who's working for us. The ladies and my son need to use a bathroom. We'd only be a minute."

There was a hesitation. Longer than one would have expected, given who I am and the circumstances I'd described.

"Okay," he said, although I could hear the hesitation in his voice.

"Thanks, Tom."

I hung up. "Fine with him," I said to the others. "He's happy to see us." I didn't know if he would be or not, but I didn't want them to feel uneasy, particularly Joan.

"Potty, Daddy," Buck called out again.

"It's happening, champ. Hold your water, one more minute."

The gate buzzed open. We drove down a long, blacktop driveway. It had been resurfaced recently. At the end of the driveway, Miller's house came into view: a low-slung affair, mission-style, similar in look to Nora's house. It was fairly new; the window frames and other such appointments were modern. Quite an impressive place. Parked in front of the garage, alongside Miller's old Jeep, which I recognized, was a Dodge minivan and a Muir County sheriff's blue-and-tan Ford Crown Victoria.

A couple of huge rottweilers came bounding out from the side of the house as we pulled up. They approached the car aggressively.

"Those are serious dogs," Riva said. "Those animals mean business. I'm not getting out of this car."

At that moment, Miller came out of the front door. He waved to us and whistled to the dogs, who sat down on their haunches, eyeballing our vehicle. "Hang on," he called out. He walked over to the dogs and put them on sturdy chain-link leashes. "It's okay now."

We got out. Riva picked Buck up. He loves animals and has no fear. She didn't want him running over to these brutes and trying to pet them.

"I'll put these two around back," Miller said. "Hang on a minute."

We waited while he disappeared around the back of the house, reappearing dogless a moment later. "They look meaner than they really are," he told us. "They're good security—being sheriff, I have to take extra precautions. You get these crazies out there, they feature taking a potshot at an authority figure is part of the drill."

We followed him inside. The interior was done in a rustic, masculine fashion. Leather furniture, several California plein-air paintings by well-known artists. There was serious money in this house.

Miller pointed to a doorway off the front foyer. "The guest bathroom's right there."

"Here we go, Buck," Joan said. She walked him into the bathroom.

"There's another toilet off the kitchen you can use," Miller told Riva.

"Thank you," she said, heading in that direction.

I looked around the living room. It was large, Western-style, with a high, wood-peaked ceiling. As I looked around, Miller's deputy Bearpaw came out of the study that was located off the back side of the living room.

"Mr. Garrison," he greeted me heartily. "How're you doing?"

"Doing fine, thanks."

"Out for a little weekend drive?"

"You've got it."

I like him. Straightforward, seems to be professional. He has a healthy distrust of outside enforcement agencies encroaching on his turf, something he's learned not only from his boss, but from firsthand experience, the compound raid being the most egregious example.

A woman trailed him out. Also Native American, wearing jeans, blouse, expensive cowboy boots. A good-looking woman, somewhere in her middle age. She could have been forty-five, or she could have been a decade older. She looked at me quizzically.

"This is Louisa Bearpaw," Miller said, "Wayne's mother. Louisa, Luke Garrison."

"Hello," I said. "Nice to meet you."

She helloed me back, shook my hand. Her handshake was firm. She gave me a good sizing-up look. "You're the special prosecutor."

"Yes, I am."

"Louisa and I are old friends, going back a long time," Miller said. "She's a tribal elder of the White Horse Nation, north of here."

"That's a coincidence," I told them. "We were just up there."

As the woman shot me a quizzical look, Joan and Buck emerged from the front bathroom.

"Hey, Joan," Wayne said, friendly.

"Hello, Wayne," she answered shyly. She looked over at Louisa. "Hello, Mrs. B."

"Hello, Joan. You with these folks?"

"I'm working for them. Helping take care of this one," she said, picking Buck up and swinging him toward the ceiling.

"I thought you had a job up on the reservation," Mrs. Bearpaw said. Her tone said she disapproved of Joan's working for Anglos in town; so I thought.

"It dried up," Joan explained.

The woman seemed upset with that explanation. "We need jobs of our own for our own young people," she explained to us. Turning to Miller, she said, "Can we continue this tomorrow?"

"Yes, we can do that," he answered.

Riva joined us in the living room. "Whew, I feel much better." Spying Wayne's mother, she stuck out her hand. "Riva Garrison."

"Louisa Bearpaw."

Another handshake. Mrs. Bearpaw's formality was impressive, if slightly intimidating.

"I hope you're enjoying your stay up here," Louisa said in an attempt to be gracious. "I understand you were up on our reservation earlier today."

Riva nodded. "We took Joan home to get some things."

Louisa turned to Joan. "How's your mother?"

"She's fine." The girl clearly was cowed by this woman.

"Well, I'll be seeing her later today or tomorrow, I reckon. Anything you want me to tell her?"

"No, ma'am."

The woman picked up her purse. "Nice meeting you all. We'll see you again, I'm sure."

As she walked out, she called back. "Wayne, you coming?"

"Yeah, Mama, I'm right behind you."

He gave Joan a wink, which caused her to color noticeably, and followed his mother out the door. We heard two cars firing up, two sets of tires squealing down the driveway.

"I'll show you around," Miller said after the front door closed on the Bearpaws, mother and son. "It'll have to be the nickel tour, I'm in the middle of my other job."

I looked at him strangely. "What other job?"

"Making money." He grinned, showing his bridge.

We walked around his house. It was quite a spread. There was a large master suite complete with Jacuzzi tub, a couple other well-appointed guest bedrooms, and a television viewing room that featured a large-screen projection TV.

"Would you like to watch some cartoons?" Miller asked Buck, bending down so his face was at Buck's level.

Buck nodded eagerly. That's one word he's known for a long time. Miller clicked on the television, flipped the channels to a cartoon show.

"I'll stay here with him," Joan volunteered quickly. She didn't feel comfortable in Miller's presence, I could feel the nervousness coming off her.

We left the two of them engrossed in Sylvester and Tweety bird and followed Miller through the rest of his house, which included a wine cellar and a shop. The cellar was well stocked, and the equipment in the shop had to be worth at least twenty thousand. There was also a small workout room, outfitted with a treadmill, a Nordic Track, rowing machine, and Universal gym.

"You get to be my age, you've got to work harder at staying in condition," Miller said as we complimented him on his stuff.

We were back in the main body of the house. "Here's where I work at my second job," Miller said as he led Riva and me into his study off the living room. The study was a small, intimate room—whitewashed walls, high-pitched ceiling, shining hardwood floors. Two computers were side by side on a long oak desk—state-of-the-art Dells, each with big nineteen-inch screens. Both running, spreadsheets on one, some kind of market analysis on the other.

"Nice computers," I commented. They were a hell of a lot better than the ones we were using in town, including the ones in his own office, which were ancient Macs.

"I'm a freak for this stuff," he said, his eyes brightening. "I've had these two a couple of months, and I'm already ready for newer ones. They're all obsolete the minute you take them out of the box. But they do the job."

"Were you working on something with the lady who just left?" Riva asked. She can put her nose right into it. Sometimes it's spontaneous, sometimes it's calculated—she can ask questions I can't and get away with it, because she's not a professional, as far as someone like Miller knows. In fact, she knows the law and its twists and turns well, from her bail-bonding days.

Miller glanced over at me. "Yes, I was, as a matter of fact."

He moved to the front of the machines and casually but deliberately cleared both screens.

"With the tribe's gambling idea?" Riva asked. "She's one of the tribal elders, isn't she?"

A frown momentarily crossed his face. "Yes, she is." He paused. "What do you know about this gambling thing?" He was trying not to sound concerned, but he wasn't entirely succeeding.

"That the tribe wants to buy the compound from the government and turn it into a little Las Vegas," she said.

"Oh," he said casually. "How'd you hear about that?"

"Everyone knows about that," I said, stepping in. I didn't want my wife exposing herself too much on my behalf; she'd opened the door, I could take it from here.

"Yeah," he said. "Well, they are."

"And you're helping them?"

"I give them my opinion, for what it's worth."

Riva put a hand on my arm. "I'm going to go in with Joan and Buck. Come get us when you're done. Nice seeing you," she said to Miller. "You'll have to come over for dinner one of these nights."

"I'd look forward to that."

She excused herself. I looked around the study. "I'd say your opinion's worth plenty, judging by the way you live."

"I do all right," Miller said offhandedly. "It's only been over the past decade, but I've managed to make some money. A little bit goes a long way up here."

Nora had told me that, too, which I knew was true. Still, though, I couldn't see this level of living on a county sheriff's salary, particularly a county as poor as Muir County, even with an FBI pension thrown in.

He was reading my mind—the question had come up before. "High tech."

"Excuse me?"

"Tech stocks. That's what I've invested in over the past ten years." He smiled like a cunning old fox. "Offhand, do you know what ten thousand dollars invested in Dell Computer in the early nineties is worth today?"

"Plenty, I'm sure."

"Over five million dollars. From a ten-thousand-dollar investment."

My jaw dropped. Literally, almost.

He grinned—he'd seen the envy and surprise on my face. "Microsoft, Intel, AOL, Amazon.com. I'm into all of them. It's been a wild ride, but I've done pretty well, I'd have to admit."

Pretty well was an understatement for the ages. The man was living like a multimillionaire, which in fact he was, to my astonishment. Every time I thought I had this old man pegged, he pulled another rabbit out of his hat to confound me. "You should have the tribe investing in those stocks, instead of gambling," I suggested. "If you're their investment guru, which it sounds like you're certainly qualified to be. Hell, I should give you some of my money to invest."

He shook his head self-deprecatingly. "I lucked out. If I'd lost the savings I put into the market, I'd still have my salary and my pensions. It was a flier that paid off. But those days are over, that kind of multiplication. Besides, the tribe can control gambling. It'll be on their property, unregulated by anyone."

"Except for the unsavories that'll be right in behind them," I put to him directly.

"Except for them," he agreed without flinching.

I pushed the conversation forward. "How do you feel about that? Being the head lawman in the county?"

"I don't like it. No one in law enforcement that I know likes gambling. Do you?"

"No."

"Well, we're in accord there." He paused. "You were up on the reservation this morning, so you've seen how these people live."

"Yes."

"It's abysmal."

"Yes, it is."

"Which would be worse for them?" he asked. "Living in abject poverty, or having to fend off outside gambling interests?"

I didn't have to answer that question. We both knew what it was.

Riva gave Joan the evening off. Buck was tired—it had been a long day for him. He went to sleep without a whimper.

"Quite a day," I declared. We were having supper. "From the outhouse to the penthouse."

She nodded. "Those poor people out on that reservation. What a crappy way to live. I hope that casino idea comes through for them."

I gnawed at a piece of French bread. "I wonder how they're going to come up with the money to buy that compound. You saw what I saw—this tribe doesn't have a dime to its name."

"Maybe they're going in business with another tribe. One that has made it big on gambling."

"That makes sense," I agreed. "Since it's the biggest thing the tribes in California have going for them now. About the only thing, according to their television commercials."

She placed a tender hand on mine. "I know you're opposed to gambling, honey, but they need money. They shouldn't have to live that way. No one should."

"I agree," I said with a heavy heart. "No one should."

PROSECUTION

Jury selection took three days, which wasn't long, given the seriousness of the indictment against Jerome. A surprising number of people in the jury pool didn't know enough about the raid and the killing to have preconceptions that would bar them from rendering a fair verdict. It's an insular world we live in now, with television and computers taking the place, more and more, of real human contact.

I was satisfied with the jury. No one on the panel had ties to law enforcement, had family members or close friends who were cops, and because of that might look favorably at a law officer killing an alleged criminal. More important, two people on the jury had Spanish surnames, and two were Native Americans. I figured those four would be inclined to be go for an Anglo cop killing a Latino, regardless of the evil of the victim's record.

Since we'd completed selecting the jury and alternates by Thursday afternoon, Judge McBee recessed until Monday morning, when I'd present my opening statement. He gave the jurors the usual admonishments about not reading anything about the trial, not watching any television shows about it, not talking to anyone—each other, family, or friends—about it. Then he sent us all on our way, wishing us a restful weekend.

I spent Friday and Saturday in the office, reviewing my notes. I was in good shape. My witnesses were lined up, my facts were in order. I knew who John Q. was calling, I had his list. I didn't see any surprises on it. Mostly character witnesses, and people who had been there that night, both DEA grants and members of Juarez's gang. Some of our witnesses overlapped, which is unusual but not unknown.

Saturday afternoon, as I was about to wrap up and go home, Kate stuck her head in the door. She'd just arrived from Santa Barbara. I wouldn't need her until later in the week, when I'd want her around to hand-hold the witnesses she'd interviewed, particularly Diane Richards, but she wanted to be present for my opening statement.

"How's it going, chief?" she sang out.

"Good as I could hope for," I answered in cheerful kind.

"That's what I like to hear." She dropped into the chair across the desk from me. "Anything last-minute you need looking into?"

I started to say, *No, everything's cool,* when a thought came to me. "There is one thing."

She perked up. "What's that?"

"One of the local Indian tribes wants to buy the compound from the government. They want to turn it into a gambling casino, a resort for high rollers."

She scrunched up her face. "Way up here? Does that make sense?"

"I don't see it, but they do. That's their decision, it's not my business."

"Then . . . ?"

"I was up there last weekend. We have this girl working for us who's from there. Helps Riva with Bucky. It's a poor reservation, from what I could see they don't have a pot to piss in, let alone enough to buy an expensive piece of property."

"You're interested in where they're getting the money."

"Their reservation abuts the compound. I'm wondering if—"

"There's a tie between them and Juarez's operation?" she said, finishing my sentence for me. We've worked together enough that she can read my mind sometimes.

"Exactly."

"You think Juarez was laundering money through this tribe?"

"I don't, really, but I'd like to know for sure. It's been nagging at me."

"I can check it out. What would it have to do with this case?"

"Nothing directly," I admitted. "I can't see where there'd be a connection."

"Although Jerome does have that mystery bank account."

"That wouldn't tie into this. They need money; if they were involved with Juarez and were moving his money for him, they sure as hell wouldn't be sending it Jerome's way."

"No, they wouldn't." She thought for a moment. "Do you think Jerome knew anything about it?"

I shook my head. "He would've brought it to his agency's attention if he did. They would have gone after the tribe as well. Another feather in his cap."

"Maybe he was going to. Bust Juarez, then go after the tribe."

"If he was going to do that, he wouldn't have killed Juarez. He would have tried to leverage him."

"Okay," she said, getting up. "I'll look into it. But if you don't think Jerome's connected, why get involved? It isn't your case. Don't you already have enough on your plate?"

"More than enough. And I don't want to prolong the agony, that's for sure."

"Then why?"

"Because I've got an itch. When I get an itch, I scratch it. Anything I can find out about Juarez could be helpful. It's probably a wild-goose chase, but what the hell, you're on the payroll." I voiced another thought I'd had. "While you're checking on that, find out if the Nevada casinos are the money behind the tribe."

"That would make more sense," she said. "Although that wouldn't have anything to do with this case, either."

"It would eliminate a variable. Old John Q.'s a crafty bastard. He's got something up his sleeve, he has to. If he could make a connection between Juarez, the tribe, outside gambling interests, anything that presents Jerome in a more sympathetic light, it could muddy the waters."

I walked her to the door. "That's our Achilles' heel, you know. We're prosecuting a cop for killing a scumbag. Some people can't get behind that. Hopefully, none of them are on our jury."

"For God's sakes, will you give it up already? That's bullshit, and you know it," she came back at me, using my own arguments. "Breaking the law is breaking the law, regardless of the circumstances or the players. You're the prosecutor, Luke, not the judge or jury. You do your job, let them do theirs. That's all you can do."

That was a good jolt of reality. Which I needed to hear.

"I know." I still couldn't help fretting. "It's there. And it's one note John Q. Jones is going to play. He's going to compose a symphony out of it, if he can."

*   *   *

"Ladies and gentlemen of the jury. Good morning."

We were into it. At last.

I stood at the podium, facing the jury. Jerome was seated across the aisle from my table, sitting next to John Q. Jerome looked sharp, dignified, professional. He was wearing a dark suit, white shirt, and tie. His hair had been cut short, marine-style. He sat ramrod straight, staring intently at me.

Behind me, seated in the first row of the gallery, were my detectives and Riva. Tom Miller and his deputy Bearpaw were also there, in one of the back rows, as was Bill Fishell, who had come up from Sacramento for the beginning of the trial. Once my opening statement and John Q.'s were over, Miller and Bearpaw would have to leave the courtroom, because they were on my witness list. This was a big case for Fishell; the credibility of his office was on the line, because he'd sanctioned and paid for this.

No DEA people were in the courtroom—they were conspicuous in their absence, but I'd expected that. They wanted to distance themselves from this as much as they could. To them, it wasn't a trial against their department. It was against one man who had broken the rules.

An assortment of reporters were present, newspaper and television. More would show up later, when we started calling some of the dramatic witnesses, such as Jerome's sister, and again when the jury went out to deliberate. The consensus was that Jerome was guilty. He'd already been tried and convicted in the press—we were putting the official imprimatur on it.

I wasn't talking to the media. No interviews, no off-the-record remarks. I wanted this to be as little a circus as possible.

As I was about to begin, the door in the rear opened, and Nora slipped into the chamber, taking a seat in the back row. I'd thought she might show up and had hoped she wouldn't. I had segregated her from the case as much as I could, giving her the dry details as they came to me, and nothing more—no strategy, no consultations. Under normal circumstances I could have used her knowledge and savvy, but these weren't normal circumstances. I was still skittish around her. She'd made a few overtures about getting together socially, with Riva and me, but I'd rejected them, offering Riva the explanation that I needed to be independent from her, which included social independence, to maintain the integrity of my investigation. Riva was fine with that; the two women hadn't struck a chord. I was hopeful that we'd finish the case without personal incident, I'd get out of Dodge, and I'd never see her again.

She tried to make eye contact with me. I turned away, avoiding her, my attention on the jury, my mind and energy focused.

"As you know, my name is Luke Garrison. I represent Muir County and the state of California as an independent prosecutor, specifically assigned to this case. That doesn't happen often; which should tell you this is an important case, a special case.

"I want to thank you in advance for the job you're going to do here, over the next days and weeks. It's a difficult task, being a member of a jury, especially in a case like this one, where the crime is so terrible and the stakes are so high. We have brought a charge of murder in the first degree against the defendant, Sterling Jerome. Murder in the first degree is as strong an indictment as the state can bring against someone."

Technically, that isn't true. We could have gone for murder with special circumstances, which would have brought the death penalty into play. But this wasn't going to be a death-penalty case. I'd made that decision, and Fishell had concurred. Nora had fought for the whole enchilada—she not only wanted Jerome on the cross, she wanted to hammer the nails in herself—but I had overruled her. Given the cast of characters and the overall situation, I didn't feel it warranted that; more importantly, as a practical consideration, I was afraid that by asking for the death penalty against a federal agent who had killed a public scourge I would force some jurors to come in with a not-guilty verdict. This way we could have what we wanted—a murder conviction—without putting these twelve ordinary men and women through more emotional turmoil than what they were already going to have to deal with.

"This trial is special, because this wasn't an ordinary murder. The people involved make it special. Now of course," I said, "any murder is heinous, awful—but this one was special way beyond that. This trial is about a law officer who decided to take the law into his own hands. He decided, all by himself, that he was above the law. That the laws you and I have to live with, including the law against murder, didn't apply to him. That the biblical commandment 'Thou shalt not kill' didn't apply to him. That it was okay for him to kill Reynaldo Juarez because Reynaldo Juarez was a criminal, a bad man. That for Sterling Jerome it wasn't enough to be an officer of the law, arrest a man, and turn him over to the system and let justice take its course. Sterling Jerome decided, all by himself, that it was okay, acceptable, *permissible and desirable,* for him to be judge, jury, and executioner.

"This isn't going to be a difficult case for you to follow. In any criminal case, you look for certain things. You look for motive, and you look for opportunity. The state is going to prove, beyond a shadow of a doubt, that Sterling Jerome had the motive to kill Reynaldo Juarez. When you hear some of the witnesses testify to that motive, it's going to knock you out. You're not going to believe that a man who had the motives to kill another man, like Sterling Jerome had against Reynaldo Juarez, could have ever been placed in the position Sterling Jerome was allowed to be placed in, so that he could carry out his motive. But it's there, and we're going to show it to you."

I paused to let them catch up with me. Then I walked to the edge of the jury box, so that I was right in front of them.

"And he had the opportunity. In fact, ladies and gentlemen, of all the people who were present when the murder of Reynaldo was committed—over sixty people—Sterling Jerome, and only Sterling Jerome, had the opportunity to commit this murder." I repeated my last sentence. "Only Sterling Jerome had the opportunity to commit this murder."

I took another brief interlude. I like to do that. It separates one thought, one piece of the puzzle from another. It's easier for people to assimilate and understand that way. Not one big idea, one overwhelming concept. Details, adding up to the bigger picture.

"We will show you . . . we will prove to you . . . that Sterling Jerome was obsessed with Reynaldo Juarez. That this obsession had gone on for decades. That it wasn't a professional obsession, a lawman going after a criminal. Mr. Jerome's lawyer is going to try to make that case, but he won't be able to. Because we will show you that this was personal, down to the gut of Sterling Jerome, a blood vendetta that consumed him, robbed him of reason, negated his ability and sworn duty to act in a professional manner. Ladies and gentlemen of the jury, this was a crime of misguided honor, and revenge."

I walked back to the podium. I wanted to put air between me and them, give them a breather.

"The defense is going to tell you that no one actually saw Jerome fire the bullet into Juarez's brain. And they're going to tell you that the actual bullet was never matched to Jerome's gun. And that's all they're going to tell you, because that's all they have."

I glanced over at the defense table. John Q. was noodling on his notepad, putting on a show of not-paying-attention nonchalance; Jerome, conversely, was staring daggers at me. I wanted him to get riled up—the jury would see the aggressiveness in his body language and assume that attitude translated into the way he lived his life. If I was lucky, I'd bait him into committing some overt physical act before the trial was over. Actually coming at me, physically, was probably too much to hope for, but I've been around men like Jerome. When you're as rigid and angry as they are, you can't bend, so you crack.

"We don't have an eyewitness to the actual murder. I admit that freely, right now. And we don't have the gun that killed Reynaldo Juarez. There's a good reason we don't, and we're going to explain that to you, and show you how that leads directly to Sterling Jerome, and only Sterling Jerome."

There's always a right place to stop. This was the right place, at this time.

"I haven't even told you about much of the other evidence we have that directly links Sterling Jerome to this crime. That'll come out during the trial. But I can promise you this: When this trial is over and both sides have had their say, you will agree with me without any question, all of you, that only one man could have committed this murder."

I turned and pointed to Jerome, my arm straight out, my accusatory finger aimed right between his eyes.

"This man. Sterling Jerome."

After a ten-minute recess, it was John Q.'s turn. He ambled up to the lectern, looking like Marlon Brando (in his present, unsvelte mien) playing Clarence Darrow, deliberately disheveled, his coat unbuttoned, snapping his bright yellow galluses, a piece of his shirttail pooched out from his trousers.

"Good morning, ladies and gentlemen of this jury," he boomed, his voice echoing in the high-ceilinged chamber. Smiling broadly, he pivoted his fleshy body so that he was looking at me, and by extension, focusing the eyes of the jury on me as well.

"Behold our distinguished prosecutor, the Honorable Luke Garrison, attorney-at-law, former district attorney of Santa Barbara County, down yonder in this fair state of ours, a hero who single-handedly saved a dozen lives in the desert last year at great risk to his own, a man admired by all in his profession."

I smiled. What a bullshit artist.

"A man who, by the way, left the business of prosecuting criminals to defend them, in large part because when he was in the business of prosecuting them, he made a mistake and prosecuted the wrong man for a particular crime, the crime of murder, and caused that man to be put to death in the gas—"

"Objection!" I thundered, jumping out of my seat.

I rarely object during an opening or a closing, but John Q. had crossed the line, big-time. He'd blindsided me. What he had just said was unprofessional, and highly unethical, which I found discomforting, especially this early in the trial, because John Q. is professional and ethical, that's an essential part of his character, one of the main reasons why he's so highly respected. And he's funny and theatrical and I'd been caught up in his act, lulled by his sonorous voice and grandiose presentation.

John Q.'s starting off on this tack was also a tacit admission, as I read it, that he had no confidence in his case and was going to try a series of end runs, smoke screens, and fancy maneuvers to try to confuse the jury. If you don't have the goods, dazzle them with footwork.

"I'm not the object of this trial, Your Honor."

"Sustained!" Judge McBee affirmed, loud and clear. "Counsel will refrain from any subjective referring to opposing counsel."

He turned to the jury. "Forget you heard those utterances about Mr. Garrison. Drop them completely from your minds." To the court reporter: "Strike all Mr. Jones's remarks up to this point." Back to the jurors: "Lawyers sometimes get carried away in their opening statements. This trial is about the guilt or innocence of the defendant. The lawyers are presenters, they are not the accused. Don't confuse them with the person on trial, because they aren't." Glaring at John Q., McBee threatened unsubtly, "Although some lawyers are held in contempt and thus become defendants in a different fashion."

"Thank you, Your Honor," I said, sitting down. I glanced over at John Q., who was taking McBee's admonition with good grace, even humor.

"Sorry, Your Honor," the old man said. "I can get off the track sometimes."

That was utter crap; he's as sharp as they come, even at his advanced age.

"Well, get back on the track and stay on it," Judge McBee warned him.

"I'll do my best."

We were off to a rousing start.

John Q. turned back to the jury. "I don't have that much to say to you, because my opponent here has already made my case for me. He's already told you there were no eyewitnesses to the killing. He's already told you the bullet that killed Juarez was never matched to my client's gun. What more do you want? A witness who *won't* tell you that my client, a highly regarded professional in his field, *wasn't* on the moon the night of the killing? Okay, I'll tell you that. Sterling Jerome was not on the moon the night of the killing. He was here in Muir County, where all of you live, conducting a raid on a drug facility. He was trying to arrest a man who was universally recognized as one of the biggest drug kingpins in the world."

He turned and looked at Jerome, who was less rigid than he'd been when I was talking about him. Jerome even managed to smile—a small, rueful smile—for the jury's benefit.

"And he did. He apprehended Reynaldo Juarez, a man on the Drug Enforcement Administration's ten most-wanted list. At great peril to himself and the men under his command. It was a great accomplishment."

A beat. Then he went on, striding from one side of the jury box to the other, his thumbs pulling at his suspenders.

"The prosecution's going to tell you that Mr. Jerome didn't play by the rules when he went in after Reynaldo Juarez. Well, in one sense, he'll be right, Mr. Garrison there. The raid wasn't conducted strictly by the book. And you know what? That's a crying shame. Boo hoo hoo. Mr. Jerome, a seasoned veteran of the drug wars, *had* to improvise when events changed. He *had* to make some quick decisions, out there in the middle of the night, in a lonely, godforsaken, hostile place, about whether or not he should try to arrest one of the most notorious criminals in the world, or let him go because of some technicalities. Not legal technicalities, mind you. Sterling Jerome didn't break any laws when he authorized the raid on Reynaldo Juarez's fortress. He bent some departmental rules, that's all. And for doing that, ladies and gentlemen, the attorney general of the United States praised him."

John Q. was going good now. I was enjoying his act. He still wasn't saying anything that would make a difference, but he was fun to watch.

"Mr. Jerome was praised because he carried out his assignment successfully. He apprehended Reynaldo Juarez. Mission accomplished. He brought him in alive. That was his mission. To capture this desperado, and bring him in alive. That's what he did."

John Q. moved away from the jury, crossing the room to stand behind his client at the defense table. Putting his hands on Jerome's shoulders like a father's on a son's, he looked at the jurors. "That's what he did. This capable soldier in the war against drugs. He captured his quarry, and he arrested him."

He waited for the moment to reach its potential, for the jurors to look at him and at Jerome. Then he walked back to the rostrum again.

"Mission accomplished. Mission wonderfully accomplished. A terrible human being—I use the word in its scientific sense, not in any humanistic way, Reynaldo Juarez was an animal, not a human being, a predator who preyed on the weak and helpless in our society—a bad, bad man was arrested. Mission accomplished. A job well done. The attorney general of the United States, waiting up all night to hear what happened, is overjoyed. Sterling Jerome, a dedicated public servant, did his job. He did it right."

Another look back at Jerome, a look almost of longing, of endearment.

"This man," John Q. said, his voice almost quivering with emotion now, "this man is a hero, not a villain. There has been a crime committed here, yes—the crime is that he's even sitting here in the dock. We should be carrying him down the street on our shoulders, singing his praises, not arresting him and locking him up and bringing these ugly, lousy charges against him. He did his job, ladies and gentlemen. He arrested a dangerous criminal."

The old warhorse was rolling, I had to give him that. A virtuoso performance.

"Then some unforeseeable horror happened after Reynaldo Juarez was arrested. He escaped. How he escaped, or who helped him escape, no one knows. The prosecution wants to pin that on Mr. Jerome—but they have absolutely no evidence, none at all. There were dozens of people there that night. It was a chaotic situation. Anyone there could have done it. Or more likely, no one did. Juarez was a hardened criminal. He had been in tough spots before. He would have foreseen his being arrested someday, and would have thought of how to deal with those consequences, including figuring out how to escape. That's a much more likely explanation. Not some concoction the prosecution had to dream up to fit the facts, after the fact.

"Brave men risked their lives to capture a group of hardened criminals. Some of them died doing their jobs—hard, thankless, dangerous jobs. We should praise them, not bury them for that. And we should never, ever, bring innocent men to trial to satisfy the needs of politicians who have to lay blame. Isn't it enough that those brave men had to die, shot down by armed desperados? Isn't it enough that for months now, an innocent man, a man whose entire life has been dedicated to wiping out the scourge of drugs, has had to sit in a jail cell, isolated from his family and friends, his career shattered? I think it is. I think that enough is enough, my friends. I think it's time to let Mr. Jerome go free and resume his exemplary life, a life dedicated to making my life, and your life, and the lives of everyone in this room, in this county, in this country, a safer place to live."

John Q. was in the homestretch now. One last hurrah.

"Sterling Jerome should never have been indicted. He should never have suffered the pain of imprisonment. He should never have had his good name smeared in the mud. What he should have, and what you should give him, is his freedom back. His freedom, and his dignity. We—all of us—owe him nothing less."

John Q.'s oration rang the bell. If an impartial observer had judged who was going to win by the opening-day performances, John Q. would have skunked me, an A or A- to my solid B+. But today was going to be his pinnacle. Despite the emotion, the appeals to a higher justice, it would be downhill for him, from here on in. Juries will swallow a certain amount of bullshit, especially at the beginning of a trial, when they've only seen the frame and not the picture, but evidence will out, unless the jury is absolutely partial to one side, and antagonistic to the other side's lawyers, which wouldn't be the case here, either.

After congratulating me on my presentation and my self-restraint (I had strong grounds for objecting several times during John Q.'s opening, but didn't, that would all be forgotten), Riva went home.

I walked from the courtroom to my office. Tomorrow I would start calling witnesses.

It was a warm and dry late-afternoon, a harbinger of a hot, late summer. The sun was low, unfiltered, a furnace door at the far end of the two-lane highway that serves as Blue River's main street. The objects in its path—buildings, cars, lampposts, pedestrians—were casting long, sharply etched shadows. There's an old-fashionedness to this town, like out of an old western movie, *High Noon* or *My Darling Clementine*.

I guess I thought of those movies because the first witness I was going to call, Sheriff Miller, reminded me of Gary Cooper and Henry Fonda.

Strong, quiet types, nothing of the bully about them. I see Miller that way, a throwback to a simpler, more humane time, although I know that's more nostalgia than reality. And Tom Miller doesn't live in the past, not with his fancy house and all the modern computer equipment.

I spent an hour with Miller, going over my questions, his answers to them, what I thought John Q. would throw at him. He was ready, he knew the drill—he'd done this innumerable times. And this was personal to him, he really wanted to nail it.

After he left, I reread, for the umpteenth time, parts of the case that were pertinent to the next few days. The butterflies were gone now. From here on in, it would be preparation, facts, and experience.

The building was empty. Everyone had gone for the day. I called Riva to let her know I'd be home soon. Then, as I was putting my papers into my briefcase, about to lock up and walk out, Nora stuck her head in the door.

"Got a minute, Luke?" she asked tentatively.

"I was just leaving, Nora." I closed my case, snapped it shut.

"I was hoping . . ."

She stood in the doorway, half in, half out.

"Was there something specific?" I asked. I didn't want to talk to her. I certainly didn't want to be alone with her, with no one else around.

"I wanted to congratulate you on your opening. You did well."

"Thanks."

"Well stated. Well structured. Not too long."

"It did the job. Today was John Q.'s day. He's got the good silver tongue."

"Maybe," she acknowledged. "People around here are meat-and-potatoes kind of folks. They're not impressed with glitz."

"That's usually the way it is." I put on my coat, straightened the pens and papers on my desk. Read the signals, Nora, it's time to go.

She wasn't ready to leave. She had come over here for a reason. "I wish we could . . . talk to each other, Luke. Confer. Like colleagues."

"We can't."

"Because you're an independent prosecutor? That's not etched in stone."

"That's not the reason. You know the reason."

She looked down at her feet. "I've put that behind me."

"I'm glad to hear that."

"But you still can't . . ."

"Share strategy with you?"

"Yes."

"I told you my attitude about that when I signed on, Nora. If I'm going to be truly independent, it has to be this way. Particularly now. I can't be alone with you, Nora. I'm uncomfortable right now."

She looked forlorn.

"I'm sorry, Nora, but that's the way it is. You may have put what you did behind you, but you can't erase it." I sized her up. "And I don't think you have put it behind you."

She stared back at me. "You're right. But that doesn't mean I'm going to make a play for you. I can control myself."

I shook my head. "Maybe you can, maybe you can't. I don't know, I don't want to find out. There's a history, and that's what I have to go by. The easiest way to make sure nothing happens is to stay out of harm's way."

She thought about that for a moment—then she took two steps into the office and closed the door behind her.

I picked my briefcase up. "Open the door, Nora."

She stood her ground, her back up against the door. "All I want is to be part of the case, Luke. I want to know what's going on. What your strategy is. How you think it's going. It's my case," she said, her voice rising, "I brought you in, damn it! You have no right to shut me out."

"Open the goddamn door. Now."

She wasn't budging. "Does your wife know about us?"

Jesus, she wasn't actually saying this.

"There's nothing for her to know."

"Maybe we should let her be the judge of that."

I took one deep breath, to compose myself. Don't back down on this now, I steeled myself, she'll run you over if you do.

"Okay, Nora. Here's how it's going to go." My voice was calm, low, clear. "You're going to walk out of this office right now, and you're never going to walk in it again unless you're invited. You want to lay some cockamamie lie on my wife, go do it. I can't stop you. I'll tell her you're lying, and she'll believe me. But if you get in my face one more time about any of this crap, I am going to call Bill Fishell and have him read you the riot act."

I stopped.

"It's up to you, Nora. Either you leave this office, right now, and stop bothering me for the remainder of this trial, or I'm picking up the phone and calling Sacramento."

She stood frozen in place for a moment—then she turned, threw open the door, and walked out.

I stood behind my desk, listening to her high heels echoing fainter and fainter on the tile floor. Then I heard the front door opening and closing.

I was shaking, my palms were wet, my heart was pounding a mile a minute, all the classic, hackneyed symptoms of distress. Except these were real. My mouth felt metallic, they were so real to my taste.

It took me a few minutes to calm down sufficiently so that I was on an even enough keel that I could feel okay to drive home and be with my family in a secure, unfreaking normality. Leaving the office, locking the door behind me, I walked outside. It was twilight time, about eight o'clock, the sun laying a final coat of blazing colors on the western foothills.

Nora's come unhinged, I was thinking. All the stress of her life had caught up to her. Riva would never believe Nora, thank God, if Nora was crazy enough to tell her about our episode in the hot tub together and try to portray me as a willing participant. She knew Nora was lonely, and although she hadn't said it to me, I assumed she felt that Nora was engaging in fantasies about me.

It was delusional, and it was sad. She wasn't a bad woman, just a desperately lonely one. I don't know if lonely women make good lovers, like the song says; I don't ever want to find out. But I knew now, clearly, that they can be dangerous.

Sheriff Miller was everything a prosecutor could hope for in a witness. He told his story clearly, firmly, decisively. And everything he said was a damning indictment against Sterling Jerome.

Q (me): "In operations such as this one, the outside agency, in this case the Drug Enforcement Administration, consults and works closely with the local agency, in this case your department. Is that true?"

A (Miller): "Yes, that's how it's supposed to work."

Q: "Is that how it happened in the raid on the drug compound?"

A: "No."

Q: "What was different in this instance?"

A: "I wasn't consulted. At all."

Q: "When did you find out that this raid was going to take place?"

A: "Late that night."

Q: "Normally, when would you find out?"

A: "Well in advance. Always long before the day or night of. Local law-enforcement agencies have to be involved. They have information that's invaluable. Plus it's their territory. You don't go into someone else's territory without letting them know about it."

Q: "How did you feel about that?"

A: "Terrible. Not from a personal point of view—I don't have an ego when it comes to capturing criminals, I'm not looking for credit. But from a professional point of view, it's wrong. People can get hurt if they don't know what's going on. Which is what happened in this case."

Q: "Once you were informed of the raid, what was your assignment, Sheriff?"

A: "I didn't have one. I was specifically instructed not to participate. My deputy and I were made to stand aside."

Q: "So even after you were notified that the raid was going to take place, you were not allowed to be part of it. Even though it was taking place in your jurisdiction."

A: "This is correct."

Q: "Did you have any role at all?"

A: "No. Jerome grudgingly allowed me and my deputy to accompany the DEA team, but we were consigned to the bull pen for the actual raid: We were not allowed to participate."

Q: "Did you ask to?"

A: "Of course. That's our job."

Q: "And the answer was?"

A: "We weren't wanted, or needed."

Q: "So where were you physically, when the raid took place?"

A: "On a hill, overlooking the compound."

I walked to one of my exhibits, a large aerial map of the area that was mounted on an easel, positioned so that the jury could easily see it.

Q: "Is this where you were? You and your deputy?" I pointed to the hill, which was far from the main raiding area.

A: "Yes."

Q: "How far away is that, approximately?"

A: "A quarter of a mile away."

Q: "How many years have you been in law enforcement, Sheriff Miller?"

A: "Between my years with the Federal Bureau of Investigation, and the Muir County Sheriff's Office, just under fifty years."

Q: "And has this ever happened to you before? Getting shut out this way?"

A: "Never. In all that time, it's never happened."

I looked at the jury. They were paying close attention. Tom Miller is the most highly respected man in this county. Jerome had picked the wrong man to disrespect, and he was going to pay for it, beyond the physical ramifications of his actions.

Q: "What did you think of Special Agent Jerome's strategy and tactics?"

A: "Highly unprofessional, reckless, and dangerous. Frightening."

Q: "Would you explain to the jury why you think that?"

A: "Yes. There was supposed to be a transfer of money for drugs. A huge amount of money, a huge amount of drugs. That's why this raid was so important. Not only to capture the drug dealers involved, including but not limited to Reynaldo Juarez, but to seize the drugs. That was the foundation of the warrant that Mr. Jerome obtained."

Q: "Did that happen?"

A: "No."

Q: "Why not?"

A: "Because the airplanes carrying the money and the drugs couldn't fly up to Muir County. There was too much fog that night, further down south."

Q: "So the raid was aborted."

A: "No."

Q: "Why not, if the objective was the bust?"

A: "Because Agent Jerome wanted to get Reynaldo Juarez, with or without the physical evidence, or the probable cause."

Q: "In your almost fifty years of law enforcement, is that common?"

A: "Absolutely not. It's almost unheard of."

Q: "So to the best of your knowledge, Agent Jerome went against normal procedures and regulations when he authorized this raid to go on."

A: "Without question."

Q: "Did you feel that Agent Jerome had a personal vendetta against Reynaldo Juarez? Beyond the fact that Juarez was a drug dealer?"

John Q. got to his feet for that one. "Objection, Your Honor. Calls for speculation on the part of the witness."

McBee agreed with him. "Rephrase your question," he told me.

I turned back to Miller.

Q: "Did you hear Agent Jerome say anything about having a personal vendetta against Reynaldo Juarez?"

A (nodding vigorously): "Yes. He said that they were going to take the compound anyway. That Juarez was not going to escape on his watch. It was obviously very personal to him."

Q: "What did you think of that?"

A: "I thought it was shortsighted, dangerous. The reason for the immediate assault was no longer applicable. The men inside that compound weren't going anywhere. The place was surrounded by over fifty DEA agents. Why mount a risky assault when you don't have to?"

Q: "Were there other reasons you were dubious about this assault on the compound, Sheriff Miller?"

A: "Yes."

Q: "What were they?"

A: "The quality of the information regarding the men inside the compound. Their degree of readiness, and so forth."

Q: "Why were you concerned about that?"

A: "It was coming from an untrustworthy source."

Q: "Untrustworthy in what way?"

A: "Jerome was relying on a drug-gang member who had been turned and was working undercover for him."

Q: "In common terms, a snitch?"

A: "That's right."

Q: "Why do you consider such a source unreliable?"

A: "Because they're not doing it for the right reasons."

Q: "Which are?"

A: "To stop a criminal activity."

Q: "Why are they doing it, then?"

A: "Usually because they've been arrested on some other charge, and they've worked out a deal to stay out of jail."

Q: "Was that how it was in this case?"

A: "Yes. I knew the informant. He was considered very unreliable. He was in it strictly for himself. Doing the right thing meant nothing to him."

Q: "Would you have used him?"

Again, John Q. stood. "Objection, Your Honor. Mr. Miller's use or disuse of this informant is not relevant."

"Overruled," McBee told John Q. firmly. "*Sheriff* Miller is a well-regarded law-enforcement officer, with a depth of knowledge and experience rarely available. His opinion is instructive. You may answer the question," McBee told my witness.

I asked Miller again if he would have used Lopez.

A: "No. I would not have. Nor would other sheriffs that I know. He was too unreliable. Which the terrible consequences in this situation proved to be all too true."

We went back and forth some more about Jerome's tactics. Then I went for the finish.

Q: "After Reynaldo Juarez was ultimately captured, were you in a position to see what was going on?"

A: "Fairly well. Once the shooting had started, my deputy and I had rushed in to help, so we were closer to the center of things. It was very chaotic, as you could imagine. Dead and wounded, nighttime, a very remote area, nobody really knowing exactly where everyone else was. But yes, to answer your question, I had a decent overlay. By that time I don't think Agent Jerome cared where I was. He'd gotten what he was after."

Q: "What about your deputy, Wayne Bearpaw? Was he with you?"

A: "No. Once Juarez had been apprehended, he went home. They didn't want us there anyway, so there was no reason for him to stay. I only did because it's my territory, and I felt I had a professional obligation to be there to the finish."

Q: "Where were you when Juarez escaped?"

A: "I was about thirty or forty yards away."

Q: "From the trailer where he was being held."

A: "Yes."

Q: "What did you do?"

A: "For a moment—no more than a few seconds—I didn't do anything. I was too shocked, it took that bit of time for it to register. Then I started running after him, like everybody else."

Q: "Did he disappear from sight?"

A: "Yes, almost instantaneously. You have to remember, it was dark out, and the moon was obscured by clouds. He made it into the woods, almost immediately."

Q: "Did you hear the gunshot?"

A: "From the bullet that killed Juarez?"

Q: "Yes."

A: "Yes, I heard it."

Q: "But you didn't see the shooting."

A: "No, sir. I did not. I don't think anyone did."

Q: "Except the killer himself."

I was waiting for John Q. to object to that—I would have, it was speculative. But he knew now how Judge McBee felt about Tom Miller. John Q. wanted this over. He stayed in his seat, quiet.

A: "Except the actual killer, that would be correct."

Q: "Go back a few minutes from when you saw the dead body of Reynaldo Juarez, Sheriff Miller, to the time when you heard Agent Jerome yelling and saw Juarez fleeing. Did you see the others chase after Juarez?"

A: "Of course. That's what I said."

Q: "Yes, you did. Do you recall if any particular agent was leading the pack? Or was it pretty much every man for himself?"

A: "It was every man for himself. The whole thing was a mess, we were lucky no one else was shot in the confusion, there could have been a terrible cross fire—like what happened during the raid on the compound," Miller said pointedly. "But to answer your question—there was one agent who was ahead of the others."

Q: "How far ahead?"

A: "Twenty yards at the beginning, I'd say. It could have been more."

I was finished. Strolling over to the jury box, I leaned on the railing, so that when Miller answered my next question, he'd be looking directly at the jurors, and they at him.

Q: "Can you identify that agent for the jury?"

A: "Yes. It was Agent Jerome. He was ahead of the rest of us."

A good lawyer knows when the best thing he can do with a witness is get him off the stand as quickly as possible. John Q.'s a good lawyer. He had a few points to make first.

"Before the raid began on the drug compound, Agent Jerome gave some instructions. Do you recall that?" he asked.

"Yes," Miller answered.

"He stipulated that Reynaldo Juarez was to be taken alive, didn't he? The entire reason for this was to capture him, not to kill him. Do you recall him saying that?"

"Yes, I do."

"Under no circumstances was Juarez to be killed," John Q. repeated. "He said it was their supreme objective, on orders directly from the attorney general. Is that true? Captured, not killed."

"That's what he said."

"He was very forceful about that. That Juarez *not* be killed."

"Yes," Miller acknowledged. "He said he wanted to take Juarez alive. That the raid would be a bust if he were killed."

"You saw the prisoner running away when he escaped, Sheriff Miller. Did you have a good view of him?"

Miller nodded. "Yes, I saw him. I wouldn't say my view was particularly good, under the circumstances. But I did see him."

"Did he have a gun—Juarez? Was he armed?"

Miller thought for a moment. "I don't think so. But I couldn't swear to it."

Kate and I reconnoitered in my office at the end of the day. Nora was nowhere in sight. For that I was grateful, and relieved. She hadn't been in court, either. Perhaps she had taken my admonitions to heart. I hoped.

"How'd you do?" Kate asked.

"Good. Miller's my kind of witness."

"A dagger to the heart, huh?"

"Dead center." I grinned.

"Well, I was busy, too." She pulled out her notepad. "The Nevada casinos are not behind the purchase. They don't want to have anything to do with Indian gambling, except to get rid of it whenever and wherever they can."

"Okay, we figured that. Any other sources? What about other tribes?"

"There are rich tribes, and there are poor tribes. Not much in between. The rich tribes are rich because they have mineral rights and get money from the royalties, or because they have gambling. The tribes with money I've checked on are the ones whose money comes from gambling."

"That sounds like the right approach."

"Thank you," she said sarcastically. "I checked with about two dozen tribes that have gambling on their reservations, both in California and other states. Some of these tribes are making an amazing amount of money. You wouldn't believe how much. Hundreds of millions of dollars. If this tribe could tap into one-tenth of that, they'd be sitting pretty."

"Anyway . . ."

"I'm getting there, hold your horses." She closed her notebook. "None of these tribes have been contacted by the White House Nation."

"None?"

"Not a one."

That was a surprise.

"Oh, and by the way, the BIA isn't funding it, either. The tribe gave them a check for a hundred fifty K recently, as a deposit on the purchase. The rest is due six months from then, and the guy I talked to in the regional office in Sacramento felt they were going to come up with the money."

"Where are they getting it, then?" I asked as another thought came to me. "Buying the property is only the tip of the iceberg. They'd have to build a casino, outfit it, the whole schmear. That's got to be millions. Maybe tens of millions."

"Well, here's a rumor that might be interesting."

I waited.

"Juarez's operation might have been funneling money to the tribe. Which is what you thought. But so far that's only a rumor."

That rocked me. "That would be a hell of a parlay. Drug running and gambling. A great way to launder money."

"You bet."

My mind was spinning. "Follow through on this connection. Maybe there's something there."

"Something with Jerome?"

"Somebody gave him half a million dollars. It wasn't for his good looks."

"Do you think they could all be connected?"

"I don't know what to think. And to be honest, I don't want to start turning over stones I don't have to turn over. I've got a good case. I don't want to muddy the waters."

The ballistics expert was one of the state's top people. John Q. and I had stipulated in advance to his expertise. He testified that the bullet that had killed Juarez could not be traced to any particular weapon, because the casings had been stripped when it had slammed into the tree. All he could say for sure was that it was 9mm., a full-metal jacket, and that it was the bullet that had killed Juarez—DNA taken from blood traces on it matched Juarez's.

*　　　*　　　*

Winston Kim was a hostile witness. He was testifying under subpoena, which meant I could question him more aggressively than is normally allowed. (He was slated to be a friendly witness for the defense, so John Q. stipulated in advance that he wouldn't be cross-examining him.)

"Agent Kim," I started out, "you are the man in charge of the DEA's investigation into the killing of Reynaldo Juarez?"

"I am the agent in charge, yes."

He wasn't going to be a good witness for me, so I wanted to get him on and off.

"Did Agent Jerome violate departmental procedures when he authorized the raid on that compound? Wasn't he supposed to be breaking up a drug deal, and capturing the people involved in the process?"

"Yes," Kim said reluctantly. He was scrupulously avoiding looking at Jerome. Jerome wasn't looking at him, either. There was no love lost between them—Jerome had disgraced the agency—but Kim didn't want to help me, either. We had trumped his investigation, and that made him look bad.

"He shouldn't have gone in there the way he did, should he?"

"I can't answer that categorically. I wasn't there."

"Going by the reports, if you had been there, would you have gone in?"

"I can't say. Judgments are made in the field. They're made fast. You go with the best information you have."

"Then why was Agent Jerome transferred to a lesser position? Isn't he being punished?"

"*Punished* isn't the word I'd use."

"Banished? Gotten out of the way? Don't bother answering that question." I moved on. "Going strictly by the book, taking the human factor out of play, meaning emotion or sentiment towards the defendant, were Agent Jerome's actions on that night grounds for discipline?"

"We don't make decisions strictly by the book. These are human beings, not robots."

"Grounds for dismissal? Again, by the written rules under which you operate."

Again, with reluctance: "Possibly."

"So he did screw up."

"He didn't follow the exact directions he was given. But he was the leader in the field, it was his call. He captured a man who had been on our ten-most-wanted list," Kim said in Jerome's defense. "That was important to us."

His agency suspends the man internally, but defends him to the world externally. The bureaucracy at its worst.

"Are DEA agents issued ammunition, Agent Kim?"

"Yes, they are."

"They don't have to buy it. It's provided for them, free of charge."

"Yes."

I glanced at my notes. "The ammunition of choice for automatic weapons in such a situation as this one was are 147-grain hydroshocks. Federal hollow points. Is that correct?"

"That is correct."

"Under these circumstances, would an agent use a full-metal-jacket-type bullet?"

"No."

"Would an agent ever use a full-metal-jacket bullet?"

Kim nodded. "For his own personal use, perhaps."

"His own personal use? Like shooting somebody when he isn't on the job? Like what, moonlighting?"

"For target practice," Kim answered angrily, stung by my accusation. "Range qualifying, that sort of thing."

"But you would provide that ammunition to him for those purposes, wouldn't you?"

"Yes," Kim admitted. "We would."

My next witness, Neil Cohen, had been Jerome's personal trainer in L.A. A tall man in his late twenties, he wore his long hair in a ponytail, sported hoop earrings in both ears, and was built along the lean, sinewy lines of a championship beach volleyballer, rather than having the bulkiness of a weight lifter.

"How many days did you work out with Mr. Jerome?" I asked.

"Six days a week, unless he was unavailable."

"How long a session?"

"Two hours. Sometimes more. If we went on a long ride, or a long run, it could go as long as four hours."

"That's a lot of working out."

"He was dedicated."

"Sterling Jerome was in good shape."

"Good shape?" Cohen scoffed at that description. "He was in awesome shape."

"Was he training for something specific, or did he just want to be in great shape?"

"Both. He was a physical-fitness freak, like me, and we were training for the Ironman."

"That's a triathlon?"

Cohen nodded. "In Hawaii. It's the Super Bowl of triathlons."

"What does it cover?"

"It starts out with a two-and-a-half-mile ocean swim—no wet suits, fins, or anything artificial that can help—then that's followed by a hundred-and-twelve-mile bike ride, finishing off with a marathon."

"You run twenty-six and a quarter miles after the swim and the bicycling. One directly after the other. No breaks in between."

"None. You power through, all the way."

"That must be grueling."

He laughed. "It's brutal, man."

"How long does it take?"

"The winner's time'll be under ten hours. A good time's twelve hours." Cohen glanced over at Jerome, who was feigning indifference. "Sterling would've busted that, easy."

I was looking at the jury as I questioned Cohen. They were agog at this kind of physical prowess, and by extension, what it indicated about the powers of the man who possessed it. "You'd have to be in fabulous shape to even think about trying it."

"It's not for the weak at heart," Cohen agreed.

"Or the weak in body."

"Definitely not."

"Jerome was in shape for something that hard? He would have finished it?"

"For sure," Cohen said enthusiastically. "Without question. He might've placed in his age group."

"What's he best at, swimming, biking, or running?"

"He's good at all of 'em," Cohen said, "but running's his main thing. He ran the half in college."

"He was a collegiate runner?" I wanted to make sure the jury heard this.

"He sure was."

"He's fast, then."

"Yeah, he's fast on his feet. Faster at running than me over the short haul, and I'm pretty fast."

"So if he was chasing after somebody, the average person, even a man in pretty good shape, he'd run him down quickly."

"The average person? He'd run that sucker into the ground."

Another hostile witness was up next—Walter Dutton, Jerome's second-in-command on the raid. My interrogation of him was brief and to the point.

"After Reynaldo Juarez was arrested and in your custody, how many people had access to him? He was locked up in your command trailer, wasn't he?"

"Yes."

"Could you answer the first part of my question, too? How many people had access to him?"

"I couldn't say exactly."

"Every agent who was there?"

He shook his head. "No."

"Only a few of you who were in charge, and needed immediate access to him?"

"Yes." He waited a moment, then added, "That was how it was set up."

"What does that mean?"

"It was a mess out there, logistically. We had wounded to attend to, the other prisoners. It wasn't a neat package."

"So what're you saying, anyone could've walked in there? This was one of the most wanted criminals in the country. What kind of security did you have, Agent Dutton?"

"The best we could, under the circumstances."

"So to the best of your knowledge, only a few of you were allowed to be in that trailer."

"Yes, that's correct."

———————

John Q. worked that one, as I knew he would.

"Only a few of you were supposed to be inside the command post with Juarez, but practically speaking, anyone might have gotten in, isn't that true, Agent Dutton?"

Dutton was a much more responsive witness with his buddy's lawyer than he'd been with me. "That's absolutely right."

"Even another member of Juarez's gang, if one of them had managed somehow to have eluded capture during the raid."

"Yes, that would have been possible."

"It was dark, it was chaotic, it was impossible to keep tabs on where everyone was, isn't that true?"

"It was bad."

"When Juarez broke out of the trailer, where was Sterling Jerome, Agent Dutton? Was he inside with the prisoner?"

A vigorous head shake no. "He was outside, about fifteen, twenty yards away."

"What was he doing?"

"Talking to me and some of the others about moving the convoy."

"So Sterling Jerome was nowhere near that trailer when Juarez broke loose."

"No."

———

I faced Dutton on redirect. "Did you or any other member of your task see any suspicious person near that trailer after the arrests had been made, Agent Dutton?"

He rearranged himself in the witness chair. "I personally didn't."

"Did anyone else?"

"I don't think anyone else did, either."

"To the best of your knowledge, were all the men who were inside the drug compound accounted for after the raid was concluded? Either apprehended, or killed in the shoot-out?"

"To the best of my knowledge, that's correct," he said grudgingly.

"Before Juarez made his escape?"

"I think so."

"You *think* so?"

"To the best of my knowledge, yes."

"Do you know the identity of the last person who was inside that trailer with Juarez before he escaped?"

"I can't say positively," he said, trying his best to stonewall.

"To the best of your knowledge," I pursued, throwing his technicality language back at him, "was it Agent Jerome?"

He looked over at Jerome, who was watching him from the defense table. Then Dutton winced. "To the best of my knowledge, that is correct."

"And to the best of your knowledge, when Juarez did make his escape, who led the charge after him? Who was the leader of the pack?"

He shook his head. "It happened too fast. I couldn't point out any particular agent for sure."

"It wasn't Agent Jerome?"

"I wouldn't swear to that, no."

"Did you chase after Juarez, Agent Dutton?"

"Yes."

"Did you see Agent Jerome during that chase?"

"For the first part of it. Everybody got separated quick, it was dark, we were running in the trees."

"During the time that you did see Agent Jerome, before he disappeared from your sight, was he ahead of you or behind you?"

"He was ahead of me."

"To the best of your recollection, Agent Dutton, did you see any other agent out in front of Agent Jerome?"

He closed his eyes, trying to bring back the memory. Or hope that when he opened them, I wouldn't be there. When after a few seconds he did open them, and answered, he had to admit that he hadn't seen any other agent running in front of Jerome.

"So to sum up your testimony, would it be fair to say that only a few people were allowed in that command-post trailer, and no one who shouldn't have gotten inside ever was inside?"

"Yes. I would have to say that's true, from where I stood."

"And Agent Jerome was the last known person to be in the trailer."

A very muted "Yes."

"And when Juarez did escape, Jerome was in the lead. You didn't see anybody in front of him."

"No. I didn't."

My final witness for the day was the gun-store owner, Ralph Harrison. He gave a wink and a nod to a few of the jurors as he took his seat—it's a small county, people know each other, especially a man with an essential business such as Harrison's. His testimony was brief and to the point: He sold Sterling Jerome a box of full-metal-jacket bullets for his Glock 17 gun less than a week before the raid on the compound. Jerome had never been in his store before, or since, nor had any of the other agents in his task force. Over John Q.'s objections, and with the help from my friendly judge, I elicited from Harrison his expert opinion that it was strange for an agent to buy ammo, stranger to buy the kind Jerome bought, and stranger still to drive three hundred miles round-trip to do so.

John Q. went after Harrison hard. "Why is it unusual for someone to buy this kind of ammunition?" he blustered.

"It isn't," Harrison answered easily.

"You testified that it was."

"I said given who was buying it, it was."

"Did you know at the time that Mr. Jerome was a DEA agent?"

"No."

"So his buying it, in and of itself, was meaningless."

"In a vacuum, you could say that. But, you know, you have to look at it in its totality."

"So from the few minutes or less that Agent Jerome was in your store, you were able to ascertain that he was a federal agent, he was buying ammunition that was unusual, and that he'd driven all the way across the county to do so."

"I figured it out later on. When I'd heard what had happened."

"All by yourself."

Harrison shrugged. "It doesn't take a rocket scientist to figure something like that out."

John Q. walked over to the defense table, leaned over to Jerome, whispered something in his ear. Jerome shook his head. John Q. walked back to the podium.

"Did Mr. Jerome identify himself as a federal agent?" he asked.

"No."

"Did he identify himself at all?"

Harrison thought for a moment. "No, I don't think he did."

"How did he pay for his box of ammunition, Mr. Harrison? Credit card, check, cash?"

"He paid cash."

"Cash. You're sure?"

"Yes. Later on I looked up his receipt, to make sure. He paid cash."

"So he never told you who he was, his name, or gave you anything, like a credit card or a check, that would indicate who he was, what his name was, or what he did?"

"No, sir."

"How much ammunition do you sell a year, Mr. Harrison?"

Harrison laughed. "A lot. That's what we do."

"On a daily basis, how many boxes of ammunition do you think you sell?"

"It depends on the time of year. Hunting season, we sell more. Other times, not as much."

"When Mr. Jerome bought his ammunition from you, was that during hunting season?"

"Yeah. It was at the beginning of it."

"So you were selling plenty of ammunition that day. Is that correct?"

"We sold a lot around then, that's right."

"Your store was pretty crowded?"

Harrison nodded. "There were a goodly number of customers."

"Did you wait on all of them?"

"No, I couldn't handle that amount of traffic single-handed. I had my usual staff on."

"How many employees do you have working for you at that time of year?"

Harrison furrowed his brow. "I think I had four on that day."

"Four including you."

"Yes."

"And all day long, people were coming in and out of your store, buying ammunition, hunting licenses, other gear, is that right?"

"Yes, that's right."

"Did you take time to talk to all of them, chew the fat so to speak?"

"The ones I know, yeah. But when it's busy, you know, you've got to keep going. Customers are waiting to be waited on, get their stuff, move on out."

"So it was more or less strictly business. A customer asked for something, you sold it to him, he paid you, end of transaction."

"More or less, yeah."

"Besides buying a box of ammunition, did Mr. Jerome buy anything else?"

"Not to my recollection." He hesitated. "No, he didn't buy anything else."

"You're sure."

"Uh-huh."

"He bought one box of bullets."

"One box, right."

"He didn't ask to look at a rifle, or a pair of boots, or anything else."

"I don't remember that he did, no."

"One box of bullets."

"Yes."

"Let me picture this in my mind if I can, Mr. Harrison. You've got a busy store. This was on a weekend, wasn't it, if I'm not mistaken?"

"It was a Saturday, that is correct."

"Your busiest day of the week?"

"Usually. It was then."

"People buying this and that, trying things on, checking equipment out, the usual."

"Uh-huh."

"So here's a man walks into your store on a busy day. He says to you I want to buy a box of nine-millimeter shells for an automatic pistol. What do you do?"

"I ask him what kind he wants."

"And then what?"

"He tells me, I get them."

"Full-metal jackets. Is that a particularly unusual request?"

"Not really. We sell a decent amount of them."

"So by itself, there's nothing suspicious about that."

"By itself, no."

"He pays you with cash?"

"In this case he did."

"And you give him his bullets, and his change, and his receipt, and he leaves. Is that right?"

"That's how it went, that's right."

"So all in all, given that your store is busy, it's a small purchase, you have other customers who want to be waited on, he isn't someone you know so you don't take a few minutes to ask him about his family, how much hunting he plans on doing this year, did he buy a new truck, nothing like that."

"No, I didn't."

"How long did this entire transaction take, Mr. Harrison? From the time Mr. Jerome walked into your store until the time he left with a box of bullets? Five minutes? Ten minutes? Half an hour?"

"No, not nearly that long."

"How long?"

"Five minutes, I guess."

"From the time he walked in the door until the time he walked out the door—five minutes."

"About that."

"How much of that five minutes would you estimate he was actually standing at the counter in front of you?"

Harrison thought about that. "One or two minutes."

"One or two." John Q. turned and looked at the jury. "So in one or two minutes, on a busy day, you figured out that he was a federal agent, that he was buying ammunition when he shouldn't have been, that it was a suspicious kind of ammunition to buy, and that he was trying to hide something."

Harrison shook his head. "No, it wasn't like that."

John Q. stared at him. "You just told us that it was. How was it different?"

"Later," Harrison said. "It was later, after I heard what had happened and saw his picture, that's when I thought about it."

I was watching this intently. This wasn't going so well. Information was coming out I didn't know about. And I was starting to think that Harrison hadn't been totally straight with me. Not a comforting feeling, with your own witness.

John Q. was going strong now. "You saw Mr. Jerome's picture? Where did you see it? In the newspaper? On television?"

"I saw it on television."

"Okay. I see." John Q. paused for a moment. "Did you see it anywhere else before you saw it on television, Mr. Harrison?"

Harrison fidgeted in the witness chair.

"Mr. Harrison. Did you see a picture of Mr. Jerome anywhere else before you saw it on television? Or after, for that matter?"

Harrison nodded slowly. "I did, yeah."

"And where was that?"

Harrison looked at me, at the back of the room, at the ceiling. Then he looked at John Q. "In the store."

"In your store? How did you come to see it in your store, Mr. Harrison?"

"Somebody showed it to me."

"Somebody showed it to you?" John Q. asked, his voice easy, relaxed. "I see. And might I ask who that somebody was?"

I didn't know what Harrison was going to answer, but I knew it wasn't going to be good.

"Sheriff Miller showed it to me."

I asked for a ten-minute recess before my redirect.

"Why in hell didn't you tell me about that?" I yelled at Harrison. We were in one of the small rooms off the courtroom, where lawyers meet with clients and witnesses. The rooms aren't soundproof—I'm sure my voice could be heard all over the courthouse. Not that I cared, I was boiling.

"I didn't think it was important," he whined. "You never asked me."

"I shouldn't have had to ask you, you moron." A sudden thought hit me. "Did Sheriff Miller tell you not to tell anyone that he'd been to see you and had shown you Jerome's picture? Including me?"

Harrison was squirming like an ant on a hot griddle. "Not in so many words."

I was outraged—not at Harrison, he didn't know any better, you don't go up against the sheriff, not when he's a load like Tom Miller and you're in the gun business. My anger was for Miller, for what he'd done with the identification after the fact of Jerome, which could be construed as witness-tampering (it was, as far as I was concerned), on top of that for warning Harrison to keep quiet about it, and most of all, for keeping me in the dark. We were supposed to be partners. I'd brought him into this, when I didn't have to. And now here I was, with a compromised witness.

Well, fuck Miller. He'd already testified, that was the end of my dealing with him. I'd talk to him about this, though. As soon as I was finished here for the day.

This in and of itself was not a big deal. Jerome had bought the bullets, he had gone out of his way to do so. My bigger concern was for what Miller might have done in other areas that I didn't know about. If this trial degenerated into a pissing match between Jerome and Miller, we could get bogged down in personalities instead of facts and lose the focus. I remembered what Curtis Jackson had said, about Miller and Nora carrying a grudge against Jerome and the DEA because they'd been shut out on their own turf. Everything Jerome had done was documented, but could Miller have been throwing extra salt on the wounds behind the scene, to insure Jerome's indictment and subsequent conviction? Small-town sheriffs can develop an overinflated sense of their importance.

I wanted to talk to Miller about this before I went back into the courtroom with Harrison, but he couldn't be found—he wasn't in his office, and he wasn't answering his pager.

It would be all right—the facts weren't in dispute, just how they'd been arrived at. But I was going to track Miller down and have a stiff heart-to-heart with him tonight. This shit would not do. I had to know everything he'd done in connection with this case. Before I got any more egg on my face, not after.

The redirect went okay. I didn't take long. Harrison stood by his earlier testimony, which was not in question: Jerome had bought the bullets. That was the important thing. It didn't appear to me that John Q.'s breaking Harrison down had been given much credence by the jury.

I was still solid. But I had to make sure.

I caught up with Miller after court had recessed for the day. He was waiting for me in my office when I got there.

"I'm sorry I was out of touch, but the battery went out in my pager," he said, taking it off his belt and giving it a hard whack against his thigh. "Damn modern technology."

I wasn't smiling. I was fuming, and I wanted him to see it.

"Look, Luke, about that picture of Jerome—"

"How'd you hear?" I asked, cutting him short. "If you were out of communication?" I sat down, but he remained standing.

"I ran into one of the newspaper reporters on the way over here. He told me."

"Great. Tomorrow's lead story," I groused.

"No," Miller said, trying to reassure me. "It was one of the local reporters. It meant nothing to him. He said the jury wasn't even paying attention. All he talked about was you, how well you're doing."

"We'll see about that," I said. "Tell me about that picture. What were you doing with that?"

"It's not what you think," he protested.

"Well, explain it, then. Because it doesn't feel right to me, and I'm sure you know why."

"It was nothing." Miller sat down across from me. "I was in Harrison's gun shop a month or two after the raid. The DEA Shooting Incident Team had been in there a few days before, he was telling me about them. Offhand, I asked him if he'd met any other agents before. Making conversation, you know? He said he thought he might have, but he wasn't sure. So he described a guy who'd been in the store a few days before the shooting, and it sounded like Jerome to me. So I went and found a picture of Jerome and showed it to him, and he ID'd him. That's all, believe me."

I looked at Miller across the desk. He didn't look like he felt guilty, but he did look like he was sorry.

"If I messed up any part of this investigation, Luke, I'm truly sorry. You know I want this to be perfect. I wouldn't do anything to hurt things. I'm on your side. You know that."

I wasn't convinced. "Why did you tell Harrison not to mention to anyone that you'd showed him the picture?"

Miller stared at me. "I never said that. Did he say that?"

"He strongly intimated it."

"Well, I never told him that," Miller said firmly. He cracked the knuckles on his old, twisted hands. "I thought you knew about it."

"No, I didn't."

"I guess I should have said something. I didn't think it was important." He looked at me. "I still don't. But I didn't tell Harrison not to tell you. I might have told him not to volunteer anything, but I never told him to lie. That was when the DEA people were swarming all over us. I knew they would try to figure out how to exonerate their own people. I wasn't about to help them do that. So that's why I might have talked about it that way with Harrison."

What could I do? Everything he'd said sounded plausible.

"Okay," I said. "Let's drop it for now. There isn't anything else, though, is there?" I asked forcefully. "I don't want any more surprises, Tom, not a one."

"No, Luke," he promised ardently. "There aren't any more surprises. You have my word on that."

Shortly after Miller left, Kate dropped by. "How'd it go?" she asked, flopping down on the small couch in the corner. She groaned as I reprised the Harrison-Miller screwup.

"Frigging amateurs. They think they're helping and all they're doing is making life more complicated."

"Miller's no amateur, don't sell him short," I cautioned her. "This is about which cock controls the barnyard. What he did won't influence the outcome, but I'm keeping him on a short leash."

I stretched—I needed exercise, after being cooped up in the courtroom all day. Maybe I'd take a run when I got home. Jerome could join me, I thought mordantly, he's in incredible shape. "Got anything new that's hot and spicy?"

"I'm running some leads down. Nothing concrete yet, but there's interesting stuff out there."

"Nothing that's going to derail us, please." I didn't need any more surprises, not until I'd processed this latest one.

"Muir County is a weird place. These backwater locales hide sinister secrets. Too much inbreeding or something."

"Since when did you become an elitist? I thought you were blue-collar all the way."

"I call 'em like I see 'em." She grinned at me.

"Give. I'm bushed, I've got to get out of here."

"Okay, but I need to get my head straight about where we are first." She flipped open her notebook.

"This is the case against Jerome, block by block." She started ticking items off on her fingers. "He went ahead with the raid when he shouldn't have, even though by doing so he blew a chance to catch Juarez's gang with the goods and break up their entire ring. The way things stand now, there may not be any convictions to come out of that, which means the drug ring can go on."

Second finger. "Then we find out this is more a personal vendetta than a conventional drug bust, because of what happened with Juarez and Jerome's sister. So far so good?"

I nodded.

Third finger. "After Juarez is killed, half a million dollars is deposited in a secret bank account that we've traced to Jerome. Our smoking gun." She looked at me for confirmation. I nodded in agreement.

Fourth finger. "Suspicious buying of unusual ammunition, right before the raid. In and of itself, no big deal, but as corroborating material, meaningful."

She cocked her thumb, item number five. "Curtis Jackson's testimony about the street rumors that Jerome had been paid by a rival gang to take out Juarez. Put it all together, it spells prime suspect."

I agreed with all that and told her so.

She put her notebook aside. "You don't see any contradictions?"

"Like what? We've got a sweet little case going here, Kate, don't start mucking it up with harebrained speculations."

"I know, and I'm not, it's just . . ."

"Just what?" I was getting impatient with this. You can overanalyze anything to death. Particularly in any case like this one, where you don't have a direct eyewitness to the crime, there are loose ends that aren't tied up in a neat bow. But I've always subscribed to the notion that if it walks like a duck and quacks like a duck and has feathers, the odds are good it's a duck. Plenty of my cases were made this way when I was a D.A., and they were solid cases.

She said, "How do you reconcile this incredibly strong, decades-old animus with a cold-blooded murder for hire? The two are contradictory, they cancel each other out. It degrades the purity of Jerome's main motive—primal hatred."

I'd thought about this myself, because I'd had to reconcile it in my own mind.

"On the surface that's a reasonable way to look at it," I agreed, "but if you examine it more carefully, the reasons aren't contradictory, they're complementary. It's uncontested that Jerome wanted to get Juarez on a pure emotional level. He was blind with hatred. Not only because of his sister, which elevated it to a fever pitch and drove him all those years, but because Juarez was a scourge. Jerome's life is committed to wiping out drug dealing. So Jerome's wanting to wipe Juarez off the face of the earth has genuine merit. I'm not unhappy Juarez is dead, are you?"

"No. It's *how* that bothers me."

"That's right. The *how* is why we're in this trial. So— Jerome's been tracking this guy for years. Relentlessly, and unsuccessfully. Finally, he has him in his gun-sights. Figurative gun-sights. But he's not allowed to kill him. That has to be maddening. He knows what can happen: Juarez hires a great lawyer and walks, or he jumps bail and flees the country to one he can't be extradited from, it's infuriating. Jerome knows Juarez is scum that should be eliminated. He wants the job dropping the pellet. But he's not allowed to. It's tearing him up inside."

"I agree," Kate said enthusiastically. "That's my point exactly. It's about emotion, not money. Money *weakens* the case, it doesn't *strengthen* it."

"No. Money is the excuse."

She gave me a "what're you, nuts?" look. "He didn't need an excuse."

"Yes, he did. This is a man who's obsessed, he hasn't thought logically about this for years. In his mind he can't let emotion rule, that goes against some bullshit sense of professionalism. He has to be cold-blooded about it. But he wants to be the man who shot Liberty Valance. Plus he's greedy. He's a career civil servant, this is a chance for him to make one big score. He knows other drug gangs want Juarez out of the way, they all hate each other. He puts the word out, like Curtis Jackson said, then he waits. And as he figures, some other gang comes to him with a deal. Could be a black gang, Asian, Aryan, he doesn't care. None of them could ever turn on him, it would be the word of a career DEA agent against criminals. Who's not going to believe him?"

Kate whistled. "Boy, that's cold. That makes him a pure mercenary. I'd think that makes it worse, not better."

"How else do you explain the money? How else do you explain mounting that raid when he should have aborted? How else do you explain Juarez miraculously escaping from custody? Jerome's the only one whose fingerprints are on everything. It has to be him."

"When you put it that way, it does make sense."

"Completely. Anyway, you said you were working on something else. What?"

She pushed some stray hair out of her face. "Nora Ray and Miller were unhappy with the way the DEA was conducting the investigation, so they decided to do their own, and they came to you."

"It was mostly Nora, but Miller was involved, that's right."

"But Miller told you they'd been suspicious about that compound before Jerome came on the scene."

"So?"

"Why didn't they do something about it then?"

"You're letting suspicion overrule reality, Kate. If Jerome's raid had been successful, we wouldn't be here and we wouldn't be having this conversation. Miller's a sheriff, it's his job to be suspicious. But no sheriff's department in the world can check out everything they think is questionable, regardless of the cost. You've been around, you know that."

I locked up. We walked to our cars in the parking lot.

"If I come up with something, you're going to want to know about it, right?" she asked, still tenacious about her hunch. "You don't want me to bury anything, do you?"

"If you discover anything directly related to the case, let me know right away. Otherwise, sit on it until we're done. It's only another couple of weeks. Let's take one thing at a time, okay? Let's finish this trial."

*　　*　　*

I would have loved to have put Curtis Jackson on the stand and have him testify about the rumor of Jerome taking a payoff from a rival gang to kill Juarez; but I couldn't, of course, it was hearsay, inadmissible, and besides, he'd appeared in front of the grand jury under a full grant of immunity. He wouldn't have testified in open court even if it had been permissible; someone would have whacked him, real fast. I would never put him in that position. McBee was aware of Jackson's testimony, of course, so I figured he would lean over backward on my behalf regarding the latitude of my two remaining witnesses.

We had a heated argument over those issues in chambers, John Q., the judge, and I, John Q. fighting to keep out anyone who wasn't part of the narrow scope of the issues, I, of course, making the opposite argument. In both cases, I won—I could present my witnesses. John Q. would use McBee's decisions to take the verdict to appeal (unless the defense won, a billion-to-one shot), but that would take years. And by then, it wouldn't matter.

The Miami bank vice president detailed how five hundred thousand dollars had been transferred into Jerome's new back account. His performance was dry, low-key, but devastating.

Jerome was furiously making notes the entire time the bank official was my witness. After I concluded, he conferred in heated, whispered tones with John Q., who listened half-attentively, then got up and strolled to the lectern.

"Did you have any conversations with Mr. Jerome concerning this bank deposit?" he asked.

"No," the man answered. "It was handled by computer transfer. That's common practice with sums of money that size."

"Then how did you know he was the one who did the transferring?"

"We checked with the bank that sent it. They verified it came from an account belonging to Mr. Jerome."

"Isn't that information privileged?"

"To the public, but not between institutions. We have to know the transfer is legitimate."

"And this one was? You're positive?"

"Of course. We wouldn't have allowed it otherwise."

"And could you tell us, sir, how that bank verified that this money had been deposited by Mr. Jerome?"

"You'll have to ask them that. I'm not privileged to give out such information. It was my responsibility to ascertain that the funds were as stated—which they were."

"Do you know how long the money had been in that account?"

"No. That wouldn't matter to my bank."

"But it was possible that someone other than Mr. Jerome deposited the money into the first account."

"I suppose so," the banker said. "What does that have to do with this situation? It's Mr. Jerome's account. Beyond that, it's none of my business, or my concern."

Exactly, I thought. John Q. was leading this in the wrong direction. He was trying to lay the groundwork for his desperate idea that Jerome was being set up, that some sinister mystery player had deposited the money. But he hadn't established that, so he wasn't getting anywhere.

Keep going, I exhorted him silently. Go way out on the wrong limb.

John Q. kept pushing this. "Five hundred thousand dollars seems like a lot of money for one party to be putting into someone else's bank account."

"You're wrong," the banker said sharply. He was not a man who suffered being doubted. "My branch alone has two or three such transactions a day."

John Q. looked at the jurors. They were as confused as he seemed to be. Unfortunately for him, he didn't seem to be helping them out of their confusion.

"Two or three a day?"

"Yes."

I was enjoying this. John Q. was on the defensive, where no lawyer should ever be. Law 101—you never ask a question you don't know the answer to, and it has to have an answer that helps you. If either of those criteria doesn't apply, don't ask. He had—now he was trying to fumble his way out of it.

"I sell a million dollars' worth of stock," the banker said, laying out a hypothetical situation. "I want to set up trusts for my two minor children. I open bank accounts for each to the tune of five hundred thousand dollars apiece. Later, I'll invest that money. Meanwhile, it's safe. Or I'm buying out a business partner. I wire money into his account. There are countless reasons."

"Okay, fine," John Q. said brusquely. He wanted to make his point and get done with it, but my witness wasn't cooperating. "I want to ask my question one more time. Could this account have been opened without my client's knowledge?"

The banker thought on that for a moment. "I suppose so," he allowed. "Although it would be unlikely."

"Because of the amount of money involved."

The banker shook his head. "Who would put this much money into someone else's account and not tell them?"

"Someone who wanted to frame the person receiving the money," John Q. said quickly, turning to the jury as he did.

I was immediately on my feet. "Objection, Your Honor! That is inflammatory speculation."

Judge McBee came down hard with the gavel.

"Sustained," he said loudly. "Strike that remark," he instructed the stenographer. He looked at the jury. "You didn't hear that. It was uncalled for, and unsubstantiated." Glaring down at John Q., he admonished him harshly. "No Perry Mason shenanigans in my courtroom, do you hear me? You're looking at a citation and a bar hearing if you keep on this way."

"My apologies, Your Honor," John Q. said morosely. He turned back to the banker. "If I wanted to set someone up, to make it look like they were taking money under the table, I could put this much money into an account I'd set up for that person and not tell him. Keep it a secret until I need to use it against him."

Judge McBee turned to me, inviting me to object. I didn't—I wanted this to get in.

The judge waited a moment more, then turned to my witness. "Answer the question, please."

"You could, but you wouldn't. Not if you had any brains," he added acidly.

"Why not?" John Q. came back combatively.

"If you wanted to set somebody up, like you're hypothesizing, you don't need to waste half a million dollars to do it," the banker said scornfully. "One-tenth of that would do the trick. Anyone who has five hundred thousand dollars in liquid money knows how to employ it wisely. He isn't going to spend more than is necessary. Half a million dollars would be overkill."

John Q. was turning crimson. If I'd been asking these questions, he would have been all over me objecting, and he would have been sustained. But because they were his questions, he was royally screwed.

He turned away, his shoulders sagging. "No further questions."

*   *   *

John Q. had done my work for me, so I passed on redirect. Judge McBee put us in recess until the following morning at nine o'clock. As I was leaving the courtroom, I noticed that they were looking glum over at the defense table: Jerome arguing with John Q., John Q. shaking his head like a dog trying to rid himself of a swarm of gnats. When the sheriff's deputies came for Jerome, they were still arguing.

I worked late into the night. One final day for me—the most important day. If I got through tomorrow as I hoped to, it was going to be a downhill run to the finish line.

I didn't get home until after ten. Riva was waiting up for me with a beer and a shot and a turkey sandwich. I ate and drank and went to bed, but I couldn't get to sleep. Too restless. Riva, lying beside me, stroked my arm.

"Calm down, Luke."

"I can't help it. I've got to get through tomorrow, it's the capper for everything."

"You will."

"People collapse under stress."

She started rubbing my shoulders. "You're tight. You need to loosen up. I don't want you getting an ulcer."

"Once tomorrow's over, I won't be like this."

She started kissing me, starting with my mouth, then moving down my body. I let go of everything, lost in her passion and caring; I only flashed on the trial a few times before I exploded and almost immediately fell asleep all tangled up in her arms and the sheets and the sounds of the winds, still nightmarish to me as reminders of the shootings in the desert, blowing through the bleak skies outside our windows.

"Call Diane Richards."

A side door opened and Diane Jerome Richards, dressed almost funereally in black, entered the courtroom. She walked up the aisle to the witness stand, her posture erect, eyes straight ahead, not turning to look at her brother seated at the defense table. Jerome, conversely, stared at her.

Diane was sworn in and sat down. Hands in lap, feet primly crossed at the ankles like a schoolgirl. I approached the podium.

"Good morning, Mrs. Richards," I greeted her.

"Good morning." Her voice was crisp, clear. No nonsense, no fake familiarity. It was painful what she was about to endure. The object was to get through it as dispassionately and unsentimentally as possible.

Riva had come to see her. So had three times as many reporters as had been around for the others. This was a red-meat story. Blood against blood, sister against brother, almost biblical in its dimensions.

She was a compelling witness, completely believable. There wasn't one false note in anything she said, recalled, detailed. It was one of the most bravura performances I'd ever seen in a courtroom, because it was so heartfelt, and so honest.

At the beginning, John Q. objected a few times, but he was overruled on each one, and he quickly realized that not only were his attempts going to be futile, they compounded the damage. The jury was with this woman, hanging on every word she spoke. They took his objections to be unwelcome intrusions, you could see the animosity in their faces. Pretty soon he gave up and sat there listening, occasionally making a note, but for the most part frozen in place.

Jerome, sitting next to John Q., looked at her some of the time, as if trying to burn a hole in her with a laser-vision stare. She paid him no attention. If she saw him looking at her at all, she gave no indication. She kept her attention on me throughout the entire time she was on the stand, unless she had to explain something to the jury, in which case she talked to them directly, or similarly to the judge.

Her testimony took over four hours. Judge McBee let us go straight through, so we didn't break for lunch until one-thirty. I had food brought in; we ate in a small waiting room next to McBee's chambers. I assured her she had done magnificently. She smiled wanly at that, knowing she was in for some trying times. Her life was public now, she was going to be living in a fishbowl. I didn't envy her that, and I admired her steeliness in facing the tough reality of it.

After the lunch recess we were back in court, and Diane took her seat on the witness stand. John Q. walked to the rostrum.

"Mrs. Richards . . ." He glanced back at Jerome, sitting at the defense table. Reflexively, her eyes followed his look, so that for the first time since she'd come into the courtroom, she was looking at her brother, which had been the cagey old lawyer's intent.

Jerome was staring intently at her. Not with evilness or in anger, but almost soulfully, the connection heavily palpable, you could feel the vibration throughout the courtroom, two beings from the same unique source.

For a brief, heart-stopping moment it looked as if her composure would crack; then she got hold of herself, gave him one brief nod, and turned away, back to John Q. No ties bound her to him. They'd been shattered on an empty beach, over two decades ago.

Diane's inner strength, so evident, took the wind out of John Q.'s sails before he'd had a chance to hoist them. She wasn't going to break; she wasn't even going to bend. He worked on her for half an hour, and then he gave it up.

Almost every day had been a good day for me, since the beginning of the trial. Today was the capper. I could see it in the jurors' eyes as Diane Richards was excused and left the courtroom. She had won them over completely; thus, by association, I had, too.

I couldn't have hoped for a higher note to go out on.

"The prosecution rests, Your Honor."

PART
FIVE

ELEVENTH HOUR

Court stood in recess until Monday morning, when John Q. would begin his defense. I reviewed his witness list and mentally checked off what I figured they'd be testifying to. There were no names on it I didn't know about, but surprises do come up at the eleventh hour, and you try to anticipate them as best you can.

I was feeling good about the case. Not only was the evidence against Jerome compelling and comprehensive, but there were no other candidates. The only other possibility was that Jerome hadn't been a lone wolf, that he'd roped others into his scheme. But there was no evidence of that, no rumors of that, nothing. Looking at the situation from a cold-blooded, practical level, Jerome would almost certainly have tried to cut a deal with me had that been the case. Misery loves company; also, when more than one person is involved in the commission of a crime like this one, it can be tougher for a prosecutor to get the jury to hand down the maximum penalty. But John Q. had ruled out a plea bargain from the outset, which to me was a clean signal that he didn't have a fallback position, such as an accomplice. Either Sterling Jerome had killed Reynaldo Juarez, or it had been done by a ghost. I stopped believing in fairy tales a long time ago.

Against my better judgment, I agreed to take Riva and Becky and Joan to Nora's house for a Sunday afternoon swim. Nora had called Riva with the invitation, and Riva had accepted without checking with me—she had no reason to, she didn't know what had gone on in that pool, or the subsequent arguments and veiled threats about that. But I couldn't come up with a plausible excuse that wouldn't raise doubts in Riva's mind, so we threw our bathing stuff in the car and drove over.

"You have a lovely home," Riva said after Nora had showed her around.

"Thank you," Nora answered graciously. "My family has some money," she explained. "When I made the decision to stay up here after Dennis died, I decided I'd live as well as I could. It's an extravagance for a single person, but what else am I going to spend my money on?"

Nora, wearing a demure bathing suit, was on her best behavior, thankfully. We swam, lay out in the sun, tossed Frisbees on her spacious lawn, and had an easy, enjoyable time. She became an instant swimming instructor, coaxing Buck to jump off the edge into her waiting arms, accompanied by shrieks of gleeful laughter.

Late in the afternoon, when Riva had taken Buck inside to use the potty, and Joan was sunbathing a distance away, Nora came over and sat down in the deck chair next to the one I was in.

"Truce?" she asked.

With my wife at hand, she wasn't going to try anything.

"As long as you behave yourself."

"I will, I promise. I don't know what I've been thinking," she apologized yet again, glancing around to make sure Riva wasn't coming up behind us. "That isn't me, Luke, it really isn't. I was just . . . I don't know what I was. It'll never happen again, I swear it."

I didn't want to talk about this. "Let's act as if it never happened and move on, okay?"

"Gladly." She shifted a bit in her chair. "Can we talk at all about the trial?"

"There's not much to talk about now. I'm finished, except for my closing. It's going to be completed within a couple of weeks."

"You've done a wonderful job," she gushed. "Everything I could have hoped for. I know Bill Fishell's thrilled, too."

"It isn't over yet, so let's cool it, okay?"

"It is over, Luke," she assured me. "What could change?"

"Don't jinx me, Nora, please. It's one of my pet superstitions."

"Not this time."

I hate being hyped in advance. "Juries can be unpredictable, Nora. This could turn not on what Jerome did but who he is—all-American crime stopper—and who Juarez was—scumbag drug dealer. Anyone on that jury could vote that Juarez got his just deserts. That's what John Q.

Jones is going to hammer, you watch. And don't for one minute under-estimate him. I've seen him do wonders with cases that looked like worse losers than this one."

She didn't want to hear my concerns. "So you'll remind them not to get confused between fact and sentiment. Juarez was an unarmed man gunned down in cold blood by a peace officer sworn to uphold the law. Use Tom Miller's authority in your closing, the people here love him. If he's against Jerome, they will be, too. Hammer that home, and you'll get your verdict."

She swept her arm, taking in her property. "I'd bet the farm on it."

"That's a chunk of change. Thanks for the confidence."

"You've earned it."

"Some fancy spread your lady friend has," Riva commented on the drive home. "It reminds me of Sheriff Miller's house, the mission style. Law enforcement pays well in Muir County," she joked.

I laughed. "Their salaries wouldn't buy the garages, let alone their houses. Miller made his money in a hot market, and hers is from her family."

"They built their houses at the same time," Joan piped up from the backseat. She could be a little chatterbox sometimes. "The reason they look like each other is because they used the same architect. He was the contractor, too. Mrs. Ray brought him up from San Francisco. The lo-cals got their noses bent out of shape, but nobody around here could put together that quality of work. Some of our guys who were working on the jobs as subs, like carpenters and plumbers, said you couldn't believe the amounts of money both of them put into their houses. One of my friends from the reservation did framing for the contractor, that's how I know."

"They're nice," I agreed, "but they don't compare to Juarez's com-pound. It dwarfs both those houses. You should see that place, honey," I said to Riva. "What's left of it. We'll cruise by there before we go home."

Joan spoke up again. "That one took a long time to build. Nobody knew what was going on up there. Guys with guns patrolling, it was scary. One time a bunch of us thought about sneaking in? Those guards must've chased us a mile. You don't ever want to mess around drug dudes, they kill for a living."

"And now your tribe's trying to buy it," I said. "It's a small world up here in Muir County."

"It sure is, Mr. Garrison. Too small, if you ask me."

Joan's remarks about the houses rattled around in my mind. After we had had dinner and put Buck to bed, I dialed Kate Blanchard. "Check on something for me. The name of the contractor who built Tom Miller's and Nora Ray's homes. They were done at the same time, five or six years ago. Get the histories for me, okay? How much they cost, how they were paid for, whatever."

"What's this about?" I could feel her getting excited over the line, like a racehorse hearing the call to the post.

"Nothing, probably. Get back to me as soon as you can on it."

"I'll try to have something for you end of the day tomorrow."

Agent Dutton, a hostile witness for me, was a cooperative one for the defense.

"Mr. Dutton . . ." John Q. got into the specifics. "You were one of the senior agents who were assembled outside the perimeter of the Juarez drug-cartel compound in order to raid the premises on the night in question, that's correct?"

"Yes, sir, that is correct," Dutton declared. "We were there to raid the Juarez drug-cartel compound, take possession of the drugs that were supposed to be there, and arrest whoever was inside."

"That was your mission. Confiscate the drugs, arrest those in possession of them."

"Yes."

"But the drugs didn't arrive as they were supposed to, by airplane. Weather wouldn't permit that."

"That's correct."

I got to my feet again. "Your Honor. The story of the drugs and the airplanes have already been well established. We don't need to rehash this over and over again, do we?"

John Q. spoke up. "I'm trying to substantiate the patterns and procedures of a correct and legitimate law enforcement operation, Your Honor. The prosecution did so from their skewed perspective. Please allow the defense to try and tell it like it really was."

"Your Honor—" I started. I didn't like the pejorative "skewed" or the adverb "really." Upon such subtle distinctions can trials be won or lost.

McBee put up a hand to silence me. "Let's move on, shall we?" he told us both. "Keep the personal feelings to yourself, please." To John Q.

he said, "You may proceed along these lines, but don't take too long, okay?"

"Yes, Your Honor. Thank you."

John Q. favored me with a smile, a small "gotcha." Turning back to his witness, he continued, "When you found out that the airplane containing the drug shipment could not come in as expected, what did you do?"

"We decided to move in anyway."

"Whose decision was that, Agent Dutton?"

"It was Jerome's, sir. He was the commander in the field."

"Did you concur in that decision, Agent Dutton?"

"I certainly did. Every many who was there agreed with that decision."

"Why was that? If the drugs weren't going to be there? Wasn't that the reason for the raid? To intercept the drugs?"

"It was *one* of the points." Dutton was aggressive in his clarification. "Arresting Juarez and the rest of them was equally important."

He swiveled to face the jury. "More important, actually. These drugs coming in that night were one shipment. A huge one, of course, but one of millions of such shipments that come into this country every year. Arresting the leaders of this important gang, and permanently stopping these shipments and the selling of these dangerous drugs into the communities of America, was a more important reason for this raid. A much more important reason."

I could have objected, but I'd wait for cross-examination.

"Good." John Q. beamed. "I wanted to make sure we got that on the record, in its proper form—these were dangerous men inside that compound, wanted men."

He walked back to the defense table, leaned over to Jerome, and said a few low words. Jerome nodded in the affirmative. Looking at his notes briefly, John Q. came back to the lectern again.

"Now, Agent Dutton. When the decision was made to go in and arrest the men inside the compound, were all the agents present given specific instructions?"

"Yes, sir."

"By Agent Jerome?"

"Yes."

"What were they?"

"To take Reynaldo Juarez alive."

"To take Juarez alive," John Q. repeated. "Alive or dead, or alive?"

"Alive," Dutton said firmly. "Not dead. Agent Jerome was clear and forceful on that. Juarez was to be captured and arrested. Under no circumstances was he to be killed."

"Explain the reasons for that, please."

"Juarez was one of the leading drug kingpins in the United States. He was a very elusive figure. It was impossible to pin him down. This was one of the few opportunities anyone had ever had to capture him. If he got away, we might never have a chance this good again."

"But why only alive then?" John Q. asked. "If he were killed, that would stop him, too, wouldn't it?"

"Yes, it would stop *him,* specifically. But alive, he could give us vital information on drug dealings all over the world. The Justice Department felt he was a key to that. So we had to take him alive."

"Those were your direct orders."

"Yes."

"Agent Jerome was clear on that?"

"Very clear. He impressed upon all of us that if Juarez was killed, the operation would be a failure. He had to be taken alive."

"So if one of you did kill Juarez, that would have severe repercussions with the Justice Department."

"Very severe."

"If, for instance," John Q. went on, "you had killed Juarez, Agent Dutton, you would have suffered some consequences?"

"Bad ones."

"Even to the point of being fired?"

"Yes, definitely. This was a command order." Dutton paused. "I already have," he said somberly. "We all have, all of us who were there."

"So if Agent Jerome had killed Juarez, he also would have suffered negative consequences?"

Dutton nodded his head vigorously. "He would have suffered the worst, because he was the team leader."

"He might have been cashiered. At least demoted."

"Yes."

"His career destroyed."

Dutton looked past John Q. to Jerome, watching from the defense table.

"It was," Dutton replied softly.

"So from a career point of view, Agent Jerome had everything to lose and nothing to gain by killing Juarez."

"Everything," Dutton concurred. "Which is what has happened."

No one in the courtroom was feeling the oppressive heat now. Everyone was engrossed in Dutton's exculpatory testimony; except me, and I wasn't sitting in the jury box.

John Q. waited a moment to let that point sink in deep, then he continued, "There has been testimony given in this trial that Agent Jerome had a personal vendetta against the drug dealer Juarez. In your opinion, knowing Agent Jerome as you do, and having worked with him for as long as you have, could he have let personal feelings supersede his professional accountability?"

I was on my feet, but before the word could leave my lips, Dutton had answered.

"Never," he said firmly.

"Objection!" I called out, a second too late.

"Sustained," Judge McBee said immediately. "Strike question and answer," he instructed the court reporter, and to the jury he said, "That is a conclusion from the witness, not a fact. You are to disregard that answer completely."

Sure they will, I thought sourly. Score one for your side, John Q.

The old jurist turned to the bench. He knew to quit when he was ahead. "No further questions, Your Honor."

———————

I glared at Dutton from the lectern.

"Agent Dutton. You've just testified that your orders from the Justice Department, as relayed to you by Agent Jerome, were to apprehend the men who were inside the compound, to capture them alive. That they were not to be killed. Is that correct?"

"Yes, that's correct."

"None of the men . . . or Reynaldo Juarez, specifically?"

"He was the focus," Dutton admitted grudgingly, "but we didn't want to kill any of them."

"Okay. You didn't want to kill any of them, but you *really* didn't want to kill Juarez. Yes?"

"Yes."

"You went into the compound expecting to make a clean sweep, correct. You'd been assured their security was down, which would enable your forces to stroll right in and arrest them all without incident, is that right?"

"You don't stroll into a drug bust. It's a dangerous situation."

"People get killed, don't they?" I asked, stating the obvious.

"Sometimes."

"But in this case, you thought you'd catch them by surprise, and escape unscathed."

I could hear his breath exhaling. So could the jury. "Yes," he admitted reluctantly.

"That was based on information supplied to you by an informant, is that right, also?"

He gave a curt nod.

"You have to speak up," I admonished him. "Was it or wasn't it?"

"Yes. It was."

He was becoming hostile again, now that it was me questioning him, instead of kindly old John Q. Jones.

"Which turned out to be wrong information, didn't it?" I asked. "They were lying in ambush for you."

Another deep breath, another deep exhale. "Yes, they were."

"With guns ablazing."

"Yes."

"You and the others in your party were caught in a tremendous firestorm that you weren't prepared for, isn't that right?"

"Yes."

"Some of the agents were killed, weren't they? Butchered."

He closed his eyes, reliving the horror of that night. "Yes."

"Good friends of yours. Men you had worked with, shoulder to shoulder, for years."

He shuddered. "Yes."

"Others were wounded."

Another involuntary shudder. "Yes."

I left the lectern and walked right up to him. Talking quickly now, I asked, "And when that happened, Agent Dutton—when you were unexpectedly fired upon with great force, what did you and the other agents do?"

He looked over at the defense table, then stared at me without answering.

"Answer the question, please," Judge McBee ordered him.

He looked at me hard. "We returned their fire."

"You shot back at them."

"Yes."

"With everything you had."

He nodded grimly. "Yes."

"To protect yourselves."

"Yes."

"And to kill them."

"Yes . . ." He caught himself. "To protect ourselves."

"And to kill them, so that you *could* protect yourselves, isn't that right? You weren't aiming to miss, were you? You were aiming to hit them. To stop them."

"Yes."

"To kill them!" I said, my voice rising.

His voice rose to meet mine. "Yes!"

"And you did kill some of them, didn't you? Didn't you kill some of the men inside that compound?"

"Yes," he snapped righteously. "We killed some of them."

"Did you know who you were killing when you started returning the enemy's fire?"

He stared, not immediately following me.

"When you started shooting at the men inside that compound with everything you had in your arsenal," I asked, "did you say to yourselves, 'We can shoot at him and him and him, but not *him,* because *he* might be Reynaldo Juarez? Did you make that distinction, Agent Dutton?"

He looked at me askance. "You can't do that. It's all happening in a split second, you can't pick and choose."

I stepped back.

"Of course you can't," I said, toning down my invective. "That's the point, isn't it? You don't know who you're shooting at. All you know is that you're shooting at the people who are shooting at you."

He didn't respond.

"Isn't that right, Agent Dutton? It's dark, you're pinned down by heavy enemy fire, you can't see a thing. You shoot at whoever's shooting you. No distinctions."

A slow nod. "That's the way it was."

"You could easily have been shooting at Reynaldo Juarez, and you could easily have killed him. Isn't that right, Agent Dutton?"

"Yes," he said woefully. "It is."

"So all this gibberish about taking him and the others alive—it flies out the window when the shooting starts. Doesn't it, Agent Dutton? It did in this case, didn't it?"

"Yes. It did."

"It was the luck of the draw that Reynaldo Juarez wasn't killed in that firefight, wasn't it?"

Dutton gave me a baleful look. "He was hiding," he said stubbornly.

"You knew that then?" I asked mockingly. "You and the forty or fifty other agents who were pouring as much fire into that compound as you could knew that Juarez was hiding, that he wasn't returning your fire? You knew that in advance of going in?" I thundered.

Dutton sat back, rubbing his temples. He was so weary from this.

"No," he admitted. "We didn't know that."

"So I'll ask it again. You were shooting to kill, including Agent Jerome. And Juarez could have been on the receiving end of one of your hollow-point bullets. Yes or no?"

"Yes," he spoke in a low undertone.

"So much for taking him alive at any cost," I said dismissively. "That was all pretense, wasn't it? Empty rhetoric." I walked to the stand again and got in his face, inches away. "Sterling Jerome would have been just as happy taking Juarez dead as alive, wouldn't he have been! Happier! He wanted Juarez dead, and when he couldn't kill him then—"

"Objection!" John Q. was on his feet, shouting over me.

"Sustained!" Judge McBee yelled, even louder.

"—he killed him later, didn't he!" I thundered on.

"Objection!"

"He was out to kill Reynaldo Juarez, and he did!"

"*Objection!*"

"*Sustained!*" *Wham wham wham!* The gavel slammed home.

I stepped back. I don't know who had the reddest face, Judge McBee, John Q., or me.

"You are out of order!" Judge McBee screamed at me. "You are this far"—he held his thumb and forefinger an inch apart—"from being severely cited for contempt! Do . . . you . . . hear . . . me?"

I stepped away. "Yes, sir," I said, properly chastened. I turned my back on Dutton and walked to the prosecution table—I'd done my damage, and then some. "I'm through with this witness," I said over my shoulder. "No further questions."

Kate was waiting for me outside my office. I unlocked the office. We went inside. I grabbed a beer from the fridge, opened one for her, flopped into my chair. "You got anything for me?"

She opened her ubiquitous notebook. "The architect-slash-contractor they both used was Dean Vaca of Connelly Associates, offices in San Francisco, L.A., Phoenix, Denver, and so forth. He was originally contacted by Nora, who turned him onto Miller."

I took a hit from the can. "The connection could be through her family in Denver. Her father's a big deal there."

"Right." Reading on, she continued, "Both paid cash. No mortgages. Nora's raw property cost sixty-five thousand, Miller's seventy-five. Her house, turnkey, was a tick under two hundred grand. His went for one seventy-five."

I marveled at the figures. "In Santa Barbara those houses would go for ten times that. Five times, minimum, back when they built them. What a deal."

"But you'd have to live here," she reminded me. "No sushi bars, no surfing, cold in winter and hot in summer. Boring."

"Picky, picky, picky."

"Anyway." Back to her notebook again. "By your standards it's a deal, that's true, but it's still a lot of cash to lay out. I'm checking on that. I'm also checking into a few other things, nothing you have to know about now, you've got your hands full with the trial. If anything jumps out at me, I'll ring your bell."

She put her notebook away. "Was there something in particular you're looking for? Why do you have me doing this?"

"Idle speculation, I guess. Sometimes coincidences happen and they make you wonder."

"I'll keep at it," she promised. "You want me to stay up here until the end of the trial, don't you? Just in case?"

"Yes. Just in case."

The air-conditioning had gone on the fritz, so the courtroom was sweltering. Repairmen were feverishly laboring to get it working, but if parts were needed, they'd have to be brought in from Reno, which wouldn't happen until tomorrow; another endearing reason for living in the outback. Coats were off—even Judge McBee was in his shirtsleeves. Contentiousness was in the air, waiting for a spark. I hoped I wouldn't be the one to strike it.

Despite the crummy conditions, Filipe Portillo looked sharp, sitting up on the witness chair, one leg crossed over the other, styling in a sharp pinstripe suit (he kept his coat on), dark blue dress shirt buttoned to the collar, no tie the way they do at the Academy Awards, and hand-tooled alligator cowboy boots, a nice touch, I thought, for up here. A simple ruby earring in his left ear completed his ensemble and made a nice statement, although it was lost on these jurors, I'm sure.

John Q., Portillo's opposite sartorially, slouched over the lectern.

"Mr. Portillo . . ." His voice sounded as if he'd eaten an extra helping of gravel for breakfast. "Were you acquainted with the deceased, Reynaldo Juarez?"

"Yeah. Me and Reynaldo were close. Like brothers, man."

"For a long time?"

"All our lives, practically."

"You worked together?"

Portillo repositioned himself to get more comfortable. "We did business together, yeah."

This is great, John Q., I thought. One drug dealer testifying about another. That's going to help you? If that's the best you're going to do, you might as well pack your bags and go home now. I'd been baffled when I'd seen Portillo's name on John Q.'s witness list; I was still baffled.

"Were you and Mr. Juarez together on the night of the raid on Mr. Juarez's property?" John Q. asked.

Portillo nodded. "We were together, that's right."

"Were there others present?"

"Yeah."

"About how many?"

"Including Reynaldo, an even dozen."

"Would you tell us where you were?"

"In Mr. Juarez's house."

"Was that here in Muir County?"

"Yeah."

"What were you and Mr. Juarez and these other men doing?"

"Hanging out. R and R, you could say. We'd been working hard, all of us, we needed to get away and goof."

"It wasn't a business occasion?"

Portillo shook his head. "Strictly recreation."

This was bullshit, as Dutton had explained earlier. John Q., of course, had anticipated the problem.

"You weren't there to receive a shipment of drugs, as one of the agents who was there has testified?"

Portillo gave him a look of disbelief. "No, man. That's a crock. Did they find this shipment of coke they're talking about? A ton? I mean, come on. There weren't going to be any drugs there. Reynaldo would never give anyone like Jerome an excuse like that."

Which was true, except for this special occasion. But John Q. had raised a little mound of doubt about the entire enterprise by bringing this lie in. What I didn't understand was the point of it.

John Q. shambled over to the defense table to consult some notes, came back to the lectern.

"Let's set the record straight. Were there drugs present on the property during that time you and the others were there, Mr. Portillo?"

"No, sir," Portillo answered vehemently. "There were not."

"No drugs of any kind."

"Well, there was booze. Beer, wine, booze."

"But no illegal substances."

"No." Portillo gave the jurors a droll look. "You can get arrested for that."

"Indeed," John Q. commented dryly. "So there was nothing illegal going on at Mr. Juarez's compound that night."

"Not a thing."

I thought about objecting to this line of questioning as irrelevant and a waste of time, but I decided not to. I was at a loss as to where John Q. was going with this, but it didn't seem to be helping his client or hurting me, so I kept my mouth shut.

John Q. nodded, as if this confirmed something important to him.

"Did you have security at Mr. Juarez's house and grounds, Mr. Portillo?"

"Oh, yeah," Portillo answered.

"What kind of security?"

"Sensors that detected if someone had come onto the property. Stuff like that."

"High-tech?"

"The latest and best equipment we could get," Portillo boasted.

"So you felt safe from intrusion."

"*Felt* safe, yeah."

"Had there been any intrusions onto this property before that night?"

"A couple."

"What kinds of intrusions, Mr. Portillo?"

"A couple times kids tried to sneak over the fence. One time a common thief, who didn't know who he was messing with. Stuff like that. Nothing heavy."

"Did the people inside respond?"

"Sure they did. That's why you have a security system."

"What was the nature of those responses, Mr. Portillo?"

"We intercepted them and asked them to leave."

"You confronted them."

"Yeah."

"With force?"

"Yeah, with force."

"So you had weapons present at this compound."

"Of course we did. Who wouldn't? Valuable piece of property like that, you got to be prepared to protect it."

"Okay. Now let's go back to that night, Mr. Portillo. You and Mr. Juarez and about a dozen other friends were in the compound. You were relaxing. You had no illegal substances with you. You were acting in a law-abiding fashion."

"That's right."

"So you didn't expect anyone to try to invade your property. Because you weren't doing anything wrong. Against the law."

"Well, we weren't doing anything wrong, but we did expect some visitors."

"Why is that, Mr. Portillo?"

I sat up. We were getting to something. Finally.

"Juarez got a call."

John Q. took a beat before going on. I was alert now, listening. This was the first I'd heard of this.

"Mr. Juarez got a telephone call? Someone called the compound?"

Portillo nodded. "He got two calls."

"About what time of the night was that, Mr. Portillo?"

"Late. The first was around three in the morning. The second came about half an hour later."

"Do you know what these calls were about?"

"I don't know about the first one. The second was that we were about to have some company pretty soon." Portillo paused. "A lot of company."

"Expected company?"

Portillo brayed. "Hell, no."

"Hostile visitors, then."

"Very."

Another pause from the old fox, another show of deep thinking. It was clear to me what the two calls were. The first was to tell them the cocaine wasn't coming in. The second was to warn them of the raid.

"These telephone calls to Mr. Juarez. Were they to his listed number?"

Portillo laughed. "Rey didn't have no listed phone numbers. He protected his privacy."

"To your knowledge, Mr. Portillo, did many people know this particular phone number?"

"No. Hardly any."

"Did you?"

"Yes."

"Did the other ten men who were present in Mr. Juarez's home that night know that number?"

Portillo nodded. "Yeah."

"Would you describe the people who knew that number as Mr. Juarez's inner circle?"

"The most inner. He changed his secure phone all the time, so people couldn't track him down."

"Would it be fair to say that Mr. Juarez was obsessed with privacy and secrecy, Mr. Portillo?"

Portillo laughed. "He made Howard Hughes look like Jay Leno. The man was totally obsessed with his security. With good reason," he added. "He'd had plenty of attempts on his life."

"What was Juarez's reaction when he got the telephone calls?"

"The first one, he was pissed. The second one, he was freaked."

"Because you were about to be invaded by a hostile force while on private property, minding your own business?"

I stood up. "Objection, Your Honor. Argumentative."

Judge McBee nodded. "Sustained."

John Q. was undaunted. "Did Mr. Juarez tell you why he was freaked?"

Portillo nodded. "He said we were going to get busted. That they were coming for him."

"Did he say who 'they' were?"

Another nod. "Federal agents. A task force that had been set up to get him."

Shit. This was new news to me. And not welcome.

"They were coming for him? Him specifically?"

"That's what he said."

"Dead or alive? Did he say dead or alive?"

"Either way. If federal agents are coming after you, they don't care. Long as they have your body in a bag. Check out Ruby Ridge, Waco, other places like them." Portillo glared past John Q. to Jerome, sitting at the defense table, as he said that.

I was utterly confused now. On one hand John Q.'s witness was saying Jerome was going to take Juarez dead or alive, on the other that he had been forewarned. The two didn't match up. I listened carefully as John Q. went on.

"I want to sidetrack for a moment, Mr. Portillo. Do you know a man named Luis Lopez?"

Portillo practically spat, right there on the witness stand. "Yeah, I know that son of a bitch!"

The courtroom buzzed. McBee gaveled down hard. "There will be no profanity in this courtroom, Mr. Portillo! You are to refrain from using such language in here! Do you understand me?"

Portillo stared up at him. "Yes, Your Honor. I'm sorry. I got carried away."

"Keep your temper in check," McBee warned him.

"I'll be careful, Your Honor."

McBee nodded at John Q. "Proceed, Counselor."

"Thank you, Your Honor. I apologize for my witness's outburst. This is a very emotional issue with him. His best friend was murdered that night, and Mr. Lopez was a party to that."

Again, I thought of protesting, and again, I decided not to.

John Q. turned to Portillo again. "Was Mr. Lopez one of the men who was at the compound on the night of September twenty-eighth?"

Portillo darkened. "Yeah, he was there." He paused. "Some of the time."

"Some of the time?" John Q. asked, pretending to be confused. "Why would anyone leave a remote place like that in the middle of the night? Unless he was trying to get away because of this impending assault on Mr. Juarez's private property."

"You'll have to ask Lopez that. I don't think that's why."

I was starting to see where this was going. The old fox still had some tricks left in his repertoire.

"Do you know who that second call was from?" John Q. asked.

That question caught me off-guard. I looked around. Nobody else seemed to realize how important this was.

Portillo answered in the negative. "No. Reynaldo didn't say."

John Q. looked at some more notes. "Did Mr. Juarez ever talk about Sterling Jerome?" John Q. turned and pointed to Jerome, sitting up straight at the defense table. "This man. Did Mr. Juarez ever mention him?"

Portillo nodded vigorously. "All the time. He talked about him for years."

"For years? Would you say that Mr. Juarez was obsessed with Mr. Jerome?"

"*Obsessed* ain't the word. It was like Jerome was a what's the word . . . succubus to Reynaldo, you know? Like that thing in *Alien* that grows inside you and eats your guts out? That's what Jerome was to Reynaldo, a virus that was trying to kill him. Like a cancer growing inside of him."

"He wasn't friendly with Mr. Jerome, then."

Portillo almost came out of his chair, he was so agitated. "He hated him! He hated him worse than anybody on earth!"

"Calm down, Mr. Portillo," John Q. begged. "Please."

Portillo was almost hyperventilating. "This is really hard for me, man. To be sitting here, in the same room with him . . ."

"I understand, I understand. Then it would be fair to say," John Q. continued, lowering the intensity, "that Mr. Jerome would *not* have been the person on the other end of either of those telephone calls with Mr. Juarez. Particularly the call that warned Mr. Juarez that he and the rest of you were about to be placed in a state of siege."

Portillo shook his head at the temerity of that question. "Jerome would be the last man on earth Reynaldo would ever talk to. They were blood enemies to the bitter end. Jerome would go to the ends of the earth to get Reynaldo. And Reynaldo knew it."

I could feel the vibe going through the courtroom: this man was saying everything I'd said, he was buttressing my case a thousand-fold. But I knew better; old John Q. was setting this up beautifully. I hated him for doing it, but I had to admire his talent.

"Okay. I hear you," John Q. said. "I want to make this point one more time, so there's no question. Sometime that night, Reynaldo Juarez was called on a telephone that almost no one had the number for and told that you were about to be heavily attacked. Is that correct?"

"Yes."

"By Mr. Jerome and other agents of the DEA?"

"Yes."

John Q. was moving closer to his target. "Obviously, whoever tried to warn Mr. Juarez had to be very close to him, didn't he? Close enough that he had Mr. Juarez's most secure telephone number."

"Yes. Whoever it was had to be real tight with Reynaldo. Super-tight."

The old lawyer leaned in to Portillo. "If you knew in advance you were going to be attacked, Mr. Portillo, why didn't you try to escape?"

Portillo stared at him. "It was too late. We were surrounded."

"You knew that."

"Yes."

"From this telephone call."

"Yes."

John Q. pondered for a moment. "You knew the attack was coming. It wasn't a breach of security in the compound."

Portillo again said it wasn't. "We knew they were coming."

"Why didn't you simply let them in? What could have happened?"

"They would have killed us. They were armed to the teeth. They did try to kill us, didn't they? We had to defend ourselves, it was our only chance for surviving." He bristled. "Why should we just let them in, anyway? We were on our own private property. We weren't doing anything wrong. Somebody comes onto your property, armed like they do, you're just going to let them? Who does that?"

I looked over at the jury. Some of them were actually nodding in agreement. Up here you don't trespass lightly.

"So your security was in place on the night in question?" John Q. asked Portillo again.

Portillo leaned forward, gripping the rails of the witness box. "It turned out it wasn't," he said. "If we hadn't gotten that phone call, they would have caught us bare-assed naked. We would've been ducks in a barrel."

John Q. turned to the jury for his next question. "What happened? Why wasn't this tight, complex security of yours working that night?"

"Because Luis Lopez disabled it."

I was up on my feet for that one. "Objection!" I called out. This was hurting me, I couldn't be a fly on the wall any longer. "Hearsay."

"Sustained," McBee backed me up. "There's no foundation for that," he told John Q.

John Q. turned back to Portillo. "You saw Mr. Lopez disarm the security system?"

"No," Portillo answered before I could object again. "But he was the only one who wasn't there at the end, so it had—"

"*Objection!*" I yelled as loud as I could.

"Sustained!" McBee turned to the jury. "This part of the witness's testimony is not admissible. Strike it," he instructed the court reporter. "Do not pursue this line of questioning any further, Mr. Jones, or I won't let you continue."

"That's fine, Your Honor." John Q. smiled as he turned away. "Because I don't have any more questions."

I had to change direction, get the jurors' minds off thinking about who had tipped off Juarez's group.

"After the attack was over, Mr. Portillo," I began, "was Mr. Juarez alive? He wasn't killed during the attack on the compound, was he?"

"No. He was alive."

"He was found in a walk-in freezer and taken prisoner, is that correct?"

"Yeah," Portillo answered in a surly tone.

"You saw him with your own eyes. You know that he was alive and was not killed during the raid on your compound. His compound."

"I saw him. He was alive."

"Did you see where he was taken?"

He nodded. "In this command trailer they had."

"Okay." I wanted to be clear on where I was going; John Q. had thrown me a curve. "Did you see who went into that trailer, after Mr. Juarez was put there?"

"Some DEA agents."

"How many do you think that was? Three or four, ten or twelve, twenty or thirty?"

"Three or four. Jerome and a couple others."

"So only a few agents had physical access to Mr. Juarez."

"Yes."

"Did you see anyone else go in that trailer, Mr. Portillo?"

"Like who?"

"Another prisoner, someone else who was out there."

Portillo scoffed at that. "All of us were handcuffed, we weren't going anywhere. There was only agents out there. Agents and us."

I nodded. "Agent Jerome was in there the most, is that right?"

"I think so, yeah."

"And at some point, after he'd been in there for some time, presumably questioning Mr. Juarez, he came out. Is that right?"

"Yeah. He came out and talked to some other agents."

"And at some point while he was talking to these other agents, Mr. Juarez escaped from that trailer, is that correct?"

"Yes."

I moved over to the jury box. "To the best of your recollection, was Agent Jerome the last person who had been in that trailer before Mr. Juarez escaped?"

Portillo thought for a moment. "I guess," he said, looking at me, and by doing so looking at the jury as well.

I repeated my question, so it would stick in the jurors' minds. "The last person who was in that trailer—before Mr. Juarez escaped—was Agent Sterling Jerome."

"He was the last one I saw."

It was too hot to continue—people were squirming in the hard wooden seats, plucking their garments from their backs and rear ends, fanning themselves with newspapers, magazines, anything stiff. The jurors, their chairs perched on risers in the jury box, looked especially uncomfortable. During the recess that followed my cross-examination of Portillo, Judge McBee conferred with the air-conditioning technicians, who promised him the replacements for the defective parts would arrive via FedEx and could be installed in time for the courtroom to be properly cooled off by tomorrow morning. With that, he adjourned us for the day.

I went home. Riva, dressed for the weather in shorts and a halter top, had the air-conditioning turned up, so our rental box was nice and cool. Joan was out shopping. I played with Bucky for a few minutes, filled Riva in on the general tenor of the action in the courtroom, then retired to the third bedroom, which I use as a home office. It's Spartan—a sixty-five-dollar, put-it-together-yourself desk from Staples, two chairs snitched from my regular office, filing cabinets, my laptop, and copies of our investigations, the grand jury proceedings, current trial information.

I found the section I was looking for in the grand jury testimony, started reading. A few minutes later, Riva popped her head in the door.

"Kate's here."

"Come on in," I called.

She came as far as the doorway. "Got a sec?"

"For you, always."

She plopped into the other chair, slipped her feet out of her sandals. "It is blistering out there. I hear the courtroom was an oven."

"About as hot as the participants." I filled her in on the day's escapades, notably the second telephone call warning Juarez of the raid. In the middle of my recitation Riva joined us, sitting yoga- style on the floor.

"Who would have made the call?" Kate asked, her interest piqued.

"There's only one person who wasn't inside the compound who would have had the information and the number," I said.

Kate nodded slowly. "Lopez."

"You've got it."

"But why?"

"Two reasons I can think of. One, he got cold feet and chickened out. He would have been scared to death about what would happen to him if Juarez survived the assault, particularly since the orders were to take him alive. He was playing both ends against the middle, hedging his bets."

"And two?" Kate asked.

"It follows one. If Juarez is alive after the raid, Lopez is screwed. He has to provoke the men inside into defending themselves. Which, of course, they'd do, being who they are. So he baits them into action. He could have lied about the size of the DEA force—underplayed it—their tactics, anything to convince Juarez that the men inside could win a shoot-out with the DEA agents who were coming in."

Riva, listening to this, shuddered. "That's diabolical. Sick. Even for a shitheel like Lopez."

"Come on," I said, "you've been there. These are men who have running gun battles in the streets. They don't give a shit about anything except their profits and their survival."

"Your theory makes sense," Kate agreed. "Unfortunately for Lopez, Juarez wasn't killed."

"No. Lopez must've been shitting bricks out there when Juarez was captured. He had to be the happiest Mexican in the world when Juarez broke out."

"Could he be involved with Jerome?" Riva asked. "In the murder?"

I shook my head. "I wondered about that, believe me, especially after Portillo's testimony." I held up one of the volumes of the grand jury material. "Lopez wasn't allowed anywhere near the trailer where Juarez was being held. Several agents stated that, independently of each other, to the grand jury. Plus he wasn't armed, also confirmed by several of the men there." I dropped the thick volume on the desk. "He just got lucky."

Kate had dug in her purse for her notebook. Now she hesitated. "Maybe this isn't the time for what I've got."

"Meaning what?"

"Sure you want to hear new stuff? You're in the home stretch, Luke. Nothing can stop you now."

"Except you, I've got a feeling."

"This can wait until tomorrow."

"Now it can't."

"Sorry. I'm trying to give you a day off. You sure?" Kate asked once again.

I motioned with my hand for her to quit procrastinating. She nodded and flipped open her book. "Some of this you already know, so I'm recapitulating. Putting things in order. So don't get antsy."

"I won't, but let's go."

"Hold your horses." She looked at her new material. "Item number one. Nora was elected D.A. before her husband killed himself." She looked at me; I nodded—that I knew.

"She contracted for her new house six weeks after Dennis died. Before that they were living in a rental house, here in town. Nothing special, what you see around here."

I shrugged. "Okay. So?"

"Not a long period of mourning. Especially when death comes so unexpectedly, so violently. I don't know how you function when that happens to you, let alone take a bold step like building a new house, with all the crap that goes with that."

"You're upset with what you think was a lack of feeling?" I asked.

"Aren't you? He was your friend."

"Not for a long time," I told Kate calmly. "And he'd been gone long before he died. The suicide made it official."

"Oh." She seemed surprised; and disquieted.

"What is it?"

"Nothing, I guess. It's just that everyone around here I've talked to said they were a happy couple. That his suicide was a shock."

I thought on that for a moment—what she'd said resonated with me personally.

Before I could reply, Riva stood up. "I'm going to get dinner ready. You'll stay?" she asked Kate. "Cold cuts, nothing fancy."

"Sure," Kate answered. "Thanks."

Riva left, closing the door behind her, giving Kate and me privacy.

"What's this about?" Something was in the air, and Kate had felt it.

"No one ever knows what's going on behind someone else's closed doors, Kate," I said. "People said the same thing when Polly and I split. They were shocked. We were a Norman Rockwell couple. Except we weren't."

Polly was my first wife. She walked out on me. The usual complaint—too much work, not enough her. Which was true, but it blindsided me, nonetheless. Losing her was a bitter pill, unexpected, and my recovery took a long time. I wasn't truly healed until I met Riva. Even then, the circle wasn't complete until we got married and she became pregnant with Buck. So I know the feeling. It helps to find something else to do with your life—you have to. I found a wife and a son. Nora's way of keeping her life and her sanity going was to build a house.

"I didn't know that." Kate blushed with embarrassment. She looked at the closed door, as if she could see my wife through it. Now she knew why Riva had excused herself. "I'm sorry, Luke."

"It's fine, now. I'm the happiest I've ever been. I'm saying, though, that no one ever knows, except the people who are living it."

"I hear you. I've been there, too. I guess we all have." She looked at her notes again, hiding further emotion behind professionalism. "Tom Miller started on his house about the same time."

"I remember you telling me that."

"They started on their houses less than six months after Juarez finished up his estate."

All of a sudden I had a bad feeling in my stomach. You can get ulcers in this job; I didn't want one, not from this.

"Guess who the architect/contractor was for the Juarez compound."

I didn't have to guess. I knew. Knowing didn't help my stomach.

"The guy from San Francisco."

"Bingo."

I sat back in my chair. "That's . . . a hell of a coincidence," I managed to say.

"Tell me about it."

"Go on. What else do you have? Anything?"

She nodded. "You also remember I told you they both paid cash. No mortgages."

"I remember."

"Which was supposed to have come from trust funds, stock investments, whatever." She flipped to the next page. "Nora's parents are both still alive. Living in Denver, like they always have. They lived a nice lifestyle, but they're not rich. In fact, they've gone beyond living off their interest. They've been eating away at their principal for years. They aren't broke, but if they live to a ripe old age, they will be." She looked up. "They don't have money to give Nora. Certainly nothing like half a million dollars, which was what the lot and the house cost."

I cradled my fingers in front of my face, forming a skeletal steeple. "You know this for a fact?"

She hesitated a moment. "Not for a fact, no. But I've learned enough about their finances to know that it doesn't fit the picture."

"Improbable, though, rather than impossible."

"Yes," she admitted.

"It's possible, for instance, that they divested themselves of their stock holdings and gave the money to her, or sold off a vacation house, or something else you haven't discovered yet."

"Yes, that's possible."

She was feeling deflated and chagrined (and probably a bit annoyed, too)—here she'd come up with what she thought was hot information, and I was dousing it with cold water.

"Go on," I told her.

New page. "Miller said he'd made his money in the stock market. But I couldn't find any evidence of his being in the market in a meaningful way until the last few years. He was living on his FBI pension and his sheriff's pay. Which isn't the amount of money needed to finance his house."

"You talked to brokers, bankers, people like that?"

"And I did some creative electronic eavesdropping," she said, a bit red-faced. "Nothing patently illegal," she assured me. "A little shady, maybe, but there's so much information out there now you can access legitimately, if you know where to look for it."

"Again," I said, "it's interesting, but far from conclusive. Maybe there was money in his wife's estate, maybe he hit big at the craps table in Vegas, there could be a variety of legit reasons. You didn't happen to get a look at his tax returns from back then, did you?"

"Now that would be clearly illegal."

"Just checking to see how far you'd go," I teased her. "Glad to see you have some scruples, after all."

"I'll walk the line, boss, but I won't cross it."

"So they say." The idea of seeing Miller's tax returns made me actually want to. "It would be nice to see those tax records."

"You're not suggesting . . ." She looked at me impishly.

I shook my head. "I'd get a subpoena if it came to that. Which I don't want to do, not now. Shit." I cracked my knuckles, one at a time. "It sure is coincidental, isn't it."

"Yes, it sure is."

This was happening too fast, too much of a jumble. My brain was already overburdened with the trial. "This connection with the contractor. That could be explained away, I suppose, but it smells bad."

"Juarez reaching out from the grave."

"There's a link between him and them." It was there, I couldn't not acknowledge it. "That can't be denied."

Kate and I continued our discourse after dinner. Riva joined us. Both women were anxious about Nora's and Miller's fishy financial dealings, and the connection with the contractor. I was, too, but I had to temper enthusiasm with other possibilities. Kate has a strong anti-law-enforcement bias, based on her experience as a cop on the mean streets of Oakland a decade ago and her work now, as a private investigator for defense lawyers like me.

Riva, too, has seen the dark side of the law. It's a sobering thought, with no foundation in actual fact (because we've never discussed it), but she and I wouldn't be together if I was still a prosecutor. She'd backed me on this undertaking because I was going after what looked like, and has turned out to be, official wrongdoing. So if there's a possibility that someone in law enforcement, be it a DEA agent, a county sheriff, or a county prosecutor, even if it's a personal friend, is dirty, she's going to believe the worst.

Kate pounded the connections hard. "Their money isn't accounted for, Nora's or Miller's. One instance you could excuse—two looks like a conspiracy. Particularly since they came up with all that money at the exact same time, right after the drug compound was built."

"Are you saying there was a financial connection between Nora and Miller and Juarez?" I put to her.

"There could be," she answered doggedly. "It should be looked into."

"I agree with Kate," Riva chimed in. "It's all too cozy."

"And what about the White Horse Nation's money?" Kate added. "Where are they getting that from?"

"You're telling me that's connected to this, too?" I asked. "You're making this out to be an Oliver Stone movie. Everybody's dirty, the world is one big conspiracy."

"It's too much to dismiss," Riva argued. "How is it that all these different entities that shouldn't have lots of money do? Nora, Miller, now the tribe. Maybe there is a conspiracy. Conspiracies exist, Luke. Even if they involve friends," she added pointedly.

"I'm not blinded by my friendship with Nora," I rejoined, stung beyond anything she could understand. "But you're taking a bunch of what I agree are disturbing coincidences, each of which, in and of itself, is a molehill, and making Mt. Whitney out of them."

Riva gave me a hard look. "You don't believe that. I know you. You don't believe there's nothing to what we're saying."

"Okay," I copped, "there could be. I know that. But whatever it could be, that's something else. That's not this trial. I'm prosecuting this trial. That's what I'm doing now, and that's all I'm doing now. I don't have time for anything else."

"You're afraid of what you'll find," Kate said challengingly.

That got my ire up, which was her intention.

"I'm not afraid of anything, and you damn well know it," I responded hotly. "If I start going after everything that's a could-have, should-have, or maybe, I won't be able to do my job. I'm in the home stretch, I can't deal with a million distractions."

"Okay, I'm sorry," Kate apologized. "You're not afraid." Not backing off, though, she added, "But you've got tunnel vision."

"These allegations are beyond distractions, honey," Riva said. "They could bear directly on your case."

"How? Did Nora kill Juarez? Did Miller? No." I continued: "If Nora or Tom Miller were in cahoots with Juarez, why would she have come to me to open an investigation? Does that make any sense? You let sleeping dogs lie, you don't light a fire under them."

"No," Kate admitted reluctantly. "That doesn't compute." She and Riva exchanged a glance.

"And if they *were* involved with Juarez, which is really going out on a limb, why would they want him dead? Killing him makes no sense at all. You don't kill the goose that lays the golden eggs."

Two nods of grudging agreement.

"What about a connection with the tribe?" Kate threw out.

I scoffed at that one. "They definitely wouldn't want Juarez dead. If he was financing them, they need him alive. Think this through. Juarez funds a casino to launder drug money. The Indians have a way to get out of poverty. Everyone gets rich. Besides, there's a hole in this. There weren't any Native Americans there that night."

Kate shook her head in disagreement. "There was one."

"Who?" I asked. "I never heard anything about that. Where did you get that?"

"Miller's deputy, Bearpaw," she reminded me. "And his mother's a White Horse tribe elder. She's the one who handed the deposit check to the BIA agent."

I'd forgotten about Bearpaw. And his mother being a tribal elder, that was interesting. I remembered her from our recent meeting, at Miller's house.

"Technically, you're right," I said as my pulse returned to normal, "but there's a basic flaw in that theory. That particular possibility couldn't have happened."

"Why not?"

"Bearpaw wasn't there. He went home an hour before Juarez escaped."

"I forgot that," Kate fretted. She prides herself on being on top of everything.

"Don't worry, I don't remember everything, either." I pushed my point of view. "Do you think Miller actually killed Juarez? Technically, he was there. But a seventy-nine-year-old man outrunning all those buffed DEA agents?"

As they shook their heads no, I said, "Of course not. And that is what this case is all about: who killed Juarez. We know who killed him. Jerome. All the evidence points to him, to him alone." I stared at them. "Doesn't it?"

"Yes," Kate admitted. "It does."

"Good. I'm glad you agree."

"I don't," Riva spoke up.

"You don't think Jerome killed Juarez?" I asked in disbelief.

"I don't mean I *don't* think he killed him. But I think this has the earmarks of an action beyond a lone gunman, and that Kate should keep checking it out."

"Thank you," Kate said in appreciative sisterhood.

I threw up my hands.

"Okay. I know when I'm outnumbered. You want to keep beating this horse," I told Kate, "whack away. But don't come to me again unless you have conclusive evidence—something that's directly tied to this trial. No more hypotheses, conjectures, suppositions. Even if they seem to add up. I've got one job to do, I'm doing it, I want to get the fuck out of here, and I don't want to get bogged down."

"So what about the contractor?" Kate asked, unable to not throw in a parting dig.

"I'll ask Nora, okay?" I told her testily. "Now I've got work to do."

I retreated to my little office and slammed the door behind me.

PIN THE TAIL ON THE DONKEY

Nora blinked in surprise—I'd caught her off-guard. "What about my house?" she asked.

"You and Tom Miller built your houses at the same time."

She nodded. "So?"

"You used the same architect-contractor. Who also built Juarez's compound."

"Is there a problem with that?" she asked, seemingly unfazed.

"Yeah, there is," I said, put off by her lack of sensitivity to the propriety of the situation. "Explain to me how a district attorney and a sheriff used the same contractor as a drug dealer who's operating right under their noses."

We were in her office, early in the morning. I'd stopped off on my way to court, calling her in advance and requesting that she meet with me. She'd assumed I wanted to discuss the trial. She'd been wrong.

"Is there something illegal with that?" she asked, moving away from me, employing her desk as a barrier between us.

"Maybe not illegal, Nora, but it looks bad."

"It looks bad to you, Luke?"

"Of course it does." This was annoying—she knew it looked bad. Why was she dancing around this?

Even though I knew there might be fire under the smoke, I had resisted Kate's and Riva's entreaties to delve deeper into connections between Juarez, Nora, and Miller, because I didn't want any distractions from the trial. Facing Nora across her desk now, I decided Kate was right—this needed deeper probing. Perhaps I had come to that decision because of Nora's behavior toward me. But it was all of a piece, lack of discretion and regard for consequences.

She frowned. "Maybe you're right. Maybe it does look bad."

"Not maybe. It does."

"There's a very simple and innocent explanation."

"What is it?"

She gestured to a chair. "Sit down, Luke. Do you want coffee?"

I shook my head. "I have to be in court in fifteen minutes. I don't have time."

"You can't sit down at least, can't you?"

I sighed impatiently. "Yes, I can sit down." I put my briefcase down next to the chair.

She walked over to her corner credenza where a coffeepot was bubbling. "Do you remember my telling you, when we first got together, that I'd reconciled myself to living here, because of Dennis?" She got a carton of milk from her cube refrigerator. "And that after he died I decided to stay on?"

"Yes." I nodded. "I remember."

"When I made that choice, which was not easy—this was and still is a foreign country to me—I decided that if I was going to be here, I'd live as well as I could. Which meant having the nicest house I could, there's not much else here for a woman like me. Unmarried. Childless."

She finished fixing her coffee and sat down across from me.

"At the time, the compound was almost finished. I didn't know Juarez was the owner. I thought it was some ordinary rich person, an oil sheik or computer whiz. Everyone did. All I knew was, whoever was doing the construction and design was doing a wonderful job. It was much better work than anyone around here does."

I recalled Joan, our au pair, saying the same thing.

"So I drove over one day, walked onto the property, and introduced myself. Complimented the foreman on the job, mentioned that I was thinking of building a house myself, and that I might be interested in using them. A few days later, I got a call from Dean Vaca, the architect, and we made an appointment. The next time he came up, about a week later, he and I looked at the property my house is on. It was empty space then, it had been part of an old ranch that was subdivided years before.

He gave me some ideas that I liked, the price was right and we got along, so I did it."

She blew on her coffee, took a tentative sip. "I didn't know about Juarez. Dean didn't, either. He'd been hired by an accounting firm from L.A. All he cared about was that the checks cleared." She drank some more coffee. "No mystery." She smiled at me over her cup. "Sometimes a cigar is just a cigar."

"So I've been told. So you started on your house when?" I asked casually.

"Soon after they were finished with the compound."

"And your parents paid for it?"

She nodded. "I'm their only child, Luke. They could afford it, the money wasn't important to them. My happiness was."

I heard the *ding* go off in my head. "What about Miller?"

"What about him?"

"He happened to meet this same architect and decided to build a new house for himself, right at the time you were? An old man in his seventies?"

She laughed. "He's only old chronologically. I have a bet going with him that he'll outlive me. I'm afraid he'll collect from my estate."

She drank some of her coffee. "Anyway—Tom. He'd made quite a bit of money playing the market, and he didn't have anything to spend it on. He'd lived for decades in this piss-poor house in town, he's always been an ascetic. He heard I'd made the plunge, and he decided to, too. Treat himself well for once. He deserved it." Another smile. "Truth be told, I talked him into it. Selfishly on my part, it helped me financially, because they used the same crew. Cheaper to build two houses at the same time than separately. And I knew it would be good for him. That's what was most important."

"So that's it?"

"That's it."

I stood up. "Got to go."

"I'm sorry if this bothers you, Luke," she said, watching me. "Maybe I should have mentioned the connection. It never occurred to me."

"No, that's okay," I said, making a show of dismissing the problem. "You can understand why I had a concern."

A head bob of understanding. "It's a hazard of our profession. You get to thinking everyone's guilty of something." She paused. "Even people you care about."

"Yes," I said as I picked up my briefcase and headed out the door. "Even them."

The courtroom was comfortably air-conditioned again, so the day's proceedings went along amiably. John Q.'s witnesses were more of the same—character witnesses, agents who had been on the raid, men and women who had worked with Sterling Jerome and vouched that he was the best Boy Scout that ever pledged allegiance. My cross-examinations were efficient and concise—there was no evidence here, just smoke and mirrors. There weren't going to be any more fireworks from the defense, unless Jerome took the stand.

Kate and I had our usual end-of-the-day rendezvous at my office. I'd called her after leaving Nora, told her to continue her snooping. That had revved her up, of course; she'd wanted to know what had changed my mind, but I didn't tell her I'd just left Nora, feeling less than satisfied. Just find out as much as you can as fast as you can, I'd instructed her.

She was champing at the bit. She had her notebook out even before she sat down.

"Been busy?" I asked.

"As a beaver. Here goes." She began reciting from her notes. "A month before Juarez's compound was finished, Nora Ray and Tom Miller each deposited half a million dollars into their bank accounts. I checked up on Nora's parents. They didn't sell any stock around then, and they didn't have any property they sold, either." She looked up, beaming.

She was smiling, and my stomach was in knots. "Go on."

"There's no record of Miller selling a sizable amount of stock, either. His holdings at the time were less than fifty thousand dollars, old blue-chip stuff. No high techs. They came later."

"This is getting ugly. What else?"

"You were right about Juarez laundering money through the Indians. They opened a special account at the time Juarez began building his Taj Mahal. There's over two million dollars in it now."

"Is there a paper trail between the tribe and Juarez?"

"I have found one yet," she admitted. "It's drug money, it was probably all cash."

"Which will make the connection hard to prove, but not impossible."

"So what now?" She looked at me, ready for new orders.

"Miller and Nora are involved in something ugly," I said with a heavy heart. "I don't know what, but there's too much lurking around for them not to be. Maybe the tribe is, too. What's eating at me is, how is this all connected? And is it related to the murder, directly?"

I slammed my hand on the desk in frustration. "This is *exactly* what I didn't want—complications. We had a nice little case going here, all tied up in a pretty bow. Now I've got a frigging Gordian knot."

Too much was happening, too fast. My head was reeling from the possibilities. "I may have to subpoena their bank records and other financial transactions, going back a decade." I gave her a gloomy stare. "Is there anything else? Any more pain? I want it all now."

She hesitated before speaking. "There is one more thing. But it's only a rumor. I wanted to check it out more before I brought it to you."

"Come on, give." I was out of patience.

"You know how you've told me that Nora stayed on here because of her husband? It was what he wanted?"

I nodded. "She hung in to the end with him."

"From what I heard—and again, this is rumor—*he* wanted out. Too many bad memories here, it wasn't panning out. Nora was the one who wanted to stay. She was the breadwinner, she made the call."

I was exhausted from the mental tension. "Do you have to be so damn competent? Why did you have to find all this out *now*? Couldn't it have waited until the trial was over?"

"Sorry, boss."

I slumped in my chair. "Forget I said that." I jumped up from my chair. "Let's take a ride."

There was a small amount of daylight still left by the time we got to the compound, enough late sun filtering through the trees for us to see the area clearly. We got out of the car and walked past the buildings to the wooded area where the DEA command post had been located. From there it took us about ten minutes to make our way through the trees to the spot by the overgrown access road where Juarez's body was discovered.

The DEA stakes were still in the ground, so it was easy to know where we were precisely. The old oak tree was dry and cracking from the summer's heat and drought. Feeling around the trunk with my fingers, I located the actual hole. I took a ballpoint pen from my pocket and pushed it in, about three inches. The rest stuck out, about three inches. I looked at the angle for a moment.

"What're you looking for?" Kate asked. She slapped at a fly buzzing at her neck. We were both perspiring.

"You've read the autopsy report on Juarez."

"Yes."

"The bullet entered his right temple, went through his brain, exited the left temple, and lodged here." I tapped the ballpoint.

She closed her eyes, recalling. "Yes, that's right."

I walked back to where the body had been found, stood on the opposite side from the tree, and lined the two up. "He's looking that way." I pointed, along the path of the grown-over road. "When he was shot. That's the angle it has to be, right? To be shot in the right temple, have the bullet exit the left side, land in the tree at this angle."

She came up behind me and sighted over my shoulder. "That's right. That's where he had to be looking."

"That was a hell of a fluke, for a bullet to enter his head and go through cleanly. All soft tissue, no bone. Then to burrow into a tree, thereby stripping the jacket, so ballistics couldn't get a match."

Kate was on the same wavelength as I was. "Unless whoever shot Juarez was standing right next to him, so he—whoever *he* is—could line him up."

"Somebody he knew?" I was talking more to myself.

"And expected?"

I nodded. "It has to be." I looked down at the overgrown pathway. "Let's walk."

We started off down the narrow old access road. It hadn't been cleared off for years. The vegetation had come back over where the cut had been, to the point that it was no longer usable for vehicles. Even walking was slow and difficult, beating a path through the grass and brambles.

"Where're we going?" Kate asked as she followed close behind me, brushing low branches out of her face.

"I don't know. I want to see if this goes anywhere."

We trudged through the thick undergrowth. After about two hundred yards, the road widened—not much, but enough for a single vehicle to drive along it, if the car had four-wheel drive. The path at this point had also been cleared. Not recently, but the signs were still there. I look back at where we'd come from, then down the road.

"I wonder where this leads," I mused.

"We can find out easily enough." She started to take her book out to make a note. "A topo map, or the locals would know."

"It doesn't matter," I said, putting my hand up to stop her. "We don't have to know where it goes." I began walking back toward our starting point, Kate beside me. "We only had to know that it does."

We were back at the killing spot. I looked at the body position again, the pen in the tree, then toward the direction from which we'd come.

"Juarez was a master at not getting caught. He'd avoided capture for a decade. Someone that slippery has a variety of escape routes, so if one is blocked, he has other avenues." I thought about that for a second. "Which, to give Jerome his due, could be an excuse for charging in the way he did. If he'd waited Juarez out, which would have been the correct procedure by the book, Juarez might have snuck out somehow, under their noses. That would have been a monumental fiasco."

I hunkered down to where the body had lain, turned my shoulders, and looked down the narrow access road.

"He wasn't running blindly when he escaped."

This was a deduction I'd dreaded coming to, but now it was unavoidable. "He was running to something. A specific spot."

Kate looked down at me, followed my gaze to the road. "Here?"

"I think so."

"To meet someone who was supposed to be here, to help him get away?"

I took a deep breath—this could fuck me up royally. "That's a logical conclusion to draw—that Juarez being at this particular spot was part of a plan."

It was almost dark. We started back to the car. The crickets and bullfrogs were in evening song now, call and response.

"And Jerome caught up to him before his rescuer showed up? Otherwise, there would have been a witness." She paused. "All the shooting could have scared whoever that was off. Ran away and left Juarez out to dry."

That was a lame justification, and we both knew it.

"One of his own?" I shook my head. "Never." I could feel it in my stomach—the tightness. "We have to look at the harsh truth—that the shooter was someone else."

We were at the buildings. As I looked back, all was in darkness in the direction we'd come from.

"It's a possibility." It was gut-wrenching to give the thought voice, but I had to. "Isn't it? A strong one?"

She sighed heavily. "Yes."

IN HIS OWN DEFENSE

Jerome, sitting straight and tall on the stand, looked like the poster boy for the DEA. Strong, straight, handsomely rugged. He was dressed in a conservative dark blue suit, his shirt was freshly pressed and starched, his black shoes were mirror-bright with spit-shine. He'd had another haircut, not a prison-barber job, clean, sleek, short, not a hair out of place.

John Q., Oscar Madison to Jerome's Felix Unger, shambled to the lectern. He looked Jerome in the eye.

"Mr. Jerome . . . did you kill Reynaldo Juarez?"

Jerome locked eyes with his lawyer. "I absolutely did not."

"Good," John Q. rumbled. "Now let's show how you *would not* have killed Juarez, and *could not* have."

He ran through the usual laundry list of awards, citations, encomiums, other tributes to Jerome as a first-rate, honorable, law-abiding agent of the Drug Enforcement Administration, a man entrusted with the most sensitive cases. It was a good recitation—it had nothing to do with the charges against Jerome, but it presented him in a good light. You could do the same with Stalin if you cherry-picked through his résumé.

I wasn't looking too good—literally. I hadn't had to confront the mirror when I'd gotten out of bed in the morning, I could feel the bags under my eyes. I'd struggled all night long about my concerns. No matter how much I went back and forth, they didn't go away.

But I wasn't going to do anything about them—not now, with the trial only a few days from concluding. Proving Jerome guilty was my job. Getting him off was John Q.'s. John Q. could have found out what I did. The reason he hadn't dug as deeply as I had was that in his heart— forget the chest-thumping regarding Jerome's sterling (no pun intended) qualities—he believed his client was guilty.

"Describe for the members of the jury, please, the special circumstances on the night in question," John Q. said, "that led to your decision to mount a physical raid on the location where Mr. Juarez and the other members of his drug ring were hiding out."

Jerome told his story. How his undercover operative, posing as an Iranian arms dealer, had gained Juarez's trust. The small, then medium-sized, then large buys of cocaine from Juarez's organization. Then the big enchilada, the hundred-million-dollar transaction.

"This was all set up over a long period of time, over a year," John Q. stated. "A legitimate operation, everything aboveboard in your agency. Everyone knew what was going on, there were no secrets."

"Absolutely."

"So it all came down to this special night."

"Yes."

"The airplanes, the money, the arrests."

"Yes, sir."

John Q. took a moment to blow his nose into a large handkerchief he had tucked into his back pants pocket. He's from the old school, he doesn't use tissues. Crumpling the snot rag up casually, he shoved it back into his pants.

"What happened then?" John Q. continued.

"The operation . . . the deal was aborted."

"Because the airplanes couldn't fly in."

"Yes."

"When did you learn that?"

"About three-thirty in the morning."

"This news was sudden and unexpected."

"Totally unexpected."

"How did you feel when you heard this?"

Jerome looked down, shaking his head regretfully. "It was terrible. Shocking, unbelievable."

"Depressing?"

"Very depressing."

"You'd been after this desperado for almost a decade. You finally had him in your sights, and then your plan went kabloooey."

I stood. "Objection, Your Honor. He's leading the witness."

"Sustained," Judge McBee agreed. "Save your conclusions for final arguments, Mr. Jones."

John Q. continued without missing a beat. "What did you decide to do then, Agent Jerome?"

"I decided to proceed with the assault."

"Was this a snap decision?"

"A quick decision," Jerome clarified, "not a snap one."

"What made you decide to go ahead?"

"If I hadn't," Jerome explained carefully, "I might never have had the opportunity again. A chance like that comes along once in a lifetime, if you're lucky. To allow, through inaction or indecisiveness, a man like Reynaldo Juarez to escape, when you have him right there—you can't let that go. If I hadn't moved on him, it would have been a dereliction of my professional obligations and responsibilities. And, I might add, highly immoral."

"Still, it was a pretty fast decision."

Jerome nodded. "It had to be. It was already almost four in the morning. Another couple hours, it would've been light. We couldn't have surprised them. We had to go in immediately."

"Your plan was to take Juarez and the others inside alive."

"Yes. I was very clear about that."

"And you had it, on good information, that the coast was clear."

"Yes, I did."

"Your informant was a member of Juarez's inner circle, who you had turned."

"That's correct."

"To bring up an earlier expression that was used in this courtroom, a snitch."

"Yes, Lopez was a paid informant."

"Does that make his credibility suspect, Agent Jerome? The fact that he was an informant?"

Jerome shook his head vigorously. "Not in the least. Informants are one of the most important tools we have. We couldn't make half our cases without them. That's a fact of life when you're working undercover, particularly in the drug business."

John Q. consulted a note. "We have heard testimony earlier, Agent Jerome, that the men inside that compound may have been warned of the impending raid. Someone called in to warn them. Could that person have been Lopez, your informant?"

"No way," Jerome answered with strong feeling. "He was by my side the entire time. It would have been impossible for him to make a phone call and for me not to know it."

I made a note for my cross.

"What about one of the other people on your team? Could one of them have called?"

Jerome regarded his lawyer balefully. "That's a ridiculous theory. We're going to call a killer drug dealer and warn him we're coming in? Forget about it."

"I agree with you, Mr. Jerome," John Q. said in his gravelly voice. "I want the jury to hear it from you. You were there, you would know."

Jerome turned to the jury. "No one in my organization called Juarez," he stated hotly. "Whoever warned him, it wasn't us. Or Luis Lopez."

John Q. walked over to the defense table, picked up some pages of earlier court testimony, walked back to the lectern. "I have to ask you some tough questions now, Agent Jerome. Questions about your motives, your credibility, your honestly. I want you to answer them in the most honest and straightforward manner that you can, even if it embarrasses you to do so. Are you ready?"

Jerome took a sip of water, nodded grimly. "Fire away." He carefully put his glass down.

I looked over at the jury. Two of the women jurors had caught the irony of that statement. Rack up one for me.

This was a dangerous strategy John Q. was pursuing. He was going to bring up the damning facts and accusations that had already been made against Jerome by strong and credible witnesses, and then, through his client's force of personality and assertions of innocence, try to demolish or discredit them. It's analogous to setting a controlled burn in a forest to prevent larger fires. The problem with that strategy is, you can't always contain the fire you set. The wind shifts direction, the undergrowth is drier, all sorts of unexpected elements can go wrong. The fire blazes out of control, and everything goes up in flames.

John Q. was going to set the controlled burn. I, coming in behind him on cross-examination, would try to be the force of nature that would turn his fire into a conflagration that would consume Jerome in John Q.'s own flames.

I wouldn't have done this if I'd been in John Q's position. There's too much risk. But he had decided that he was holding a losing hand,

and he was betting the farm on one bold move. Ironically, if he'd known of the fresh details I'd discovered recently, he wouldn't have played it this way. But early on, his case had turned negative so hard and so fast that he hadn't dug deeply enough. It happens to the best of us—no one can cover all the bases. So now he stood at the lectern, a box of matches in hand.

John Q. looked at his pages, then at Jerome. "A few days before the raid, you bought a box of full-metal-jacket bullets for your handgun from a gun-shop owner named Harrison, whose store is on the far side of the county from where you were located. Why did you buy the ammunition, considering you get your ammunition free of charge? And what were you doing all the way over there, anyway?"

Jerome took his cue.

"I'll answer the second part of your question first," he said smoothly as if he were an expert witness in someone else's trial. "I needed to get away by myself, so I could clear my head. You can't do that when you're surrounded by four dozen samurai, which I consider my men to be, in the finest sense. I meditate every day," he added, which I'm sure surprised everyone in the courtroom as much as it did me. "I like to be in a private space before I'm about to go into battle. I often go into the hills alone, wherever I am, to be at one with myself."

At one with myself? I believe in meditation and contemplation as much as the next man, but this was a crock of shit. Now he's a flower child? What's next, dropping acid on the top of Mt. Everest?

"So you were in that part of the county to get away," John Q. said. "Nothing sinister."

"The opposite is true," Jerome replied unctuously.

"And the first part of the question," John Q. continued. "Why did you buy the ammunition? You get free ammo."

"That's a simple explanation," Jerome answered easily. "I wanted to get some target practice in while I was out there, and I hadn't brought any ammunition with me."

John Q. nodded. "That seems reasonable to me. But why full-metal jackets instead of hollow points, since that's what you normally use?"

Jerome smiled. "Full-metal jackets are cheaper."

"Well, I'm glad we cleared that up," John Q. pronounced solemnly, as if Jerome's buying the bullets was no longer an issue. "Now to the other two damaging areas that have been raised, which are more complex. What can you tell us about this phantom bank account you purportedly opened with a five-hundred-thousand-dollar deposit shortly after Juarez was killed?"

Boy, I was up fast for that one. "Objection. This bank account and deposit—"

Judge McBee put up a hand to restrain me from going any further—he'd figured this was coming, he had it covered. "Objection is sustained," he said sharply.

He looked to the jurors. "A stipulated witness has testified that a bank account was opened, that the account was Mr. Jerome's, that five hundred thousand dollars was deposited into it."

McBee looked down at John Q., using the height of his perch for obvious intimidation. "We already went through this, with the bank official. Don't bark up this tree again."

John Q. looked properly chastised. "Yes, Your Honor," he muttered. Turning back to Jerome, he asked, "Do you have any idea who opened this bank account?"

"Objection!"

"Sustained."

"Did you open this bank account?" John Q. asked. His face was flushing. He was losing composure. Not a good sign when your lawyer get flustered.

"No," Jerome answered adamantly. "I did not. I never even knew about it until I was informed in the grand jury."

"What was your reaction?"

"I didn't believe it," Jerome said as convincingly as he could, which certainly fell short of anyone having full confidence in him, if I could read the looks the jurors were giving each other. "I still don't know anything about it."

"Or the five hundred thousand dollars?"

"I don't know anything about this five hundred thousand dollars, or this bank account, or any of this. I didn't open it, I didn't deposit any money in it, I didn't do anything about it." Jerome was almost whining now, he seemed so frustrated and beaten down on this point.

"Once you found out there was a bank account in your name, with five hundred thousand dollars in it, what did you do?"

"I didn't do anything. It isn't my account, so it isn't my money."

"That is your sworn testimony," John Q. declared. "You did not open this bank account, nor did you deposit any money in it."

"Like I said," Jerome answered, his voice rising in anger, "I didn't know it existed, so how could I have?"

"How, indeed," John Q. rumbled. He shuffled some papers around, then asked quickly, "Why do you suppose anyone would set up a bank account for someone else, like this one?"

Before I could get to my feet, Jerome answered in a loud, powerful voice, "To frame me."

"Objection!" I literally jumped out of my seat, knocking my chair over. "This is outrageous, Your Honor!" Pointing to Jerome, I cried, "What is he, a soothsayer? This line of questions and answers is nonsense and highly prejudicial to the fairness of these proceedings."

"Sustained." McBee looked down at John Q. with a weariness that belied his building impatience. "Any ideas like these are for final argument only. Stay with your examination, please. Or I'm going to have to terminate it."

That caught the old man off-guard. "I'm not pushing for that," he apologized. "I'll be careful."

"Do so," the judge remonstrated him.

John Q. turned back to Jerome again. "You've known . . . you had been aware of Reynaldo Juarez for many years."

Jerome nodded grimly. "Yes."

"Before you joined the DEA."

A murmur: "Yes."

McBee looked down from the bench. "Speak up, please. The jurors can't hear you, or the court reporter."

"Yes," Jerome said more loudly, not bothering to conceal his anger.

"You had a dispute with him over your sister, while they were in college together?"

"Yes."

Dispute? I thought. He almost killed Juarez. I made a note—that was not going to get by unchallenged.

"Tell us about that, if you would, from your perspective."

Jerome rearranged himself in the witness chair. He'd been looking forward to doing this for years. This was going to be a good one.

"We heard Diane was dating someone in her class. We figured it was fine. A student at Stanford, one of the finest universities in the world. How bad could that be?"

His face darkened; he took a sip of water.

"Then we started finding out bits and pieces, things about this kid, this Juarez. Him being Chicano, we didn't give a damn about that. That's like being Irish, two generations ago. If anything, you give a person like that credit, pulling himself up by his bootstraps, you know? How many Chicanos from east Los Angeles wind up at Stanford? Hardly any, I'll bet. So you figure he's got plenty on the ball."

He paused again. This was sickening, I thought as I listened to these lies. He was a bigoted Irish prick from a low-rent family, all of whom hated Juarez precisely because he was Chicano, no other reason.

"But then we started hearing stuff about him. What he'd been doing in L.A. before he went to Palo Alto. The more we heard, the uglier it got. The guy was a common criminal, a thug. How he ever got into Stanford I'll never figure out. Affirmative action or some such crap, I guess. Tells you everything you need to know about affirmative action, doesn't it?"

I looked at the Latinos and Native Americans on the jury. They didn't seem put off by Jerome's ethnic smears. Maybe they believed that propaganda, like other rural, suspicious people. Or maybe they just didn't get it; not a good omen.

"What did you do then?" John Q. interjected.

"We talked to Diane about him, over the telephone. My mother, my father. Begging her to listen to the facts. We told her about this person she was so blind over that she couldn't see, who he really was." He shook his head sadly. "She didn't hear us. She couldn't. She was blinded by love. It was so pitiful, to listen to her."

Jesus, I thought, this bastard has more blarney in him than all of Dublin. And he was doing it so convincingly. He could, because he believed it: not the facts, but the emotions. No greaser was going to be his kin, he'd kill the fucker first.

Not that he said that. Under John Q.'s easy prodding, he went on with his story.

"Finally, we had to go out there. My brothers and me. We didn't want anything bad to happen. He could stay at Stanford, we didn't care. All we wanted was for him to leave go of Diane. She didn't know any better, we were her family, we had to protect her. That's what families are for, isn't it?" he asked, looking up plaintively.

"Yes, they are," old John Q. assured him. "That's exactly what they're for. To take care of each other. Go on, son," John Q. said kindly.

I really felt like laughing. I could have objected to this nonsensical display, this third-rate dinner-theater emoting, but to what point? It was such obvious crap. All the facts were in direct contradiction to this self-serving bullshit. It's the same old story—when you don't have the truth on your side, lie.

"We met up with him—Juarez. We went someplace private, to talk to him."

"He went with you willingly?"

"He wasn't happy about it."

That was good strategy, I thought. John Q. had rehearsed that with Jerome. Admit to a few small damaging details, they'll believe you on the big ones.

"That's understandable," John Q. said. "Go on."

"We convinced him it would be the right thing to do, to come talk with us."

"Did you use force to convince him to come with you?" John Q. asked cagily, anticipating my cross.

Jerome shook his head. "No, we did not. We didn't want to *pound* sense into him, we wanted to *talk* it into him."

"Then what happened?" John Q. asked as if he were truly interested in finding out. "How did Juarez get hurt so badly?"

Jerome shut his eyes for a moment, rubbed his temples as if he had a terrible headache.

"He pulled a gun on us."

"He what?" John Q. asked, glancing at the jurors as he did.

"He pulled a gun on us," Jerome said again, louder.

"That must have been frightening. None of you were in law enforcement yet, were you? You and your brothers."

"No, we were just kids. Of course it scared us. Some guy from east L.A., you already know he's a criminal, he pulls a gun? You figure he's going to kill you."

"So then what did you do?"

Jerome shrugged, the easy shrug of a man who does a hard job and doesn't like to brag about it. "We disarmed him."

"You managed to get his weapon away from him."

"Yes."

"Then what?"

"We beat him up. He pulled a gun on us, for crying out loud," he said defensively. "What were we supposed to do, let him go his merry way?"

John Q. paused before asking his next series of questions. Walking up to the witness box, standing right next to Jerome, he said, "Your sister has testified that you forced her to get an abortion."

Jerome shook his head firmly. "That isn't true. We didn't force her."

"She didn't get an abortion?"

"Abortion is a sin. My family is antiabortion. That goes against our strongest core beliefs. Only God can decide that."

"Are you telling this court that your sister did not have an abortion?" John Q. asked again.

Jerome buried his head in his hands. When he looked up, he whispered, "She had one."

"But you didn't make her?"

Jerome's voice was choking. "No. She decided to do it on her own. We tried to talk her out of it, but she insisted. She didn't want to have any part of his life, especially his child."

I watched Jerome, writhing in fake agony. At that particular moment I wanted to kill him myself. There are lies, and then there are unforgivable lies. This was an unforgivable lie. Thank God Diane Richards wasn't here in the courtroom to hear this.

"And that's it?" John Q. placed a comforting hand on his client's shoulder.

"That's it. After that, we figured we'd done what we could, Diane could do whatever she wanted. She chose to come home, thank God. But it was her free choice, I swear it."

Judge McBee gave us a ten-minute piss break. John Q. was loitering by himself in an out-of-the-way hallway outside the courtroom. No one else was around. I ambled over to him. He looked up, gave me an old pro's smile.

"You're going to hell, you know that, don't you?" I said, smiling back at him.

"We're all going to hell, Luke. Whatever hell is."

"Lying is a sin, John Q. You've got this good Irish-Catholic boy up there lying his brains out."

"That's for the jury to judge. Isn't that what you've been preaching? Let lawyers try cases, let juries decide them?"

I wagged a finger at him. For some reason, I was feeling good about this, my knowing Jerome was lying through his teeth, John Q. knowing I knew. It made me feel better, as I regarded my own doubts. I still had them, but Jerome was such an arrogant prick I was going to be happy to see him get shafted. And he was going to be.

"You asked him if he killed Juarez, and he said no. You know the obligation of a lawyer to disclose the truth, if he knows his client's lying. Especially about murder."

John Q. looked away for a moment, then turned back to me. "The man swears to me that he didn't do it, Luke. I have to believe him, he's my client." He paused. "And you know what? I think I do."

"You're the only one who does, then."

"We'll see what the jury has to say about that," he gravel-voiced his soft reply. "You never know what's going to happen in that cramped little room, once we pros leave it to the amateurs." One more smile. "That's the beauty of the system, isn't it. The sheer and terrifying unpredictability."

John Q. was almost finished. "There's one last section we have to cover. An important one."

Jerome, looking refreshed, nodded, almost eagerly.

"You went to college and got your degree in criminology."

"That's correct."

"And then you joined the Drug Enforcement Administration."

"I was on the Chicago police force first for a few years. Then I joined up."

"You moved up the ranks quickly."

A self-deprecating shrug. "I worked hard. You work hard, you get rewarded."

"At some point you began tracking a large drug ring. Juarez's drug ring."

"Yes, that's right."

"When you got involved investigating this terrible drug ring, did you know that Juarez was the leader? That your sister's former boyfriend was, in fact, the same man?"

Jerome shook his head. "No, I did not."

"You were just going after a vicious drug lord."

"That's my job. That's our job, all of us in the agency."

"At what point did you realize Juarez was that same person?"

Jerome looked up at the ceiling, as if in deep thought. "I don't recall."

"A few weeks later? A few months?"

"Oh, no. It was years later. Several years later."

"At that point, when you discovered the connection, did you think you should take yourself off the case? Hand it over to another agent?"

Jerome nodded slowly. "I thought about it. I gave it a lot of thought."

"Why didn't you?"

"By then, it didn't matter," Jerome answered. "My focus was on who he was, then, not who he had been. And I had compiled a huge dossier, I had contacts working for me I'd spent years cultivating. You can't hand something that big and important over to a fresh team. You'd lose years of momentum. We couldn't afford that."

"So your going after Reynaldo Juarez for as long and as hard as you did wasn't about revenge?"

"No, sir," Jerome answered forcefully. "It was about justice." He paused. "But it confirmed the truth of my family's feelings from twenty years earlier. Juarez was an evil, corrupt, dangerous criminal. My sister should get down on her knees every night and say a prayer thanking her family that we cared enough about her to take care of her, when she was too blind to take care of herself."

It was late in the day, so Judge McBee recessed court until the following morning. I went back to the office to begin preparing my cross-examination. Jerome's attempts to right his ship, which had already been three-fourths underwater, hadn't done much for him, despite John Q.'s attempts to put positive spin on his actions. Either everyone in the world was engaged in a great conspiracy against him, or he was lying through his teeth. If he'd killed Juarez during a misguided raid, and that was all there was to it, the jury might have let him off—a mercy verdict, because Juarez was evil. But when revenge, premeditation, and killing for money were factored in, he didn't stand a chance.

Aside from the events in the courtroom, I was on an emotional roller coaster. If I hadn't found out all this new stuff, I would have lit up a victory cigar. I still could, because no one else knew, only me, Kate, and Riva. But because of this fresh information, my impending win—I was going to win, I had no doubts about that now—was leaving a sour taste in my mouth. All the evidence pointed to Jerome as the killer. It's what hadn't been placed into evidence that was disturbing me, more and more. The smoke was blacker and thicker, but I shall hadn't found a fire.

I reread bits and pieces of all the material I'd accumulated since the first time I'd come up to Blue River to meet with Nora. It was a mess, because it was complicated, and because the two elements that would have tidied everything up—witness and weapon—didn't exist.

Thinking back to the trip to the compound the night before with Kate, I again read the autopsy report: shot at close range through temple, high-caliber 9mm automatic, full-metal-jacket bullet, no ballistics. The killer could still be Jerome—he had the weapon and the bullets. He could have caught up to Juarez and assassinated him in cold blood before any of the others reached the scene—his prowess as a runner bolstered that scenario. His dodging and lying on the stand had reinforced that possibility for me—if he could lie so brazenly about his own sister's abortion, and about the kidnapping and beating he and his brothers had given Juarez, he could certainly have faked his dismay upon finding Juarez's body that night.

All the stuff with Miller and Nora and Juarez and the Indian tribe bothered me greatly; but it was still possible that they weren't related to this killing.

The other possibility, of course, which is what I believed in my gut now, was that they were. But how, precisely? What real evidence was there?

So far, I hadn't found it.

Again, I read the autopsy report. Nothing new jumped off the page. Something about it, though, was tickling the back of my brain. It was trying to speak to me. But what was it trying to tell me?

I couldn't come up with anything, so I put the folders back in the file cabinets and went home.

Jerome might have been able to put on a show of looking comfortable yesterday, but he couldn't pull it off today. He was clearly nervous—he'd shot his wad during his examination by John Q. There was nowhere to go now but down, and he knew it.

"Agent Jerome," I began.

He looked at me sullenly.

I stood still at the podium, arms folded across my chest, staring at him. I did this long enough that he started fidgeting, looking from me to John Q., to the back of the room, around the room. I could feel Judge McBee watching me, waiting for me to get on with it.

After what was to Jerome an interminable wait, I leaned over the lectern toward him. "How many DEA agents were on the scene that night?"

"Sixty-two, counting myself."

"Isn't that a large force for a drug bust?"

"Not for one this size," he answered. "This was going to be one of the biggest takedowns in the history of the department. You can't have enough men on an assignment like that."

"Would it be correct to say that your group was ample for the assignment?"

"There were enough of us to do the job."

"The job being to intercept a huge shipment of drugs and arrest the people involved."

"The orders were to . . ." He caught himself.

I walked over to the evidence table and picked up a document. Showing it to Judge McBee, who nodded, I crossed to the witness stand and handed it to Jerome.

"Do you recognize this?"

He looked at it. "Yes."

I took it from him, walked it over to John Q., who gave it a quick glance and waved it away. Taking it with me to the lectern, I said to the jury, "This is the federal warrant that was issued for that arrest. It's been stipulated to by all parties, meaning we all agree it's what it says it is."

I turned back to Jerome. "This warrant is to seize drugs, isn't it?"

"To seize drugs and arrest the dealers."

I looked at it again. "But it doesn't say to arrest the purported dealers if there aren't any drugs, does it? How can you prove they're drug dealers if they aren't dealing drugs?"

He stared at me, his lips, chalk white, tightly pressed together.

"One element is dependent on the other, isn't it? No drugs, no evidence of dealing. No evidence of dealing, no arrest. That's why the warrant required the drugs be present before you could raid the place, isn't it?"

He shook his head, but he didn't reply. I looked at the bench.

"Answer the question," Judge McBee ordered Jerome.

"Technically, that's correct," Jerome gave it up.

"Technically?" I echoed. *"Technically?"* There's no such thing as *technically* when it comes to warrants, Mr. Jerome. What does that mean—if it's only technically, it really doesn't count? You don't have to obey it?"

"You have to abide by the conditions in a warrant," he grudgingly agreed.

"Whether you like them or not. Whether you *agree* with them or not."

He nodded, muttered, "Yes."

"But you don't always abide by the provisions in your warrants, do you, Agent Jerome? Sometimes you decide to make your own decisions, with or without the warrant."

"I obey the law as much . . ." He caught himself.

"As much as you can? As much as you want to?"

"I do the best I can, under the circumstances."

I shook my head in disgust. Partly it was for show, for the jury, but I truly felt it. This man believed he was above the law.

"You violated a warrant. That is a crime. You are a law officer, you are aware of that, are you not?" I hammered him.

"I . . . what was I supposed to do, let him go free?" he blurted out.

I stepped back and smiled. Gotcha, pal! "So you admit you violated that warrant."

"There were extenuating circumstances," he said doggedly.

"There were? What were they?"

"Juarez was in there."

"So?"

"I couldn't let him get away. I've already explained that."

"Who said anything about letting him go? Did I say anything about letting him go?"

He looked at me. He wasn't following fast enough. He'd used too many brain cells spinning yesterday's lies.

I answered for him. "You had over sixty agents at that compound. There were no more than a dozen men inside, you knew that for a fact. Sixty crack DEA agents surrounding twelve drug dealers. Those are pretty good odds, aren't they, sixty crack DEA agents versus twelve druggies?"

He breathed in and out deeply, his eyes closed.

"Are you being at one with yourself, Agent Jerome?" I asked caustically.

His eyes popped open. He was gripping the arms of the chair, hard. I thought of a pit bull at the end of a chain, straining to break loose. The pit bull inside Jerome was dying to come at me. Only the surroundings, the public forum, prevented it.

"The odds," I repeated. "Sixty against twelve, plus the advantage of surprise. Aren't those damn good odds? Or are twelve trapped drug dealers more powerful than sixty DEA samurai?"

"The odds were in our favor," he reluctantly admitted.

"They sure were." Leaning forward, I asked, "So why go in at all? You don't have a warrant, given the changes in the circumstances, and you have the place surrounded. Why not wait them out? Where could they go? Where could they hide?"

I looked over at the jury box. One juror in the back row leaned over and whispered something to her companion. *In the freezer,* I'm sure she was saying. Both smiled before turning their attention back to Jerome.

"I couldn't take the chance," he said.

"Five to one against them, you've got the place completely surrounded, and you couldn't take the chance this one man might elude you? That doesn't speak well for your operation, Agent Jerome. Or your opinion of yourself and of your men."

"Objection." John Q. lumbered wearily to his feet. "He's browbeating the witness, Your Honor."

I put a hand up, signifying I'd back off, even as McBee said, "Sustained."

I looked at the notes I'd made during Jerome's direct testimony. "You stated that the purported phone call or calls to the compound could not have been made by your snitch, Lopez, because he was in your sight the entire time. Yes?"

"Yes." He nodded tightly.

"You were coordinating this raid, correct? You were in charge of everything. You had the big picture in your head, you were the axle, all the spokes were revolving around you."

"I was the leader, if that's what you mean."

"Yes." A glance at the notes again. " 'Lopez was by my side the entire time.' That's your direct quote."

"He was."

I pursed my lips, looked up at the ceiling, looked at the jurors, shook my head again. "You're in charge of sixty men, you're about to raid a drug compound where the man you've been stalking for ten years is hiding out—twenty, really, ever since the incident at Stanford—and yet you're attentive enough to Lopez, whose work was done by then, that you never left him out of your sight. Not for a minute, not for thirty seconds, which is all it would have taken for him to make a call. He was never out of your sight for even thirty seconds. Is that what you are swearing to, Mr. Jerome? You are swearing, under oath, that with all this going on, you never took your eyes off Lopez for thirty seconds? You're swearing to that?"

Now it was his turn to gaze upward, but in supplication, not disgust.

"To the best of my recollection, he was always . . . right there."

I glanced at the jurors. They were shaking their heads.

"Okay," I continued, "let's talk about the raid itself. How many of your men were killed on that raid?"

"Three," he said softly, almost inaudibly.

"Three," I repeated. "Three good men. They were good men, weren't they?"

"They were excellent men."

"Do you feel responsible for their deaths, Agent Jerome? Since you were the one who led the charge of the light brigade? In violation of your warrant, I have to add."

He nodded. This was becoming excruciating to him. "In some ways," he acknowledged meekly.

"They died because of a decision you made that night."

One long nod. "Yes."

"Well, let me ask you this. You were raiding a known drug stronghold, whether there were drugs there at the moment or not. Didn't it occur to you that these men would be heavily armed, that they would have tight security? Didn't you think they might try to fight you off? Didn't you think there was any chance of that *at all*?"

"I . . ." He worked to regain his composure. "There's always a chance of that. Of course. But we were working on the best information we could get. Which was that we were going to be able to surprise them."

"Information provided by a snitch. A Judas. A criminal looking out for himself."

He shook his head as if to say, *You don't get it. You weren't there.*

"In fact," I went on, "you could've taken them later. You could have kept the drug transaction alive. The planes could have come in later. It would have been a better choice to take them down during a huge drug transaction, wouldn't it? When their attention is on the drugs and the money?"

He shrugged. "In hindsight, maybe. I didn't think Juarez would stick around. That wasn't his style. He came and he went, he didn't tarry."

"So instead, you led your men into an ambush."

Even the out-of-town reporters, who had migrated back to Blue River for Jerome's testimony, froze over their pens.

I didn't need or expect an answer to that. The question was damage enough.

"Let's get on with this," I said. "You've moved in, you've encountered massive fire, you're under attack, some of your men have been killed and wounded almost instantaneously. What did you do?"

"We returned fire."

"With every piece of weaponry you had."

"Once you're committed, you're in all the way."

"I agree, you can't go at something like this halfway. You and the surviving agents shot into that compound with everything you had."

"I said that."

"You certainly did. As have others. That's my point, Agent Jerome."

I left the lectern and walked halfway to him. "What guarantee did you have, once you started firing into that compound, that you wouldn't kill Reynaldo Juarez, the man you were under strict orders to bring in alive? What do you use, smart bullets? Bullets so sophisticated they can differentiate between who to kill and who not to kill?"

"No," he said wearily. I was beating the shit out of him, blow upon blow. He was actually sagging physically.

"So the whole reason for going in was negated, wasn't it? You weren't going to get any drugs, you lost three of your men, and you easily might have killed the man you were under strict orders not to kill. What was the point, man? What in God's name was the point?"

I walked back to the lectern and took a drink, letting the dust settle. Then I went on the attack again.

"You bought ammunition at Harrison's because you were out of ammunition. That's your contention."

"That's what happened," he said stubbornly.

"You were driving a government car? You didn't have your personal vehicle up here, did you?"

"I had a government vehicle."

"If you were in a government car, you were on duty. Technically," I couldn't resist digging.

He was numbed to insult by now. "I was on duty. On a job like this, you're never off duty, officially."

"Uh-huh. So if you were on duty, you had to be armed. You have to be armed when you're on duty, don't you?"

"Yes, you're always armed when you're on duty."

"You had your gun with you. Your nine-millimeter automatic."

"Yes."

"So either you had bullets on you, in your gun, on your person, in your car, or you were derelict in your duty. Would that be a fair statement to make? I want to be fair here, Agent Jerome. If you aren't armed when you're supposed to be, is that not dereliction of duty?"

"Tech—" He twisted in his chair. "I was not derelict in my duties as a DEA agent."

I'd trapped him. "Then you did have bullets on you."

"I . . ."

"You didn't."

"No."

"So you were derelict of duty."

He bent over, elbows on knees. "Yes."

Man, was I going to have a field day in my final summation with this. And I wasn't finished with him.

"You've stated you have no idea who opened that bank account in your name. Is that true?"

"Yes."

"You have no idea who deposited *five hundred thousand dollars* in that bank account. Is that true?"

Again: "Yes."

"It's all a mystery to you."

"I . . . I don't know anything about it. That's all I can say."

"It's all part of a frame-up, is that your contention?" I asked bitingly.

"It has to be," he whimpered.

"It has to be," I repeated, using his whining tone. "I don't think it does have to be. Do you want to know why, Agent Jerome?"

Before he could answer, I gave my own: "It wouldn't take half a million. You would have killed Juarez for nothing. Fifty thousand would have been more than enough. Isn't that right!" I hollered. "You could've been had cheap, and everybody knows it!"

As John Q. was crying "Objection!" Jerome was lunging out of his seat, coming at me.

He didn't get far. You don't easily jump out of the witness box, there's a railing right in front of you. By the time he'd gotten to his feet and was making his first move, the courtroom deputies had grabbed him, each by an arm, and flung him backward.

I wasn't worried—to the contrary, I was elated. I'd broken through his brittle barrier, as I had hoped I would.

Judge McBee called for a thirty-minute recess. John Q. and I met with him in chambers.

"He's baiting the witness," John Q. complained.

"Give me a break," I shot back. "I'm handling this asshole with kid gloves, considering the bullshit he's spewing in there."

McBee was livid. "Jungle conduct will not be abided in my courtroom. I'm talking to you, sir," he said, pointing a trembling finger at John Q. "I don't care how famous you are or how many big trials you've done. I respect you, and you and your client had better respect me. Don't think you can treat me or my courtroom with disrespect because we're small-time here. I will hold you and your client in contempt of court if anything like this ever happens again. Do you understand me, Mr. Jones?"

John Q. was both contrite and pissed-off. "I *do* understand you, Your Honor, and I apologize for that outburst. Believe me, that's the last thing I want to see happen. That doesn't help my client, or me."

McBee straightened his robes. "Okay." He turned to me. "Can we cut down on the theatrics, Mr. Prosecutor?"

I gave him one of my better sincere smiles. "Yes, Your Honor. I'll tone it down."

"Your sister, Diane Richards, testified against you. You were here, you heard her."

Jerome was in the witness chair again. He had been handcuffed and hustled out of the courtroom following his outburst, but the cuffs were off now. I didn't want them on—he wasn't going to come after me again, he knew the damage that had done. And I didn't want him to have any advantage of pity. I had gotten what I wanted, in spades.

"She testified under oath that you and your brothers kidnapped Mr. Juarez. That the reason was not to talk to him, but to teach him a lesson. To make sure he never came near her, ever again."

"That isn't true."

"You stand by your version."

"It's true."

I stared at him. "So she lied. Under oath."

He stared back at me. He was under control now; it was hard for him, I could see his body tensing, but he wasn't going to blow again. John Q. had read the riot act to him, after our session with Judge McBee.

"What I said was the truth," was his response.

"And the abortion. She did that of her own free will, you didn't force it on her. That's the truth as well?"

"Yes."

"And years later, when you went after Reynaldo Juarez with a single-minded passion that bordered on obsession, that had nothing to do with your sister. You were merely doing your job."

One more "Yes."

I gathered up my papers. "I'm done with him," I said disdainfully. "Take him away."

John Q. was finished. Jerome was his final witness, his parting shot. He stood in place at the defense table, his wilted client slumped in the chair next to him. I'd cut Jerome to ribbons, and they knew it.

"The defense rests, Your Honor," the old man said, his voice even lower and gravelier than usual. There was no end-of-presentation enthusiasm in him.

Judge McBee looked at the clock behind him, made a note on his calendar. "Are there going to be any rebuttal witnesses from your side?" he asked me.

"No, Your Honor."

"Then we will stand adjourned until tomorrow at nine o'clock, when you will begin your closing arguments."

With that, he gaveled the session to a close.

The Killers

It was late now, well after dark. I was in my office. I had gone over my closing argument until I had it down pat. Now, for perhaps the final time, I went over all the documents, transcripts, interviews, grand jury testimony. Everything that had a bearing on this case.

I was still dissatisfied. Kate's and my recent trip to the compound, to the spot where Juarez had been killed, kept rattling around inside my head.

The autopsy report was buried deep in my files. I fished it out and read it. Nine-millimeter bullet entered the right temple, exited the left temple. Full-metal-jacket bullet entered the right temple, exited the left temple.

I looked at the date on the report: April 20, 1995. Two days after Dennis Ray had killed himself. Shot himself in the right temple with an automatic. The owner of the gun was listed, along with some other physical details.

I flashed back to law school. Dennis and I used to play tennis together. I was the better athlete, but he was a terrier, he never gave up. We nicknamed him Laver, after the great Aussie pro. They had two things in common, Dennis and Rod Laver. They both chased after everything. And they were both left-handed.

I looked down at the report once again. Deceased's wife found husband in their bedroom, when she came home from work. Shot in the right temple.

Dennis was a southpaw. Logically, he would have held the gun in his left hand. And shot himself in the *left* temple, not the right.

My hunch was not evidence that Dennis's death was anything other than suicide, but God, did this realization shake me. I picked through my papers and found the other autopsy report, the one on Juarez. Shot in the right temple. Nine-millimeter bullet. Full-metal jacket. The same caliber and type that killed Dennis.

I had to do something. What, I wasn't sure. But I had to act.

Riva had waited dinner on me. I picked at my food, but it tasted like cardboard. I was too jumbled inside to eat.

I told her about Dennis's autopsy report, how similar his suicide was to the way Juarez had been killed. She listened somberly.

"That's . . . pretty heavy," she commented when I was finished.

"Yeah." I felt heavy myself, heavy and tired, as if I were carrying hundred-pound sacks of cement on my shoulders.

From the living room could be heard the sounds of a *Seinfeld* rerun on television, coupled with girlish giggling. Joan had a friend over, another girl from her tribe, Maria. Maria was a few years older than Joan—cute, slender, a mane of black hair down her back to her waist. The two girls were lying on their stomachs on the floor, feet sticking up in the air, eating popcorn and talking back to the screen. I'd said a quick hello when I came in—they were already absorbed in the tube.

"What are you going to do?" Riva asked.

"Nothing, for now." God, I felt tired. "We're about to go into closing arguments." I pushed my plate away, took a healthy swallow of chardonnay.

"One thing's sure," she said. "Jerome didn't kill Dennis Ray."

"No."

"It could be suicide." She was trying to take some of the load off me. "Dennis could have used his right hand. Was there any consideration of foul play at the time?"

I shook my head. "Everyone knew how depressed Dennis was. It was open and shut." I got up and refilled my wineglass. "This is more than I can handle now. I'm going to put everything aside until the trial's over. It's just a couple more days. Than I'll figure out what I want to do." I pounded my forehead with my knuckles. "Have to do."

"This isn't your fight," she reminded me.

"That's what I'm hoping." I looked into the living room, at the girls on the floor watching television. "Dreading."

She started clearing the table. I usually help her, but I needed to veg out. I went into the living room and flopped on the couch, looking stupidly over the girls' backs at the television screen.

Joan sat up. Her friend followed suit. "This is Maria Waters," Joan said, introducing us. "This is Mr. Garrison, Bucky's father."

"Nice to meet you," I said. I wasn't paying attention to them, or the television. My thoughts were inward.

"Your little boy's a dreamboat," Maria said.

"Thanks." I smiled weakly.

"Mr. Garrison is the lawyer in the trial downtown," Joan pronounced proudly, my esteem rubbing off on her. "You know all about that, don't you?" she said, poking her friend in the ribs.

Maria yelped, pinning her arms to her sides. Joan poked her again.

"Don't." Maria giggled, pushing Joan's hand away. She looked up at me, almost blushing.

"Maria knows a lot about that, don't you?" Joan said again, giving another rib-tickle.

"Stop it already!" Maria squealed, grabbing the offending hand.

"Maria used to go with Wayne Bearpaw," Joan said as if divulging a juicy secret.

"The deputy?" I perked up a little.

Maria nodded. "We don't go together anymore." She frowned. "He broke it off, last month."

"Wayne's had a million girlfriends." Joan laughed. "Him and Maria went together for a whole year, though. That's a world record for Wayne."

"He's too wired to settle down," Maria said. "That's what makes him a good deputy. He loves action. He's an action junkie."

She gobbled a handful of popcorn. "That night? The raid? He was bouncing off the walls, talking about all the shooting, the blood all over the place, all the guns and stuff, finding that Juarez guy hiding out in the freezer, like half-froze. It was like in a war, the way he described it, everything blowing up. Like when the ammunition inside blew, it was like bombs over Kosovo, you know?"

"He talked to you about it?" I asked.

She nodded, her eyes wide, excited. "Like, he was electric, it was like he had his finger in a light socket, he couldn't stop moving, like he was bouncing up and down in bed, drinking whiskey straight out of the bottle, then like . . ." She blushed furiously.

"Like what?" I asked, my curiosity aroused, but not over her sex life.

"Well, we were like, you know . . ." Her blush deepened.

"Yes." I smiled, to put her at ease. "Go on," I urged her, trying not to show my impatience.

"So, like, he couldn't stop talking about it, until the middle of the morning practically. Especially about how that Juarez dude escaped, and they went chasing after him. I finally had to kick him out, because I had to be at work at eleven o'clock."

I gripped the edges of the couch for support. "Eleven in the morning?"

"Uh-huh."

"So you saw Bearpaw the night of the raid? After the raid? It wasn't another night?" I was questioning her as calmly as I could, but my mind was reeling.

"It was that night." Another blush. "I remember 'cause nobody was home at my house that night. My family had all driven up to Klamath Falls, to supply up. They were spending the night there, so I was alone in the house. Which Wayne knew, that's how come he came over. He couldn't stay over when my father was home, my father's old-fashioned that way."

"I know," I said understandingly. "Fathers are like that."

I called Bill Fishell at home. I could hear the shock in his voice as I gave him the bad news about my recent discoveries.

"You're running the show. What do you want to do?" he asked.

"You better get out here."

"As soon as I can."

Fishell's chartered airplane landed on the compound tarmac at five in the morning. I was there to greet him. I hadn't slept—I'd spent the rest of the night reviewing everything again. Bits and pieces of information that had seemed irrelevant and immaterial to the case suddenly took on new meaning, now that the picture had changed shape.

Fishell had brought four state marshals with him, one of them a woman. We stopped off to pick up a second vehicle. The marshals drove it, following me—we would need a second car. As we headed in the direction of the reservation, I filled Bill in on how the trial was progressing.

"Sounds like you've got a win." He took a hard look at me. "You look pretty ragged, boyo."

"I hope it's the right win," I answered. "And you're right, I'm beat. I didn't sleep last night. A lot of reading to plow through. Yet again."

"The evidence still points to Jerome—doesn't it?"

Bill's a prosecutor, he wants to win cases. I hadn't disrupted my life for a hollow victory.

"We'll find out pretty soon, one way or the other."

We reached the reservation at first light. Fishell looked out the windows as we bounced over the bleak terrain. The car jostled on the hard-baked bare-dirt ruts. Six in the morning and we could already feel the heat rising.

Louisa Bearpaw's house was dark, one light on over the porch. A sheriff's department Pathfinder was parked in the front yard next to a dusty Dodge Caravan. I pulled up next to the station wagon, the marshals right behind me. We all got out of our cars and walked to the front door. Down the street, unseen, dogs started barking, and farther off, a rooster answered with a raucous crow.

I knocked on the door, three hard raps. For a moment, it was silent within. Then a woman's voice, heavy with sleep, called out, "Who's there?"

"Luke Garrison, Mrs. Bearpaw," I announced through the closed door. "The special prosecutor."

I heard some fumbling around inside; then the door opened. She was wearing a light cotton robe, wrapped tight around her. Her hair was un-braided, she was barefoot, wore no makeup.

"What's up?" she asked, peering through slit eyes at the six of us, four in uniform.

"Is your son Wayne here?" I asked, looking into the house over her shoulder.

"He's sleeping. He worked late last night."

"Can we come in?"

She could tell from my look and tone that no was not an option. "Okay," she said, stepping aside so we could enter her small living room. "I'll put coffee on."

"Don't bother." This from Fishell. "Would you wake your son up, please?"

She stared at him, hands on hips. "Who are you?" She turned to me. "Who's he?"

"He's the attorney general of California. Now would you wake up Wayne and tell him to come in here?"

She cocked her head, gave me a quizzical, confrontational look. "What's this all about, Mr. Garrison? What's going on?"

"Get your son," I said curtly. "I'll explain when he's here."

She turned and walked to the back of the house.

One of the male marshals leaned in to Fishell. "I'll be outside," he said quietly.

Fishell nodded. The man let himself out, softly closing the door behind him.

I could hear Louisa's voice coming from a bedroom in the back of the house. Then silence.

Fishell and I exchanged a glance. "Mrs. Bearpaw?" I called. "What's going on?"

The three remaining marshals unsnapped their holsters, put their hands at the ready on the butts of their automatics.

Another thirty or forty seconds went by; then she came back into the living room. "He isn't there," she said with a look of surprise. "He mustn't have come home last night."

"Mind if we take a look?" Fishell asked. He nodded to the marshals.

She hesitated for a moment, then said, "Go ahead."

Fishell and I waited in the living room with Mrs. Bearpaw while the marshals headed for the back.

"He isn't here," she repeated in an angry voice. "Don't you believe me? What're you doing here, anyway, this time of the morning?" She glared at me.

"You'll know, soon enough."

"I should call Sheriff Miller about this." She went to pick up the telephone.

"I'd prefer you didn't," I said, placing my hand over the telephone.

She bristled. "Now look, Mr. Special Prosecutor. This is my house and I can do anything I want in it."

From the rear of the house, one of the marshals called out, "He isn't here."

"See?" The woman was in my face. "Now I want you and all of you—"

The roar of a gun being fired shook the house like an earthquake tremor. We all ran outside.

The trail marshal had his magnum pressed up against Wayne Bearpaw's ear. He pushed the deputy rudely against my car.

"Spread 'em," the marshal barked. "Now." He grabbed Bearpaw by the belt and jerked him back, placing a leg against the deputy's thighs, spreading his legs. With a practiced move he snapped handcuffs on Bearpaw's wrists, behind his back. Bearpaw was bleeding from the left shoulder. A 9mm automatic lay on the ground nearby.

"He had the weapon in his hand, he was ready to fire," the marshal explained.

"No problem," Fishell assured him. "Where was he coming from?"

The marshal pointed. "Around the back. Came out through a window. He was going to try sneaking to his vehicle, get away."

A few people in the nearest houses, aroused by the gunfire, were watching from a careful distance.

Louisa ran to her son. "Are you all right?" She hovered next to him.

He nodded, grimacing. "Stupid move," he said under his breath.

Fishell turned to Louisa Bearpaw. "We're not going to cuff you, Mrs. Bearpaw, but we have to take you in. You can go inside and get dressed, but no funny business, okay? We have your son."

She nodded dumbly. The woman marshal escorted her into her house. Not long after, dressed in a stylish cotton dress, heels, and panty hose, makeup on, hair combed, she emerged with the female marshal. Even though she was on her way to jail, she was going to look good.

Fishell read them their rights.

"Are we under arrest?" Louisa asked. Her bravado wasn't so aggressive now.

"Yes," I told her.

"What for?" She came on as if she were bewildered, but I saw through her act now.

"Perjury in front of the grand jury." I looked over at her son. "Resisting arrest."

We watched as the marshals assisted mother and son into the car. "And whatever else we can hang on you," Fishell said as the door closed on them. "Money laundering, racketeering." As he and I walked to our car, he said to me, "And if we can prove it, accessory to murder."

We stopped at the county hospital to get Bearpaw patched up. His wound wasn't bad, no arteries or bone had been hit, only muscle. After that we drove mother and son to my office, parked in back, and hustled them inside. I didn't want anyone to know what was going on—not

Tom Miller, not Nora, certainly not the press. I'd have to let Judge McBee in on what we were doing, but that could wait.

I stashed Louisa in a room with the female marshal in attendance.

"I want to talk to my lawyer," Louisa demanded.

I picked up the telephone. "What's his number? I'll dial it for you."

She glared at me. "I'd like some privacy."

"When your lawyer gets here, you can meet with him privately."

She looked away. "I . . . I want to talk to Sheriff Miller."

I shook my head. "That's out of the question. You can talk to a lawyer, but no one else."

She rocked in the hard metal chair. "I can't call the tribe's lawyer. I can't involve them in this, more than they already are." She realized that what she had just said could hurt her badly. "I don't mean we've done anything wrong, it's the publicity," she backtracked quickly, trying to cover. "Tom will know a good lawyer for me to talk to." She looked up at me. "Has he been arrested, too?"

"No."

I let her twist in the wind for a moment, then I asked, "Do you have information that might be incriminating against him?" Playing one of my hole cards, I said, "If you do, and you tell me, it could help you."

Could Miller be the killer, after all? He'd been there. He knew the area, he'd lived here for thirty years. And he hated Jerome. He would have loved to pull something like this off and then pin the tail on Jerome's ass. And what about the alleged telephone calls to the compound, late at night? Could they have come from him, too? If he was in Juarez's pocket, he'd have the number. He'd lied about where he'd gotten the money to build his house. Could Miller be in this all the way up to his neck?

Louisa shook her head. "I don't know anything about him that could help you." She paused. "Or help me."

I told her I'd call a lawyer for her anytime she wanted. Leaving her in the custody of the woman marshal, I went into an adjoining room, where Bearpaw, his bandaged arm in a sling, was being guarded by the marshal who'd shot him. Bill Fishell joined me.

"Why'd you run, man?" I asked Bearpaw.

He was hangdogging, his head lolling between his legs. "You were going to arrest me."

"How'd you know that?"

"A gypsy fortune-teller told me." He stared up at me. "What do you think, I'm stupid? Special prosecutor shows up at six in the morning with the attorney general and four state marshals, it ain't to wish me happy birthday."

"Stupid is running, so I guess you are," I rejoined. "Where'd you think you were going to go?"

He shook his head forlornly. "Anywhere. You give me half an hour head start, you'd never find me, dude. I'd make Eric Rudolph look like a day-hiker."

"You're a police officer," I said in disgust. "How can you even think like that?"

He just shook his head and looked down at the floor.

"You want a lawyer, tell me who, I'll call him, or I'll get you one," I told him. "But here's the deal: You were at the compound when Juarez was killed. I have a witness who puts you there. It's ironclad. So that's perjury before the grand jury, which is a crime; I'm going to indict you for it. And for resisting arrest, and pulling a gun on a peace officer. I could put you away for years on those charges alone. But knowing you were at the compound and lying about it tells me you're involved in that killing. Now we're talking murder."

I leaned in close to him.

"You were there, you have the right kind of gun. I don't know where you were when Juarez broke out, but I'll make odds you were out in the woods, waiting for him to come to you. Your tribe's connected with Juarez, your mother is singing her heart out," I lied—an easy lie, I knew he'd buy it. "My bet is that you were waiting for him. He thought you were going to help him escape. But you assassinated him instead and ran away."

I grabbed him by the hair, pulled his head up. "Look at me! You were there! You know that terrain like the back of your hand, it's right next to your reservation. You've probably hunted there a million times, camped out, fucked there."

I let go of him. He collapsed. I turned to Fishell. "I'm bringing an indictment against him. For the murder of Reynaldo Juarez. I'll go see the judge, right now."

I turned to leave. I could hear Bearpaw rustling in his chair. Walking slowly to the door, I thought to myself, stop me, man. I've done my part, now you do yours.

"Wait a minute."

My hand hadn't even reached the doorknob.

*   *   *

He crooned better than Elvis.

"I was there," he confessed. "After I told Sheriff Miller I was leaving, I circled around and snuck up from the back side. Nobody saw me." He shook his head disdainfully. "All that bullshit from Jerome about knowing where everyone was? Jerome didn't know jack shit, he was so fucking hyper he couldn't count the fingers on his hands."

"Go on," I prompted.

"These trailers they were using to lock the prisoners in? They got them from county welfare. I've been in those trailers. They've got these little trapdoors in the back, for fire escapes. You can open those locks with a pocketknife."

I listened, enraptured. All the pieces of the puzzle were fitting, finally.

"You freed him."

He nodded. "I watched until I saw Jerome leave the trailer. He was being sloppy, he left Juarez alone in there—he was hogging the glory, he didn't want anyone else near his prize. Which was lucky for me, otherwise I'd have had to try some intricate diversion, which might not have worked. But I was able to sneak in and unlocked the cuffs. Anyone could've unlocked them, they're standard issue."

"I know," I said. "Go on."

"I told him to wait a couple minutes, until I could create a diversion. It wasn't going to be much, just enough to give him a jump. Once he took off, he was on his own. He'd planned it out in advance, in case something like this ever happened. Where he was going to run to, and who was going to meet him there to help him get away."

"And that's what happened."

He nodded grimly. "That's what happened."

"And you got there first, and murdered him."

He shook his head violently. "No way, man! I cut him loose, that's all. I wasn't anywheres near that murder scene."

"What about the phone calls to the compound? Did you make them?"

Another head-shake. "No. I didn't know the number."

I sat on the edge of the table, looking at him closely. "Was Sheriff Miller involved in any of this? Was he Juarez's secret accomplice?"

"No, man," he said indignantly. "Sheriff Miller's straight as a ruler. He didn't know shit about any of this."

"Does he know you're dirty?"

He was in pain now. "No."

"It's going to hurt him to find out."

The look on Bearpaw's face was indescribable. "It's going to kill him." He gave me this sickly smile. "You don't know, do you?"

"Know what?"

"About Sheriff Miller and my mother."

Fishell and I exchanged a look. Wasn't this already crazy enough?

"What about them?" I asked. I almost didn't want to know, especially if Miller wasn't involved in Juarez's killing, or with Juarez in general.

"They're lovers. They've been lovers forever, way before his wife died. She was a cold bitch, his wife. She hated living out here, she hated him for fucking up his FBI career. My mother was good to him. A real woman, what he needed. And he was great to her." He paused. "He still is."

Fishell and I gave each other looks of pure disbelief. "Now I've heard everything," I said.

Bearpaw shook his head. "No, you haven't." Then he smiled. "Sheriff Tom Miller is my father."

Once Louisa Bearpaw knew her son had broken, she came clean, too.

Juarez, through an emissary, had contacted her when he decided to buy the land next to the reservation. They were supporters of Native American causes, they told her, and they wanted to help her tribe. In exchange, the tribe could do them a service. It would work out well for both sides.

"The service being to launder their money."

"I prefer the phrase 'invest in our future.' We weren't involved in dealing drugs," she said self-righteously, as if being once removed whitewashed the crime. "I wouldn't cross that line."

I felt dirty, listening to this ugly, self-serving excuse. "Don't ask, don't tell."

"Precisely." She wasn't going to back down an inch.

"How much did Juarez *invest* in your future?"

My irony was a gnat on an elephant's ass to her. "Twenty million dollars a year. It wasn't much to them, they spread their money around."

"Investing in futures. Especially their own."

"One hand washes the other."

"And both get dirty."

I was getting angrier and angrier—the woman had no remorse, and seemingly, no comprehension of the consequences of her actions. "What did the tribe get out of it? How much of his bloody money did it take to corrupt you?"

"We kept five points." She was talking as if we were in an accounting seminar. "And we weren't corrupted. We were never in the drug business."

"A million a year. No taxes, of course. That's five million, so far. Which is where you got the money to buy the compound."

She gave me a savvy look. "Once Juarez was dead and the government took the property, we had to do something. They weren't going to be around anymore, our revenue had dried up. We needed the money," she said matter-of-factly. "Gambling's legit, it would solve all our problems."

"And how much of it did you skim?"

"Nothing," she said angrily. "Not one dime. It all went to the betterment of my people."

"The betterment of your people. That's a wonderful excuse." I paced around the desk. "Does Tom Miller know about any of this? He's your financial adviser, isn't he?" I gave her a hard look. "Among other things." She knew her son had told me about her and Miller.

She smiled. "He isn't, really. He plays with a little bit of our money. It makes him feel good, necessary. He's a trend-follower, but he's not in this league."

"Not many are. What's going to happen when he finds out?"

"He'll be hurt."

"Hurt? That's all? He's a lifer cop, you betrayed the heart and soul of what he believes in."

The glare she gave me would melt icebergs. "Life isn't always tidy, Mr. Garrison. I have no regrets about anything I did. We've been poor for a hundred and fifty years, ever since you stole our land from us, stole our lives. Drugs aren't the worst thing that's ever happened, Indians have been doing hallucinogens forever, it's part of our religion. It hasn't killed us. Poverty, disease, high infant mortality, alcoholism, all the shit you gave us—those are real calamities. Who cares if some bored Anglo housewife in the San Fernando Valley wants to snort powder up her nose, or a junkie in Chicago chooses to smoke crack? What business is that of mine? My people are my business. And I was helping them. You don't like it, give me back my country and I'll abide by my own laws."

I backed away from her. She could be contagious. "Tom Miller isn't your people."

"He'll understand," she said unwaveringly. "He's seen the poverty up close for thirty years. You'd be surprised."

I already was.

"What are you going to do now?" she asked. "There's no records of the money, we've been super-careful, you'll never get us on that. And I didn't kill Juarez, and neither did Wayne. Reynaldo was our savior. I cried when I heard he'd been killed."

"Who did kill him, then?" By now I was almost positive I knew who it was, but when you're in the middle of the lake already, it doesn't cost anything to throw out another line.

"Jerome," she said with certainty. "You've got him dead to rights."

Whether I did or not, she was bullshitting me. Even now, after she'd caught both tits in the wringer.

"You'd want it to be Jerome."

"Jerome cut down my money tree. Of course I want it to be him. It *is* him," she declared fiercely. "It has to be."

"What if it isn't?" I hadn't said that to anyone outside my brain trust.

"It is, even if it isn't," she insisted. "If he hadn't done what he did, Juarez would be alive, and we'd all be better off for it."

Her rationale was twisted, selfish, destructive. "Maybe you weren't dealing drugs directly, but you helped enable Juarez's people to. You're not clean, Ms. Bearpaw—you're filthy. I know the way your people have to live is shit, it's unconscionable—but that can't justify doing business with drug dealers. And it didn't solve your problem, did it? You and your son are going to jail, and your tribe will never get that property now."

Her hollowness was too twisted for me to handle. I had to get out of here.

"I'm going to get who killed Juarez, you and I both know that— but it's far better for the world that he's dead."

She clung to her attitude like a barnacle. "Not for me."

Tom Miller was waiting for me in my office, slumped in a chair. He was ashen.

"You've arrested my deputy."

"And his mother."

His look was pure distress. "You know about us? Louisa?"

I nodded. "Your son told me."

"Aw, Jesus."

"It's nothing to be ashamed of. They both think you're the greatest guy in the world."

"No, I'm not." He shook his head from side to side. "I betrayed my wife, and had a child out of wedlock."

"If those are the worst sins you've ever committed, you still have a fighting chance of getting into heaven."

"I'm not religious that way."

"One less problem to worry about."

"I lied about my investments, too." This had been quite a morning for confessions. "I didn't make that money playing stocks. I wouldn't have the guts to do that, or the foresight. That money was from my wife's life insurance policy. From an old policy I bought back when I was with the Bureau. It had nothing to do with being smart." He gave me a sideways, embarrassed look. "I wanted to look like a big shot. Like I was modern. Not a relic, which is what I've become."

He was so down in the dumps it was terrible. I couldn't even fake trying to make him feel better—I had to fill him in on my conversations with Louisa and Wayne. It got worse and worse. He kept shaking his head.

"For the record"—I had to do this officially—"it wasn't you, was it? You had nothing to do with it?"

"No, it wasn't me."

"For a long time, I thought it was."

"I know."

"You never said anything to me."

"What was I going to say, 'I'm innocent of a crime I haven't been charged with'? You're a smart man, Luke. I knew that sooner or later you'd figure it out."

"It took me a long time."

He grimaced. "Me, too."

"When did you?"

He was sheepish. "Only now. Hearing about Louisa and Wayne."

I threw him some rope. "Wayne says he didn't do it. That he freed Juarez from the trailer, but didn't pull the trigger out there."

Miller leaned over, burying his head in his hands. "I hope that's true." His shoulders were shaking from his crying, this rock of a man. "This is a nightmare. How in the world did this ever happen?"

"It's a long story, Tom. You know more of it than I do, I'm sure."

He nodded.

"What about Juarez laundering money through the tribe? Did you know about that?"

He shook his head. "No. Louisa kept it from me to protect me, I'm sure. She said it was money out-of-state tribes were donating to them, to get a piece of the Prop 5 action when it happened. I bought it."

He paused. "I didn't want to look under the rock," he berated himself. "Man, did she play me for a fool. An old fool's the worst fool, isn't he? You're not supposed to be blinded by love when you get to be as old as me."

"I think you were right the first time," I consoled him. "She was protecting you."

He kept shaking his head. I could see that my attempt at solace was small comfort.

Nora was my final call before I went to the judge. I caught her at home; she was on her way out the door for the courtroom, to hear the final arguments. She agreed to wait for me. She was curious, of course, about why I wanted to see her. I told her there had been a big break in the case, involving Jerome. That excited her—she was eager to know what it was, right then. I told her I'd be there in a short while, that it would be better to hear it all in person.

I picked up Kate Blanchard en route. I wanted a witness with me, preferably a woman, when I broke the news. I was clear with Miller about not tipping Nora in advance—this was my show. He was fine with that.

Kate arched an eyebrow as she got into the car and saw me. "What cat dragged you in?"

"One with sharp teeth."

She was beside herself with glee as I recited the predawn events. "Goddamn Sam!" She pounded the dashboard, she was so jazzed. "This is major high drama. I mean, it's insane!"

"You're a big reason for all this. You're a dogged detective, lady."

"Thank you, kind sir. As long as I'm not a dog."

In another life, she'd be a hell of a fine old lady. I already have one of those; besides, we're great friends, also something to be prized.

Nora was surprised that Kate was with me—maybe *disappointed* is a better word. She was wearing a clingy dress that showed her figure to good advantage—this was going to be her day in court as well as mine—the culmination of her efforts to find justice.

We sat in her living room, Kate and me on one couch, Nora across the coffee table from us, perched on the edge of the cushion. She was having coffee; Kate and I had declined. This wasn't a time to have anything fragile or liquid in my hands.

"What's up?" Nora asked, looking from me to Kate and back. "What's new with Jerome we don't already know?" She glanced at her watch. "You start closing arguments in less than an hour." She took a sip of coffee. She was drinking from a china cup, a good one.

"You might want to put your coffee down," I cautioned her.

"What?" She was antsy, wanting to know. She put the cup down on the table.

I leaned toward her. "We arrested Wayne Bearpaw this morning."

That froze her. "Wayne Bearpaw? Deputy Bearpaw? For what?"

"Perjury. Resisting arrest." I paused. "Accessory to murder."

She rocked in place. "Jesus." Another look at Kate, back to me. "Wayne was in cahoots with Jerome? How in . . . what in the world is that all about? How did he and Jerome hook up?"

"I don't know exactly, yet," I said. "It's complicated. One piece of it is, Bearpaw's mother's been laundering money for Juarez. Ever since he built the compound. Before, even."

"That's incredible. Louisa Bearpaw? You know that for a fact?"

"She's confessed to it."

"Oh my God!" Her hands fluttered above her waist. She pushed them down into her lap, one on top of the other. "Louisa's one of my closest friends." A look of consternation crossed her face. "This isn't going to screw up the trial, is it?"

I gave an anything-goes shrug. "It's all up in the air now."

That was the last thing she wanted to hear. "That's great!" she spat. "That's fucking wonderful! All this time, and money, and energy. Does Judge McBee know?" she asked, her mind spinning.

I shook my head. "I told him I needed to push my closing back an hour, but I didn't tell him why. I wanted to tell you first."

"Thanks. I appreciate that." She jumped up. "Bill Fishell. He has to be told. I'll call him." She ran toward the phone in the kitchen.

"He already knows."

She stopped cold, turned back to me. "He does?"

I nodded. "I called him last night."

She came back, sat down slowly. "What did he have to say?"

"He was as surprised and shocked as I was." I leaned toward her. "You can talk to him directly, yourself. He's here in town, in my office."

She frowned. "Bill Fishell is here in Blue River? When did he get here?"

"Five this morning. He was with me when we arrested the Bearpaws."

I could see her mind going a mile a minute. "Does Tom Miller know about this?"

"He knows."

She was thinking on the run. "He must be in shock, he's so close to them."

"He's taking it hard," I told her, greatly understanding Miller's grief. "But he understands. And yes, it was a terrible blow to him."

She looked at me, her body rocking. Slowly she said, "Then you know about—"

I cut her off. "Thanks for clueing me in." I was being deliberately curt with her.

"How was I to know that would matter?" she bristled. "And what are you so mad about?"

"Everything matters, Nora," I said darkly. "I've found that out, the hard way. Everything."

She was defensive and unapologetic simultaneously.

"Like what, Luke? I'm not sorry I didn't tell you about Miller and the Bearpaws. No one knows about that, it's a well-kept secret. Anyway, that has nothing to do with Juarez's murder. I can't be expected to tell you the history of everything that's happened in Muir County over the last thirty years, can I?"

"Anything that touches on this, even remotely, you should have."

"Well, like what? Besides that."

I sat up straight. "Things about you."

She gave me a funny look. "What things?"

Her eyes darted to Kate for a second, as if seeking some kind of woman-to-woman bonding coalition against me. Kate returned her look with a noncommittal stare.

"What things?" Nora asked me again.

"There are an awful lot of coincidences here, Nora. They're piling up."

I pulled a few sheets of paper out of my back pocket on which I'd scribbled some notes the night before.

"This connection with Juarez's contractor. It still bothers me."

"Oh, come on, Luke," she said, clearly exasperated. "We've already gone over this. I'm sorry I don't have twenty-twenty hindsight, okay? How was I supposed to know? I wouldn't have used Dean if I'd known. But how could I have? Juarez was never there."

"Remind me again—how did you get on the property? Juarez's man Portillo said it was heavily guarded, from day one."

She shrugged—too nonchalantly, I thought. "Not when I was there. That must have been later, after they finished it." She took a sip of coffee.

"So you met the architect before it was finished."

"Yes. You know that."

My eyes flicked over at Kate for an instant. "That's funny."

"What is?" Nora asked crossly.

"The first time you ever showed me the place, the day after I came up here, you said you had never been there until after the killings. But you'd been there plenty of times before, hadn't you?"

"No. I mean . . . yes, of course I was up there before. I told you that. I never said I hadn't been there before Juarez was killed."

"I must be mistaken," I said, staring at her coolly. "You sure you didn't say that?"

"I'm positive, Luke," she said firmly. "I had been there before it was finished. What I said, I'm sure, was that I hadn't been there since it was built. Before Juarez's group moved in."

"Okay," I said. "Obviously, I misheard you."

"Obviously," she said tartly.

I looked at my notes again. "And paying for the house, all in cash. Why didn't you take out a mortgage?"

"Has anything I've ever said registered with you? I told you, my parents gave me the money in a lump sum. I could have gotten a home loan, I suppose, but this way I don't have the debt." She was becoming increasingly agitated with my questions. "It's my money, what concern is it of yours?"

I felt Kate tensing, next to me. "We couldn't find any documentation of your parents giving you any money, Nora. Not in that amount."

She put her cup down hard, rattling the saucer. "You've been investigating *me*?"

"I've been investigating everyone. Including you."

She stood. "I find that offensive, Luke. I find that ugly."

"Where did the money come from, Nora?" I wasn't going to stop.

"My parents, like I said. You want me to get a letter from them to give the principal?" She was livid—a vein was popping involuntarily in her neck. "I don't want to have any more of this conversation," she said abruptly. "I want you to leave. Both of you. Now." She pointed to the door.

I waggled my head back and forth slowly. "That's a bad idea. It could give me a worse impression that I already have. I don't feel good, okay? I was up all night, watching my case go up in flames. *So sit down and answer my questions.*"

She hesitated, considering possible courses of action. Then she came around the couch and sat back down, perched on the edge.

She tried a new tack. "You're tired," she said calmly. "I understand. You've had a monkey wrench thrown into the works. Go ahead. Ask me whatever you want to ask me. I have nothing to hide from you." She paused. "From anyone." She smiled at me, almost lasciviously. "Do you?"

"No," I answered, feeling the churn in my gut, "but we're not here for me."

"You mean I have to show you mine, but you don't have to show me yours."

She was coming on to me. Not for the reasons she had before, but to embarrass me in front of Kate.

I forced a smile. "I don't have anything to show you."

She looked at Kate again. This time, she winked. "Oh, I'll bet you do."

Kate glanced at me, like asking, *What's this?*

I wasn't going to get caught up in Nora's emotional machinations. I threw her a curve. "Let's talk about Dennis's suicide."

My tactic worked—she turned pale. "Dennis's suicide? What does that have to do with anything? My God, Luke, isn't that low? At a time like this?"

I took the autopsy report out of my pocket. "You found him."

"Yes," she said between clenched teeth, staring at the document in my hand.

"He shot himself with a gun. In the temple. A nine-millimeter Sig Sauer." I looked up from the page. "Your gun."

"I know all that!" she cried. "You don't have to remind me. I've been living with it for five years." She turned to Kate. "Please make him stop."

Kate shook her head.

I carefully laid the autopsy report on the coffee table. "You never told me you had a gun, Nora. Why didn't you tell me you had a gun? Why didn't you tell me your husband killed himself with *your* gun?"

Her nails were digging into the palms of her hands. "What in the world does that have to do with any of this case?" She snatched up the report, crumpled it in her hand. "Yes, I have a gun. All D.A.'s in this county have guns, they're given to you when you take the job, whether you want one or not. This is the old West up here, Luke. Everybody has a gun."

She threw the paper across the room at me. "I didn't want the fucking thing. I hate guns, they scare the shit out of me. They kill people." She started crying, her face in her hands, loud, racking sobs. "Like Dennis," she cried from behind her hands. "It was in a drawer, I'd forgotten I even had it."

She sobbed harder.

Kate put a hand on my arm. "Should we stop for a while?" she whispered, concerned.

I was fresh out of pity. "Get her a glass of water."

Kate went into the kitchen and came back with a half-full glass. She pressed it into Nora's hands. Kate looked over at me—she was feeling sorry for Nora.

I wasn't. "Come on, Nora. Pull it together."

Her crying turned to sniffles. She took a swallow, handed the glass back to Kate. Kate put it on the coffee table and sat next to me again.

"I don't know why you're doing this, Luke." Nora's eyes were red-rimmed.

"You brought me up here to do a job. This is part of it."

Her sigh came from way deep down. "Okay. Go ahead. I'll be all right." She reached for the water.

I went to my notes again. "Where were you the night of the raid?"

She looked at me incredulously; then she broke out laughing. "Now you're really reaching."

I sat there staring at her.

One of her legs was crossed over the other. Her foot jiggled up and down involuntarily. "I was home, of course. In my bed, asleep. It happened at four in the morning, for God's sakes."

"You didn't know it was going down? Tom Miller didn't call and tell you?"

The expression on her face told me I'd caught her in a lie.

She backtracked hastily. "I'm sorry. I wasn't thinking. Yes, he called me."

"When?"

"Around twelve or one. Somewhere in there. Of course he called me."

"What did you do?"

She snorted a laugh. "Cussed. That bastard Jerome had cut us out until the last minute. But what could you expect?"

I was a metronome. "Then what?"

"Nothing." Her foot had taken on a life of its own, twitching up and down. "There was nothing I could do. I hoped it would go all right. What else could I do?"

I rubbed my fingers on my forehead. "What does 'go all right' mean?"

"You know. That the raid would be successful."

"That they'd catch these guys, the dealers," I paused. "Including Juarez."

"Of course including Juarez," she answered. "He was the reason for it."

"Okay. So then what?"

"I went . . ." She hesitated. "I didn't go back to sleep. I stayed up."

"You were up all night."

"Yes."

"Here."

"Yes. I sat by the phone. With a glass of Jack Daniel's close at hand, I might add. It was a very tense time, as you can imagine."

I was staccatoing my questions. "Until when?"

She thought for a moment. "Around six-thirty. Tom called and told me what had happened."

"The raid. Juarez being caught. Escaping. Being killed."

She nodded. "Everything."

"So from midnight until six-thirty in the morning you were here, waiting by the telephone to hear what had happened."

Another nod.

"You didn't go out at all, make any calls, anything?"

"No. I stuck right here, by the telephone. I wanted to make sure I was here when Tom called back."

I looked at the last page in my hand. "According to your telephone records, you made some phone calls between midnight and four in the morning. From your phone, here."

I angled the page to Kate, out of Nora's vision. She looked at it carefully, her eyes following my finger down the page.

There were no phone numbers in my notes. Records aren't kept of local phone calls in California. I was counting on Nora not knowing that, or that I'd rattled her enough that she'd forget. Kate did a convincing job of playing her part, mouthing the phantom numbers to herself.

"Who were they to?" I asked.

Nora started shaking.

"I . . . I think . . . I don't remember, but maybe I did. I think I was trying to call someone from the DEA to get more information, or . . . I don't remember exactly, it was such a nervous time."

Next to me, Kate's body was vibrating. I could feel it, an electric impulse. I put my notes aside and threw my haymaker.

"You killed him."

Nora fainted dead away. Kate propped her up, applied a damp dishtowel to her forehead until she revived. She sat on the couch, slumped over, her body limp. We sat close by, flanking her.

"When did you know?" she asked dully. Her eyes were glazed over, spittle was dribbling out the side of her mouth.

"Not until this morning, for sure. But last night, when I pulled Dennis's autopsy report out and read it again, it hit me. The missing piece of the puzzle. A left-handed man would shoot himself in the left temple, not the right."

She shook her head mournfully. "Nobody ever caught that. You're the only one."

"It was a lucky break. Although by itself, that wasn't enough. It wasn't until we arrested Wayne Bearpaw that I put it all together. I knew there had to be someone else involved, someone Juarez knew and would trust to help him get away."

I looked at her. "That had to be you."

Her head barely moved in acknowledgment.

She made a pact with the devil. Money for access and protection. It had taken a long time, his people feeling her out, plying her with small favors, making certain she was corruptible.

When the big offer came, it was too good to resist. Fifty thousand dollars a month in cash, for as long as they operated out of there and she was the D.A. She would see to it that they could run their business without police interference. Dennis was a bust, her parents had no money to leave her, she couldn't go anywhere else and start over, she was too old, too many bridges had been burned. It was her only chance to ever make real money.

Tom Miller had been suspicious of what was going on out there. She had restrained him from investigating, citing financial considerations.

Louisa Bearpaw was in on it from her end, and Wayne. A Luciferian threesome.

When Jerome came on the scene, she was worried, but not as much as Juarez. Jerome had dedicated his career to find Juarez and nailing him. Juarez had been staying away from Muir County since Jerome had centered his operation there, until the night the drug deal was supposed to go down. He had to come, the buyer had insisted on it. Too much money was at stake for him not to. It was going to be a one-night stay-over, gone before dawn.

The timing of the raid caught her completely by surprise. She had assumed the DEA would notify her and Miller well in advance. The feds always work with the locals.

When Miller called her the first time and told her he was going on a raid with Jerome and his men that night, right away, she had called the compound to warn Juarez, but it was too late for him to run. The compound was surrounded, his avenues of escape were blocked. He was going to have to stay and fight it out. He had a huge cache of arms, and Jerome wasn't expecting resistance. They had outfought the DEA before, they could do it again.

But they didn't. He was caught and arrested.

All this she knew because Tom Miller, the consummate pro, was constantly in touch with her.

Wayne Bearpaw was on the phone with her as soon as he left the war zone. She gave him his instructions: Find a way to sneak into that trailer and break Juarez loose—take the handcuffs off, unlock the trailer door. Kill whoever's guarding him if you have to, Juarez has to be sprung loose. If Juarez could get out, he might be able to make his way to a pre-arranged spot and get away. It would be risky, but it was his only chance. That's what she told Bearpaw. She didn't say who might be at this prearranged location, or where it was.

Bearpaw was scared out of his wits to do it—the place was an armed camp, those agents would shoot at anything that moved. But she forced him to. If he didn't, all three of them—him, his mother, her—were finished.

Somehow, he did his part.

She was at the designated spot, waiting. Juarez had planned this out before, long ago—I may have to come to you for help, he'd said. She'd agreed to it—she hadn't thought it would actually ever happen. But it had, and now she had to fulfill her end of the bargain.

She was standing at the edge of the grown-over fire trail, in the clump of trees. She knew the area well—she had selected it because of its proximity to the fire road.

Juarez came running to her. He was shaking with exhaustion and fear. He bent over, hands on knees, gasping for breath. She leaned him up against the tree for support.

They could hear the DEA agents chasing around, running in all different directions. The feds didn't know this terrain as well as she did, they weren't close enough to find Juarez and her before the two of them could get to her car and get away.

Juarez never saw her raise her automatic, point the barrel an inch from his head, and pull the trigger.

I was numb. "You have no soul."

She didn't respond.

"You have no comprehension of your own depravity, do you?"

She shrugged, as if to say, *So what?*

"I have a question." Kate spoke. She was trembling.

Nora turned to her blankly.

"Why did you kill him?" Kate asked. "Why didn't you spirit him away, like you'd planned?"

Nora laughed harshly.

"What was I going to do with him, stick him in the guest bedroom? I couldn't take the chance he wouldn't get caught again. That was the strongest thing he had going for him—that he could never be captured. But now he had. His shield of invulnerability had been shattered. He was just another drug dealer on the run now. Sooner or later, Jerome would have caught up with him. Or one of many others who had been after him."

She continued. "After that night, he was useless to me. Worse than useless, he was dangerous. He wasn't going to be paying me anymore, his people wouldn't be able to operate out of Muir County. And he would have turned on me if he'd been caught. A district attorney on a drug dealer's payroll? They would have sent me to jail forever."

She took a sip of her water. It was incredible how calm and detailed she was in telling us this. It made the situation, and her, even harder to take.

"I thought for sure he'd be killed, trying to escape. I had to think Jerome could get that much of it straight. I never thought he'd actually get away." She sighed. "But he did. With sixty men at his disposal, Jerome couldn't even do that one thing right. Talk about a loser."

She smiled at Kate and me, as if we were all sharing a wonderful secret.

"Killing him was my only option. Surely you understand that."

I didn't want to hear any more. I didn't want to be in her sick, loathsome presence. But I had to know the rest.

"But why did you kill Dennis? He wasn't involved in any of this . . . was he?" I asked fearfully. How deep did this go? I thought. How widespread was this corruption?

Her face was a dark mask of pure contempt.

"Dennis involved in this? That fucking pussy. By the time this chance came he was so beaten down he didn't have the guts to cross the street by himself, let alone take any kind of risk."

She shook her head as if trying to clear away a bad memory. "I wanted him to be with me in it, I begged him. It was a chance for us to have the kind of life we'd always wanted, the only chance we'd ever have."

She cleared her throat, took a sip of water. "He didn't want any part of it. After all I'd done for him."

Her voice was thick with vitriol. "In all the years we were together I only asked him òne goddamn thing. One lousy favor. And he wouldn't do it. He wouldn't lift one lousy finger to help me." The scorn was in her eyes. "He was going to blow the whistle on me, all of us. It wasn't enough that he wouldn't be there for me when I needed him the most. He was going to stop me. His own wife, who had sacrificed everything for him. My career, my chance at having children, everything."

I looked over at Kate. She was trembling, shaking her head, back and forth.

"You killed your husband because he was against this deal? Against breaking the law?"

Her answer was flat, unfeeling of anything. "He was already dead by then. His brain hadn't passed the message to his body, that's all. I did him a favor."

I put a hand on Kate's, human reassurance.

"That bank account of Jerome's. That was your doing, wasn't it? Everything with Jerome was your doing."

She nodded.

"Once Juarez was dead, I had to figure a way out, some donkey to pin the tail on. Jerome was the perfect ass. I discovered the background of him and his sister and Juarez, it set him up beautifully, particularly since he'd hidden it from his agency and they'd never known about it. The money was the clincher. Sure, it was a lot, but it had to be, so it couldn't be explained away. Fifty thousand wouldn't have caught your attention, Luke. Five hundred thousand had to. I could afford it. Juarez had made me rich. I still have plenty left. Which no one's ever going to find."

She paused. "I put in half. Louisa Bearpaw put up the other half. It hurt—a quarter million apiece is a lot of money, but the way we looked at it, it had been free. It was an expensive insurance policy. And it worked."

She smiled. "We even got lucky with things we didn't plan, like those bullets Jerome bought. The way he said it happened is true, I'm sure. One more lucky coincidence in a perfectly planned piece of work." She frowned. "Almost perfectly."

There was one question left unresolved—the most important one, for me.

"Why did you bring me into this?" I beseeched her. "Why didn't you leave it alone? Why take the chance of exposing yourself? Nobody suspected you."

She stared at me like I was the village idiot.

"The DEA wasn't going to give up. Sooner or later, they would have found a weak link. The tribe, probably. Do you think Louisa and Wayne Bearpaw would have protected me? They would have thrown me to the wolves."

Her eyes were gleaming now, like she was rabid.

"I had to deflect it. I knew I could pin it on Jerome, if I had someone smart enough ramrodding the case."

She smiled tenderly at me. "That was you, Luke. I knew you'd find all the clues I'd sprinkled around. And I knew you'd feel so sorry for poor Nora, your old friend, that you wouldn't quit until you did."

I stood there, swaying. She'd been conning me from the beginning, and like the trusting sap I am, I'd flown right into the center of her web.

"Let's go, Nora."

She ignored me, turned to Kate.

"Luke loves me. We're lovers. Do you know that?"

Kate's jaw dropped. She looked at me in shock. I shook my head sadly—*she's crazy, can't you see that?*

"We've been in love since we were in law school. It wasn't meant to be, then. Dennis swept me away. But then, when Luke came up here, it was like we had gone back in time." She smiled dreamily, her eyes closed. "We became lovers, the very first night. And we've been lovers ever since."

This was painful, for reasons beyond Kate's knowing.

"Nora." I was pleading, with her and for myself. "Let's go."

She wasn't here. Wherever "here" is.

"He was going to leave his wife. We were going away together, me and him and his son. Where no one would ever find us."

"Nora . . ." This was horrendous now, made more so because of that tiny kernel of reality I'd been a part of.

She looked at me with an otherworldly expression. "I lied to you, Luke. I told you there was no one else but you, except for Dennis, and he didn't count. But I lied. There was someone else."

Don't say it, I thought. You've already said too much. Way too much.

"Reynaldo was unbelievable. Such a man. When we started, it was business. I didn't even meet him for over a year. But once we did, we couldn't get enough of each other. While his men were screwing around out there, he was here with me. In my bed."

She laughed, an insane braying. "Jerome was in town once, looking for the legendary, elusive Reynaldo Juarez. Who was in bed with the district attorney." She laughed again. "We thought it was the most delicious thing in the world."

Her eyes were open now. She was looking at me, but she wasn't seeing me, not the me who was standing here in front of her. She was seeing something else—her fantasy.

"I thought he was the best I'd ever have. And he was, Luke. Until you. You're the best. The best there ever was. The best there ever will be."

She moved toward me, as if to wrap me in an embrace. I recoiled in horror.

"Nora. For God's sakes . . . !"

A guttural sound came from deep in Kate's throat—she couldn't handle the sickness anymore. Stepping between us, she hauled off and slapped Nora across the face, as hard as she could.

"Shut up, you sick bitch!" Kate was shaking. "Shut your filthy, lying mouth!"

I pulled Kate away. We were both shaking, uncontrollably.

"Don't. Can't you see?" I turned to Nora. "It's time to go. We have to go."

She rubbed her mouth where she'd been hit. "I can't go to jail in something like this." She fingered her dress, the fine material.

Her voice was matter-of-fact now—she was back in the real world. "Let me change into something more comfortable and get my toilet things. I'll only take a minute."

I wasn't thinking—I was emotionally wasted.

"Go ahead." I wanted her out of my sight, if only for a few minutes.

She walked down the hallway into her bedroom, closed the door. I sagged onto the sofa. Kate, equally devastated, dropped down next to me.

We heard drawers opening and closing. Then metal slamming against metal.

Kate leaped up before me, both of us running for the bedroom door.

The explosion from Nora's automatic rocked the house to its foundations.

PART

SIX

PART

SIX

HOME

I stood at the prosecution table.

"The state is dropping its case against Sterling Jerome, Your Honor. We move the defendant be released immediately."

My motion was a formality. After the ambulance came to Nora's house, and the police, and the coroner, and Kate and I had given our statements, I went into town and met with Judge McBee and John Q., in the judge's chambers. Bill Fishell came with me. I recounted what had happened, all the back story, up to Nora's suicide.

They were all thunderstruck, including John Q., who really had thought he had a loser. Not only the case, the client.

It was ironic in a terrible way. If I hadn't done John Q.'s job for him, I would have won, hands down. Now I was flushing it all away.

"You're filing charges against Louisa and Wayne Bearpaw, I presume?" McBee asked me.

They were being held in the jail, no bail.

I looked over at Fishell.

"Racketeering and money laundering," Bill confirmed. "Assisting in the escape of a prisoner, against Deputy Bearpaw. Resisting arrest against him, too. Whatever else we can come up with."

"What about murder?" the judge asked.

"That was Nora's doing. Hers alone," Fishell said.

They wouldn't go to prison forever. Although for Louisa, at her age, it was basically a death sentence. Maybe she'd pull something out of the hat. She was a survivor. And a great con artist.

"You'll be the prosecutor?" McBee asked me. We'd come to like each other.

I shook my head firmly. "I'm done here."

"This will be filed in federal court," Fishell said. "It's their jurisdiction." He was happy to pass the buck this time.

Outside chambers, John Q. pulled me aside. "You did my job for me. You should get a cut."

"No, thanks. You showed up, you did your best. He was lucky to have you."

"I gave up on him," John Q. insisted. In the dim light he was looking old, even older than he was. I suspected this was his last big case.

"He was a crummy client," I said.

"Well . . ."

We shook hands.

I signed the release documents in open court. As I was turning to push through the gate and leave the courtroom, Sterling Jerome blocked my exit.

"I hope you're satisfied," he said in an ugly voice. "You fucked my life up, really good."

I tried to move around him. He moved with me.

"You almost convicted an innocent man," he ranted. "You ought to be sick of yourself. I ought to sue you, you cheap shyster."

I stepped back. He was contaminating my air.

"If it wasn't for me," I said, maintaining my calm, which wasn't easy, "you would have been convicted of premeditated murder."

He wanted a fight. "If it wasn't for you, there wouldn't have been any case in the first place. You should have checked your facts better."

I wasn't going to oblige him. "I'm not getting in a debate with you. But let me ask you one question."

"What?" he gibed.

"How many of your men died on that raid?"

The muscles of his jaw were working. His neck swelled, the veins pulsing. "Fuck you."

I pushed him aside and left the Muir County courthouse for the last time.

Tom Miller was drunk. I don't think he'd ever been drunk before in his life, but he was drunk now.

"It's not your fault," I said. "You couldn't have known."

It was small consolation.

He kept shaking his head. "I should have known," he insisted stubbornly.

We were in the study of his house. He poured himself another shot.

"The money Louisa was giving me to invest for the tribe. I should have been suspicious of where it was coming from."

"Where did you think?"

"From other tribes. That's what she told me."

"That's what she told everyone. It's plausible."

"I should have known." He drank from his tumbler.

"She didn't want you to know. She was protecting you."

"I know. That makes it worse."

He looked up. "Wayne was the son I lost. I loved him." The despair on his face was heartbreaking. "I loved them both."

"I know," I said. "That makes it harder."

"What a web of lies." His hand was unsteady, reaching for his glass. "Even me."

"How you?"

"I lied to you about how I got the money to pay for this." His arm took in the room, and beyond. "I said I made it from investments. I didn't."

"I know."

"You know everything."

"More than I want to," I said with real regret.

"It was my wife's money. She left it to me when she died."

The bottle of Jim Beam was over half-empty, but he was still drinking. I should have stopped him, but I didn't. Everyone deserves one good drunk in his life, when the reasons are as good as these.

"I didn't want to admit to that. Vanity of vanities, all is vanity. Pride goeth before a fall."

He drained his glass, corked the bottle. "I'm done here. I was retiring anyway, but I'm going to quit now. I'm not going to wait."

"You might want to give it a few days to make sure."

"No. I'm finished. There's no gas left in the tank."

"What are you going to do?"

"Go somewhere else. Finish up my life. Whatever there's left to finish."

I got up. So did he. He was shaky on his feet. We shook hands.

"I'm glad I met you," I said to him. "You're a good man. A good cop."

"I wasn't good enough to stop this," he lamented, flagellating himself.

"Nobody was."

That was the truth.

"The best we could do was pick up the pieces."

Riva and Bucky and I flew home courtesy of the state, one last time. A trucking service would drive down the stuff we'd left behind.

Everyone who wasn't from Blue River was gone now. I didn't think any of us would return. I knew I wouldn't.

By the time we got home and unpacked, we were wiped out. I made a Taco Bell run. We ate out on our balcony. Riva put Buck to bed. He went without a fuss, for a change.

I'd forgotten how blissful Santa Barbara is in the evenings. Cool, clear. La Fiesta, our homegrown bacchanalia, was coming up soon. The city, spread out below our house high on the Riviera, seemed to be swaying to a cosmic rhythm in anticipation. Or maybe that was merely my imagination, a projection of my desire.

Riva poured two flutes of champagne. Veuve Clicquot, the good stuff. We always drink champagne at the end of a case. We clinked glasses.

"It wasn't the win you wanted," she said sagaciously. "But justice did prevail." She drank, her dark eyes checking me out. "Didn't it?"

"There was punishment for the crime, so you could say yes, by the book. But real justice? I don't think so. There was too much corruption for true justice. All around."

"I know you don't want to hear this—but I feel sorry for Nora."

I had told her about Nora's final ravings, her sexual love fantasies. Riva had dismissed them as the product of a sick, sad woman. "She was so lonely and miserable it melted her mind."

Riva was right—I didn't want to hear it. She didn't have to know the reasons why.

"She could have solved her problems another way, short of killing," I said. "Not Juarez—we're all better off he's dead. And if Jerome's career is finished, that's fine with me, too. He's shit, another rotten cop who believed he was above the law. Three of his men died to satisfy his ego."

I sipped some champagne. It tasted great—a well-earned benefaction to myself. "But not Dennis. There's no justification in the world for that." I twirled the delicate glass in my fingers. The pale liquid fire sparkled.

"I remember him and Nora together, back in the old days," I reminisced. "She worshiped the ground he walked on, and he felt the same about her. They really loved each other, once."

"That's why she thought she had to kill him," my bighearted wife said. "When it's like that, it's all or nothing. And if it's nothing, it can't exist anymore. You have to try to leave it behind, and move on. She was moving on, the best she could."

I thought about that, sitting on my own balcony again, looking out over my city. Maybe if I tried hard enough, that's how I'd remember Nora: as a keeper of the flame, until the fire burned out and only the ashes were left.

I spent a couple of days in Gentle Ben's shop, tuning up my motorcycle—it isn't easy getting parts for an old bike, they had to be shipped in from halfway across the country. When I was satisfied with my work, I drove out of town and rode over the pass into the Santa Ynez valley. Past Rancho San Marcos golf course, past Lake Cachuma, through Los Olivos and Los Alamas, all the way to Foxen Canyon Road.

It was a beautiful early autumn day. It was on a day like this that I had bought this motorcycle. My pride and joy, of the non human species. I hadn't had a chance to ride it very much. This was a delayed christening.

It was the middle of harvesttime for grapes. I could see the pickers in the fields. In a couple of years I'd be drinking wine made from these grapes.

I stopped at the Foxen Winery tasting room and bought a bottle of pinot noir. I stashed it in my saddlebag, along with some cheese and bread I'd brought from home.

I doubled back partway, then headed up Figueroa Mountain Road, cruising high into the Los Padres National Forest, catching the Happy Canyon cutoff to where it ended. I got off the bike, grabbed the wine, cheese, bread, a corkscrew, and a crystal Riedel wineglass wrapped in a dishtowel. It's a special glass, for special occasions. I hiked a couple of hundred yards up the foot trail, until I came to a good viewpoint.

The entire valley was laid out below me. I could see forever, all the way to the ocean. I unfolded the towel, laid the bread and cheese on it, uncorked the bottle, and poured myself a glass.

Sometimes simple pleasures are the best. I cut off a hunk of cheese, ripped a handful of bread from the loaf, and ate them with the wine— a lunch fit for a king.

High above, a red-tailed hawk was circling in the wind. Birds catch the hot thermals in these low mountains and ride them for hours without ever once having to flap their wings. I tracked it as it drifted southward, growing smaller in the distance. It looked, from down below where I was watching, to be completely free.

That's how I felt. I work in a profession where people do bad things, get into trouble, hurt each other, sometimes even kill each other, and men and women like me have to clean up afterward. I don't mind being the guy with the broom trailing the circus. It's the job I've chosen, and I get plenty of rewards from it.

But sometimes I like to lead the parade. Standing here in the warm sun, my wineglass in hand, I knew that right now, this moment, I was. I could eat and drink and lie down for a nap to sleep it off, and then I could go home. My son would jump into my arms, my wife would kiss me on the lips, we'd make love. And If I was lucky, when I fell asleep in her arms, all my dreams would be sweet.

ACKNOWLEDGMENTS

Special Agent Sharon Carter of the U.S. Drug Enforcement Administration assisted me regarding DEA procedures and methodology. In those instances where she was unable to convey specific information, because of departmental policy (or any other reason), I used the best data available. Any mistakes or misrepresentations are the author's, not hers.

Terry Cannon, J.D., of the San Diego District Attorney's office, formerly with the Santa Barbara County District Attorney's office, read the manuscript several times and advised me in all the phases of the workings of a D.A.'s office, including the protocols regarding a state special prosecutor. Terrence L. Lammers, J.D., and Robert L. Monk, J.D., helped in answering questions I had about other legal matters. Rick Dodge of Dodge City Gunshop, Santa Barbara, assisted me in weapons research.

Lori Lipsky, my editor, did an excellent job in helping me maintain my clarity and writing voice. Bob Lescher, my agent, was supportive of this effort, as he has been on all of my books. Al Silverman, my former editor (now retired, but still a part of my creative life), also read the manuscript and weighed in with his usual astute observations.